"COME HERE, JILLIAN," JACOB SAID QUIETLY.

He pulled her onto his lap and cradled her against him. When her arms tightened around him he shuddered and buried his face in her hair. "I've missed you so much, Jill. If you only knew how many times I've dreamed of holding you like this...."

Jillian's tears were warm against his cheek as she clung to him, her body shaking with repressed sobs. "Oh, Jacob, I thought I would never see you again!" she whispered brokenly.

With a low groan he covered her trembling mouth with his own. She returned his ardor with an uncontrolled hunger. He might break her heart again, but for the moment she didn't care. Jacob was holding her, needing her and that was what mattered beyond all else....

AND NOW...

SUPERROMANCES

Worldwide Library is proud to present a
sensational new series of modern love stories—
SUPERROMANCES

Written by masters of the genre, these longer,
sensuous and dramatic novels are truly in keeping
with today's changing life-styles. Full of intriguing
conflicts, the heartaches and delights of true love,
SUPERROMANCES are absorbing stories—
satisfying and sophisticated reading that lovers
of romance fiction have long been waiting for.

SUPERROMANCES
Contemporary love stories for the woman of today!

JUDITH DUNCAN

TENDER RHAPSODY

A SUPERROMANCE FROM
WORLDWIDE

TORONTO · NEW YORK · LOS ANGELES · LONDON

Published February 1983

First printing December 1982

ISBN 0-373-70051-2

Printed in Canada

CHAPTER ONE

LITTLE BEAMS OF REFLECTED LIGHT danced across the black counter top as the door to the restaurant swung open. A hot draft of summer wind ruffled the covers of the magazines on display by the cash register as a very tall and attractive woman entered. Three truck drivers, slouched at the counter eating their lunch, turned in unison to stare.

The woman took off her sunglasses and perched them on top of her head as she paused to scan the restaurant for an empty table. As she turned and moved toward an empty window seat, the sun caught and glistened in her auburn hair. The thick windblown tresses, which tumbled past her waist, shimmered and swayed like a cascade of burnished copper.

There was a long low whistle of approval from one of the drivers, and he was rewarded with a quick amused grin that dispelled the haunted lonely look from the woman's large hazel eyes.

Jillian Lambert was still smiling to herself as she settled into the padded bench of the booth and slipped the menu from its place between the chrome napkin holder and the mismatched salt and pepper shakers.

She wasn't really that hungry, but she always stopped in Vegreville on her way home. It made a break from the three-hour drive, and the Ukrainian food that was served at this particular café was excellent.

Jillian smiled at the pleasant, plump waitress who came to take her order. "Could I have the pirogi-and-kielbasa special, please?"

The waitress nodded. "And what would you like to drink, miss?"

"A large iced tea, please—and could I have that now?"

"Certainly."

Jillian sighed gratefully when the tall frosty glass was placed before her, and she quenched her thirst with a long refreshing drink. It was so hot outside. June was an unpredictable month in Alberta. It could be either hot and dry or cold and wet—and today was definitely hot and dry.

She rested her elbow on the table and propped her chin in her hand as she gazed out the window. A group of elementary-school students was racing exuberantly across the vacant lot next to the restaurant. One small boy was gleefully shredding a notebook as he ran, and Jillian couldn't help grinning. She would bet all she had that it was his English-composition workbook.

She knew exactly how he felt. She had been teaching music in a large elementary school in Edmonton for the past five years, and she'd soon discovered that no matter what your age, whether student or teacher, summer vacation was summer vacation. The enthusiasm at its arrival was shared by all.

She had very little planned for the two months that stretched lazily before her, but she was going to spend at least two weeks at home with her brother and his wife. Ken and Sylvia lived on the farm where

Jillian had grown up, and since she had always enjoyed rural life, the time there would be relaxed and casual. She needed that kind of break, the year had been a hectic pressured one. The entire music program for the five hundred students enrolled in the school was her responsibility, so her workload had been demanding. She had also taken two evening courses at the university and had been heavily involved in the Edmonton Theatrical Association. Taking the lead female role in a very successful musical production in the spring had used up the remainder of her free time. From the end of March on she'd had barely time to think, but that was how she liked it.

Now, however, she was looking forward to having no plans, no pressures, no deadlines. She almost regretted the fact that she had committed herself to an audition in mid-July for the female vocalist lead with an up-and-coming group from the States. Jillian was realistic about her chances. It would be rather farfetched to expect anything to come of it—a country girl from Lloydminster, Alberta, simply couldn't expect that degree of success. That would be tempting fate beyond reason! But the audition would be an interesting experience, no matter what the outcome.

Jillian smiled at the waitress, who was placing a heaping plate before her. The food looked tantalizing. . . .

THE MEAL had been delicious, as usual, and Jillian had enjoyed it despite her initial lack of appetite. She slipped on her sunglasses as she stepped out of the air-conditioned building into the blinding bright sun. The dry wind whipped her hair across her face. She unlocked the door of her compact car, and she grimaced as a blast of stifling heat hit her. Rapidly she rolled down the windows. It was a scorcher of a day.

Driving to the eastern outskirts of town, she pulled into a neat, attractively landscaped park that bordered the highway, and she climbed out of the car. Jillian seldom drove through Vegreville without stopping at the park. As usual she walked over to the monument that was the colorful focal point of the grounds and stood staring up at it, fascinated as ever by the engineering marvel before her.

The community had considered a number of possibilities to honor the hundredth anniversary of the Royal Canadian Mounted Police and because of its rich multicultural background had selected a monument that was as distinctive as it was unique—a massive Ukrainian Easter egg. The actual construction of the aluminum egg had presented considerable challenges, but Jillian felt it had been well worth the frustration for all those involved. The end product— twenty-five feet long, eighteen feet across and towering thirty feet in the air—was truly spectacular. The exquisite design in bronze, gold and silver, true in every detail to the original folk art that inspired it, was magnificent, but it was the engineering feat that fascinated Jillian the most. Viewed from the ground the egg seemed to be constructed of thousands of individual triangles, but it was impossible to tell how it had been assembled.

Jillian's heart filled with patriotic pride as she read the dedication message.

This Pysanka (Easter Egg) symbolizes the harmony, vitality and culture of the community and is dedicated as a tribute to the One-Hundredth

Anniversary of the Royal Canadian Mounted Police who brought peace and security to the largest multicultural settlement in all of Canada.

An ardent scholar when it came to the history of Alberta, Jillian knew that the Vegreville district had been settled in the late 1800s by English-speaking pioneers. In 1894 a colony of French people had arrived from the United States, and then at the turn of the century Ukrainian immigrants had begun to arrive. At the time Canada was encouraging the colonization of the west by means of the Homestead Act, whereby 160 acres of land was granted to anyone settling there, with the stipulation that the landholder would clear the land and make it productive.

For the Ukrainians, who were fleeing from oppression, this opportunity was their hope, their shining dream for a bright future. They came in droves, bringing with them a colorful culture and a proud heritage. By the time the Canadian Northern Railway was built in 1905, settlers from Germany and the Scandinavian countries were also homesteading in the Vegreville area. But despite the variety of mingling cultures, the Ukrainians managed to maintain their language, their old-world traditions, their distinctive culture. Jillian was filled with a deep sense of respect for their persistence, their stoicism, their dignity.

Her own great-grandparents had immigrated from Britain. Members of the Barr Colonists, they had faced incredible hardships and disappointments before they settled around Lloydminster. Jillian had grown up with the stories about their sacrifices, their challenges and their successes. Her roots, her sense of belonging, were deep. The farm where she had been raised was the original Lambert homestead. It had always been Lambert land.

Because of immigrants and settlers like the Ukrainians and the Barr Colonists, who had played a vital role in the early development, Alberta had developed into a dynamic progressive province. Those pioneers had given Jillian her birthright, and she was fiercely proud of it.

Glancing at her watch she walked slowly back to the car. A final look at the towering monument sent a warm flood of satisfaction through her. Whoever had originated the idea had a finely tuned perception of history, and the district of Vegreville had to be commended for championing such a brilliant plan.

Jillian climbed into her car and switched on the ignition. She had dawdled long enough....

The final stretch of her trip was over almost too quickly for Jillian. The panorama of rolling farmland never failed to touch her, especially at this time of year. She loved to drive through the lush green fields that were checkerboarded with rich black summer-fallowed strips and hay crops of purple alfalfa and pink and yellow clover. The bright yellow fields of rapeseed lay across the fertile land like blankets of summer sunshine, its sweet perfume reminding her of fresh honey. The landscape was liberally sprinkled with stands of poplar and aspen trees, as well as the occasional clump of towering spruce. Willow-ringed lakes and ponds shimmered silver blue in the sun, and the earthy clean fragrance of clover and moist soil that wafted through the open window was the sweetest perfume on earth to Jillian.

A whirlwind of thick dust hung behind her as she

sped down the familiar gravel road. She geared down as she approached the grove of spruce trees that marked the long sweeping driveway of the Lambert farm, then geared down again as she swung into the drive and headed slowly toward the huge old brick house.

The Lambert farm was situated on the crest of a hill, offering a spectacular view of the surrounding farmland. The house itself was a massive structure that had been built some fifty years before by Jillian's great-grandparents. It was a two-story building with a large ivy-covered veranda around it, its white-louvered shutters and fresh white trim giving it a stately but homey appearance. A thick green carpet of lawn swept down to the honeysuckle- and lilac-lined drive. Tall old trees formed a beautiful but practical windbreak around the house, while off to the side a large area of fruit trees and shrubs was bordered with splashes of rich color from carefully tended perennials.

Jillian's oldest brother and his wife lived in the "big house" with their two small sons. Well aware of the impulsiveness of four-year-old Kenny, the newcomer was not surprised when a curly blond head came bobbing through the shrubs beside the lane. She braked and threw open the passenger door as the handsome lad reached the car. Scrambling in and throwing himself into his aunt's arms, he cried, "I've been waiting and waiting for you, Auntie Jill!"

She hugged him close, tears welling up in her eyes. She loved this little man dearly, but every time she saw him it was a reminder of a face from her past. He looked so much like—

She pushed the thought away and grinned into the

dancing brown eyes before her. "I'll bet you've been waiting and waiting just so you could help me drive the rest of the way to the house!"

The blond head bobbed vigorously as the boy squirmed onto Jillian's lap. She leaned across the seat and pulled the passenger door shut, then put the car in gear, keeping her hands unobtrusively at the bottom of the wheel. Kenny grasped the steering mechanism in his own chubby tanned hands, and Jillian had to struggle to keep from laughing out loud at the deadly serious concentration on the little boy's face as they weaved their way up the drive. She took over with an ease borne of experience as she parked the car in the space between the garage and the house. Opening the door she set Kenny on the ground, then slid out behind him.

Kenny dashed through the gate, slamming it loudly behind him. "She's here! She's here! She's here!"

Jillian was lifting her luggage from the trunk when a very pretty and radiantly pregnant blond-haired woman appeared on the veranda, a welcoming smile on her face. "Thank heavens you're here, Jill. He's been driving me crazy all afternoon with 'Is it time yet? Is it time yet?' "

Jillian laughed as she gathered together her belongings and elbowed her way through the white picket gate. "Well, Sylvia, I was just as anxious to get here myself. You have no idea how much I've been looking forward to this."

Sylvia Lambert hugged her sister-in-law warmly, then burst out laughing. "I was watching you come up the drive. Either you've been drinking or you had underage help!"

"Oh, I had help, all right!"

They were both laughing as they walked into the house. There was a genuine deep affection between the two women based on a long solid friendship. Sylvia had been born and raised on the neighboring farm, but her parents had immigrated from Poland many years before. Both her mother and father had come from old influential families there, but when the political situation had become threatening they had fled to Canada with little more than a few personal belongings. Mike Holinski had worked as a hired man for one of the farmers in the district until he had enough saved for a down payment on what had been a small rundown farm. Olga, who had studied classical music extensively in the old country and was an exceptionally talented pianist and vocalist, had subsidized her husband's income by teaching music, soon developing a far-reaching reputation as a teacher. Jillian and her two brothers had experienced the privilege of studying for many years under her tutorage.

The two families had been especially close, as an unusually strong friendship had blossomed over the years between the three Lambert children and the five Holinski offspring. The youngsters had grown up together, performed together, worked and played together, shared good times and bad. They had on occasion squabbled noisily among themselves, but they had always presented a united front to those outside their circle. Music had been the basic commonality. Olga Holinski had nurtured and cultivated this talent, which all of them shared. Because of the constant interaction between the two families, everyone had been ecstatic when Sylvia and Ken had decided to get married.

The two women entered the house to the welcome of an exuberant Kenny. He was leading a sleepy-eyed, pink-cheeked toddler by the hand.

"I gotted him up, mommy. He wants to see Auntie Jill, too!"

Jillian laughed as she knelt down and held out her arms to the carrot-topped little boy. He grinned sleepily, then threw his dimpled arms around her neck and snuggled his face against her shoulder.

"Oh, thanks a lot, Kenny. That is just what we need—a cranky Scott!" Sylvia's voice was dry but tinged with amusement.

Jillian flopped into one of the old maple captain's chairs at the big round kitchen table with little Scott still cuddled against her. Her sister-in-law went into the pantry and promptly reappeared with a tray of glasses and a huge pitcher of lemonade. On the tray were two frosty Popsicles for the children.

"Here you go, boys." She passed them to her two sons. "Why don't you eat them outside on the veranda? *That* I can hose down." She grinned as the two small boys scampered out. "And, Kenny, don't let Scott feed his to the dog, okay?"

"Okay, mommy." The screen door slammed behind them.

Sylvia collapsed in one of the chairs across the table and ran her fingers through her short curly hair. "Honestly, Jill, I'm beginning to feel like a pumpkin, and this heat is driving me nuts."

Jillian chuckled as she stretched her long legs out in front of her. "That doesn't sound very appetizing, Sylvia—pumpkins and nuts. Unless you're going to be a pie."

"Sympathy! I try to squeeze out a little sympathy

and all I get is a flip retort!'' Sylvia grinned impishly. "Ah, but I'll get revenge. I'll mark you in for hours and hours of baby-sitting.''

"Anytime!'' Jillian filled the tall glasses on the tray before her with the icy lemonade and passed one to Sylvia. "Well, what wild, wonderful and scandalous things have happened since I was home last?''

"Let's see now. Rosie Peters had a baby boy a week ago—that makes four. Henry Jackson lost one whole quarter-section of wheat in a freak hailstorm. . . .'' Sylvia's face lighted up and she clapped her hands excitedly. "Oh, Lord, and guess what? The Freedman-Connor feud has exploded again!''

Jillian threw her head back and laughed, her eyes sparkling with delight. The Freedman-Connor dispute had been an on-again off-again thing in the community for the past decade. It had started when George Freedman's utility bull broke through a line fence and dispensed his affections among Will Connor's purebred Hereford cows, thereby eliminating the purebred calf line Will had been counting on that spring. Will had retaliated by hooking his tractor to George's fence and ripping it up, post by post, for over half a mile. George, who felt indignant about Will's hostility, dammed a stream on his property and effectively flooded Will's best hay field.

"What happened this time?''

"Oh, Jill, you won't believe it. Do you remember that old gray horse that Will has had wandering around the back pasture for the last hundred years?''

Jillian nodded, her eyes gleaming with anticipation.

"Well, the poor old thing escaped through an open gate and somehow managed to haul its tired old body the half-mile to Freedman's. Wouldn't you know it, it wandered into that beautiful big greenhouse of theirs and upset half the flats, ate nearly all the tomato plants, then managed to shatter a whole wall when it came crashing through.'' Sylvia's eyes were dancing and Jill's shoulders shook with suppressed laughter. ''So Will loaded up his big grain truck with manure and dumped it on George's front doorstep the very day that Tina Freedman had all the UFW ladies there for tea. That really upset George, of course, and he went storming up to Will's with murder in his heart and blood in his eye. He figured he'd find Will in the barn, so he went stomping in. And guess what he found?''

Jillian shook her head helplessly as she went into paroxysms of laughter.

''Apparently George let out a mighty roar and there was this mad flurry in one of the box stalls they use to store hay. Out staggered Bill—that's Will's oldest boy—and Penny Freedman! Can you imagine? I guess there was an awful scene to end all awful scenes, with Will and George bellowing at each other. Until Penny stepped between the two of them and in that sweet gentle way of hers said, 'You two are just going to have to stop this nonsense because Bill and I are getting married!' ''

Sylvia was wiping tears of mirth from her eyes as Jillian finally managed to gasp, ''What happened then?''

''Well, the kids are getting married in late August, and you can bet they are going to be the best equipped newlyweds this district has ever seen. George and Will are trying to outdo each other.''

Jillian finally managed to calm down but her eyes

were dancing. "Who said life was dull down on the farm?"

The remainder of the afternoon was spent in casual chatter. The two women lounged on the veranda until five o'clock, when Sylvia picked up the large wicker hamper and carried it into the kitchen. Jillian knew the ritual. It was haying season, so her brother would remain out in the fields to take advantage of every moment of good weather. Sylvia would load up the hamper with food and take it out to him.

Most farm wives loathed the extra work, but Sylvia accepted it in her usual good-natured manner, confessing that she enjoyed it. "I would get stoned to death by the other farm women if they ever heard me say it, but I've always liked doing it. It's a picnic every day!"

Jillian smiled as her sister-in-law loaded the basket with fried chicken, potato salad, baked beans, fresh buns and a mass of other food. She topped it off with two delicious-looking pies and closed the lid.

"You can take that out to the station wagon, Jill, while I put some cold drinks in the cooler."

Jillian lugged the heavy hamper out to the car and called the two boys, who were playing in the paddle pool. She helped them into jeans and cowboy boots, well aware of what the stubble of a hay field could do to bare legs. She herself changed into blue jeans and boots, for a field was not the place for a dainty sun dress and sandals, either.

She found Sylvia leaning against the car waiting for her. "You drive, Jill. I have to push the seat so far back from the steering wheel that my arms barely reach. I feel like a menace on the road."

Jillian laughed as she opened the door and lifted

the two boys into the back seat, then slipped behind the wheel. She turned to Sylvia as she started the vehicle, her voice teasing. "And where will we find Ken, Pumpkin Lady?"

Sylvia pulled a face and grinned. "He's in the field by the swimming hole."

The drive out to that field had always been a favorite of Jillian's. It was a narrow dirt road, with the encroaching poplar trees forming a green sun-dappled arch overhead. The saskatoon and chokecherry bushes crowded close against the car, their blossom-laden branches brushing the sides of the vehicle as it passed.

The fifteen-minute drive passed in a comfortable easy silence as the two women enjoyed the natural beauty that surrounded them.

Finally Jillian pulled into the field and parked in the shade of a stand of spruce and aspen. Ken acknowledged their presence with a hearty wave from the baler and Jillian waved back. She helped Sylvia unload the car, then sat with her back propped against a tree, braiding her tangled hair. She watched Ken approach, the baler moving slowly through the thick scented windrows of grass and clover. It was a lazy, hazy scene as the heat waves shimmered, blurring the landscape.

Ken finished the row, then pulled to a halt and climbed down from the cab. Jillian's heart was full of pride and affection as she watched him stride toward them. He was a giant of a man, with rugged hawklike features and thick wavy auburn hair.

He tugged at Jillian's braid with a fond brotherly gesture as he stretched out on the grass beside her. "Hi, Auntie Jilly."

Jillian loathed being called "Jilly" and Ken knew it. She stuck her tongue out at him. He laughed up at her. "That's a nice thing to teach my sons."

"Teach them to call me 'Jilly' and I'll teach them something worse than that!"

Sylvia came over and sat beside them, handing Ken a cold bottle of beer.

"Thanks, honey." He took a long thirsty swallow, then rolled to his side. "Come lean against me, Syl. It's too hard on your back sitting like that."

A flash of envy washed through Jillian as Sylvia moved over and leaned comfortably against Ken's massive chest. He rested his hand possessively on her thigh. Jillian fought down the wave of loneliness and gibed lightly, "Why don't you ever call her 'Sylly'?"

Ken laughed. "I do sometimes, but it's with a small *S*."

Sylvia grinned down at him and slapped his shoulder playfully. "That's a lie. The way you say it, it sounds as though it's all in capitals!"

Jillian joined in the laughter. It was so good to be home!

It was nearly seven o'clock by the time they returned to the house. Ken would remain in the field until the dew formed or until it became too dark to work. The summer days were at their longest now, with the sun setting very late in the evening. Even then, the nights seldom became really dark as they did in the winter. Jillian helped Sylvia clean up, then she repacked the hamper with clean dishes and cutlery. She spent a riotous half hour with the boys while they splashed in the tub. She had them shiny clean and ready for bed when Kenny asked for a special favor.

"Auntie Jill, will you teach us a new song?" For his age he had a remarkable voice, and he loved to have her teach him the bouncy funny songs she taught to the lower grades in school.

"Come on, then. Let's go," she agreed, taking one plump dimpled hand in each of hers. The three of them strolled through the immaculate kitchen into the living room.

The rustic room was dominated by a vast field-stone fireplace and enormous bay windows. Sylvia had refused to modernize the house when she became Ken's bride seven years before. She had laboriously restored the beautiful oak woodwork, and the oak floors now gleamed in their beautiful natural hue, accented by cheerful area rugs. In spite of the overwhelming size, Sylvia had achieved an atmosphere of warmth, friendship and congeniality in her home.

Jillian walked through the shuttered room to the piano and switched on the rattan swag lamp above it. A second later a wave of almost unbearable nostalgia swept over her as her eyes were transfixed on a large color photograph.

Sensuous brown eyes smiled back at her with such warmth that it was almost as though he was sitting there, smiling that smile for her. His sun-streaked blond hair was longer than she remembered, but it was still thick and curly. It was the face from her past. The picture blurred as tears filled her eyes.

"I'm sorry, Jillian." It was Sylvia's voice, quiet and contrite. "I didn't think it still bothered you—"

"It's all right. Really." She continued to stare at it, drinking in every detail. He had on a rust-colored turtleneck sweater that highlighted the amber flecks in his eyes. He was seated at a grand piano, his arms resting casually across the top, his hand hanging relaxed. In his other hand he held a sheaf of music. It was a perfect setting for him.

"Sylvia?"

"Yes?"

"How is he?" She could barely talk for the tight constriction in her throat.

"He's fine, Jillian."

Jillian turned to Sylvia, her face pale and pathetic with unshed tears still clinging to her long lashes. "Is it a recent picture?"

The other woman sighed heavily and ran her fingers through her hair. "We received it just after you were here at Easter."

Jillian again turned to the photo, trying to clamp shut that part of her mind where all the memories stirred. There would be periods of time when she would begin to believe that she was over him completely, then something would happen and all the memories would come rushing back, bringing with them all the heartaches.

"Why are you crying, Auntie Jill?"

Jillian tilted her head and looked down at the worried little face that was watching her. She scooped Kenny up and hugged him tightly as she wiped away the tears with the back of her hand.

"Sometimes I'm a little sad, love. That's all."

Her nephew wasn't really satisfied with that answer. His Auntie Jill never cried, she always laughed. "Can we still sing a song?"

Jillian laughed weakly and sat him down on the piano bench, then picked up Scott and held him on her lap as she, too, sat at the piano. She forced herself to concentrate on the two small boys as she taught Kenny a song about a frog, two fish and a turtle, one that amused him vastly. He learned quickly and was soon singing it in a piping-clear sweet voice.

She smiled ruefully as she ruffled his hair. This child, too, had music in his soul. She sighed deeply as she looked down at the two-year-old nestled against her. Scott, his eyelids drooping, was tugging sleepily at his eyebrows. She kissed the riot of red curls and cuddled him against her as she sang him to sleep with a soft tender lullaby, her mind locking out the memories that would shatter her composure.

She found Sylvia puttering at the kitchen sink when she came downstairs after tucking her two nephews in bed.

"Anything I can do?"

"You already have. You have no idea what a treat it is to have someone else take over at bedtime."

Jillian slid into one of the kitchen chairs while Sylvia opened one of the drawers and took out a thick envelope, handing it to Jill.

"It's the last letter we had from Karin. She said the two of you talked for nearly an hour on the phone a couple of weeks ago. I'm glad I don't pay your long-distance phone bills!"

Jillian grinned at Sylvia's mock horror as she unfolded the letter. Karin Holinski and Jillian had been practically inseparable all their lives. There had been only a few weeks' difference in their ages, so they had been in the same grades together all through school. Karin was in Vancouver now, but even that fact had little effect on their very special friendship. The long-distance phone bills were, in fact, often horrendous.

Jillian finished reading the newsy letter, then folded it and replaced it in the envelope. "When will mom and dad be back from Banff?"

Sylvia polished the taps, then draped the tea towel over her shoulder and sat down across the table from Jillian. "They don't know for sure. When their mini home was delivered they were like a pair of kids with a new toy."

"I'm so glad that they're enjoying themselves."

"So am I." Sylvia paused and began to fold the towel into a precise square. "Jill?"

"What?"

"Why have you never talked about what happened?"

Jillian swung around and faced her sister-in-law squarely, her arms resting on the table. She sighed deeply. "Because it hurt so damned much. And I really couldn't see the point of making everyone else miserable."

Sylvia continued to toy with the towel. "We all felt pretty rotten about it."

"I know."

Sylvia looked at her, her brown eyes disturbed. She wadded up the tea towel and flung it angrily at the sink. "Damn."

Jillian fingered the chain around her neck, her face reflective.

"Jill?"

"Yes?"

"We never knew why he left."

Jillian's eyes were cloudy as she looked up. She heaved another deep sigh and rubbed her forehead with a weary resigned gesture.

It was true that nobody knew the real reason why Jacob had disappeared so abruptly. Only Sylvia's consideration and deep compassion had kept her silent for so long. It had been an unwritten law that Jacob was never discussed in front of Jillian.

Jillian had been so confused and so hurt when he left that nothing had made sense. She probably would never have known the truth herself if her brother Allan hadn't been in medical school. He somehow managed to get his hands on Jacob's medical files several weeks after Jacob had bolted, and the information he found there finally shed some light on the muddle. Even when he told her what he had discovered, Jillian had not been able to believe that there was any merit to it—in fact she still didn't believe it.

"Jillian?"

Jillian glanced again at her sister-in-law, her eyes unwittingly communicating her grave reluctance to talk.

But Sylvia's chin thrust forward with tenacity. "I think you'd better tell me what you know, Jillian."

Sylvia had every right to know, Jillian realized, but it was going to be very difficult to tell her. When Allan discovered what the doctor had insinuated to Jacob, both he and Jillian had been stupefied. They had agreed to keep that bit of information from the rest of the family, however, as it would have upset everyone and made them even more distraught.

Jillian rubbed her temples with her fingers, then took a deep breath. "We're pretty certain that Jacob left because he had been told by Dr. Paulson that the bruising in his spine was healing. That there was a very real possibility that his remaining paralysis was psychological."

"*What!*" Sylvia's face registered her absolute disbelief. "I don't believe it!"

Jillian shrugged one shoulder with a desolate gesture, her sagging posture revealing her dejection. "I couldn't believe it, either. It didn't make sense then and it doesn't now. That prognosis simply doesn't mesh with Jacob's character or his personality. Allan couldn't accept it, either, but that's what the records said. There were several references in Jacob's charts to his suppressed emotional reaction and his obvious withdrawal. He refused to discuss his psychological attitude with any of the doctors, and there was concern about that. One comment stated very clearly that Jacob's mental attitude might be interfering with his recuperation."

Sylvia stood up and began pacing back and forth across the kitchen, her face set in a deep frown. "How did you find out all the information you did?"

"Allan did some detective work after Jacob disappeared. He had a hunch that Jacob had been told something that had hit him hard—he suspected that Jacob might have developed a tumor, for apparently that sometimes happens. I don't know how he managed to gain access to Jacob's records and I didn't ask. We were both so upset about the pyschosomatic diagnosis—it just didn't make sense."

"I can imagine how Allan reacted!" Sylvia sat down and rested her arms on the table, her hands clasped tightly together. "Did he find out anything about Jacob's treatment?"

"Yes, he did. When Jacob was admitted, the doctors' prime concern was to keep him alive. Initially they were most concerned with the internal bleeding and the damage his broken ribs had caused. It wasn't until he was out of intensive care that they paid much attention to the paralysis. They knew his back wasn't broken. The severe tensor shock—that's what caused that awful rigidity in his body in the beginning—indicated specifically that his spine had suffered an intense trauma. The neurological examinations that they did later, and the blood that was discovered in his spinal fluid, told them he had extensive spinal hematoma, or bruising.''

"Then it was the spinal shock that totally paralyzed him for the first month, wasn't it?''

"Yes, but by then they were aware of the extent of the hematoma in his spine, and they knew the damage was in the lower lumbar region of his back. The neurosurgeon told me that such extreme bruising could take months to heal, if it ever did heal. He also warned me that there might be permanent paralysis in Jacob's legs because of the shattered pelvis. He was concerned that bone fragments might have severed the sciatic nerves in Jacob's legs. They just didn't know. Until the spinal bruising healed—''

"*If* it healed.''

"Until it healed, there was no way they could determine if the sciatic nerves had been damaged.'' Jillian felt suddenly as though all the warmth had been drained from her body, and she wrapped her arms across her breasts in an attempt to ward off the inner chill that was seeping through her.

Sylvia was watching her with bewilderment. "But. . . I just don't understand, Jill. When he had two such specific and extensive injuries that could cause paralysis, why were the doctors so quick to suggest that the problem might be psychological?''

"I have no idea. It seemed like such a stupid assessment.'' Jillian stretched her legs out under the table in an attempt to relieve the tension in her rigid muscles. She stared off into space for a long time, her thoughts centered on Jacob's recovery. "Do you remember when Jacob began to regain feeling in his hips and the doctors were so pleased?"

"I'll never forget it—he had been hospitalized for nearly eight months, and it was the first sign that there was hope for recovery."

"That's right. It was the first indication that there was regeneration of the damaged tissue. That's when Jacob's physiotherapy was intensified so dramatically. From then on, there was slow but steady improvement."

"Wasn't it shortly after they stepped up his physio that he moved back to the apartment with John and Allan?"

"A few weeks later, I think. I know that he still had to go to the hospital every day for therapy. Allan said that as more and more feeling returned to his legs, they were able to do sensory tests that indicated that the nerves in his legs had not been damaged when his pelvis was smashed."

"But there was still the spinal hematoma."

"Apparently Jacob was slated for another myelogram in a few weeks, but Dr. Paulson recommended that the psychiatric treatment be started in the meantime."

"And Jacob bolted as soon as that was suggested." It was a flat statement. Sylvia sat glaring out the window, her face cast in fury as she burst out in an explosion of indignation. "How could Paulson ever arrive at that damned stupid conclusion when he did?" She turned to face Jillian, her eyes flashing. "Why didn't he give Jacob a little more time. It just doesn't seem fair that he assessed Jacob the way he did because of how he was coping with his crisis. Why didn't he just give him more time?"

Jillian gestured weakly with her hands, her face deadly pale.

The following silence was smothering. Sylvia pressed her hands against her face and closed her eyes tightly. Jillian watched with concern. She knew the awful shock and disbelief her sister-in-law was experiencing; she had experienced it herself. Even now her entire body felt numb and lifeless, and she rubbed her hands up and down her arms in an attempt to dispel the feeling. It just did not fit that Jacob's paralysis was psychosomatic. He had fought too valiant a fight for his life and had struggled too courageously through the grueling and often painful physiotherapy—and he had never once complained. He had borne the frustration, the discouragement, the boredom, the intense pain with controlled patience and cold determination. Once he was conscious and off the critical list, he had never faltered. He had been very withdrawn and reserved, but he had not given way to the deep grim depression that so often accompanies a disabling injury.

Sylvia's usually quiet voice was laced with restrained anger and suppressed tears. "My God, Jillian, how could they do that to him? Couldn't they see what kind of person he was?"

Jillian stared at her sister-in-law, her face grim and her voice bitter. "I never liked Dr. Paulson, Sylvia. I know he was supposed to be brilliant and the best there was, but he always gave me the impression that the only thing he gave a damn about was Jacob's spine. He wasn't even aware of Jacob as a person. I'll bet my life that he dropped that cold diagnosis on Jacob without one shred of compassion."

Sylvia sighed and pulled distractedly at her tousled hair. "Well, this revelation of yours certainly clears up several unanswered questions. Jacob could never accept something like that. He could surmount anything that was dumped on him and he knew it, but for a doctor to insinuate that he was paralyzed because of psychological reasons would be just too much—especially after what he had been through."

"I know. I went to see Dr. Paulson after I found out what the last prognosis was, but he wouldn't talk to me. He pulled his professional ethics out of the bag and told me that anything discussed between a patient and his doctor was confidential."

A look of disgust swept across Sylvia's face. "How convenient!" She stared vacantly at the floor, her brow creased with perplexity. She didn't say anything for a long time, then she looked at Jillian. "It was because of this that Allan decided to specialize in neurosurgery instead of pediatrics, wasn't it?"

"Yes. He was never really satisfied with Jacob's final assessment. He felt that something had been overlooked."

"God, what a mess!" Sylvia rested her head on her hand and heaved a deep sigh. "Did Jacob ever talk to you about the accident or about his convalescence?"

"No, he refused to discuss it or even acknowledge it. He would become very distant and cold if I asked him anything about his treatment, so I stopped pressing him. As long as I didn't push, he was fine."

"Jill?"

"Hmm?"

"Was there some specific incident that you think may have influenced Jacob to leave when he did?"

Jill leaned back in her chair and abstractedly

picked at a loose thread in the hem of her blouse.
When she spoke her voice was flat and was resigned.

"I had been selected to fill a vacancy as music
specialist to develop a new music program for the
elementary schools. It was the last part of June, but
my job didn't begin until the middle of July. Allan
made a comment that since we had postponed the
wedding for a year—" Sylvia winced. Both of them
knew that Allan would have cut off his arm before
causing his only sister any pain, and yet he had done
it unwittingly. "And since I didn't begin work for
another two weeks, it would be a perfect interlude for
a honeymoon."

"What did Jacob say?"

"Nothing then. After Allan left, he became more
withdrawn than usual." Jillian could feel a tightness
growing around her heart as she recalled the despair
and hopelessness that had engulfed her that night.
She had, out of sheer self-preservation, obliterated
the memory from her mind.

"He must have said more than that, Jillian."
Sylvia's voice was gentle but probing. Jillian understood her need to know.

"He said there would come a time when I would
resent being tied to a cripple and that it would breed a
bitterness that would destroy us both. He felt it
would be better for us to make the break then, while
we still had happy pleasant memories to cherish."

"What did you do?"

"I tried to reason with him, but he just sat there
with that cold distant look on his face. Finally he told
me he wanted me to leave. I refused."

"Then?"

"He seemed to relent a little. He said he wanted me

to go home and think about it and we'd talk about it again in the morning." The memory was becoming more and more vivid. Jillian had knelt in front of him and put her arms around his waist. She had told him how much she loved him.

He had looked so vague and distant, but he had leaned over and taken her face in his hands, kissing her gently. He had sat gazing at her, his eyes tender, almost as though he was memorizing her face. He had whispered, "You will never know what you have meant to me."

"Jillian?" Sylvia's voice was insistent.

Jillian fought down the urge to cry as the desolation she had felt that night became a near reality once again. "Next morning I went to the apartment, but he was gone."

"That was when mom and dad received the note from him?"

"Yes. Later that week," Jillian whispered.

Jacob Holinski had disappeared, leaving his family, his friends and especially his fiancée in a state of total shock.

CHAPTER TWO

SILENCE INTENSIFIED the ticking of the cuckoo clock as dusk infiltrated the room and cast its long gloomy shadows.

"Sylvia?"

"What?"

"Is he still in California?"

"Yes."

"Has anyone been down to see him?"

Sylvia sighed and shook her head. "No, he still refuses to see anyone, although he writes more frequently now. We tried to coax him to come home for mom's and dad's anniversary, but he said he has made a new life for himself and wouldn't even consider it."

Jillian dreaded asking the next question, fearful what the answer would be. But she had to know one way or the other. "Is he married?"

"No." Sylvia glanced at Jillian's face, but the lengthening shadows masked her expression. "Jill, are you still...?"

"I don't know. I honestly don't. I'll probably never know for certain." Jillian stood up and stretched, then walked around the table. She hugged her sister-in-law affectionately, then ruffled her hair. "There's no sense even thinking about it. It's past history and we simply can't change it. Come on, cheer up. I'm going upstairs to have a bath. Why don't you make a pot of coffee and we'll eat the rest of the pie when I come down?''

A few minutes later Jillian lay in the tub, luxuriating in the comfort of the warm water. Leaning her auburn head against the plastic headrest, she closed her eyes.

It was a damned stupid accident that should never have occurred, but it had. It had happened six weeks before their wedding date. Jacob had just returned from California.

The Holinskis had been moving two hundred head of cattle from one of their pastures onto the shared government lease land for summer grazing. It was a difficult operation, so Jacob, John and Mark Holinski were all there, with Ken and Allan helping them out. Since the move would take all day, Sylvia and Jillian had driven over in the truck with their lunch. It had been a beautiful spring day, the grassland a riot of color with bright yellow buttercups and purple spring violets.

The men had decided they would prefer to delay lunch until they had the herd within the lease boundaries, so they had stopped only for a quick coffee break. Jillian herself had mounted Ken's big bay gelding and had helped round up the scattered herd.

Jacob was riding a magnificent three-year-old black stallion named Rogue. The animal was highstrung and skittish, but Jacob was a superb horseman and could handle him easily.

There was one particular location on the trail that always presented difficulties. The cattle had to be driven down a steep bank to the river, then forded across. It was hard work for both riders and horses, and Jacob's stallion, not accustomed to the demands required of him, had become unruly and difficult. They had successfuly moved the herd across the river and were giving the horses a breather when the stallion began prancing about and throwing his head nervously. Jillian spotted the garter snake that was spooking him the same time Jacob did, but it was too late to avoid trouble. Rogue fought Jacob's control fiercely and reared up, his forelegs slashing violently as he went over backward. Jacob was thrown clear, but the fall knocked the wind out of him.

Jillian was alarmed when Jacob and the horse went down, but she was totally unprepared for what happened when the horse scrambled to its feet, crazed with fear. If only she had anticipated that Rogue would panic, she could have been off her horse immediately.

Jacob was still lying facedown on the ground, trying to get his breath, when Rogue went into a mad frenzy. By the time Jillian had dismounted, grabbed the reins and thrown her weight against the chest of the terrified screaming animal, the pounding hooves had done their damage. She knew bones had been broken; she had heard them snap. Because of a tragic accident that she could have prevented, Jacob had suffered severe internal injuries, a smashed pelvis, several broken ribs and extensive spinal injuries.

It had happened six years ago, but Jillian had never quite erased the guilt, the fear and the unbearable unhappiness that had sprouted from that one seed of awful misfortune. Everyone had suffered so much; it had marked each one of them.

She sighed and crawled out of the bath, wrapping herself in a fluffy towel. As the tub drained she watched the water being sucked down in a long lazy swirl. Past history—was it? He had taken away a large part of her life, of herself, when he left, and Jillian knew that no one else could ever completely fill the void. He was gone; she would never see him again, but she would never forget him, either.

She shook her head and slipped into a soft cotton nightie and matching housecoat. Hanging up the towel, she picked up her hairbrush from the vanity and went downstairs.

She was sitting in the kitchen brushing her hair when her brother came in. "Rapunzel, Rapunzel, let down your hair!" he chanted when he saw her.

Jillian gave him an insolent look. "You must be one of the Snow White group. Dopey, isn't it?"

He grinned at her as he slipped his arm around his wife's shoulders. "My, my, sharp tonight, aren't we?"

Jillian grinned back at him.

SHE AWOKE in the middle of the night, unnerved and shaking. She had had the same terrifying dream that had been haunting her for years, and as always, it was so real and so frightening that it left her damp with sweat. Jacob had been walking in slow motion across a field toward her, his arms outstretched, a warm welcoming smile on his face. He was just going to catch her up in his arms when a dark threatening shadow appeared behind him. The shadow turned into a fierce black horse with red eyes and steaming nostrils, with hooves that spurted blood. The gruesome animal overtook Jacob, absorbing his image. Jillian was sucked into a slow swirling stream that carried her away into blackness. It had been awful.

She bolted from the bed and knelt in front of the window, trying to push away the horrible reality of the dream. Clasping her shaking hands in front of her she willed herself to relax her painfully tense muscles. She longed desperately, so desperately for that face from the past. She had been told a thousand times that it would all fade in time, but it hadn't. It hadn't faded at all. Her memories, her feelings, her desires were as vivid now as they had been then.

"Auntie Jill, are you still sad?"

Jillian turned around to find little Kenny standing at her door, a bedraggled stuffed owl clutched in his arms. She quickly wiped away her tears and drew the little boy against her. "I'm feeling sad and a little lonely, pet."

"Can I sleep with you? Then you won't be all by yourself."

Jillian smiled weakly in the darkness. "That's the best offer I've had in a long time."

KEN ROSE EARLY the next morning and slipped quietly out of the master bedroom so that he wouldn't wake his sleeping wife. Peeking in on his sons, he smiled knowingly when he saw one empty bed. Silently he walked down the hallway and opened the door to his sister's room. Little Kenny lay sprawled on his tummy, one fat chubby hand tucked beneath Jillian's cheek, her arm curled around the boy.

Ken shook his head sadly when he saw the dark circles beneath her eyes. He went down the stairs and walked directly to the piano. Picking up the photograph, he opened the hinged top of the piano bench and buried it deep beneath a stack of music.

Jillian herself awoke a bit later to the sounds and

smells of breakfast. A warmth fused through her as she gazed at the small sleeping figure beside her. She leaned over and dropped a soft kiss on the top of his head, relishing the smell of the clean shining hair.

The outside door slammed. That meant Ken had finished his morning chores and had returned from the barns. She quietly rolled over onto her back, contemplating the hollowness in her stomach. The tantalizing smell of breakfast finally tempted her and she eased herself from the bed, gathered up her housecoat from the cedar chest and tiptoed soundlessly from the room. Downstairs in the living room her eyes were drawn to the piano, even though she knew the picture would be gone. It was.

Sylvia was just pouring coffee as Jillian strode into the kitchen.

"Ah-ha—Sleeping Beauty!"

Jillian made a face at her brother as she slipped into the chair across from him. She flashed an apologetic smile at her sister-in-law. "I had planned on surprising you with breakfast in bed, but I certainly bungled that plan!"

Sylvia patted Jill's back affectionately as she eased her cumbersome body into the chair beside Jillian. "You can do it tomorrow. By the way, Ken tells me you had a strange man in your bed last night."

Jillian didn't want to think about last night; she wanted to blot it from her mind. She had learned to hide her feelings most of the time, however, and none of her inner turbulence was visible on her face as she replied, "Oh, I did, and what a charmer!"

The three of them laughed together as they dug into the pile of food on their plates.

"Well, Jill, what are your plans for the holidays?" Ken asked after a companionable silence.

Jillian grinned mischievously at her brother, knowing that he would pull the big-brother routine when she told him. "I have an audition in a few weeks for the female vocalist with a band," she said casually, then laughed out loud at the look of horror that swept across his face.

"Jillian!"

"Now, Ken, give me a little credit before you dish out a lecture. I'm twenty-five years old, and you have to admit that so far I've managed not too badly."

Ken grinned wryly and shook his head. "Okay, no lecture. I guess you're getting to be a big girl—even if you *are* my little sister."

"A very big girl!" Jillian retorted wryly.

THE PHOTOGRAPH HAUNTED JILLIAN all that day. Even so she knew she didn't dare dig it out from under the stack of sheet music in the piano bench, where she was certain Ken had hidden it.

She had gone down to the vegetable garden to do some of the weeding, partly to ease the load of chores that were difficult for Sylvia and partly because she needed some time alone.

Six years had passed since the tragic accident, five years since Jacob had left, yet she could still recall his image to mind as clearly as if she had seen him only yesterday. They had been so happy—too happy perhaps. They had shared so much, but their love of music had been the magic bond that had drawn—no, welded—them together. They had been so close, so compatible that it seemed they could even read each other's minds.

Then Jacob was gone like a puff of smoke. For a long time after he had disappeared, Jillian wished she could simply die to escape the awful hurt and the awful emptiness that plagued her constantly. Bit by bit she had reconstructed her shattered life to the degree that it was once again tolerable, but she always felt that part of her inner being had been ripped out of her—the vital part.

She sighed and stood up, brushing the dirt from her bare legs. Damn. Would she ever completely recover?

"I knew if I sneaked up behind you I would catch you lazing around!"

Jillian turned to find Ken striding across the garden toward her, a satisfied grin on his face. "Look who's calling the kettle black. I thought you were supposed to be haying. You know, 'Make hay while the sun shines'?"

Ken laughed and whacked her soundly on the bottom. "Cheeky thing, aren't you?"

Jillian laughed in turn. "I have this odd feeling that that comment was double bladed."

"Perhaps. One doesn't always find a bikini-clad female in his garden. You'd better watch it, though. It looks like you're beginning to burn."

Jillian slipped into the blouse Ken handed her, then squinted up at him. "Did you stop at the house?"

Ken nodded as he draped his arm across his sister's shoulders. The two of them fell into step. "Everyone was having an afternoon nap. What did you do to get Sylvia to lie down in the middle of the afternoon, drug the pudding at lunch?"

Jillian grinned and shook her head. "Nothing as

drastic as that. I just told her that if she didn't have a
rest when the boys did, I'd pull up all her cucumber
plants and step on her tomato sets. I guess my . . . suggestion must have worked.''

"You are such a bully at times!"

"I know," Jillian replied. "I had a great teacher.
But you never answered me—how come you're
home? Did you have an equipment breakdown?''

"No, I finished the big field, but the one on the
other side of the creek is a little wet yet. I'll leave it
and pray like hell it doesn't rain for a couple of
days.''

They walked on in silence until they approached
the long low stable with its attached indoor arena.
Their father was justifiably proud of the fine line of
Arabian horses he raised. His dedication to his hobby
had paid off over the past few years; his services as a
trainer and breeder were in great demand due to the
renewed interest in pleasure riding. In fact, the horses
had become a major financial asset to the farm.

Jillian had always been keenly interested and involved in that aspect of farm life. She had become an
accomplished rider and trainer over the years, but she
hadn't been on a horse since Jacob's accident.

"I was just going to ride over to the north pasture
to check the cattle. Why don't you saddle up a horse
and come with me?''

Jillian shivered as she walked into the barn alongside her brother. A strange barren feeling settled over
her as she moved slowly down the alley between the
well-kept box stalls. She paused, a pensive look on
her face as she watched the dust motes from the loose
hay climb up the shafts of light that penciled in
through the small windows. She inhaled deeply,

savoring the familiar smells of clover and hay, oiled tack, the stale sweat from the saddle blankets.

"How about it? Dad has been working that liver-chestnut gelding in the second stall. You'd like him."

Ken was right. The gelding was the kind of spirited mount that, years ago, Jillian would have loved to work. "He's gorgeous, Ken, but—no, I don't want to."

"Come on, Jill." When she shook her head he coaxed, "Try him in the arena if you like, but just try."

"Ken, please...." She knew the uneasiness and vulnerability she was experiencing were the result of the clutter of old memories stirring in her mind. Over the years her brother had been persistent in his attempts to get her riding again.

"Hi, Auntie Jill," a young voice interrupted. "Are you finally going to go riding with daddy?"

"Well, hi, there, sport. No, I'm not. I'm going up to the house to help mommy."

"Can I go, daddy?"

"Sure can. Maybe Aunt Jill will help you saddle that fierce, wild mustang of yours while I saddle the chestnut. Okay, Jill?"

Jillian had to struggle to keep from laughing out loud as Kenny manfully led a docile, sleepy-looking pony out of a stall. Wild mustang? Hardly!

In no time at all the horses were tacked up, and father and son led them out into the hot blinding sunlight. Jillian stooped to hoist the little boy into the saddle but drew back as she caught a gesture of restraint from Ken. After a struggle, Kenny managed to mount on his own, then settled deep in the saddle as he gathered up the reins. He threw his aunt a beaming look of self-satisfaction. By coaxing and threatening, the lad managed to nudge the lazy pony into a reluctant trot, displaying his horsemanship.

"Good grief, Ken, where do you insert the key to wind up that overgrown stuffed toy?"

Ken chuckled, "Oh, come on, Jill, Gracie isn't that bad!"

"With a name like Gracie, no wonder the horse won't move. Well, I'm giving you fair warning. I'm going to buy that child a decent pony. Just look at him ride. His equitation is excellent—he has light hands and a dandy seat!"

Ken's eyes danced. "Ah, just like his Aunt Jill!"

She tossed him a menacing look. "You and your innuendos again!"

As she watched Ken and his son amble off, a memory crowded out the present moment. It was of a snow-covered landscape, of a blond-haired man with dancing eyes and a devilish smile astride a steaming black stallion. He was galloping through drifts of fresh snow and she was riding at his side. . . .

Jillian shut her eyes. Her breathing was rapid as she fought to close the door on her memories, once again to shut away from her past the face that assailed her thoughts and rode like a hurricane through her emotions.

THE NEXT MORNING Jillian had breakfast ready and waiting for Sylvia. She would dearly have loved to pamper her sister-in-law by serving her breakfast in bed, but she knew Sylvia would have been horrified.

Jillian had brought her guitar with her, and she was sitting with her feet propped up on a chair, the instrument cradled in her arms, her fingers strumming softly as she waited for the steaks to grill. When Sylvia entered the kitchen Jillian welcomed her with a few resounding chords of Spanish music.

Sylvia looked at her wryly. "Am I supposed to holler, *'Ole!'* or something?"

Jillian laughed as she swung her legs down and stood up. "I think just a plain 'Good morning' would suffice.

"Good morning, then."

"Good morning, yourself." She propped the guitar against the wall and stirred the potatoes that were browning in a heavy cast-iron skillet. "I see you didn't shrink overnight!"

Sylvia shot her a rueful look as she poured herself a cup of coffee. "Why is it that you big tall broads always pick on us short ones?"

"I wasn't referring to your height, sweet sister. I was referring to your girth."

Sylvia's face was perfectly straight. "And to think I was going to *let* you clean the attic today."

Jillian tossed her head back and laughed, her amusement bubbling out with a rich throaty sound. "I thought I cleaned the attic at Christmastime!"

"You did, but—"

"But my wife has this fetish for cleaning whenever she's pregnant," interjected Ken as he entered the kitchen. "I haven't figured out if it's a nesting instinct or if it's because it's easier to get someone else to do it for her then."

Sylvia whirled to face her husband. "Why, Ken Lambert, you are a horrible man and I've a good mind—"

Jillian raised her hands. "So, children! You have a need to make sour notes?"

Ken and Sylvia both laughed. It was a flawless takeoff of one of Olga Holinski's favorite sayings when she was teaching music. It had become a catch phrase that they all used frequently when someone's temper was riled.

Ken ruffled his wife's hair affectionately as he sat down at the table beside her. "Don't worry about it, Syl. If the house turns into a shambles after we quit having babies, we'll know that you're just plain lazy."

Jillian grinned as she placed their plates before them. There were steaks broiled to perfection, fluffy scrambled eggs, crisp fried potatoes and a wedge of cantaloupe.

Ken looked at his plate and sighed. "Well, at least you aren't a rotten cook like my sister."

Jillian's eyes narrowed threateningly as she neatly whipped the plate away from him. "There's corn-flakes in there," she said, pointing to the pantry. "After all, we can't expect you to eat this slop!"

Ken caught her wrist and laughingly apologized. "Okay! Okay! I'm sorry. I promise I'll quit torment-ing you!"

Jillian handed him his plate, then brought her own to the table as Ken turned toward his wife. "What are you two going to do after you finish harassing the spiders in the attic?"

"I don't know," answered Sylvia. "Maybe we'll drive into town."

Ken caught her hand gently in his, his face sober-ing with warm concern. "Please take it easy today, honey. You didn't sleep much last night, you know."

Jillian looked from one to the other. "Haven't you been feeling well, Sylvia?"

The other woman shrugged. "Nothing really specific. This pregnancy has been different from the other two, but I don't think it's anything to worry about."

"The doctor did tell you to take it easy," Ken admonished gently. A look passed between him and his wife that made Jillian ache inside. The image in the photograph flashed into her mind and she swallowed against the sudden contraction in her throat. She left the table under the pretense of getting more coffee, but the real reason was to give herself some time to compose herself.

After Ken left for the fields Sylvia and Jillian indulged themselves in another cup of coffee. They both enjoyed the peaceful quiet time before the two little boys awoke and arrived on the scene with questions, interruptions, distractions and laughter.

As she cradled an earthenware mug of hot coffee in her hands Jillian looked at her sister-in-law with masked concern. "Look, Sylvia, you have only five or six weeks to go before the baby is born, and then you can work like a dog if you want to. While I'm here I want you *please* to take it a little easy." She grinned, her eyes sparkling. "Besides, I'm looking out for my own interests—at present, you're my only source for nieces and nephews. Allan's too busy, as mother would tactfully put it, 'sowing his wild oats.'"

Sylvia made a prim shocked face. "Our Allan?"

"Our Allan!"

Both women laughed, but Sylvia's eyes registered her genuine appreciation for her sister-in-law's concern. "It's only been the last couple of weeks that I've felt a little off. Once your mother comes back from holidays it will be okay—she's such a help with everything. I've been grateful a thousand times over that they built another house out here and stayed on the farm after Ken and I were married." She reached out and touched Jillian's hand in a conspiratorial gesture. "Ken's right, you know, I couldn't care less if the house filled up with old eggshells and dried orange peels. But I cannot abide those spiders in the attic!"

Jillian laughed and flexed her arms. "Here I am— your very own spider fighter!" Then she squinted thoughtfully. "Do you suppose if I told Kenny that, he would believe his Auntie Jill was really Spider-woman?"

Sylvia rolled her eyes heavenward. "Go and dust, Jillian. Your humor makes my stomach hurt!"

Jillian actually enjoyed cleaning out the attic. She had just vacuumed it at Christmas, but today she was planning to give it a thorough cleaning. It would give her an excuse to poke through the boxes of discarded items, chests of old clothes and trunks of keepsakes.

She spent the morning digging through everything—sorting, discarding and repacking. As she thoroughly cleaned and vacuumed everything she discovered that Sylvia wasn't exaggerating about the spiders.

She had deliberately left two boxes until the last, knowing full well that once she opened them, her work would come to a grinding halt. Now she carried them over to the dormer window and sat cross-legged on an old braided rug, opening the flaps and lifting out several of the old family photograph albums.

She flipped through the first one slowly. Some of the pictures were very old, taken in the early settlement days of the Barr Colonists. From a historical point of view they were very valuable. She laid the leather-bound album aside; she would take it downstairs to show Ken. It really should be on display in the museum in Lloydminster, with the exhibit of other memorabilia from the pioneer days donated by the Lambert family.

As her fingers absently caressed the monogram engraved on the cover of the album, Jillian's thoughts drifted back into family history.

The story of the Barr Colonists was a fascinating one. It had begun in England in 1902, when Reverend George Lloyd, who had spent twenty years in Canada, decided that emigration to the Dominion was a golden opportunity for troops returning from the Boer War. Jobs were scarce in the old country and opportunities were few. He had no funds with which to publicize an emigration scheme, but he decided to write a letter to the London *Times* to promote his idea of a new life in the West.

Lloyd had expected to receive some responses, but he wasn't prepared for the deluge of letters from hopeful people seriously inquiring about emigration. He was overwhelmed and at a loss about what to do, until Isaac Barr, who was also a clergyman, contacted him and informed him that he was organizing a settlement party to emigrate to western Canada. Reverend Lloyd turned all the letters he had received over to Barr, who sent information outlining his plans to those interested. Applications poured in, including money for homestead fees, supplies and shares in some of Barr's proposed ventures. Reverend Lloyd had been concerned about the haphazard way Barr handled the money. It was on his insistence that a clerk was dispatched from the Canadian offices to help with the affair.

Basically Lloyd left the organization and planning to Barr while he dealt with another troublesome issue. Many of those planning on emigrating were deeply concerned about the religious aspect of their new life, and the minister felt responsible for providing an experienced chaplain to accompany the settlers. But time ran out and a suitable candidate could not be found. Although he was reluctant to leave England, Reverend Lloyd could not with clear conscience let so many settlers strike out on such a monumental venture without a clergyman to provide for their spiritual needs. With reluctance but with a deep boundless commitment, he, his wife and their five young children joined the expedition.

In March of 1903 a throng of nearly three thousand hopeful men, women and children had boarded the S.S. *Lake Manitoba*, a converted troop carrier, in Liverpool. In their quest for a better life and a more optimistic future they were leaving everything familiar behind them. Amidst the crush was Kenneth Lambert, a carpenter by trade and a determined industrious man by nature. He left behind him a wife and two small children, who, if all went well, would join him the following year. And so it all began.

The trip was a nightmare of seasickness, overcrowding and inadequate meals, but through it all Reverend Lloyd and his dedicated wife administered to their flock.

By the time the ship docked at Saint John, New Brunswick, in April, many of the emigrants were experiencing some doubts about the integrity of Isaac Barr. Their suspicions were compounded when they discovered that he had bought up all the flour on board the ship and had had it baked into bread by the ship's cooks. He was actually proposing to sell it to the passengers for ten cents a loaf, knowing full well that in port bread was five cents a loaf. Reverend Lloyd was enraged and he intervened.

Incident after disastrous incident further exposed the man as an uncaring profiteer. On arrival in Saskatoon it was discovered that few arrangements had been made to provide for the massive influx of people into this small community. The green unseasoned settlers were forced to rely on their own inadequate resources. Had it not been for provisions given by the government and for the farsightedness of merchants in Saskatoon, the inexperienced colonists would have suffered indescribable hardships. Not only was there inadequate food and little in the way of transportation and protection; Barr had bought up all the available grain at a few cents a bushel and was selling it at a grossly inflated price.

With countless mishaps the colonists managed to trek from Saskatoon to Battleford. Once there they revolted, and Isaac Barr was removed from his position as leader. By unanimous and enthusiastic agreement, Reverend George Lloyd was elected as the new director of the colony.

From Battleford, Reverend Lloyd led the settlers on an arduous trek to the fourth meridian, where they were to homestead. The town site was named Lloydminster in honor of the man who had provided the colonists with such dedicated leadership.

Jillian sighed as she looked out the attic window. The rolling farmland below had remained in the Lambert family since her ancestors settled there. She knew that her awareness, her sense of being had been enriched by their legacy.

Stretching out her legs, she clasped her hands behind her head and smiled broadly to herself. How would she have fared if she had been Isabella Lambert, she wondered. Her great-grandmother had been the only daughter of a landowner in England and had had a rather coddled childhood. Yet as a young woman she had traveled halfway around the world in less than ideal conditions, with two very small children in tow. The railway had been constructed as far as Edmonton by the time she arrived in 1904. She landed there with little more than the necessities— barrels of dishes and household items, trunks of clothing and linens, a hand-crank sewing machine. By river barge she traveled down the North Saskatchewan River to Hewitt's Landing, where she hired a wagon and a team of horses and drove herself and her two babies the twenty-five miles to Lloydminster.

There Isabella discovered that her husband had not expected her for another month and that their log cabin was not yet completed. She didn't bat an eye, however. With sweetness and charm and a fair amount of determination, she blatantly commandeered a completed cabin from two bachelors and moved her family in, bag and baggage. When the two gentlemen came to their senses, they found themselves willingly housed in the Lambert tent.

Jillian smiled once again and picked up another album. It was stifling hot in the attic but she didn't really feel like carrying the box downstairs.

This album was dearly familiar—school pictures, birthday parties, Christmases. She shifted into a more comfortable position, her face alive with anticipation.

The first picture was of Ken, Allan and herself lined up on the back step, dressed in their Sunday best. Jillian's hair was in fat pigtails and she had a front tooth missing; she must have been five or six when the photo was taken. Ken was standing ramrod straight, definitely the "big brother," and Allan had his head turned slightly, trying valiantly to hide a black eye. Jillian laughed out loud.

"Who are you today—Little Miss Muffet or Cinderella?" a masculine voice drawled. Ken's head and shoulders were poking through the trapdoor opening to the attic, his muscled arms resting on the board floor.

Jillian gritted her teeth at him, her face twisted into a mock grimace. "Ken Lambert, if you don't quit this awful nursery-rhyme stuff, I'm going to put arsenic in your porridge!"

"One of the pitfalls of being a father," he sighed. "What do you have there?"

She stood up and dusted her hands on her jeans. Carrying the album over to Ken she knelt on the floor beside him. "Look at this—it really is priceless. And look at Allan's eye. Remember? He had been bugging me, so I took a swing at him. Remember how he bawled all through supper because he didn't know how he could go to school and tell the guys his kid sister had punched him in the eye? He wanted dad to let him say he'd been kicked by a horse."

Ken chuckled as he studied the snapshot. "Lord, yes, I remember."

"And look at you—you look as though someone had stuck a pole up your back!"

"It was that damned sweater. It itched like hell. But mom had knit it, and I knew I'd hurt her feelings if I refused to wear it."

He flipped a few pages of the album. "Let's take it downstairs. I haven't looked at these in years!"

Jillian went back to the window and closed up the boxes. "Why don't we take them all down?" she suggested. "If nothing else, they'll keep the kids amused for hours."

Ken took the two boxes from her. "Here—I'll take that and you get the light."

Jillian caught the dangling string of the single light bulb and pulled it. She picked up the vacuum cleaner and followed Ken down the steep attic stairs. "I'd better burn the vacuum-cleaner bag or Sylvia will have spiders crawling all over the house," she said.

"So you eliminated all the little varmints, did you?"

"Every one. Oh, Grandma Lambert's old album is here, too, Ken. Don't you think we should take it to the museum and display it with the other things we have there?"

"By all means. Mom was looking for it last winter but she couldn't find it. She thought it must have been packed in one of the old trunks. You know, I don't even know what's up in the attic anymore."

"It's a treasure house. Do you know that Mom kept all our old baby clothes? I love attics!"

"Well, you can have this one," offered Sylvia dryly as they entered the kitchen.

"Look at this, Syl. Jillian found the old photograph albums. Some of the pictures are a riot."

Jillian set down the vacuum, opened the canister and slid out the bag, which she handed to Kenny.

"Would you take this out to the burning barrel for me, pet? It's full of spiders."

Kenny looked at the bag curiously. "Can I open it, Auntie Jill? I want to watch them."

Sylvia grimaced with distaste as Jillian nodded her head. "Sure you can—just promise me you won't bring any back into the house, okay? Your mommy turns a funny color when she sees spiders."

Kenny giggled and took the bag. As Jillian put the vacuum away in the broom closet she said, "I should have a shower—I'm covered in dust."

"I don't care what you're covered in as long as it isn't spiders!" Sylvia replied, handing her sister-in-law a frosty glass of iced tea. Jillian sighed gratefully as she took a long thirsty swallow.

Ken had opened the book and was slowly turning the pages when he let out a hoot of laughter. "Look at this one. How did mom ever stand us?"

The picture had been taken in the garden after a heavy spring rain. Allan had said that Ken had splashed him on purpose, and he had flung a handful of mud at his older brother in retaliation. The action had started a mud fight to end all mud fights. Initially Jillian had been an innocent bystander, but when she had been smacked on the side of the head by a misdirected throw, she, too, had retaliated. The three of them had been a mess by the time their father had unsympathetically hosed them off with ice-cold water.

Ken turned to the next page and all three of them burst out laughing at a picture of Allan and John Holinski taken at a Farmers' Day picnic. The two lads had been disqualified in the boys' three-legged race because they had cheated, so they had decided to disguise themselves and enter the girls' event. They had tied ribbons in their hair and, raiding Mrs. Lambert's makeup kit, had plastered themselves with cosmetics. The judges had good-naturedly allowed them to race, but Jillian and Karin had beaten them by a large margin, anyway.

There were murmured comments over the next few pages but the big newspaper clipping on the last page claimed all their attention.

"Lloydminster group takes top award in provincial music festival," read the headlines. Beneath was a picture of the Lamberts and Holinskis dressed in green-and-white plaid vests with white turtleneck sweaters and white slacks. Jillian had to admit they looked very sharp.

"Ken, you couldn't have been fourteen," argued Sylvia. "I'm sure we won that award when *I* was fourteen, and you're a year older than I am."

Jillian unfolded the bottom of the clipping. "Well, you're both wrong. The paper says, 'The group, directed by Mrs. Olga Holinski, consists of—' now, get this you two '—Mr. Jacob Holinski, age 17; Mr. Kenneth Lambert, age 16; Miss Sylvia Holinski, age 15; Mr. Allan Lambert, age 13; Mr. John Holinski, age 13; Miss Karin Holinski, age 11; Miss Jillian Lambert, age 11; and Mr. Mark Holinski, age 9.' So there. If the paper says so, it must be true!"

"Let me see that." Ken pulled the album closer. "Well, how come we competed two more years after that? Jacob would have graduated from high school the following year—"

"Remember, Ken, he was home for two years before he went to university," Sylvia interrupted. "He stayed home the first year because dad was so sick, and then he worked a year before he went to Edmonton.''

"That's right, too! I'd forgotten about that. Then how old were you when you started university, Jill?''

"Karin and I had just turned seventeen.'' She pointed to the clipping. "We certainly were a spiffy-looking bunch and we certainly did our parents proud.''

Ken nodded his head. "We did damned well for a bunch of country bumpkins.''

"Naturally!'' Sylvia stood up and despite her condition made a graceful curtsy. She started gathering up the albums. "We'd better clear the table. Lunch should be ready. I threw a casserole in the oven—''

"God, I hope you put it in a dish this time!''

"Oh, go away, Ken, and find your boys!''

Ken laughed and kissed his wife on the cheek. "Right, chubby!''

Sylvia shook her head as she watched him go, but her eyes danced with suppressed laughter. "One of these days I'm going to do that man bodily harm!''

"I take it that the comment about the dish was some sort of dig?''

"Oh, yes! But it *was* funny. One night I took two frozen meat pies out of the freezer and popped them in the oven on a piece of tinfoil—they weren't in pie plates because I had used all the ones I had to make rhubarb pies. Anyway, something sharp in the freezer must have sliced through the bottom crusts and I never noticed it. Once they started to thaw, all the filling oozed out. I didn't discover the mess till I went to take them out of the oven. We had to have omelets for supper.''

Jillian tossed her head and laughed. She knew her brother; he'd never let Sylvia forget that.

AFTER SHE HAD PUT the boys to bed that evening Jillian went for a walk. There was a little hollow in the pasture, about a quarter of a mile from the house, that nurtured a bountiful wild-strawberry patch. For years the Lamberts and the Holinskis had picked baskets of the succulent berries there, and strawberry shortcake made with the sweet wild fruit was always a special treat.

Bound for the hollow, she wound her way through the copse of poplar and aspen trees, the leaves of which rustled softly. There was the soft hum of insects, and Jillian could hear a meadowlark trilling in the distance. She watched a large dragonfly flit from a wild dogwood bush, its blue gauzy wings flashing silver in the evening light. A little patch of white wood violets filled her with delight, and she knelt down to caress softly the fragile, creamy, blue-veined blossoms. They were her favorite flower. She took a deep breath, savoring the clean outdoor smell of damp moss, the pungent smell of the balsam poplars, the elusive fragrance of wild roses.

Suddenly she felt wistful for the happy uncomplicated days of her youth. There was a dull ache inside her as she thought about the man who had disappeared from her life, leaving her alone and confused by his rejection. It had taken her a long painful time to reconstruct her existence to a degree of tolerability. Their time together had been so rich with love and laughter that she hadn't yet been able even to consider other romantic attachments. Unconsciously she compared every man she met to Jacob, and they always seemed shallow and dull compared to him.

She fingered the chain she wore around her neck. She had worn it for over six years and had taken it off only once. Jacob had given it to her to symbolize his deep commitment to her....

If it hadn't been for that damned accident, she would have had a home and a family of her own now. There would have been purpose to her life instead of this vague feeling of discontent that plagued her. Seeing the photograph of Jacob had unlocked a door to her mind that had taken her years to close, and she didn't dare allow it to swing open. She couldn't let all the memories and pain come tumbling out.

Resolutely she got to her feet and continued toward the hollow. But when she got there the strawberry patch was barren and empty.

THE TWO WEEKS sped by too quickly for Jillian. She had kept herself very busy, taking over many of the outdoor chores that were difficult for Sylvia. She had spent hours and hours in the huge garden, her light dusting of freckles giving way to a deep golden tan. Ken had teased her that she was now covered by one massive freckle, and Jillian secretly admitted he was probably right.

"I've filled the car with gas, Jillian, and I've checked the oil. I think that old heap will get you to Edmonton, God willing."

Jillian grinned at her brother's good-natured needling as she carried her empty coffee cup to the sink. "Thanks, Ken. I guess I'm ready to go, then."

"I wish you could stay longer. It's been terrific having you here." Sylvia leaned against the sink, her expression dejected.

Jillian hugged her sister-in-law. "It's been great being here. If this audition is a flop I'll come straight back, I promise. I know it's a coward's way out to sneak off before the boys are up, but I'll bawl all the way to Vegreville if I have to say goodbye to them.'' She smiled weakly as tears burned the back of her eyes. ''I've left a present for each of them on the foot of their beds. Be sure to tell them that Auntie Jillian will be back.''

The tears had come in spite of her determination to suppress them. She wasn't a mile down the road before she was overcome with homesickness and loneliness as once again the old memories stirred, like a sleeping dragon waking up.

CHAPTER THREE

JILLIAN PULLED INTO the long drive beside the house and slid gratefully out of the car. She couldn't believe the change in the large, attractively landscaped yard in the two weeks she'd been away. The long sweeping flower beds were now a riot of color. A number of flowering shrubs were in blossom, while a profusion of petunias, lobelia and ivy spilled out of the window boxes at the front of the house. Honeysuckle climbing the wrought-iron trellis by the front door was in full bloom, the sweet perfume from its trumpet-shaped flowers permeating the air.

Jillian loved the house she lived in. It was a low sprawling cedar bungalow that nestled among tapering cedars and spreading junipers. Two blue spruce and a stand of birch beside the curved flagstone walk added to the natural beauty of its setting.

Mrs. Olsen, Jillian's landlady, had been widowed several years before, so she had remodeled the house slightly inside to accommodate an apartment for extra revenue. Jillian and Karin had shared it while they were attending university, and after Karin moved to Vancouver, her place had been taken by Allan. Jillian's brother was presently in Boston doing postgraduate studies in microsurgery.

Jillian unlocked the front door and set her suitcases inside the dusky corridor. Dropping the other paraphernalia she had clutched in her arms on top of the luggage, she searched for the right key to her apartment door.

A long wide hallway divided the house; at the end of it was a screened sun room that opened onto a large patio surrounded by a vivid array of flowers. Jillian opened the door on the right and pushed her luggage inside the door.

A deep sigh escaped her as she leaned against the door frame, surveying with satisfaction her spacious living room. She had spent many spare hours in the past few months redecorating her apartment and had definitely managed to create a warm and friendly atmosphere. The decorating spree had been initiated by a chance to purchase new carpeting at such an exceptional price that Jillian simply could not resist. She had installed the off-white broadloom throughout, with the exception of her cozy kitchen. She had covered the walls of the large living room in a heavily textured pampas-grass fabric that complemented perfectly her green-and-beige striped sofa. Her occasional tables and wall unit were dark teak, while two deep comfortable easy chairs were upholstered in a darker green. A forest of lush healthy plants added a finishing touch to the decor.

On the wall beside the brick fireplace was a grouping of miniature pen-and-ink drawings, three excellent watercolors and one beautiful mid-sized oil painting. Jillian went over and stood before the collection, studying it as she so often did. They were all landscapes of the Lloydminster area and as usual Jillian felt a knot of homesickness as she gazed at them. Jacob had painted them for her, and she treasured them above all her other possessions. The old familiar stirring of pain around her heart churned again as she stood there drinking in the beauty before her.

Finally she shook her head in a resigned gesture, then walked into her white-and-yellow kitchen and made herself a tall, ice-filled glass of lemonade. Glass in hand she sat down in the breakfast nook to watch a fat robin tugging at an earthworm in the garden.

As Jillian stared out the window, she forced her wandering thoughts to concentrate on what she had to do. She would go out for a few groceries and then she'd prepare a résumé for her audition the next day. But she really didn't feel like doing either right now.

Her mind began to drift aimlessly, straying from one inconsequential thought to another until it focused on the photograph on Sylvia's piano. She sighed deeply.

Was she still in love with Jacob Holinski. . .or only with a memory? She and Jacob had been friends, good friends for many years before they had ever become involved romantically. That had definitely struck like a bolt of lightning.

The memories came rolling in like breakers on a beach, pounding away at the frail sand-castle barriers of her mind until they were washed away. . . .

Jacob had still been attending the University of Alberta when Jillian and Karin enrolled. They had all spent a great deal of time together. Jacob, Allan and John had visited the girls often and had frequently studied there.

Jacob had applied earlier in the term for a scholarship to a university in California. It would provide him with sufficient financing for the additional year he required for his master's degree in fine arts. He had almost given up hope of being selected when the good news finally arrived.

Jillian had been making lunch in the kitchen when the door to the apartment slammed open and a shout of jubilation rang out in the living room. She raced into the other room, knowing immediately who it was and why he was so elated. She found herself caught up in Jacob's arms as he whirled her around the living room, singing at the top of his lungs, his face alive with delight and relief. She flung her arms around his neck and laughed ecstatically as she hugged him.

But suddenly the playful friendly embrace was charged with a current of emotion that swept them into something much, much more. Jacob's eyes darkened as a charge of electricity curled around them, polarizing their intense feelings until they were living magnets, bound by a force that defied description. Jillian was filled with a strange breathless anticipation as he lowered his head, his mouth warm on hers in a searching kiss that ignited a flame of desire within them. The flame blazed up, leaving them both stunned and trembling. Jacob caught her face in his hands, his eyes wide with incredulity and disbelief. Then slowly he lowered his head again, his mouth searching hers. The fierce yearning that carried both of them into a swirling vortex obliterated any doubt that might have remained in their minds.

He groaned as he pulled his mouth away from hers, his heart pounding wildly as he cradled her head tenderly and possessively against his broad chest, an embrace that was all encompassing. "My God, Jillian," he whispered huskily, his voice shaking, "it's like waking up to find yourself hopelessly in love with your sister." They stood staring into each other's eyes, completely staggered by what had happened to them. He held her hard against him, her body trembling with a passion that she hadn't known existed, as he buried his face in her hair and whispered her name over and over again.

Jillian's eyes were filled with tears as she forced her disturbing thoughts back into the present. She sighed heavily as she stood up and walked to the sink, where she poured her now-tepid lemonade down the drain. She wished she had never seen that damned photograph.

"Oh, hell!" Her voice echoed loudly in the quiet apartment as she stomped into the living room and grabbed her suitcases. She spent the next half hour unpacking, her mood definitely black.

Her thoughts didn't begin to brighten until the mail arrived, bringing with it a long humorous letter from Allan. She read it twice, then tossed it onto her desk. She would answer it later, but first she must compile a résumé. She loathed doing it, but it had to be done. At least it would be professional.

By the time she went for groceries, she had managed to clear her mind of the sad gloomy thoughts that had been plaguing her.

Since she needed only a few items, Jillian decided to walk the two blocks to the supermarket. Sylvia had sent along a large box filled with fresh garden vegetables, farm eggs, a jar of thick cream, plus several cuts of meat from her well-stocked freezer.

Jill enjoyed the walk. Her apartment was located in an old residential area of the city. The tree-lined boulevards gave the area a picturesque quiet serenity that she very much appreciated. Most of the yards were neatly landscaped, and the vivid hues from the early-blooming flowers added splashes of color that satisfied an essential need within her. Someone had recently cut their lawn and Jillian breathed deeply, savoring the fragrance of newly mowed grass. She stopped to chat briefly with Mr. Williams, the minister at the charming old church on the corner, who was fussing with his roses.

The supermarket, Jillian found, was nearly empty so it took her only a few moments to complete her shopping. On the way home from the store Jillian decided to phone John Holinski and invite him over to share the spoils from his sister's garden.

John was a petroleum engineer with one of the major oil companies in Edmonton. He was only two years older than Jillian, but his outstanding intellect and ability had elevated him into a very responsible position within his company. At the moment he was a group leader for a crucial pilot project investigating methods of recovering oil from the Athabasca tar sands in northern Alberta.

Jillian saw John frequently. They enjoyed a comfortable relaxed friendship that allowed room for natural open feelings. John was also a member of the theatrical group Jillian belonged to, and she was very aware that there was quiet speculation among the other members about John and herself, something both of them found amusing. They were friends, close friends, but that was all.

Her phone was ringing as she opened the door to her apartment. She set her bags of groceries on the coffee table, then bounded across the living room.

"Hello." Her voice, breathless from hurrying, was husky.

"Jillian, if you always answered your phone in a sensuous voice like that, I'd phone you more often!"

"John, you idiot. I just came in the door."

"Well, you can just turn around and go out again. I'm picking you up for dinner in fifteen minutes."

The receiver clicked in Jillian's ear as she stood looking at the phone with dumbfounded amazement. Then she smiled wryly as she replaced the receiver and glanced at her watch. It was two-thirty in the afternoon and he was taking her to dinner? She picked up the groceries, carried them to the kitchen and started to put them away. There was no sense in changing until she knew more about John's plans. Dinner to him could mean a hamburger and milkshake or an eight-course meal in the most elite dining establishment in town. With John you just never knew for certain, but that was what made him so much fun.

She had finished putting the groceries away and had a large pitcher of lemonade chilling in the fridge by the time John arrived. She let him in, whistling appreciatively at his appearance. John smirked as he did a ridiculous pirouette in the middle of the living room. He was very much like Jacob, except his hair was a lot darker.

"You aren't ready." His tone was slightly accusing.

Jillian laughed, then pulled a face at him. "You didn't tell me where we're going. I didn't know whether I should put on jeans or an evening dress!"

"How would you like to go to Calgary?"

"For dinner?" Jillian's voice came out a squeak of surprise. Calgary was a four-hour drive away.

"Why not?"

Jillian shrugged, her face completely dumbfounded, and John laughed, thoroughly enjoying her stupefied reaction. "Well, why not, Jill? We could catch some of the events at the stampede. It's Friday night—we wouldn't have to hurry back. Besides, I was talking to Lyle Martin today and he and Alice extended an invitation to you and to yours truly. We could come back on Sunday." He sat back on the chesterfield, a smug look on his face, his eyes dancing.

Jillian threw up her hands in a gesture of complete confusion and surrender. "Okay, John, but I have that audition tomorrow night. I would have to be back for that—"

"Oh, hell, I forgot about it. I'll have you back in time for that, then."

Jillian still looked at him, her face a study of uncertainty. "Are you really serious? Going to Calgary for dinner is a bit far out, even for you." This had to be one of the wildest stunts John had ever dreamed up. Surely he must be teasing.

"You have fifteen minutes to get ready, girl!"

He definitely wasn't teasing and he seemed to be enjoying himself immensely. Jillian hesitated for a moment, staring hard at his face, then she flew into the bedroom.

John's face sobered instantly. He stood up and walked quietly to the phone, lifting the receiver gently off the hook and laying it quietly on the desk. Then he jammed his hands in his pockets and stared at the floor, his face perplexed.

Jillian was ready within the allotted time. She grabbed her overnight bag off the bed, fervently hoping she had remembered to pack everything she would need. As she entered the living room she found John leaning against the wall, the telephone receiver at his ear. He was staring vacantly at the ceiling.

"What are you doing, John? Making obscene telephone calls?"

He laughed as he made a threatening gesture. "I'm phoning for the time—I think my watch is slow. Are you ready?"

"Ready!"

"Well, let's go!" He paused, checked his watch, then replaced the receiver.

JILLIAN WAS DEFINITELY PREOCCUPIED as she parked her car in the underground lot beneath the Centennial Library. Something had been troubling John deeply during the time they had spent in Calgary. As he'd promised, they did have an uproarious time, but there had been a strange air of restraint about him. They had met their friends for dinner, then had attended the wild and exciting chuck-wagon races and the other evening events of the world-famous rodeo. They hadn't returned to the Martin home until dawn, exhausted but in high spirits.

John and Jillian had left Calgary about three in the afternoon, arriving back at her apartment in plenty of time for her to change for her interview. John had been unusually quiet on the drive back, and she had had a feeling that he was going to tell her what it was that was bothering him. He had held back for some reason, however, and that was not like John.

She sighed and dismissed the puzzle from her mind. She had other things to think about that required her full concentration. She would call John as soon as she returned to her apartment—after the audition was behind her.

The wind caught Jillian's breath and whipped her hair across her face as she opened the door and left the parkade. A whirlwind of paper scraps and dead leaves caught her up in its eddy as she rounded the corner. Dark storm clouds had rolled across the sinister sky. It was hailing somewhere, she knew; she could smell the telltale coolness in the air.

Her thoughts drifted toward the interview that was facing her, and her heart started hammering with anticipation. Perhaps, just perhaps, this unexpected opportunity might be her golden chance to break out of her present tedium and find something new, something exciting, something that could develop into an important part of her life.

Music was a passion with her and she came alive when she was performing. She had been teaching music for five years now. It had been a very rewarding experience and she had learned a great deal from it, but she was beginning to find that she was becoming dissatisfied. Jillian genuinely enjoyed working with children, but she was developing an unprofessional attachment to a number of her students. Children of her own didn't seem to be a part of her future, yet she found herself, time and time again, longing for the permanence of a home and family. She got along well with her co-workers, but she deliberately discouraged involved friendships from developing. Instead she kept her old, close friends who understood her feelings. And she had found that loneliness could be tolerable as long as she kept herself fully occupied. . . .

Jillian smiled to herself as she silently blessed her role in that season's theatrical production. It had been the springboard to this audition. She had just completed an evening's performance when an usher appeared with a message for her. It was from a Mr. Watson, asking her if he might have a chat with her concerning a possible position as a professional singer with a group. She had told the usher that the gentleman could come to her dressing room in ten minutes to talk to her.

Jillian had just finished changing into her street clothes when a knock sounded on her door. She had opened it, expecting to find a young man, but had found instead a short balding one with protruding eyes that made him look like a worried frog. He had been very brief and to the point: he had been impressed with her voice and, as a booking agent for one of the major hotel chains across Canada, had wanted to set up an audition for her. One of the bands that was booked at the lounge of the chain's hotel in Edmonton was going to be losing its female vocalist and was looking for a replacement. Would she consider having an audition with the band manager? She had been stunned but had jumped at the chance.

Jillian found that the butterflies in her stomach were becoming impossible to ignore as she approached the main doors of the hotel. She wanted this job badly. A career in singing could give her an outlet for all her energies, and it would certainly be a change. She shuddered at the thought of being an old-maid schoolteacher for the rest of her life.

She gave herself a mental shake and forced herself to smile at the uniformed attendant who held the big ornate door open for her. As the door hissed shut behind her, closing out the violence of the wind and the clamor of the traffic, she felt as though she had stepped into a total vacuum. In vain she tried to smooth down her wind-tossed hair as she approached the friendly-looking clerk at the main desk.

"Good evening. I have an appointment at nine

o'clock with Mr. Watson and Mr. Norm Kent. I wonder if you could tell them that Jillian Lambert is here?'' She shuddered silently. She hardly recognized her voice as her own. She knew if she started trembling now, she wouldn't be able to stop.

The clerk eyed her speculatively and nodded. ''Oh, yes, miss. Mr. Kent left word that you were to be shown up when you arrived. I'll ring for a bellboy to take you.''

''Thank you.'' Jill winced inwardly at the sound of her breathless seductive-sounding response. *Damn, don't have a case of stage fright now and come across as a flighty addle-brained schoolgirl,* she scolded herself inwardly.

The bellboy nodded as he approached her. ''Would you care to follow me, Miss Lambert?''

She nodded and picked up her shoulder bag from the desk as she smiled her thanks to the clerk. Then she grinned ruefully and swore softly to herself as she walked away, for she knew without turning around that he was watching her with a calculating expression on his face. Her amused chagrin at her lack of self-discipline helped her gather her poise and perspective, so that by the time she was shown through the door of the hotel sitting room she was collected and calm, her sense of humor intact.

''Ah, Jillian, right on time! It's so refreshing to find a young person who is prompt these days,'' beamed Mr. Watson as he bounced across the room. Jillian felt laughter welling up within her as she smiled at him and took his extended hand. She speculated silently that maybe he was an enchanted frog, and if she kissed him he would turn into a prince.

Mr. Watson led her into the room. ''Jillian, I would

like you to meet Norm Kent. Norm is the manager of the band, Firefly. Norm, Jillian Lambert.''

The first impression that washed over Jillian was that Norm Kent was reacting strongly to her name or her face. Yet she knew that she had never met him before. It was a strange feeling.

He was a tall slim man. Jillian herself was five feet ten inches in height, and he was a good deal taller than she—probably six feet four. He was a handsome man, most likely in his early forties, with dark hair that was liberally sprinkled with gray. He had a friendly, relaxed manner, but the lines etched into his face showed the effects of a life that had not always been easy.

Jillian reached out to shake his hand and was instantly aware of an odd guarded sensation. Yet she had the strangest feeling that here was someone who could be trusted, who could become a close friend. Their eyes held as he clasped her hand and smiled down at her. Something passed between them that was completely intangible but nevertheless very real.

''Hello, Jillian. Arthur has been singing, if you'll pardon the pun, your praises ever since we arrived yesterday.'' He continued to hold her hand firmly in his as he laughed down at her. ''If you sound half as good as you look, you'll be sensational!''

Jillian grinned up at him. ''It's a wonder I'm still in one piece. I half expected I would either shake myself to death or crumple into a heap on the floor by now!''

''Nervous?''

''Yes! It's the first time I've had an opportunity to audition for anything as exciting as this, and to be perfectly honest, I'm scared half out of my wits!''

He let go of her hand. "Here, let me take your raincoat." She noticed as she slipped out of her trench coat that Mr. Watson had disappeared. Norm draped the coat across the back of a chair and motioned her to sit down on the sofa.

"Now, Jillian, I'd like to know a bit about you, what experience you have, your musical background—things like that. Then I'll tell you a bit about the group before we go down for the audition." He sat down in the armchair closest to Jill and looked at her expectantly.

Jill shrugged her shoulders and clasped her hands in front of her in an uncertain gesture. "There isn't really much to tell. I was raised in rural Alberta. I graduated from university five years ago with a bachelor of education and a major in music, and I've been teaching music for the public-school system ever since. I've since picked up my master's degree at night classes and summer school, and I've been involved in a number of musical productions in the city." She opened her bag and pulled out a folder. "I've compiled a résumé, if you would like to see it." He nodded silently, but for some reason his face was again guarded and reserved as he opened the portfolio and started to read. The silence unnerved Jillian and she started playing nervously with the chain around her neck. Her fingers slipped down the long gold strand to the delicate circular locket, which she caressed unthinkingly. An Oriental jade ring set in beaten gold dangled freely on the chain.

She lifted her head to find Norm watching her intently. To her surprise he reached forward, lifted the locket out of her hand and held it between his thumb and forefinger.

He spoke very quietly, his face intent. "These are very beautiful pieces, Jill. Are they special?"

Jillian nodded, keenly aware that he had been able to read some of the despair that she knew was evident in her eyes.

When he looked at her questioningly she shook her head. "It was something that happened a long, long time ago, Norm." She was surprised to find that her fingers were trembling as she combed them through her hair. "I'm sorry."

"There's no need to apologize." He smiled lop-sidedly when she finally looked up at him. "There are a few of us with ghosts in our past that come out to haunt us at awkward times." The guarded look had left his face as he patted her hand and grinned warmly. "Now, to get back to current affairs." He flipped through the papers he held in his hand. "I see in your résumé that you were Klondike Kate for Edmonton's Klondike Days. How did you find that experience? And who in hell was Klondike Kate? I'm a Yank and I've never heard of her."

Jillian laughed as she thought back to the episode that two years before had projected her into the role of the infamous Kate. Taking a deep breath she explained, "Some years ago the city of Edmonton selected the Klondike Gold Rush in the Yukon as the theme for its annual exhibition. Klondike Kate was one of the notorious dance-hall girls of that era." She always felt embarrassed when she talked about her part as Kate, and she could feel the beginning of a flush on her cheeks. "The whole thing started out as a dare, actually. They were auditioning for someone for the part and there had been a big furor in the press because local talent had never been employed.

The subject was being discussed in the staff room at school during one lunch break.''

Jillian hesitated as she looked at Norm. "Are you certain you want to hear all this?"

The band manager stroked his chin reflectively. "Yes, I think I do. I'm curious to find out what happened that would make you blush like that."

Jillian shrugged reluctantly and silently cursed her expressive face. "Well...four of my music classes had just finished putting on an operetta based on the gold rush. One particularly talented twelve-year-old girl had vamped the part of Kate with absolute perfection, so I said that maybe I should hustle Donna down to the auditions. The principal of the school thought it was a brilliant idea, so there was some bantering about it. Then someone commented that maybe they should send me, since I had coached Donna so well."

Jillian laughed self-consciously at the recollection. "One thing led to another, and by the time the noon bell rang, there was an ante on the table from the staff amounting to nearly two hundred dollars. If I went down to audition, the money would be mine to fund the next operetta. So down I went. My accompanist was an old friend who thought the whole episode was an incredible gas. The staff had dreamed up the stage name 'Amber Blaine.' It was a huge joke as far as I was concerned, so you can imagine my reaction when I landed the job. I nearly died. I would have backed out if John, my pianist, hadn't dashed over to the school where I worked and told everyone. So...." Jillian shrugged with embarrassment.

Norm's eyes were twinkling with restrained laughter by the time Jillian finished telling her story. "Was it fun?"

"Oh, it was," she returned brightly. "I had to go to all these weird and wonderful places at weird and wonderful times, singing torchy barroom songs. The audiences were everything you could imagine. One critic commented that I was the 'most un-Katelike Kate' he had ever hoped to see. I was never sure what he meant by that. Actually, after a few performances I overcame my terror and really enjoyed myself."

"And probably picked up some damned good reviews while you were at it." Norm was shaking his head, a broad smile on his face as he flipped through the pages of her résumé. "Now, about your singing the Canadian anthem at the National Hockey League games—did you get railroaded into that, too?" He had pursed his lips, a knowing gleam in his eyes.

"Well, sort of. One of the people involved with Klondike Days and the Edmonton Exhibition Association was also indirectly involved with the Oilers Hockey Team. He approached me and asked me if I would consider doing it. The only problem was that he came to school to talk to me about it, and the news about why he was there spread like German measles. The principal in fun—or at least I thought it was in fun—told him that he was sure it could be arranged, especially if some season tickets were part of the deal. Consequently, about a week later, four season tickets arrived at the school—so now I sing the anthem at home games."

Norm was chuckling out loud by this time, his eyes dancing. "Jillian, I think perhaps Lady Fate keeps herself amused with you!" He reached out his hand and helped her to her feet. "Come on, let's go down and meet the guys. They should be practicing by now."

Jillian gathered up her purse and coat and walked

in front of Norm as he opened the door for her. She felt reassured and confident as she tucked her arm through his and they walked down the corridor to the elevators.

She could hear strains of music as they approached the large banquet room at the end of the hall. Norm stopped and faced her.

"I just realized that I haven't given you any info about the band. There are five members. Jake's on keyboards and backup vocals—he also does all the arranging. He's well known in the States as an arranger, and he's an up-and-coming composer. In fact, he makes a damned good living at it. This tour is a swan for him as he's filling in as a personal favor to me—our regular man had to take a few months off because of personal problems. We're damned lucky to have him.

"Then there's Keith, the drummer. All this kid needs is a little maturity and exposure for him to develop into a top-flight performer and musician. Dan and David are brothers. David plays lead guitar and is also our lead vocalist. He has a good voice, but if you have any power at all you may find you have to pull back a little. He's good, though. Dan plays rhythm guitar and does backup vocals. These two can handle any instrument you give them, but their strongest suit is brass—and they are *good*. David acts as our emcee, Keith as our ham—which is no act, by the way. They're a good bunch and as serious as hell about their music. Oh, yeah, David's and Dan's wives travel with us. They do most of the offstage stuff.

"They are all good people, and I know you'll like them. The girl we had before quit us in Vancouver and ran off with a tugboat captain, so we were left in a bad way. Watson wired for us to hang loose, as he had someone who might do.''

Jillian nodded, a frown of concentration on her face. ''What type of music have they been using?''

''Well, all types, actually. A lot of upbeat stuff with good harmonies, thanks to Jake, but absolutely no punk rock. Jake has composed a few pieces but we haven't really promoted them yet. Deanne, the girl we had before, wasn't the right vehicle. I'll tell you this, though. Both Jake and I think this group has potential, and they are a good decent bunch. I'd like to see them take off.'' He grinned down at her. ''You could be on your way.''

Jill clenched her hands together and looked heavenward. ''I hope you're right!''

He laughed and squeezed her hand. ''Now, kid, there's a bathroom right there. Go and brush your teeth, practice yoga, have hysterics or do whatever girls do before something like this. I'm going in to talk to the guys for a minute and I'll come back out to get you.'' He started to walk away, then paused. ''Oh, Jake won't be there for a while, so I'll be filling in on the piano. Have patience; I'm nowhere near his class. I'll be out in ten minutes, okay?''

''Okay. I think I'll settle for hysterics, if there's no objection.'' Jillian grimaced up at him. ''The butterflies are trying to get out again.''

Norm laughed as he patted her shoulder. ''You'll be fine, Jill. Not to worry. Ten minutes!''

She watched his retreating back with definite reluctance, wishing she could go with him and get it over with. Instead she shrugged her shoulders and walked toward the women's washroom.

Once inside, Jillian combed her hair and suddenly

regretted her decision to leave it down. Her back felt so hot and sticky. She reapplied her lipstick, then stepped back to appraise herself in the full-length mirror, staring at her face within its frame of thick auburn hair. Her eyes were large and hazel, accentuated by gently arching dark brows and long sweeping lashes.

After a moment she grinned at herself and stuck her tongue out at her reflection. She touched the locket and ring and felt strangely comforted when she felt the cold metal slide between her breasts as she dropped it down the neck of her blouse. "I'm wearing my lucky colors, anyway," she whispered, taking one last glance at the emerald green blouse and matching slacks before she turned to go out the door.

The introductions with the band members and the wives went well. Jillian felt instantly comfortable with them and inwardly heaved a sigh of relief when she discovered for herself that they were indeed serious, hard-working musicians. They had already run through a number of songs with instrumentals and harmony backups when Norm rose from the piano, walked over to where she was standing and handed her two scores.

"These are Streisand's 'Evergreen' and Manilow's 'Looks Like We Made It.' We'll do them with just piano, Jill, and I want you to give them all you've got, okay?"

She looked up at him, her eyes dark. They were two love songs that moved her every time she heard them; she knew she could sing them no other way than with everything she possessed. She also knew what kind of state she would be in at the end.

"Can you handle it, Jill?"

For some reason he understood that this was going to be an emotionally difficult thing for her to do, but she also understood that he had to test her on something that would push her emotionally. She laid the mike down and turned toward the rest of the group, who sat at the side of the stage.

As Norm did the lead-in introduction, Jill closed her eyes and let her mental picture of Jacob obliterate all else. Jacob. Jacob with his tawny hair and laughing eyes. The image of the rugged face became vividly real and her inner loneliness grew. Then she sang, her deep rich contralto filling the room, throbbing with the power of emotion, an aching, crying melancholy that pulled her into the haunting music. She sang and it all came pouring out. She sang for the past; she sang for Jacob.

The last tremulous notes faded into the total silence of the room. Jill bent her head and fought for control of her runaway emotions. Then she turned to face Norm at the piano, her face streaked with tears, her heart tormented by a gripping pain within her. But when she raised her head, she instantly froze. Everything seemed to be sucked into a dense spinning fog, her whole body trembling with shock as she looked into the cool impersonal eyes of Jacob Holinski. Without a word, without a gesture, he turned his wheelchair around and left the room.

CHAPTER FOUR

Norm had somehow managed to get Jillian out of the hotel, back to her car and home. She was still stunned and very much shaken by the encounter with Jacob. His cold rejection had brought all her emotions from the past rushing back, sweeping away the mental defenses that had taken her years to erect. She simply did not have the strength to rebuild the barriers now.

Something hot was thrust into her trembling hands. She looked up dazedly at Norm.

"I've made myself at home, Jillian. It's coffee with a damned good shot of brandy in it. I want you to drink it all." He spoke quietly as he sat down on the sofa beside her. "Have a drink, kid, and then I think maybe you and I should have a long talk. Have you ever talked about it?"

Jill shook her head numbly, then raised the cup of steaming coffee to her lips. The hot biting brew had an almost instant calming effect. She had nearly finished the cup before Norm spoke again.

"Honey, first of all, let me tell you something. I can see the agony you're going through. Hell, I can feel it. Believe me, Jill, I know what it's all about. As I said earlier, some of us have ghosts that come out to haunt us at awkward times.... Well, I have a ghost, too."

Jill raised her head and looked deep into Norm Kent's pain-riddled eyes. She could sense that this man had been through his own living hell and had survived. She recalled her earlier intuition that Norm was a man who could be trusted.

He stood up and began to pace back and forth in front of the sofa. "Twelve years ago, Jill, I married a woman who was everything to me." His voice broke slightly. "She was my life. We had two kids—two beautiful little girls. They were five and three years old. I was the managing director of one of the big recording studios in L.A. at the time. I was really snowed under at work, so Paula had taken the girls down to our beach house for a week. I was going to join them for a few days once I had some of the work cleared away. She phoned one rainy Tuesday morning and said she had loaded up the car and was coming home. The weather had been miserable and she was lonely. I was so damned glad she was coming home. I had missed her like hell and told her so."

He stopped pacing and stood with his hands rammed into his pockets, his jaw clenched, staring at the floor. "She was going to pick me up at the studio about five o'clock. At four o'clock I received a phone call from the hospital. There had been a four-car pileup on Interstate 5. A big semi had gone out of control on the wet pavement and had smashed into Paula's car, and she and the girls were in the hospital. I found out later that the two girls were actually dead on arrival, but Paula lived for three days."

Norm's voice was no longer even and controlled. It was costing him a terrible price to relate this story to her. "Paula's back was broken in three different places and she would have been paralyzed from the neck down. She had sustained severe internal injuries, as well, but the doctors felt there was a slim chance. The night before she died, she had a long stretch of consciousness and we talked.'' At this point in his grim story, Norm sat on the coffee table facing Jill, his face buried in his hands, his body rigid.

The recollections came pouring back of the numbing terror and helplessness Jillian herself had felt during the days that Jacob's life hung suspended by a delicate thread. There had been that awful horrifying feeling of being unable to do anything but wait. Here was someone who had experienced it, too, and something even far worse—the loss of the entire family that he had obviously cherished. Yet he had survived somehow.

Jillian was unaware of tears trickling down her face as she knelt down in front of Norm. She took his hands in hers, pulled them away from his face and held them tightly. He looked up, his face white and scarred with an anguish that was almost unbearable to watch. He grasped Jill's hands in his, his body shuddering as he forced himself to take a deep breath.

His grip tightened as he went on. ''We talked about our love for the girls, our very special love for each other, the six unbelievably happy years we had had together. We gave each other comfort and solace that night. God, every word we spoke was indelibly etched in my mind.'' Norm looked deep into Jillian's eyes, conveying a message that she understood. ''At times, I wish I had the guts to end it all, but there are times when I feel her presence, and there is a kind of peace.''

Norm rose and sat down beside Jillian on the chesterfield, still holding her hands. "It was about a year and a half later that I met Jake. I guess it must have been about six months after he left here. Anyway, he was working for a friend of mine as an illustrator for the wildlife books Fred was writing. We hit it off immediately, probably because we were both trying to cope with a major and very painful adjustment in our lives. We each understood exactly how the other felt. Eventually I found out about his extensive musical background, and he's been working with me ever since." Norm let go of Jillian's hands and ran his hand through his hair. "He's brilliant, you know. I've never met anyone with as much natural talent as he has."

"That explains it," whispered Jillian.

"Explains what?"

"When I met you tonight, I had an immediate impression, one that registered rather strongly."

"And that was?"

"That you recognized me or my name when Mr. Watson introduced us. It was weird at the time."

Norm smiled and patted her hand. "Oh, yes, I recognized you, but I didn't think I had let it show."

"How did you recognize me? You couldn't have seen a picture of me because Jacob took only his clothes when he left."

"I'll tell you all about that later, Jill, but now I would like you to tell me what happened when Jacob left. Did you know he was going?"

Jillian shook her head and clasped her hands together to still the trembling. "He told no one. We were all frantic. It was two weeks before his family heard from him, and all he said was that he was fine and to please let him have some time to sort out his life.''

Jillian shuddered at the memory of the six weeks of hell they had gone through before they heard from him again. Then that cold distant note had arrived, saying that he could never be a part of her life under the circumstances.

It was over, and he would never see her again.

"Jillian?"

"What?"

"Would you mind thinking out loud tonight?"

"What do you mean?"

"Well, you were deep in a memory, and I know that it's really none of my business, but I would like to know what happened—at least your side of it. I'll be quite frank. If I hadn't recognized that pendant and ring tonight, you would never have found out through me that Jake was part of the band. He only once talked about his accident, and I had come to the incorrect conclusion you had walked out on him.''

Jillian's head flew up and anger blazed in her eyes. "Left him? Did he tell you that? I went home one night and he was gone in the morning—''

"Hold it! Hold it! I never said he told me that! It was my own assumption. Now, will you tell me what happened, the whole story? Then afterward I'll tell you what I know and why I want to know what happened. Okay?"

Jill leaned back against the loose cushions of the sofa and shut her eyes. She pushed the hair back off her ashen face, the strain of the evening already etching dark circles beneath her eyes. She sighed heavily and nodded her head. "All right, Norm, I'll tell you, but you had better have an ample supply of cigarettes and that coffeepot had better be full. It's going to be a long drawn-out affair, and I'm not too sure how well I'm going to handle it.''

Norm leaned back against the other end of the sofa and fished his cigarettes out of his shirt pocket. He opened the pack, took out two, lighted them both, then handed one to Jillian. He reached for the ashtray on the coffee table and set it on a cushion between them. "I didn't think you smoked.''

Jillian gave him a rueful look. "I don't normally, but I think tonight is going to warrant it.''

Norm stood up and stepped over the coffee table, picking up the mugs on his way by, and strolled toward the kitchen. "I'm going to get us some more coffee, sans brandy, or we'll both be so loaded in three hours that we won't remember what in blazes this was about.''

Jillian was beginning to feel dizzy and slightly light-headed. She wasn't sure if it was from the cigarette, the previous cup of brandy-laced coffee or all the tension that had engulfed her this night. She shut her eyes and made her mind go blank. She heard Norm set the coffee on the table and walk over to the wall unit opposite the sofa.

"This is an impressive stereo setup you have, Jillian.''

"My one extravagance.''

"And worth every penny, I'll bet.''

"I would have gone insane without it.''

"What's in the cassette?''

"It's a tape of Spanish guitars—one of my favorites.''

Norm switched on the set and the rich vibrant music filled the room. He came back, settled himself and picked up his coffee. "Jill?"

She looked up, her eyes clouded with doubt and uncertainty as she thought about the ordeal that lay before her.

"How long have you known Jake and where did you meet him?"

Clasping her arms around her knees she took a deep breath. "I've known Jacob all my life. We grew up in the same farming community—in fact, his family's farm is next to ours."

Norm's face registered surprise. "He's never mentioned his family or his personal background. How did he manage to accumulate the extensive musical background he has, stuck out on a farm?"

Jillian laughed for the first time all evening, enjoying Norm's bewildered yet cosmopolitan outlook. "Oh, Norm, that's a very citified statement." She tapped the ash off her cigarette as she explained, "Jacob's mother is a brilliant and very talented pianist and vocalist who was European trained. She taught music in the district, and my two brothers and I were pupils of hers. Jacob's entire family is extremely talented. He has two brothers and two sisters, who have had extensive training, also. It was his brother John who acted as my accompanist when I did Klondike Kate. The eight of us used to sing together as a group for public functions, but we used to do it for fun, too. I can remember all of us sitting on a haystack, creating our own harmonies to popular songs. Allan, my brother, maintained that we could have been famous if only we'd managed to sing one song the same way twice. We were all very close."

Jillian's voice softened and became husky as she recalled the happy fun-filled times the Holinskis and Lamberts had spent together.

"Don't tell me you and Jake were grade-school sweethearts!" Norm's voice was disbelieving.

"Heavens, no!" Jillian was amused at his reaction to the information she had passed on to him. "Jacob was always like another older brother, until university."

"Tell me about it."

She shook her head. "That is definitely off limits, Norm. I will tell you that it caught us both...off guard." She reached for her coffee, her thoughts caught up in a net of memories that hadn't blurred with the passage of time. They had been so young and so ridiculously happy.

"You must have some very special memories, Jill."

Jillian was drawn back to the present, her face pensive. "You know, Norm, I have the uncanny sensation you can read my mind."

He laughed, then lighted another cigarette. "Maybe it's because I can identify with you and Jake." He took a long drag on his cigarette and looked at Jillian. "Will you tell me about the locket, Jill? Jake gave it to you, didn't he?"

Distractedly she began to pleat the striped fabric of the armrest cover. "Yes, he gave it to me for my birthday the year we were to be married." Her voice was a bare whisper. The memories, the beautiful sweet memories were clamoring within her mind and she had little will to resist them. Her hand slipped down the long gold strand to the delicate circular locket, which she caressed. It had been so perfect.

The mental picture became clearer and clearer as it swept her back in time. It had been her birthday....

Jacob had been attending a university in California and she was at the University of Alberta. It had been a particularly rotten day for Jillian, and she returned to the apartment to find there was nothing in the mail from Jacob—no letter, no card. Disappointment sliced through her. She stormed into the apartment and dashed through to her bedroom, where she threw her books violently on the floor and ripped off her coat. She flung herself facedown on the bed and gave way to stormy tears.

"Don't, love. Is this what you're crying over?"

She twisted around to find him standing there with a devilish grin on his face, waving a birthday card in his hand. She whispered his name, unable to believe he was really there until he was on the bed beside her, holding her hard against him. He held her so tightly, his hand buried deep in her hair as he whispered her name over and over in an agonized groan. She clung to him with a desperation born of loneliness. An overwhelming longing for him pushed her to the brink of uncontrollable desire. His mouth was on hers, insistent and possessive as their bodies were welded together with a need so strong that it obliterated all else. He groaned as he gathered her closer against him and rolled her under him. Her arms encircled his neck as she drew him down.

"Oh, God, Jacob, please," she pleaded huskily against the wildly beating pulse at the base of his throat. She pressed against him, wanting him, as she felt the hard masculinity of his body burning against hers. The knowledge that he wanted her just as much inflamed her more. His mouth crushed down on hers, insistent and demanding. Their passion drove them out of control, pressing them to the point of no return.

Suddenly Jacob groaned and bolted from the bed. He stood with his back to her, his hands clenched and shaking at his sides. Jillian struggled to smother the flame of desire that was surging and boiling within her as she rose, weak-kneed and shaking, and laid her hand on his back. He turned to face her, his face ashen, his breathing heavy and labored. Tears filled her eyes as she took his taut face in her hands. Her mouth was trembling and wet from her tears.

"It's all right, babe. It's all right," he murmured as he gathered her in his arms and tenderly held her to him. He stroked her back in long soothing motions as they stood quietly together in the shadows, completely overwhelmed by the intensity of their yearning. Jillian shivered within the security of his arms, knowing full well the massive effort he was exerting to restrain their emotions. She tried to quell the unsatisfied hunger that gnawed within her. She reached up and touched his face with her fingertips and gazed into his eyes, knowing his concern was for her above all else. It made her feel secure beyond belief, but it was little comfort for raw ragged nerves. She smiled at him ruefully.

"Oh, Jacob, I've missed you so much that I thought I would die, and now that you're here playing the White Knight, I could wring your neck!"

He took her face in his hands and kissed her softly on the forehead, then grinned, his brown eyes sparking with a wicked gleam. "There are a few things I would like to do to you, Jillian Lambert, but wringing your neck isn't one of them."

By that time she was clad only in her slacks and bra. He let his eyes slide down the full length of her body, and as he did she went weak at the knees and felt the color rising in her cheeks. He cradled her against him as he leaned over and swept her blouse off the bed. Keeping her within the circle of his arms he slipped it on, his hands lingering on the soft swell of her breasts.

"I think it might be a good idea if you were dressed, Jillian. You are too damned hard to resist standing there like that." His voice was deep and husky.

She wanted him so. She ran her hands across his bare muscular chest, slipping them seductively up his neck, running her fingers slowly through his thick tousled hair. He shut his eyes, his jaw clenched, as he reached up and caught her hands. He lowered them to his lips and kissed her palms, sending ice and fire coursing through her veins. His body was tense and rigid as he fought to control the hunger that was rising once again.

"Jill, baby, don't. For God's sake, don't make it any more difficult than it already is." He whispered hoarsely, "I want you. It's more than I can stand." He looked deep into her eyes. "But Jillian, you are very much worth loving and I know you are going to be very much worth waiting for."

"Jacob, I want you so...."

He gave that smile that turned her bones to water and made her heart pound. "Listen, Jill, I know. This waiting has got to be a special hell, but, babe, I want to be able to watch you come down that aisle to me in bridal white." He held her close to him as he whispered softly in her ear. "You will be a vision,

Jill, and I want to know that I was man enough to give you the honor of wearing it. I want you to have a wedding night that is special, that will be the beginning, not the continuation of something." He lifted her head, his hand gently caressing her cheek, his eyes so full of love and tenderness that it brought tears to her eyes. He ran his hand slowly and lovingly through her tangled hair, letting it slip like molten copper through his fingers. He kissed her softly, then released her.

When he swung his jacket off the bed, he retrieved a blue velvet box from the pocket. He opened it, slipped out the beautifully crafted locket and clasped it around her neck.

His voice was low and tremulous with emotion. "I love you, Jillian, and I will forever. I can't always be here to tell you. I wanted to give you something to wear that would say, by its presence, that I do." He traced the square-linked golden chain with his fingers down to the locket where it lay nestled between her breasts. "It marks my claim, Jillian." He bent down and kissed her where the locket lay. "As long as you wear it, I'll know that you love me...."

"Jill?" Norm's questioning concerned voice dragged her back to the present, the awful stark present. Her face was drawn and ashen from the impact of the recollection from her past. She wiped away the tears that had trickled down her face and reached out numbly for the lighted cigarette that Norm was handing her.

"Jill, please. I know this is a living nightmare for you but I need to know what happened, all about his accident, why he bolted."

"Why is it so important? It's over, Norm, and

nothing can change what has already happened.''
The defeat and hopelessness in her voice rang hollow-
ly in her head.

"I promise I'll tell you what's happened since, but
I want to know what drove Jacob into his shell and
why he has made the decisions he has. Okay?''

She nodded, again unconscious that she was caressing the golden pendant between her long slim
fingers.

"You do that all the time, do you know that?
Every time you're reflective or scared or tense, you
touch that as though it's a source of strength.''

Jillian smiled wanly. "I guess I do it because it's
my one physical link with that portion of my life.''

"Have you ever taken it off?''

"Only when I put our engagement ring on the
chain.'' It had been a cold, rainy, desolate spring
evening when she had finally admitted to herself that
it was over and had taken off the ring.

"There was another reason why you hung the ring
with the locket, wasn't there?''

Jillian's head flew up, her cheeks pink, her eyes
wide with amazement. "He told you about that?''

Norm chuckled, his eyes sparkling. "Jacob told
me nothing about you, Jillian, but I know him very
well and I know he's a sensitive person with a strong
sentimental streak. And I'm a good guesser. The
chain is longer than on most pendants, and I'm perfectly aware of where it lies when you wear it next to
you.'' He cocked one of his heavy black eyebrows, a
knowing grin on his face. "Am I right?''

Jillian blushed and lowered her head, letting her
hair fall forward to cover her face. She composed
herself, then unwound her long legs, stood up and

looked down at Norm, who was sprawled at the end of the chesterfield, a wicked gleam in his eyes.

"Are you ready for a refill?"

"May as well."

Jillian went into the kitchen and filled the coffee mugs. Norm followed her and leaned against the cupboard, his long legs crossed as he took the steaming cup from her.

"How did Jake wreck his back? I know it was a riding accident, but that's all I know."

Jillian sat down at the table, her head propped on one hand as she idly traced the geometric patterns in the yellow-and-white woven tablecloth. She began to relate the account of the accident, her voice controlled and even. She told Norm what had happened—of Jacob's battle to survive, the long convalescence, his withdrawal and finally his disappearance. She told it all, except what the final prognosis was; that, she kept to herself.

Norm listened quietly, not interrupting the account as he watched her with a reflective look on his face. Finally she finished and fell silent. Norm continued to watch her as she sat staring vacantly at the bowl of fruit on the table, her hands clenched into tight fists. He set his mug on the counter as he pushed himself away from the cupboard and walked over to where she sat. When he picked up one of her hands he winced as he saw the angry purple indentations that her nails had made in her palms.

"Jill, how do you feel about him now?"

She stood up, her shoulders drooping as she walked slowly toward the living room. "I don't know, Norm. I miss him terribly sometimes, and it was an awful shock seeing him tonight, I can tell you.'' She swept her hands through her hair in an exhausted gesture as she sat down on the sofa. ''I don't know. I honestly don't know. I don't even want to think about it. I don't think I could stand to go through that hell again, and until Jacob comes to terms with his disability I don't think he's going to allow anything to change. He can be very stubborn.''

''I know.'' Norm sighed as he sat down beside Jillian and draped his arm across the back of the chesterfield. He opened his mouth to speak, then paused for a moment before he said, ''Did you ever try to find him?''

Jill closed her eyes and leaned back against the cushions as she propped her feet up on the coffee table. ''Yes. We were able to trace him to California after he left here. I contacted some of the people Jacob had introduced me to when I went down to see him when he was attending university. Word must've reached him that I was trying to locate him. Anyway Sylvia and Ken received a letter saying that if we tried to find him, he would disappear and no one would hear from him again. The same warning applied if they gave me his address. He didn't want to hear from me or about me ever again!''

''Did you believe that, Jillian?''

''I believed he would disappear, and I couldn't risk cutting his family off from him because of me. It was bad enough for them as it was without my making matters worse. You say you know him. Don't you think he would have carried through with his threat?''

Norm sighed, ''Yes, he would have. You were in one hell of a tough spot.''

Jillian sat up and looked at Norm. ''So that's my

story. Now are you going to tell me what has happened to him since?''

"Yes, I will. As I said, the fellow he was working for was a mutual friend. When I met him, he was exactly as you described him—withdrawn, isolated, totally cut off from people. He had rented a little beach house along the coast and was very nearly a hermit. He went out only when he had to, wouldn't associate with anyone, did all his work at home. I had gone down to Jacob's to pick up some things for Fred. We started drinking and it seemed to be the catalyst we both needed. I told him about Paula and he told me a little about his accident. I asked him if there had been a girl and he said there was. It was because of her that he had come to California.''

"And you thought I had deserted him?''

"Yes, I did. But I was certain that he was still really hung up on you. Anyway, a friendship developed and I found out about his musical ability. We've been working together ever since.''

"He never mentioned me.'' It hurt to know that he had completely and effectively dismissed her from his life.

"Just hang on a minute, Jill. Don't jump to any conclusions until I finish. Anyway, he really got involved with arranging music, and it wasn't long before he had built himself an impressive reputation. Within two years, commissions for Jake literally swamped the studio. He had incorporated himself under Jacco Music Incorporated. Sometime when you have nothing to do, go through your recent records under our label and see how many were arranged by him—the guy is a genius.

"Then about two years ago he started painting. He

wouldn't show anyone, not even me. I went down one weekend for a break. We were sitting on his sun deck when he asked me, like a bolt out of the blue, if I wanted to see what he had been working on. I said I did. He took me into the sun room he uses for a studio and there was this huge canvas of the most inspired, impassioned work I had ever seen—and I've seen a few. It was a painting of a beautiful girl sitting on the rail of an old wooden bridge. She had on an ice-blue sun dress, but the thing that hit me was her hair.'' Norm reached out and lifted a thick strand of Jillian's hair and wound it around his finger. He grinned at her as realization dawned on her face. ''It was the most incredible auburn hair I had ever seen. It hung nearly to her waist and it was alive with golden highlights.''

Norm was obviously beginning to enjoy himself. ''The next thing that hit me were her eyes. They were fantastic—they sparkled like emeralds, and they were so full of love and joy that it made me ache inside.''

Tears were threatening to overflow from Jillian's eyes as she covered her trembling mouth with her hand.

''I didn't say anything for a long, long time and then I said I wanted to buy it. Jake told me to go to hell, that it wasn't for sale. Then I said I didn't want it anyway because no one could possibly have hair like that, and besides, a guy could lose his soul in those eyes. Jake looked up at me with a look so loaded with emotion that I felt as if someone had slammed me in the chest with a block of cement. He said, and I quote verbatim, 'She's real, Norm—God, is she real—and you're right about the eyes. I should know.' We stood looking at that painting for ages, not saying anything. Finally I asked him if he would tell me about her. He didn't say anything for a long time, then he said, 'There's not much to tell, except she was my whole life.' ''

"Oh, Norm." Jillian could no longer hold back the tears, and they spilled over and coursed down her cheeks.

Norm chuckled as he let go of her hair and lifted the chain from around her neck with one finger. "I recognized both the ring and the locket from that picture. He did another painting where you were galloping this magnificent black horse across a snow-covered field. You had on a woolly sheepskin jacket and high leather boots. With your hair wound around your head in a thick braid you looked like a Cossack princess. The damned picture radiated a power, a freedom, a wildness that was nearly tangible. Jillian, it was so real, so very real that I could almost hear you breathing."

"Then that was how you recognized me." Her voice was a ragged whisper as she tried to quell the surge of hope she was experiencing.

"Yes, that's how." He hesitated for a moment before he went on. "It takes him about four to six months to do one, Jillian, so you know it's a labor motivated by more than loneliness. You have been very much on his mind—and don't you ever doubt it—but I don't know how, or if, you can reach him. Jake's biggest problem is his pride. In his heart he has never accepted the fact that he is crippled. He thinks his disability makes him some sort of monumental burden, and he cannot tolerate that."

Jillian felt as though someone had lifted a weight off her chest. She had carried around such a load of guilt and doubt after he left, for she had always blamed herself harshly for the outcome of the accident and for Jacob's withdrawal afterward. It would help to know that he hadn't come to hate her or resent her.

"Norm, why did he take this tour? Do you think his only reason was because you needed him, or do you think it was because he wanted to come home?"

"Right now I think one of his main reasons for coming back is you. I think he felt he had to see you once more and to find out what happened to you."

"But why now?"

"That's why I'm so concerned. Jake has found out about a new treatment that's been developed in Israel. I don't know anything about it—in fact, I didn't know until we left Vancouver that he was considering any treatment." Norm stood up and started pacing. "He told me then that he was definitely going to Israel as soon as this tour is over. Apparently the arrangements are being made now."

Studying Norm's anxious face, Jillian experienced a twinge of guilt because she hadn't told him about Dr. Paulson's final verdict on Jacob's paralysis. She rubbed her hand across her eyes and tried to sort out her jumbled thoughts. If Jacob had wanted Norm to know that his remaining paralysis had been diagnosed as psychosomatic, he would have told him.

She looked up. "Do you think this treatment might involve some risk, Norm?"

"I don't know, Jill. I don't have a clue what's involved, but I do have a gut feeling that something isn't quite right." He began pacing again, his head bowed, his arms folded tightly across his chest. "I'm

almost certain that Jake Holinski would risk anything, even his life, to be able to come back here a
whole man. I'm even more certain of that since I've
met you. I thought at first he had agreed to come to
Edmonton as some kind of self-punishment, but
when he dropped this bomb on me about the trip to
Israel, I began to really wonder. He was so close-
mouthed about the actual treatment that I have to
assume it's a high-risk technique. To put it very
frankly, I'm as scared as hell that he's going to do
something stupid.''

Jillian felt sick. It didn't help that her mind was
swimming in a haze of confusion. Too much was
coming at her at once, and nothing made any sense—
nothing—except Jacob was back and had turned her
world upside down with the force of a hurricane. She
closed her eyes against the pain that was spreading inside her.

''Jillian?''

She glanced up, her expression fixed. Norm sat
down beside her and held her cold hands in his.
''Don't worry about this treatment, kid. There's at
least four months before he can go, and one hell of a
lot can happen in that space of time.'' He squeezed
her hands, his eyes communicating a warm depend-
able reassurance. ''I'll be damned certain whatever
he's planning is safe, so don't worry about it.''

She smiled at him then, the firmness in his voice
calming her inner turmoil. Her instincts had been
right: she could trust this man. ''I won't worry about
it, Norm. My brother is a neurosurgeon and I'll be
able to find out from him what sort of treatment is
being done in Israel. He's in Boston now on post-

graduate work, but I'll write him immediately. Between you and Allan, I know that Jacob is going to be in good hands."

Norm smiled at her and gave her hands another squeeze before he released them. "Good girl." He took out a cigarette, lighted it and inhaled slowly. "You've had a lot dumped on you tonight, kid, and I imagine you're feeling swamped. I hate to pressure you at a time like this, but I'd like to know if you're still serious about signing on with Firefly."

Jillian looked up and gave him a lopsided smile. "Right now I feel totally incapable of making any kind of rational decision. What do you think I should do?"

"You have the job with the band if you'll take it— and I think you should. Hell, I'd give you that job even if you couldn't sing a note."

Jill raised her eyebrows, a slightly cynical look on her face. "You really know how to build up a person's ego, don't you? Now, on top of everything else, I'm not sure if I have the job because you think I can handle it or because of Jacob."

He patted her cheek and chuckled. "You can handle it, kid, believe me. I could hardly believe my ears when you started to sing. I figured you must be good to get Watson all excited, but I wasn't prepared for what I heard." He paused for a minute, obviously reluctant to voice his thoughts.

"Say what you're thinking, Norm."

"Well, you may be letting yourself in for a lot more heartbreak, you know. I won't even guess how Jake is going to react to all this or to you. He may accept you as part of the group, but on the other hand he might just walk out of your life again. I don't really want to subject you to any more hurt than you've already experienced. It's going to be a hard decision, and it's one only you can make.'' He was watching her, his eyes penetrating.

She sat staring back at him with a worried frown on her pale face. ''If Jacob wasn't part of the group I would definitely take the job. But since he is, I think it gives me all the more reason to take it.'' She rubbed her fingers across her forehead in an attempt to relieve the headache she was developing. ''He was my friend for a long time, Norm—a very special friend. We have so much in common, but it's even more than that—I don't think I could ever explain it adequately. I don't want to see him risk his life on some foolish move. I guess what I'm trying to say is that I always felt somehow I let him down before, and maybe this time I can actually help. Do you know what I'm trying to say?''

''You don't have to try to explain. I can see it in your eyes, and believe me, I understand. Nevertheless, I know it isn't going to be easy because of Jake's attitude about himself. And in all honesty I can understand how he feels. If I were in his shoes nothing—absolutely nothing—could break me faster than feeling that someone I cared for might someday resent me because of what I had become. I know it doesn't matter to you, but that fear is there in him. You're going to have to be completely honest with him, because I'm certain he can read you like a book. He can cope with honesty, but he could never handle doubt.''

Jillian was beginning to realize just how well Norm understood Jacob. She also realized that she would have to be very careful not to compromise his friendship with Jacob. She would be on her own in an emotionally charged and complicated situation, one that could erupt at any moment. No, it would not be easy, but it was her only chance to reestablish any contact with Jacob....

"Now, Miss Lambert, why don't you make me some breakfast and send me back to the hotel? It's three o'clock in the morning and I'm almost starved!"

CHAPTER FIVE

JILLIAN AWOKE to the midmorning sounds of children riding their tricycles on the sidewalk outside her bedroom window. The noise penetrated her stupor and she rolled over slowly. She forced her eyes to focus on the dainty porcelain clock on her bedside table. Eleven-thirty.

She groaned as she struggled to a sitting position; she had never slept in this late before in her whole life. She brushed back the loose tendrils of hair that had escaped from her braid, then leaned against the padded headboard of her bed, her forehead pulsating with a muffled ache.

Slowly the drowsiness diffused and her thoughts focused sharply. Jacob was back—a cold distant Jacob. Swift raw panic drilled through her. It twisted her insides, wringing the breath from her as she remembered the unyielding hostile look on his face as he deliberately turned away from her.

No, not again! Not again, screamed her mind. *God, I can't stand it again.* She stiffened her body against the rising mental hysteria. Gritting her teeth she battled down the awful feeling of desperation, and little by little the panic ebbed. Willing her body to relax she closed her eyes and made her mind go blank until a detached calmness settled upon her.

She pressed her cool hands against her throbbing

head. She had lain awake long after Norm had left, trying to come to terms with the agonizing uncertainty and the acute loneliness that had swamped her. Just seeing Jacob had rekindled all the feelings she had smothered for so long—and she was hurting far more than she wanted to admit.

Yes, he was back. It was hard to believe, but harder yet to believe was the fact that she had a job that was going to throw her into a close intense relationship with him. Music was an intoxicating stimulus for both Jacob and herself, one that could arouse them emotionally as nothing else could—except, perhaps, each other, she concluded wryly. It was a feeling that came from deep within, that caught them completely and totally within its spell. For the two of them to perform together would definitely create difficulties under the present circumstances. Their profound feeling for music had been a captivating magic between them in the past. What type of power it would unleash now was uncertain. Jillian shook her head and forced herself to think of other things.

Norm had told her before he departed that they would begin rehearsing at two that afternoon and that she should expect to put in long grueling hours for the next few days. The band had managed to arrange for a four-day layover before they started performing so they could break in their new vocalist, but they had to be ready for their first engagement the following Tuesday evening.

Jillian crawled out of bed and headed for the shower. She wouldn't be able to waste any time, for she had a number of things to do before she left for the hotel. She would have to contact Mildred, the wardrobe mistress of her theater group, to see if she could borrow some outfits to wear onstage. She would also have to go through her own closet to see what she had that could be remodeled. And it was her turn for Sunday brunch. She and Mrs. Olsen had long ago fallen into the habit of having the noon meal on Sunday together. It was just as well, because she wanted to tell her landlady what had happened. She would have to make some arrangements about keeping the apartment until Allan was back. Firefly would be performing in Edmonton for six weeks, and Jillian didn't want to give it up until she knew for certain what she was going to do.

She showered quickly and slipped into a cool caftan. She had plugged in the coffee percolator and had just finished preparing a fresh fruit salad when there was a knock at her door. Her heart skipped a beat in anticipation, but she knew she was being ridiculous thinking it might be Jacob. It was probably John, as he and Allan were the only ones who had keys for the outside door.

It was John. She opened the door and stood with one hand on her hip, the other barring his way. "You might at least have warned me that he was in town."

John stood looking at her, his face sober and slightly drawn. "Would you believe me if I told you I had no idea he was involved with that damned band until I went down to see him last night?"

Jillian stood back and motioned him in, then closed the door behind him and walked into the kitchen. John followed her, his shoulders slumped and his hands rammed deep into the back pockets of his jeans.

"But you knew he was in town." She knew now

what had been troubling him while they were in Calgary; Jacob's unexpected appearance was probably the reason they'd gone to Calgary in the first place.

"Yes, I knew. He phoned me Friday at noon. I nearly fell over when he called—I couldn't believe it. I had lunch with him." John sat down in the kitchen nook, obviously dispirited. "I'm sorry, Jill, I really am. I didn't know whether I should tell you or not. I didn't know what in hell to do."

Jillian patted his shoulder and, sitting down across from him, smiled crookedly. "I imagine it was just as much of a shock for you as it was for me." She looked at him as she chewed nervously on her lower lip. "How was it, John?"

"It was an awful strain at first, I can tell you. I could have cried like a baby when I saw him, and I think he felt the same way. God, he's been gone five years." John's voice was choked with emotion, and Jillian could tell he was really struggling with his feelings. She was doing some struggling of her own, but she was losing. John smiled lopsidedly, a knowing compassionate look on his face as she wiped the tears away.

"If it's any consolation, Jill, I think it's ten times worse for him. But he has that tremendous self-control and discipline and he *seems* to handle it so much better than we do." John rubbed the back of his neck wearily, then took a sip of the hot strong brew Jillian placed before him. "I feel really rotten about your walking into that audition as you did. When I went down to the hotel to see him Friday afternoon he never said a word about the band or the reason he was in Edmonton. I just assumed he had finally relented and had come home to see everyone. It wasn't until I phoned Karin when I got back from Calgary that I found out he was the pianist with Firefly. I came tearing over here to warn you that he was with the group, but you'd already left for the hotel. I went over to the hotel to try to catch you before you walked into that audition, but. . . .''

He reached out and caught Jillian's hand in his, his eyes dark with regret. "I didn't want you to see him face to face without being prepared for the shock, but I was too late. When I got to the hotel I ran into Jacob in the lobby, and I could tell by the look on his face that he had already seen you. He said that you had left with the band's manager." John squeezed her hand, then raked his fingers through his hair. "Jillian, I'm so sorry I didn't tell you he was here as soon as I found out, but I just didn't know what was best."

Jillian laid her free hand on top of his as she tried to swallow the growing painful lump in her throat. "That's the reason we made the flying trip to Calgary, wasn't it—so I wouldn't be here in case he tried to contact me?"

"Yeah, that's why. I wanted to get you out of town so I'd have time to try to sort through the muddle I was in. I had decided to tell you after the audition. I knew how much you wanted that job and I didn't want you to blow it because I hit you with this bit of news beforehand."

"You said Karin knew he was back?"

"Jacob went to see her just before the band left Vancouver. At that time he didn't know if he was going to contact me or anyone else in the family. Karin thought it would be best if she kept to herself that he had been to see her. She didn't want to upset mom and dad—or you—by laying that trip on anyone. She thought it would just bring back a lot of memories and hurt everyone all over again if he decided not to contact anyone.''

Jillian laced her fingers tightly together, her voice barely audible for the tightness in her throat. ''Poor Karin. She would be so upset about it. As much as I wish I had known, I can't blame her for her decision. Had I been in her shoes, I probably would have done the same thing.''

''I couldn't believe that something like this could happen in real life. You and Jacob running into each other the way you did was just too remote a coincidence.''

''Not remote enough, apparently.''

John grinned at the dryness in Jillian's voice and hunched his shoulders in a slightly derisive movement. ''Did he say anything at all to you?''

''Not a word. He turned around and left the room when he saw me there.'' Her voice broke treacherously. It had hurt. It had hurt unbearably when he left without a single gesture of acknowledgment.

''Are you taking the job?''

''Yes.''

''It's going to be damned difficult if he doesn't soften a bit, Jillian. You know that.''

Jillian flexed her shoulders and stood up abruptly, suddenly overcome by a pressing claustrophobic sensation. ''I know, John. I feel so...so out of my depth. I can't walk away; I couldn't make myself turn away from him now. I don't have that kind of strength simply to dismiss him from my mind and pretend it doesn't matter anymore.'' A tight sob escaped from her tense stiff body as she clenched her hands into fists in an effort to choke back the rising desperation within her. "I can't pretend I don't care, because I still do. Damn it, I still do." She buried her face in her hands, unable to control the flood of wretched tears.

John stood up, put his arm around her shaking shoulders and gently led her into the living room. He sat down on the chesterfield beside her, then brushed a wisp of hair from her tear-dampened face.

He held her for a moment, then wiped the tears from her face with the back of his hand. "I'm not going to give you any big-brotherly advice because I know damned well if I was in the same situation I'd feel the same way." He leaned back and stretched his long legs out in front of him, clasping his hands behind his head as he stared at the ceiling. "I wish the repercussions from that lousy accident would simply stop—for both of you." He hesitated for a moment, his face set, as he considered something. Then he looked at Jillian. "He asked Karin about you, Jill. At least he was interested enough to ask."

For a split second there was a tiny flutter of hope within her, but it was smothered by her despair. "That doesn't mean anything. For all I know, he may have left because he blamed me for the accident. He wasn't exactly communicative during the year of his recovery."

John frowned with stunned disbelief. "*Blame* you! Why blame, Jillian? You reacted faster than anyone else when it happened...."

"If I had reacted faster, instead of just sitting there, I could have had Rogue under control before he scrambled up, before he ever had a chance to get near Jacob—''

"Now hold on just one damned minute, Jillian Lambert!" He caught her taut ashen face in his hands and groaned in horror at the guilt he saw in her eyes. "That is the most ridiculous.... Jillian, don't you ever, ever think that it was your fault he was crippled! Ever! We'd all been thrown so many times that none of us was too concerned when Rogue went over with Jacob. You're no more to blame than anyone else. If you hadn't acted as fast as you did, Jacob would have been killed and you know it. It was a stupid freak accident—that's all. Sure, we could have prevented it, but not one of us expected the horse to go into a crazy frenzy." He shook her in mild rebuke. "We can't spend the rest of our lives tormenting ourselves with 'if only'—and that goes for Jacob, too." His face was deadly earnest as he made her look at him. "We can't change the past, Jillian; we can only influence the future."

Jillian rested her head against the cushions behind her and closed her eyes. She was so exhausted that she couldn't marshal her thoughts into any order. Her sleepless hours during the night had been spent in a struggle to shore up the gaping breaches in her mental barriers. It had been a futile battle. The memories seeped into her consciousness, unbidden, unwanted, yet so very special. She had finally broken beneath the shock, the hurt, and had cried herself to sleep.

"Jill?" John's voice had a peculiar tremor to it. "Jill, we don't know what kind of a life Jacob has had since he left. It's a very real possibility that the

Jacob we remember may be very different from the Jacob who's returned.''

She frowned slightly, her eyes very solemn. ''You've talked to him, John—do you have some reason to believe that's the case?''

John shook his head as he roughly rubbed his face with his hands. ''No, I don't. But maybe that's because I don't want to see. I idolized him, Jillian, and I was always as proud as hell of my big brother. Maybe I don't want my idol to come crashing down.''

Jillian sat quietly, staring at the beam of sunshine that splashed across the hearth, her thoughts riveted on what John had said. Finally she looked at him. ''Are you trying to tell me in a roundabout way that maybe I need to know, to find out if I really do still care about the Jacob who has returned?''

''I don't know if I'm trying to say anything or not. Maybe I'm just airing some of my own personal doubts. There was a moment—just a flash—when I thought, *I don't know this person.* It was after the audition, and he seemed so cold and hard and distant. It just wasn't like him. That feeling really threw me.''

Jillian sighed as she rubbed the dull throb in her temple. ''It's possible he has changed a great deal, John. I suppose anything is possible.'' She patted his knee companionably. ''Do you want another coffee?''

''Okay.'' He followed her into the kitchen and sprawled out on the padded curved seat that encircled three sides of the dining nook. Jillian refilled his coffee mug, poured one for herself and placed both cups on the table. She opened the fridge and took out the large bowl of fruit salad.

"Would you like a dish of fruit salad and whipped cream, John?"

"Skip the cream. I'll have it with a little sugar, please."

Jillian filled two cereal bowls with the delicious tangy fruit and set them on the table, then slid the sugar bowl and a spoon across the table to John. She stretched out on the seat opposite him, her eyes thoughtful.

"You talked to him right after the audition?"

"Yeah. As soon as I started questioning him about you, he clammed up. What I can't fathom is why, after all this time, he's decided to come back. I spent all night trying to rationalize the possible reasons, but nothing really makes sense to me—especially the way he's treating you. Knowing Jacob, he had a reason for coming besides his position with the band."

Jillian was on the verge of telling John about the treatment Jacob was planning on having in the fall, but she decided against it. She would say nothing until she found out from Allan what it was all about.

"Didn't he say anything about going home?"

John munched his way through a spoonful of fruit before he answered her. "That's why his being here baffles me. I asked him if he was going home, and he said that he was considering it but didn't want me to tell anyone he was here until he was sure he'd go. I could see him coming back if he was planning on going home but...."

Jillian's eyes filled with tears as she thought of Jacob's self-imposed exile from his family. The

Holinskis had been a particularly close-knit family, and she knew that his isolation from them must have left a very painful void in his life.

John seemed to read her mind. "He must miss home more than we can ever imagine, Jill. He really cared so much about all of us and now he's alone. At least the rest of us had one another to lean on when he disappeared—but he had no one."

Jillian surreptitiously wiped away the tears with her fingertips and looked out the window so John couldn't see the distress in her eyes.

"I know. I was thinking the same thing myself." She shook her head in bleak bewilderment. "I feel as if I'm caught in a house of mirrors. I don't know which way to go or how to find my way out of this maze— and I don't know how well I'm going to handle the situation when I'm working with him every day."

"Give him some time, Jill. This must be one hell of an ordeal for him, no matter what. He must feel like a stranger, an outsider."

They sat in silence, both of them preoccupied with their own thoughts. Jillian finally stirred. "John, will you do me a favor?"

"Sure—what is it?"

"Please don't attempt to discuss me with Jacob."

John shot her a questioning look. "Why? Somebody needs to pound some sense into his mule head."

"Please, John. Don't. I think he'd really resent it. Besides, there's no point in your alienating yourself from him."

John sighed and dropped his shoulders dejectedly. "I guess he wouldn't appreciate it." He paused. "Jill, don't let his attitude get to you."

It was excellent advice—if only she could follow it.

THE TIME SPED BY so quickly that Jillian hadn't had a moment to dwell on anything since John left. Mildred had brought over four outfits that would be suitable, then she and Mrs. Olsen, who was also an experienced seamstress, had rifled through Jillian's closet and found four more that they could restyle. When Jillian finally left for the hotel, the two women were enthusiastically designing costumes. Jillian had some misgivings that their enthusiasm might carry them beyond the point of good taste, but they assured her that she could have every confidence in them.

Right now her major concern was trying to still the awful churning that was twisting her stomach. She caught a glimpse of herself in the hotel window as she walked by. She had worn her hair up in a massive coil at the back of her head and had put on a simple white sun dress because it had been so hot. But she was beginning to wish she had put on something else, for she suddenly felt icy cold. *I feel like I'm on my way to the dentist,* she mused inwardly.

She entered the plant-filled lobby and marched determinedly across to the elevators. Norm had managed to obtain the use of an empty banquet hall for practices, so she was to meet the rest of the group there. Jill wished fervently she could get a grip on her shaking nerves, but she doubted if she would settle down until she started singing. She wondered desperately what was going to happen when Jacob saw her again. What was worse, she had no idea how she would handle the situation.

By the time she reached the large foyer adjacent to the banquet room she was pale and trembling. She could have cried with relief when she rounded the corner and found Norm leaning against the wall. He pushed himself erect and strolled over to her, taking her shaking hands in his. He grinned down at her warmly.

"You look marvelous, Jillian."

"I feel terrible." Her voice was shaky and low.

Norm squeezed her hands. "Be cool, kid. Everything is going to be okay."

Jillian entered the room completely on edge. She really had no idea what to expect.

David walked across the small stage to greet her. "Hi, Jillian. Ready to go to work?"

Jillian smiled weakly at him and nodded, keenly aware that Jacob was totally ignoring her. She took the sheaf of music that David handed her.

"This is the material we'll be using. We won't go through it all today, I don't think. We'll work on three or four pieces and get them down pretty good. Okay with you?"

"Okay."

"Let's get started then."

They accomplished a great deal during the practice. Jillian had been relieved to find she knew most of the lyrics to the songs, and the music wasn't going to be difficult to learn. By the time they broke for supper, her confidence had been partially restored, even though Jacob's cool aloofness was still very unsettling. But there was nothing she could do about that now.

They decided they would have second cups of coffee after dinner, which dragged into thirds. Keith, the drummer, was an outgoing individual, a natural clown who kept them laughing with his stories.

He turned to Jillian. "But one of the best stories

I've heard in a long time was when Norm told us about how you got railroaded into some of the things you've done.''

Jillian laughed with him and shook her head. ''Sometimes I'm not too sure how it all happened. It must sound like a fabrication, but it wasn't.''

''Did you really grow up around here?''

David's innocent question stirred the knot of uncertainty that had been growing in the pit of her stomach ever since they had sat down to dinner. It was a question she had been dreading, as she knew she would have to answer it honestly. But she was aware that the answer would open a whole area of speculation for the members of the band. She laid her hands in her lap and clenched them tightly together, striving for a casualness she definitely did not feel.

''Yes, I did.'' She raised her head and looked at David squarely. ''Actually, Jacob and I grew up in the same community. His mother taught me everything I know about music.''

A dumbfounded silence fell over everyone seated at the table. Jillian knew for certain that this was all news to them. She forced herself to take a sip of coffee, attempting with all the strength she had to keep things light and casual.

Elaine, who was sitting on Jill's immediate right, was a relaxed warmhearted person. Jill suspected that she had sensed her anxiety, but she was totally unprepared for Elaine's attempt to ease the strain.

''That's a beautiful locket you're wearing, Jill.'' The woman lifted the chain with her fingers. Jill wanted to snatch it away from her, but instead she sat with eyes downcast, her hands clenched into tight white fists in her lap. "And what a beautiful ring. It must have sentimental value."

Jillian raised her eyes to find herself trapped by Jacob's dark cold stare. Her voice was a husky whisper, "Yes, it does." She couldn't tear her eyes away from Jacob's as he sat there, his jaw clenched, the muscle in his cheek twitching violently. She felt the color leave her face and she could feel herself beginning to shake. She had to get out of there before she went to pieces, so she pushed her chair away from the table. "Excuse me, please."

She nearly ran out of the room. By the time she reached the corridor leading to the banquet room she was in full flight, her body racked with sobs. She burst through the door of the ladies' room, flung herself into one of the cubicles and stood there shaking violently as she tried to stem the flow of tears. After a few moments she leaned back against the door, her head thrown back, her breath coming in deep gasps.

She was standing in front of one of the sinks splashing cold water on her face when she felt a hand on her back. She raised her head to find Elaine watching her in the row of mirrors above the sinks. There was a concerned expression on the woman's face as Jillian silently accepted the paper towels she handed her.

"I'm sorry, Jill, I really am," she said.

Jillian gave her a shaky smile as she blotted her cheeks dry, then tossed the wadded towels into the garbage can. "You didn't know, Elaine. It's all right, really."

Elaine stood in front of Jill, one hand on her hip, the other one toying with the paper dispenser. "You and Jacob had something going once, didn't you?"

Jillian stared at her reflectively for a long while, then nodded mutely.

"Do you want to talk about it?"

When Jillian shook her head Elaine patted her shoulder understandingly and turned to leave.

"Elaine?"

"Yes?"

"Could I ask a big favor of you?"

"Sure."

"Do you think you could smooth over the episode at dinner with the guys? I would rather not have to answer a swarm of questions, and I know Jacob won't like being questioned."

Elaine grinned and nodded. "I'll tell them I hit a sore spot with you and that you had been uptight with the first rehearsal and all."

"Well, that certainly wouldn't be far from the truth."

Elaine laughed. "I have enough sins without adding lying to the list!" She slipped her arm through Jillian's and led her out into the corridor. Elaine was a bouncy happy person, so much so that by the time they entered the rehearsal room, Jillian was collected enough to act as though nothing was wrong. As she approached the stage, however, she was keenly aware that everyone was watching her. She forced a smile and hoped that no one would notice her reddened eyes. Elaine caught David's eye and signaled frantically for him to begin the practice.

"We'll start with this piece, Jill, and we'll do it as a duet," he said, picking up on the message. "It has some difficult spots so it might take some time."

Jillian scanned the sheet of music as the band went

into the instrumental introduction. But her concentration was definitely off as she started rehearsing. They worked at it for some time before Norm interrupted. He walked out onto the stage stroking his chin.

"I think I know what the problem is, Jillian. You tend to expect a pause in this phrase here." He took the music from her hand and pointed to a certain bar. "Don't anticipate it and you'll be fine."

Jillian raised her head to find Jacob staring at her, his face set. His voice was cool and impersonal as he said, "That's good advice, Jill. Don't anticipate anything."

Jillian felt as though someone had slapped her. She understood perfectly what Jacob had meant. A sinking hopeless feeling settled upon her, and only her determination not to break beneath Jacob's coldness kept her going.

The practice was very nearly a disaster. The distant stiffness that radiated between Jillian and Jacob spread throughout the rest of the group. Everyone was making the most ridiculous errors.

They tried to get the introduction right to one particularly difficult piece of music. Each of them had a different beat on which to come in, and they were supposed to blend together in a fabulous five-part harmony. Jillian could tell that this arrangement was definitely one of Jacob's and that if they ever managed to master it it would create a spectacular sound. Finally Jacob lined up David, Dan, Keith and Jillian in front of the piano like a group of glee-club members and with strained patience, made them go over it again and again and again.

Finally he tipped his head to one side and stared at

them with thinly disguised exasperation. "Let's take five."

Keith winked at Jillian and grasped her hand in friendly reassurance. "Hang in there, Jill. We dummies with the tin ears will get it eventually!"

Jillian smiled at him, her eyes dancing with amusement and a certain amount of relief at his casual unconcerned banter. She whispered conspiratorially, "I'm beginning to feel like the kid with the big booming voice who perpetually sings off-key!"

Keith laughed. "Spoken like a true schoolmarm." He looked at her slim hand, his voice echoing sharply into a lull in the conversation. "Hey, how did you get this scar on your hand? It looks as though someone bit you!"

Jillian could feel herself blushing wildly as she quickly snatched her hand away. She stood there transfixed, staring at the white scar that stood out so dramatically against the tanned skin on the back of her hand. Tentatively she traced the mark with her fingers, and the present faded away into a dreamlike mist as a memory came rushing in to push aside all else.

It had been quite a party, she mused wryly. Allan, John, Karin, Jillian and Jacob had been invited to an end-of-the-year barbecue at the country home of one of the girls John occasionally dated. They had all piled into Allan's somewhat battered and undependable car and had driven the thirty miles to Lynda's home. By the time they arrived they were in high, flying spirits. After the weeks of intense studying they were more than ready for a fun-filled evening. Everyone there was feeling the same way. They had eaten their way through a mountain of food and had been dancing to disco music on the massive patio when the party was crashed by a group of acquaintances who had deliberately not been invited.

Jillian and Jacob, who were enclosed in shadows in a secluded corner, were unaware of the intrusion. They were so wrapped up in each other they would have been unaware of a raging battle. Their bodies had been moving to the heavy sensual beat of the music, their eyes locked on each other as they swayed to the heady rhythm. Jacob had had just a touch too much to drink and his iron control was slipping. He was watching her with dark smoldering eyes that left her breathless with surrender. He moved closer to Jillian, their bodies brushing together suggestively, arousing them both to a fever pitch. A hot surge of desire boiled through her as Jacob bent his head and covered her mouth with his, the tip of his tongue sensuously brushing her lips.

The heat of the moment was figuratively dashed with cold water when Georgia—Jillian's face softened into an amused reminiscent smile as she thought, *Who in their right mind would name a daughter Georgia Brown*—sauntered over to them and somehow managed to impose herself between Jacob and Jillian.

Georgia Brown, who was anything but sweet, had let it be known across campus that one way or another she was going to get Jacob Holinski into her bed and out of the clutches of the redheaded Lambert bitch. Needless to say, Jillian had developed an intense dislike for the curvaceous and definitely sexy brunette. Her temper still flared when she thought of how Georgia had pressed her very adequate bosom against Jacob's chest and had provocatively moved her body against his.

"Jacob, honey, you'll dance with me, won't you?"

Jacob, who was heartily sick of Georgia's unsolicited attentions, moved away from her and draped his arm possessively around Jillian's rigid shoulders. "No, I won't." He pulled Jillian against him and laughed at her fury as they walked back to the brightly lighted patio.

"Damn her! I'll kill her," seethed Jillian through clenched teeth.

"Forget her, babe." Jacob leaned over and softly bit the sensitive hollow at the curve of her neck. "If you keep on tormenting me the way you have been tonight, I'm apt to drag you off into some dark and hidden corner and ravish you on the spot." He was laughing that low husky laugh that always made Jillian feel like warm butter inside. He kissed her behind her ear, his tongue teasing, and pins and needles of desire shuddered through her. She melted against him, his hand caressing her hip as he pressed her firmly against him. Jacob knew very well the state she was in and he knew very well that he was tormenting her even more. There was a heated hungry gleam in his eyes, but his control had not totally dissolved. He took her hand in his and led her over to Allan and John, who were lounging against the outdoor brick fireplace. Several people joined them and they were laughing helplessly at one of John's hilarious impersonations of a very pompous, very stuffy professor.

The atmosphere became strained and awkward as

Georgia and several of the other gate-crashers joined the group. It became charged with tension as Georgia elbowed her way through the crowd, a drink in her hand, and sidled up to Jacob, her hips swaying. She stopped in front of him, her blouse unbuttoned to the navel, revealing considerably more than just cleavage.

Her voice had been low, sultry and very suggestive. "Come on, Jacob. Why don't you come move with me, baby?" She caught his hand and tried to draw him toward her.

Jillian's anger burst into a magnificent flaming fury and she glared at the girl, barely able to control her rage.

Jacob disentangled his hand from Georgia's and pointedly rammed it in the back pocket of his jeans. His voice was deadly quiet but there was a quality to it that was like ice. "I'm not buying what you're selling, Georgia."

With a flash of viperous anger Georgia flung the contents of her glass in Jacob's face. That, for Jillian, was the very last straw.

With the swiftness and agility of a spitting cat, she threw her weight into a resounding backhand that caught Georgia across the mouth, her teeth slashing Jillian's hand. The blow sent Georgia sprawling.

Jillian's strength was fed by fury as she grasped the flattened girl by her arm and hauled her to her feet. She ignored Georgia's bruised mouth and bleeding nose as she snarled in a voice like hard cold steel, "Touch him again, Georgia Brown, and so help me I'll wipe your nose right off your face." She flung the girl away from her, her voice seething, "He's *mine* and don't you forget it!"

Everyone was shocked into stunned silence. There wasn't a sound as Jillian turned to face Jacob. He was watching her with a lazy half-smile on his face, his eyes hooded with a vibrating virility that drained her of all anger and left her trembling. Slowly Jacob reached out, caught a handful of Jillian's tumbled hair and dragged her into his arms. She reached up and gently wiped the beads of moisture from his face with her bloodied hand as his arms encircled her with the authority of possession. His eyes flashed a warning, challenging anyone to deny his right.

The intensity of the charged current that crackled between Jacob and Jillian mesmerized everyone around them. The trance was finally shattered when John motioned to Jillian's slashed hand and commented in a deadly serious voice, "Allan, you'd better do something about that. Your sister has just been bitten by a dog of one sort or another!"

On the way home that night Jillian and Jacob had to suffer the merciless teasing the other three heaped upon them. John shook his finger at Jacob with a slightly inebriated warning.

"You'd better watch out, Jacob. Every guy on campus is going to be ogling that lusty Lambert broad."

"And," interjected Karin, "you'd better be on guard, Jillian, because all the 'Sweet Georgia Browns' on campus will be panting after that Holinski hunk who drags his women around by their hair."

The three in the front seat had burst into gales of laughter when Jacob and Jillian had responded in perfect unison, their voices resolute. "Just let them try!"

Jillian was standing in a daze, her fingers tracing the scar as a soft smile played around her mouth. She glanced up, and the bottom dropped out of her stomach when she realized Jacob was watching her with piercing eyes. For a brief breathless moment she thought she saw a sparkle in his eyes and an amused twitch at the corners of his mouth as he looked at her hand.

"Are you ready to start now, Jillian?" His voice was as cold and caustic as ever.

CHAPTER SIX

JILLIAN SPENT A RESTLESS tormented night. She knew that the tension between her and Jacob could not continue or it would have a demoralizing effect on all the members of Firefly. Jacob had made it perfectly clear that he had no intention of changing his position as far as she was concerned. But unless they came to terms with the situation, the friction would soon turn into open hostility. That would be disastrous for them as individuals as well as performers.

She had no choice. She would have to talk to Jacob. Perhaps they could come to some understanding that would make it possible for them to work together. Jillian was beginning to think she had made a serious mistake taking the position with the band.

A dismal feeling of futility settled upon her. She doubted if she would have an opportunity to speak to Jacob alone, and even if she did, she was almost certain he would refuse to discuss anything with her. He had cut himself off from his past deliberately and totally, and she knew him well enough to know that he would not likely reverse his position. It was such a senseless mess.

She arrived at the hotel to find Elaine waiting for her in the lobby. "Hi, Jill. I've been posted out here to try to catch you. The banquet room is booked for this afternoon so we'll have to delay the practice until it's cleared."

Jillian raised her eyebrows questioningly as she slipped her sunglasses off. "And how long will that be?"

"Another half an hour, I guess. Come on upstairs."

For a second Jillian stood staring vacantly at the garish carpet that covered the lobby floor. She raised her head to find Elaine watching her speculatively. "Is Jacob up there, Elaine?"

The other woman sighed heavily and shook her head. "No, he left when he found out I was coming down to wait for you. I saw him go into the small cocktail lounge by the dining room as I came across the lobby."

Jillian clasped the shoulder strap of her bag with clammy hands and smiled ruefully. "I think maybe I had better talk to him before the tension reaches a dangerous level."

Elaine grinned as she wiped her hand across her forehead in an exaggerated gesture of relief. "Thank heavens! He's been like a bear. And rehearsal! I don't know how you stood it."

Jillian felt tears burning her eyes but she blinked them back.

"We'll see you later then, Jill. Good luck!"

As Elaine strolled toward the elevators, Jillian turned and walked toward the lounge. As she entered she had to pause for a moment to allow her eyes to adjust to the dim lighting. The small intimate room was nearly empty. Then she saw Jacob sitting at a table in the corner, his wheelchair shining in the gloom.

It was the first time she had had an opportunity really to study him. His upper body was definitely more muscled since he'd left five years before. His expensively tailored clothes, which he wore with a casual ease, suited him. He was wearing his hair longer than he used to and had obviously stopped trying to straighten the flaxen curls. His face had changed, too.

A strange melancholy feeling for the lost years swept over Jillian as she realized with a sharp pang that he was nearly thirty-one years old. She tried to quell the nervous trembling as she took a deep breath and moved toward the table. "Hello, Jacob."

He continued to stare at his drink as he turned the glass around and around on the table. "What do you want?" His voice was cool and unfriendly.

She tried to ignore his hostility as she sank into the armchair opposite him. As the waiter approached her she shook her head, then fixed her eyes on the wet rings left by Jacob's glass. "Jacob, I think we had better talk."

His head jerked up, his eyes flashing angrily. "About what? About the marvelous life we could have had?"

Jillian bent her head to hide the terrible hurt he had inflicted. She fought to keep her voice level as she said, "It's been five years, Jacob—"

"Then why are you still wearing that damned necklace?" His voice was tight, for he spoke between clenched teeth.

Jillian shut her eyes and prayed silently that she would say the right thing. She forced her face to relax and tried to quiet her thumping heart. "Because I haven't met anyone who made me want to take it off."

He stared at her, his face set into hard unreadable lines.

"Jacob, you were a big part of my life. You were a very special friend long before you were my lover." Her voice caught on the word "lover," but she forced herself to go on. "Either we can make this tour a living hell for everyone, including ourselves, or we can make some kind of decision that we can live with."

He was still staring at her, but Jillian could see he was considering what she had said. He dropped his eyes and began toying with his drink again.

She watched him in silence for a moment, trying to gather her courage. "Jacob, would it be best if I didn't take the job?"

He took a deep breath and leaned back in his chair, then looked at her for a very long time. She could feel herself going weak under his scrutiny. "No."

At his gruff statement a sense of relief rushed through her. She hadn't even been aware that she'd been holding her breath until he had answered. Suddenly she wanted to touch his hand, but she was desperately afraid to make physical contact. Instead she slid out from behind the table, stood up and started to walk away.

"Jillian?"

She turned to face him. He looked at her again for a long time, then shook his head. "Never mind." He picked up his drink. "I'll see you at rehearsal."

Jillian's legs felt like rubber as she walked out of the lounge. She could feel Jacob's eyes on her back and would have given anything to turn and study the look on his face, but she didn't dare. She leaned weakly against the wall outside as she fought back the lump in her throat. *Oh, Jacob, why,* she whispered to herself.

She straightened and forced a smile onto her face as Norm and the others appeared at the far side of the lobby and started to walk toward her. By the time they reached her she had full control of herself and was able to act naturally when Norm approached her.

"Ready to go, Jill?"

"Yes." She hiked the strap of her shoulder bag farther up on her shoulder as she fell into step beside him. As was his habit he draped his arm casually across her shoulders, and they immediately became involved in a conversation about the city.

Jillian wasn't aware that Jacob had joined the group until they approached the banquet hall. She stepped to one side as Norm reached in front of her to open the door, and as she did so she caught a glimpse of Jacob sitting there with a hard unreadable look on his face, his eyes narrow. Again she caught her breath. She could hardly wait for the rehearsal to begin so that she could forget the uncertainty that was spreading through her.

Jacob rolled himself up the makeshift ramp to the stage, the muscles across his back and in his arms bulging with the strain. He positioned his wheelchair, then swung himself effortlessly onto the piano bench with the smoothness and technique of a gymnast. Jillian stared at the hard lines of his profile, then sighed as she tossed her purse onto a chair. She brushed a few wisps of hair off her face, then walked to the stage, picking up her music from the top of the piano. As she lifted her head she found Jacob watching her. Almost instantly she was mesmerized by those eyes, which held her bound in their dark brown depths. She could read nothing in them; they were completely expressionless, devoid of all feeling. Yet he was thinking something. Jillian knew it, but she wasn't too certain if she wanted to know what it was. Then his gaze lowered and Jill knew he was watching the telltale pulse that was throbbing wildly at the base of her throat.

It seemed like ages before he raised his eyes and regarded her with a mocking coolness once again. Mutely Jillian turned and walked over to where David sat tuning his guitar. She knew that Jacob had been about to say something sarcastic to her, and she felt as though she simply couldn't cope with any more of his animosity. He resented her intrusion into his life, but if his attitude was going to continue, she would have to reconsider her decision. He had come back simply to reestablish family ties, not to see her. As far as Jacob was concerned, everything the two of them had once shared was over and finished. It was dead.

What had been an uncertainty before suddenly became crystal clear—Jacob wanted nothing to do with her ever again. But the cold terrible reality for Jillian was that for her it was not over. She still loved him with every fiber of her being. There could never be anyone else for her except Jacob.

The icy numbness that settled around her heart was almost a relief. She prayed it would continue forever, for she knew the pain, when it came, would be unbearable.

THE FOLLOWING AFTERNOON Jillian was standing in the middle of her living room, her forehead creased with a frown. For the life of her she couldn't remember where she had put her old white satin pantsuit. She had paid a fortune for the damned thing, and now when she wanted it she couldn't remember what she had done with it. She had worn it only twice because she felt so conspicuous in it, but it would be perfect to wear onstage. She sighed with annoyance. It wasn't in any of the closets upstairs so she must have packed it away in one of her trunks.

She went into the hallway and opened the door to the basement. Flipping on the light she ran quickly down the stairs. She really didn't feel like rooting through the trunks of odds and ends she had accumulated over the years, but she was certain it had to be packed in one of them.

She had nearly emptied the second trunk when she finally uncovered a familiar bundle wrapped in blue tissue paper. Nodding her head in satisfaction she lifted it out. One more stage outfit accounted for!

A second later her face drained of all color as she saw the large blue Birks box stored at the bottom of the trunk. With shaking hands she pulled the box out and set it on her lap. A low moan was torn from her as she closed her eyes. The numbness she had prayed would last was swept away like mist and a dull throbbing ache rolled in like a tide.

Jillian barely remembered repacking the trunk or coming up the stairs. Carelessly she dropped the satin suit on the chesterfield, then carried the blue box into her room and placed it on her bed. She crawled onto the middle of the bed and huddled there, her arms wrapped around herself in an attempt to ward off a chill that suddenly shivered through her. For a long time she looked at the box, then she slowly ran her nail under the brittle yellowed Scotch tape and lifted the lid. This was her Pandora's box.

Inside there were several bundles of old letters tied

with red ribbons. There was another huge bundle in a plastic bag. On the very bottom of the box were several old snapshots and photos of Jillian.

The letters in the plastic bag were the ones she had written to Jacob while he was attending university in California. He had left them behind, along with his many pictures of her, when he had disappeared from her life. The letters tied with red ribbons were from him. She pressed a bundle of them against her breast as she tipped her head back, her face twisted with anguish. Tears seeped out beneath her clenched eyelids, and she was filled with such a sense of loss it nearly strangled her.

She had forgotten all about them—no, that wasn't the truth. She had deliberately not remembered them. Tenderly she caressed the yellowed envelopes with her fingertips, then slowly untied the bow on one package. Handling them like rare, priceless documents she carefully slipped the folded white sheets out of one envelope. She opened them, and another twist of pain shot through her when she saw the bold, dearly familiar writing.

My love, I'm lying on my lonely bed, my arms so very empty, my mind trapped by thoughts of you. I've been tormenting myself with the haunting, beautiful memory of my last night in Edmonton, with you asleep in my arms. Oh, babe, I knew I'd miss you like hell, but the real loneliness is far more excruciating than anything I could ever imagine. I look at the calendar and it seems like an eternity until Christmas. The thought of all those empty days and lonely nights before I can hold you again nearly drives me—

Jillian couldn't read any further. Her tears were falling so fast and the ache around her heart was so intense that she could barely breathe, but there was a poignant warmth within her, too, as she recalled the time he had referred to in his letter.

It had been the night before he left. She had already started classes at the university, and he had come to the city to spend three days with her before he left. But their time together had turned into a disaster of edginess; they were both dreading the long separation. Jillian had made a supreme effort to hide her melancholy, but her despondency seemed to contaminate every moment they had left together.

He was to leave Sunday morning. By Saturday night her nerves were shot, and Jacob was acting like a caged cat. They ended up having a blazing row over some insignificant incident that she could no longer recall. He slammed out of her apartment in a rage, and Jillian herself was in such a fiery temper that she didn't even try to stop him. It was nearly eleven o'clock before she cooled off enough to put everything back in perspective. At once she dialed John and Allan's apartment but there was no answer. She had just replaced the receiver on the hook when there was a soft knock on her door. She flew to answer it, silently praying that it would be Jacob. Sure enough, he was standing there, his shoulder propped against the door frame, a look of misery in his eyes. She threw herself into his arms and buried her face against his chest.

"Oh, Jacob, I'm so sorry I've been so bitchy, but I don't think I can stand not having you here." Her shoulders shook with repressed sobs as he pulled her into the apartment and kicked the door closed.

"Don't, babe! God, don't cry." He held her tightly as he tried to soothe her. "I don't want to go, Jill. If I hadn't won that damned scholarship—" he laughed, his voice tinged with amused irony "—if I hadn't won that damned scholarship, I might never have discovered you." He stroked her head as he eased her away from him slightly and looked down at her. "I don't want to leave you—it's going to be a lifetime until Christmas."

The thought of all those long empty days without him destroyed what little control she had, and she gave way to her pent-up tears. He cradled her against him and let her cry. After a long while her stormy weeping subsided, and he eased her away from him and wiped away her tears with a Kleenex.

"Don't baby me, Jacob." There was a touch of petulance in her voice, and his eyes sparked with humor when he recognized it for what it was.

"Shut up. I want to baby you." He lay the tissue across her nose. "Blow." She shot him a look of defiance but complied.

He laughed and chided her softly as he wiped her nose. "Runny-nosed kid!"

For an instant there was a glimmer of temper snapping in her green eyes, but it gave way to humor and she hugged him fiercely. She rested her head on his shoulder as he drew her against him. She felt so safe in his arms.

"Jacob?"

"What, babe?"

"Will you stay here tonight? I'm going to be here by myself and I don't want you to go."

He kissed her softly, then smiled at her. "You'll be branded a scarlet woman and your father will have my hide."

She smiled up at him, her eyes dancing. "I've always wanted to be a scarlet woman! And don't worry about dad—I have a sneaking hunch he never was an innocent.'' She laid her hand on his cheek, her eyes beseeching. ''Will you?''

''I'll stay.''

And he had. She had lain in his arms all night, secure and content until dawn....

She tipped back her head, the tears coursing down her neck as she clutched the letter to her heart and whispered, ''Oh, Jacob, how could you do this?'' Harsh sobs racked her body as she grieved her loss. The wounds were too deep, too raw. They would never heal.

She wept until she was exhausted. Then she lay on her bed for a long time, totally spent, before she wearily sat up and tried to rebundle the letters. One slipped free from the package and skittered onto the floor. As she picked it up, her eyes caught the words.

Jillian, my red-haired wench, it's hard to believe that only yesterday I put you on a plane for Edmonton. I don't think I could ever find the words to express what I felt inside when I walked out of my class and saw you standing there. I didn't know how I was going to make it to the end of May without seeing you....

Jillian stretched out on her stomach and let her thoughts once again carry her back in time....

Jacob had been unable to come home for Easter. Good Friday was his only day off from classes, and he really couldn't afford the airfare. Jillian had understood, but that hadn't eased the disappointment.

A week before the break, her parents had present-ed her with an airline ticket in the guise of a belated birthday gift. She had been ecstatic. She had very nearly phoned Jacob to tell him she was coming, but she decided to surprise him instead.

It was a beautiful bright day in late March when she arrived. She strolled through the campus, her suitcase in her hand, on her way to the faculty of fine arts. She was afraid that she would miss him, but the secretary at the registrar's office was a gem. When Jillian told her why she was trying to locate him, the woman found out which class Jacob was attending and when it would be dismissed.

Jillian waited outside and was leaning against a light standard when she spotted him among a group of students. He hadn't seen her and was nearly beside her when she called out his name. He scanned the faces around him, and when his eyes rested on her he stopped dead in his tracks, his face registering his disbelief. After elbowing his way through the crowd he nearly cracked her ribs as he caught her in his arms and swung her around exuberantly. She blushed furi-ously at the good-natured hooting from the other students who stopped to watch.

Those five days she spent with Jacob in California were the happiest five days of her life. He took her home to his boarding house, and Mrs. O'Malley, his landlady, was horrified when she found out that Jil-lian planned to stay at a hotel. Instead she absolutely insisted that Jill stay there.

Mrs. O'Malley, the original mold for an old-fashioned Irish grandmother, deputized herself as the guardian of Jillian's innocence, much to Jacob's amusement. She tucked her into the guest room in her own private quarters, her eyes snapping a warning at Jacob as she did so. Jillian was well aware that the devilish sparkle in his eyes belied his very serious expression.

Because of Gran O'Malley's shrewd common sense and her wise advice, the tenor of Jillian's stay had been carefree, happy and relaxed, her time with Jacob flavored with contentment. She blessed the old woman and her infinite wisdom many times.

The wise advice was shared the very first morning of Jillian's stay. Gran and Jillian were in the kitchen, busily preparing breakfast for Gran's twelve boarders. Jacob strolled in, his eyes warm with love as he slipped his arm around Jillian's waist and dropped a soft kiss on her mouth. "Top o' the mornin' to you, my lovely lass," he greeted her in a perfect Irish brogue.

Jillian's smile turned into laughter as Gran brandished her spoon. "Now, you big tawny devil, don't you go tormentin' me helper or I'll whack you with me spoon!"

Jacob caught the old woman around the shoulders and kissed her wrinkled cheek. "Gran, you wouldn't really."

"I would! Now be a good lad and trot down to the fruit stand on the corner. Fetch me a big bag of oranges and a bag of grapefruit."

Jacob winked at Jillian as she squeezed his hand, her eyes sparkling like emeralds as she tried to suppress a bubble of laughter. He made a point of ogling her shamelessly as he disappeared through the door.

Gran was standing at the huge worktable measuring ingredients for pancakes. She looked at Jillian, her bright blue eyes twinkling.

"He's my favorite, lass—you know that."

Jillian smiled softly as she patted the old woman's shoulder. "He's my favorite, too, Gran."

"Aye, I know." Gran flashed her a knowing smile and nodded her head in approval. She began to stir the batter, her face wrinkled with a frown. "Aye, lass, I know. He misses you somethin' terrible, Jillian. He comes down in the evenings to play the piano in the parlor, but he often ends up starin' out the window, and you can tell his heart is a thousand miles away."

Jillian was so touched by Gran's comment that her eyes misted with tears. "It seems like such a long time until July and our wedding," she whispered.

Gran patted her cheek. "You're a lucky lass. He's a man of deep passions, is Jacob. And he's been torn, lass. In his heart he wants to fly home to you, but his head tells him to remain so he can provide for you well. There's a dozen times he's been ready to quit because he's been achin' for you. Did you know that, Jillian?"

Jillian nodded as she wiped her tears away with the back of her hand. Gran smiled at her, her flashing eyes warm with understanding.

"Jillian, your man needs some gentleness and comfortin' now, above all else. Soothe him with as tender a love as you would give a wee babe." She stopped stirring the batter as she looked out the window, her face soft. "Jacob is as deep as a river and just as strong—and lovin'. He has love unmeasurable and he's givin' it all to you. You'll never love another once you've given your heart to a man like that."

Those words came back to haunt Jillian now. She knew that Gran O'Malley had forecast her life for her when she had made that observation. It was true. She would never love another. She had totally committed herself to Jacob....

Jillian rolled over on her back and tucked her hands beneath her head as she stared into space. Gran had been right about Jacob's need for gentleness. A tension like static electricity had crackled within him that first day. Jillian, with the magnified vision Gran's gentle warning had given her, realized he was fighting one hell of a battle with his emotions.

She had little opportunity to talk to him alone until late that evening; he had an evening job as pianist in a lounge. She had gone with him to work, and after much coaxing from him and the lounge manager, she had relented and performed with him. The music had caught them within its turbulent spell and inflamed them both. When they arrived back at the boarding house Jacob was edgy and tense, and Jillian sensed that his usually rigid willpower was practically nonexistent.

He avoided touching her when they entered the darkened house, and he sprawled out on the old-fashioned sofa in the parlor with one arm draped across his eyes. His teeth were clenched, the muscle in his jaw tensed with restraint. When Jillian knelt down on the floor and slipped her arms around his shoulders, he swore softly and crushed her against his rigid body.

He was vulnerable, and it hurt her so to see him in such desperate turmoil. She cradled his head against her breast and very quietly began telling him about the preparations for their wedding. Little by little she felt the tension ease from him as she combed her fingers gently through his hair.

"We have only three more months to go, Jacob, and we can put all this behind us."

His arms tightened around her with such strength that she felt her breath being squeezed out of her. "It seems like such an eternity, Jillian."

She buried her hands in his hair as she pressed his head tightly against her, her eyes brimming with unshed tears at the desolation in his voice. Desperately she tried to think of something to spark his humor and dispel his dark mood. "You know, love, if Gran O'Malley should stroll into her parlor and see the two of us lying together on her horsehair sofa, she'd beat us both senseless with her shillelagh."

She felt him smile against her as he hugged her close. "Well, lass, we'd be behavin' ourselves." Sitting up he pulled her onto his lap, nestled her head on his shoulder and wrapped his arms around her.

"Oh, Jacob, it feels so good to be close to you."

"Three more months, babe, and I can hold you all night through and I won't have to leave you." He loosened the thick coil of her braid and idly combed his fingers through her hair. "I wish I could afford to take you on a spectacular, unforgettable honeymoon, Jill—"

"It will be unforgettable *and* spectacular, Jacob."

He tipped his head back and laughed at her dry tone. "Oh, Jill. . . ." He kissed her softly on her temple, then began to stroke her hair again. "*That* part of the honeymoon isn't what I was referring to. I just wish I could take you someplace special."

She caught his face in her hands, her eyes shining with genuine sincerity and a touch of mischief. "But you *are* taking me someplace special, love. You're taking me to our own little apartment at Mrs.

Olsen's. That's all I want—that and a bed. You can take me on a wildly expensive and romantic honeymoon for our twenty-fifth anniversary; we may need a dash of excitement and romance by that time!''

Jacob grinned, his eyes flashing. ''It's a deal.'' Their eyes locked and Jillian felt as though she was being drawn into a weightless world as she lost herself within his soul. His eyes suddenly became very dark and passionate. ''Have I told you how very much I love you, Jillian Lambert—and how very much I need you?''

She felt smothered by that look and closed her eyes as she pressed against him and whispered into his ear. ''Don't look at me like that, Jacob. It makes me hot and cold and weak inside, and I don't want to torment you.'' She clung to him for a long time until she was able to control her spiraling emotions.

His voice was husky and thick with longing. ''Jillian, babe, I want you so bad, but I know I would hate myself afterward and I'm so afraid that you'd regret it.''

The desperation in his voice strangely calmed her. She took his taut face in her hands and softly kissed his eyes, then smiled at him. ''Then we won't run the risk. We'll keep my virtue and your honor intact, and we'll spend these next few days just simply enjoying the fact that we're together.''

And they had. The days had been beautiful and special. Their future had stretched before them like an intricate mosaic, but like a fragile thing it had been shattered by the dark hand of fate.

With a sad heaviness inside her, Jillian tied up the letters again. But instead of packing them back in the blue cardboard box she slipped off the bed and left the room, returning with a Chinese chest inlaid with jade and mother-of-pearl. Dumping the contents of the chest on her bed, she carefully stacked the letters inside. With an air of finality she closed the lid, carried the chest into the living room and placed it beside the fireplace.

Minutes later she was jarred out of her reverie by the chiming of the door bell. Sighing, she went out into the hallway and opened the outside door.

Norm was lounging against the wrought-iron rail watching a group of children playing across the street. His unguarded eyes were filled with pain and sadness, and Jillian swallowed hard, her throat tight with compassion as he glanced at her. "Hi, Jillian."

"Hi. Come on in," she answered. "Would you like a drink?"

"Would I! A long tall cold one with lots of ice." He followed her into the kitchen and sat down at the table, smiling warmly at her as she handed him his drink and sat down across from him. He took a long swallow, then his gaze became penetrating. "So how's it going?"

She sidestepped the issue by replying, "You've been at all the rehearsals—how *is* it going?"

Norm smiled at her lopsidely. "You're avoiding the question and you know it."

Jill turned and stared out the window. She was feeling too raw to discuss Jacob with anyone right then. Talking about it changed nothing.

Norm watched her set face as he lighted a cigarette and slowly exhaled a cloud of swirling smoke. "I know you think it's none of my business, kid, but I'll debate that point with you."

At his words Jillian snapped her head around to look at him, her eyes glimmering dangerously.

Norm's smile was both shrewd and doleful, his voice earnest. "Look, Jill, if you aren't going to be able to handle the pressure, I need to know. This kind of tension can splinter a group if it's allowed to continue. Can you cope? That's what I need to know."

She stared at him for a long time, her expression vacant as she honestly attempted to view the situation from Norm's position. Finally she shrugged her shoulders in a gesture of weariness and confusion.

"I don't know, Norm. I've never been in a situation like this before. I know I can handle the music and I think I can cope with the demands made of a performer. But I don't know how I'll handle working with Jacob. I just don't know."

Norm ran his finger tentatively around the rim of his glass for a moment, then he laid his hand on hers. "We normally have new members sign a contract to ensure that we maintain the quality of the group for the duration of a tour." He squeezed her hand reassuringly. "I think you have a very special talent, Jill, and I would certainly like to have the opportunity to promote it. But I think we'd better give you a month's trial period before you commit yourself. The end of the tour is four months away, and if you can't resolve this problem between yourself and Jake, it could be the worst time of your life. I want you to be very sure before you sign that contract."

Jill looked at their joined hands and felt a pang of remorse at the sight of his gold wedding band. It was his own grim reminder.

"I think perhaps that would be wise," she said finally. "I need some time."

Norm's expression was grave. "I realize that this leaves you up in the air about your present job, and I feel badly about that. It certainly isn't a very solid commitment on my part but—"

"Don't worry about that, Norm. I've already made arrangements with the school board to take a year's leave of absence. If this doesn't work out, I honestly wouldn't mind taking a year off from teaching. I need a break, no matter what."

He patted her hand, then drained his glass and leaned back. "There's something else, Jillian. I want you to move down to the hotel. I really don't like the idea of your driving back here alone at two in the morning. Besides, if you were with the rest of us we could work in a rehearsal on the spur of the moment."

Jillian didn't like the idea, not a bit. Avoiding Jacob's hostility would be much more difficult and his proximity would only add to the tension and the strain.

"Norm, I don't think—"

His eyes were piercing as he interrupted, "If you sign on with the group, you're going to have to move sooner or later. I think the sooner the better."

She met his level gaze with troubled eyes; he was right, of course. "Very well. When do you want me to move?"

"I would like to have you moved in by the time we begin our regular performances."

Jillian nodded reluctantly, then shut her eyes as a terrible knowledge churned within her. The nightmare was only beginning.

CHAPTER SEVEN

IT WAS TUESDAY, and the first performance was that night. Jillian didn't experience the burst of excitement that normally stimulated her before a performance. The past three days—had it been only three days since her world had been devastated by Jacob's return—had seemed like a lifetime of anguish. Since then she had been so emotionally exhausted that she felt drained of all enthusiasm.

The strained atmosphere between Jacob and herself was still nearly intolerable, but she was becoming adept at avoiding him and his caustic attitude. She was grateful that he remained aloof and detached at rehearsals, for it would have been disastrous if he had been openly hostile toward her. The pressure was beginning to grind away at her, but she was determined to persevere.

Jillian had felt disquieted and uneasy over Norm's insistence that she move down to the hotel. The more she thought about it, however, the more she realized it was the logical thing to do. She was having difficulty adjusting to the different hours she was putting in now, and she knew that it was going to get worse. Their actual working day would begin at seven at night with the first of four sets, the last one ending about one-thirty in the morning.

All the necessary arrangements were beginning to

fall into place. Jillian was immensely grateful to Mrs. Olsen and her friend Mildred for the fabulous costumes they had created for her. She had been delighted with every one of them. Then Kathy, Dan's wife, had offered to help Jillian with her costume changes. It was soon apparent that Kathy had a flair for styling hair, so Jillian was relieved from worrying about that chore.

John had spread the news far and wide that she would be performing with Firefly, so the phone had rung steadily with calls from friends and co-workers congratulating her on her success. She'd had to wring promises from all of them that they would give her until the weekend to settle in before they came to see her perform.

Jillian was mentally going over the list of things she had packed to see if she had forgotten anything when the front-door bell chimed. Racing through the living room and into the front foyer she yanked open the door, then laughed delightedly as John gave her a sweeping bow.

"I have come to collect Miss Jillian Lambert, alias Amber Blaine, alias Klondike Kate, alias—"

"You're totally ridiculous, John, but I'm glad to see you anyway." Jill reached up and gave his nose a healthy twist, then patted his cheek affectionately.

John caught her hand and bestowed a gallant kiss upon it. "At your service, ma'am. When I heard you were moving down to the hotel today I thought I would come over and give you a hand. I know you're hopeless when it comes to packing, and besides, I had this awful mental picture of your suitcases bursting open in the middle of the lobby."

"Bless you, John, boy. I could do with some moral

support right now. Come on in. I still have some iced tea in the fridge. We'll finish that off before we go.''

By the time they reached the hotel lobby, John had Jillian in high spirits. They were standing in front of the elevators, laughing helplessly, when the elevator door opened and disgorged the entire retinue of Firefly. Jacob was definitely taken aback at seeing his brother there with Jill, but John ignored his reserve. Grabbing the handles of the wheelchair, he spun Jacob around and headed across the lobby.

''I guess I've been deserted,'' laughed Jillian.

Elaine giggled and made a face. ''Tell you what, Jill. You explain what goes where, and Kathy and I will stow it away upstairs for you.''

''Thanks, Elaine, I'd appreciate that,'' Jill replied warmly. ''This all goes up to my room—'' she gestured at the two suitcases ''—but I'll take these two garment bags with me and put them in the dressing room backstage.''

''Good enough. We'll see you later. Kathy and I are going out shopping for a while. We'll be back about five.''

Jillian smiled and waved as the two women sprinted toward the closing door of the elevator. Norm had waited, and he fell into step beside her.

''Nervous about opening night?''

''Not yet, but that doesn't mean a thing. Ask me again about half past six; I'll be shaking so badly by then my teeth will be rattling.''

''That has to be Jake's brother who went wheeling off with him.''

''It is. That's John, my undoing or my uplifting or whatever. He's only slightly demented. He and my brother Allan were the two who kept things interesting when we were kids.''

"Still does, by the look of things."

Jillian felt a pang of loneliness and isolation as she looked ahead to where the brothers were waiting. Jacob had his head thrown back and he was laughing up at John, who looked smug and pleased with himself. She desperately wanted to be included. She and Norm joined the group just as Jacob was introducing John to the band.

"And this is Norm Kent," he said then. "He's our manager." Norm reached across Jacob to shake John's outstretched hand. "I hate to admit it, but this is my brother John."

Jillian followed as John pushed Jacob up a ramp, which led into the lounge where they would be performing. He was puffing affectedly when he reached the top. "I'll bet it would be a hell of a lot more fun going down then going up. You know, Jacob, you'd move along at a pretty good clip if I gave you a push from up here."

"Skip it. Going down the ramp might be fun but flying through the plate-glass window at the bottom would be a drag." Jacob was actually laughing.

Norm looked at Jillian, his eyes registering disbelief. She nodded slightly. No one but John, and perhaps Allan, would ever be able to make a flip reference to Jacob's disability without incurring his cold withdrawal. She knew that.

The lounge turned out to be a very large room, but pleasant. Raised booths ringed the three walls that formed a hollow square opposite the stage, which was draped in glimmering silver lamé. Another table-filled balcony was at stage level, its edges fenced with decorative wrought-iron railings. Below that was a large sunken area that was normally a dance floor. The space was now filled with about twenty extra

tables to accommodate the large crowds expected for
their performances. Jill had been to the lounge before, but now she was seeing it through the eyes of a
performer. It would be a good setup in which to
work.

"We'll have one complete run-through of the first
show, more to get the feel of the place than anything
else," directed Norm. "Would you like to stay and
watch, John?"

"No!" It rang out in horrified unison from both
Jill and Jacob.

John laughed and pretended to cower, his arms
covering his head in a protective gesture. "All right!
All right! You don't have to beat me over the head to
make your point—I can tell when I'm not wanted!"

"John Holinski," laughed Jillian as she stood in
front of him, her hands on her hips, "you can foul
up *anything* faster than anyone I know! I love you
dearly, but I want you out, *now!*"

John grinned back and roguishly cocked one eyebrow at her. Then he reached out and touched her
lips with his fingers, his eyes dancing with pure devilment. "Don't tempt me, Miss Lambert! The idea of
falling in love with you has crossed my mind before. I
came to the conclusion that it wouldn't work—it
would be like falling in love with my own sister."
With that John laughed and walked out of the room,
totally unaware how Jillian had reacted to his teasing
words.

And Jillian did react. She felt herself go white and
she had to clutch the bar to keep her knees from
buckling beneath her.

"Jillian?" It was Norm's voice.

"Leave her alone for a minute!" Jacob was sud-

denly close beside her, a strange look on his drawn
face. Jillian managed to sit down on one of the bar
stools, her body trembling.

Jacob's voice was low and flat. "That was rather a
bad choice of words, wasn't it?"

She forced herself to look at him directly. Their
eyes met and held, both of them remembering that
moment of discovery so long ago that had been the
beautiful, overwhelming beginning.

IN SPITE OF THE EPISODE with John the rehearsal went
without a hitch. Jillian glanced at her watch as they
left the stage and was a little surprised to see that it
was only four-thirty.

"Are you coming for some lunch, Jill?" David
asked companionably.

"I don't think so, thanks," she answered. "I think
I'll go up to my room, if I can find it, and lie down
for a while. I still haven't managed to switch my
hours around, so if I don't have an hour's nap now,
I'll likely crash on you after the second set." She
paused at the doorway. "Do I pick up the key from
the front desk?"

David dug into his pocket and fished out a hotel
key. "Why don't you take mine? The hotel has a
large suite for entertainers on the second floor,
number 219. You go through the common sitting
area to the individual rooms. It's a good setup. We
have a place of our own to relax and there isn't a big
hassle over individual keys. Elaine will have put your
things in one of the empty rooms."

"Thanks, David." She raised her hand in salute as
the musician headed down the ramp and turned toward the hotel coffee shop. Then she walked quickly

across the lobby. She simply had to have some time to herself to collect her nerves, or she would never make it through the evening.

As she reached the elevator she had the sudden feeling that she was being watched. Before the door closed, she caught a glimpse of Jacob staring at her from across the lobby.

As she unlocked the door to suite 219 she was feeling totally unsettled. She would have given anything to know what was going on in Jacob's mind. . . and why he hated her so.

It wasn't until Jill had pushed these thoughts away that the familiarity of the place registered. The sitting room was the one where Norm had interviewed her. A pleasant room, it was decorated in orange, rust and dark brown. It was furnished with two loveseats covered with bold plaid upholstery, plus four large cozy-looking armchairs in accentuating tones of rust and orange. The furniture was arranged around two large coffee tables into a comfortable conversation area.

Jillian sat down on one of the loveseats and propped her long legs up on the coffee table. Wearily she swept her hair back off her face and rested her head against the cushions. She was tired and discouraged beyond description.

She felt as if she had been swimming against the current for a long time as her mind drifted within a haze of sleep. A sound, a motion or perhaps an intuition that someone else was in the room watching her penetrated the swirling fog. She opened her eyes, soft with slumber, to find Jacob watching her from the open door. Their eyes met and held, then he wheeled around and closed the door quietly behind him with a gesture of finality.

Jillian covered her face with her arm as despair settled upon her like a familiar cloak. He had left her five years before; now he was rejecting her again, but this time there was an element of hate in him that made it far worse.

Jillian raised her arm at last to find John standing at the door, his eyes solemn and concerned. She sat up and brushed her long tangled hair off her face, her motions indicating her dejected state.

"Do you feel like going downstairs for a coffee with me, Jill, or would you rather I got lost?"

Jillian heaved a sigh and grinned up at him halfheartedly. "Let's try the coffee. I've been trying to lose you for years and years, John, and I haven't succeeded before. Do you really think I'd have any success today?"

He made a face as he grasped her hands and hauled her to her feet. "Come to think of it, why should I ruin a perfect record?"

Downstairs in the coffee shop they found the two couples from Firefly still there. Before long, John had everyone laughing helplessly as he recalled some of the experiences he, Jillian and the others had shared as children and young adults. He had just finished recounting a story about Jillian training one particularly wily stallion when Norm and Jacob joined the group.

Every muscle in Jillian's body tensed. She was seized with uneasiness as an ominous premonition swept through her.

Elaine wiped tears of mirth from her eyes as she said, "I didn't realize you were an accomplished horsewoman, Jillian. You'll have to take us greenhorns riding one of these days while we're out here in ranch country."

Jillian forced a smile but shook her head. Jacob was watching her, his eyes revealing the coldness that he constantly directed toward her. "Oh, I'm sure Jillian will take you riding, Elaine, if you coax her a little. She really is quite good, you know."

Jillian felt the blood drain from her face when she realized that he wasn't going to drop the topic. "You will take them out, won't you?" he pressed. "I'm sure they would enjoy it." His manner was even and controlled, but Jillian was aware of the hostility that was hovering beneath that thin veneer.

"I'll gladly take you out. Why don't we go next Sunday?" John suggested casually. But Jillian could detect the tension in his voice. Her own muscles tightened defensively, almost as though she was preparing herself for a physical blow. Everyone at the table was waiting for a response from her, but she knew if she unclenched her teeth she would cry.

Jacob's voice was razor edged. "I'm sure Jillian can be persuaded to go along."

John covered her clammy hands with one of his, then looked directly at Jacob. "Leave her alone, Jacob, and quit tormenting her." He spoke very quietly, but his voice rang with a barely controlled anger. "Jillian hasn't been on a horse since your accident. For some reason she developed an aversion to riding that left her—"

"John, don't!" Jillian's voice, low and shaking, pleaded for a rescue from the situation, which was becoming intolerable.

John looked at her, his jaw set and tense as he stood up, pulling Jillian up with him. "Come on, red, let's go and get drunk!" His tone had softened as he put his arm protectively around her and led her away, knowing that she could barely see through the blur of tears.

Through the entire evening's performances that night Jillian felt hollow and detached. It was as though part of her mind had gone into hibernation, leaving her to function with a peculiar vacancy.

She joined the others for a drink after the last set, her mind registering vague impressions that left her only half-aware of what was happening around her. Her remoteness was shattered by a heavy hand on her shoulder.

She turned around to find a man standing behind her, the same man who had been sitting at one of the tables directly below the stage all evening. His breath reeked of rum as he bent low over her shoulder, his hand gripping her painfully. She reached up to push him away, but he caught her fingers and squeezed them so hard she cried out in pain.

"Don't try to give me the brush-off, sweetheart." His voice was slurred and insinuating. "I know your type. Why don't we just skip the act and go on up to my room?"

Jillian's face twisted with a mixture of disgust and disbelief. Norm sprang to his feet as the drunk caught a handful of her hair, twisting her head around with a vicious, savage yank. Then she felt her hair released suddenly as a grunt of pain exploded behind her. She whirled around, white and shaken, to find her tormentor doubled over, his hands clutching his midriff.

Jacob was there, too, his face livid with fury. He reached out and grabbed his opponent by the hair and with one violent powerful motion threw him onto his back.

"Don't you ever touch her again, or I promise you, I'll smash your skull!" His voice was quiet and deadly. As the lounge staff arrived to remove the troublemaker, he turned his wheelchair around and approached the table again.

The entire group sat in dumbfounded silence, stunned by Jacob's wrath. In the vacuum Jacob turned to Jillian, his eyes cold with anger. "You know you're asking for trouble, flaunting that—" he flicked her hair disdainfully "—around the way you do."

Jillian stared at him in disbelief. Then fury—hot boiling fury—surged within her, reviving her. Without saying a word she rose from the table, her rage radiating from her like heat from a fire as she turned and stormed out of the lounge.

Minutes later she burst into her room, her temper still overriding all other emotions. Yanking open a dresser drawer, she rummaged through it wildly until she found what she was searching for. Then she slammed the drawer shut and ripped open the sewing kit. She was standing there with scissors in hand, ready to snip a thick lock of hair, when her door flew open and Jacob barged in. He propelled himself across the room in a flash, the scissors clattering against the wall as he struck them from her hand.

"I might have known you'd resort to childishness." His face was livid with anger.

Jillian reacted without thinking and slapped his face with a resounding backhand. "Go to hell, Jacob," she snarled through gritted teeth. "You washed your hands of me, remember?"

He caught her wrist and twisted it brutally, forcing her down on her knees in front of him. His eyes were narrowed threateningly as he growled, "Cut your hair, and so help me God, I'll give you the beating of your life.''

''Why don't you, then, if it will make you feel any better?'' Anger flashed from her eyes as she glared up at him.

He stared back at her, his expression unreadable. ''I might at that!'' In one swift movement he caught her by the arms and yanked her against him. ''Yes, maybe it *would* make me feel better. So don't push me, Jillian. Just don't push me!'' It was no idle threat.

JILLIAN FELT ODDLY REVITALIZED and cleansed after a surprisingly good night's sleep. She smiled wryly at herself as she applied the little makeup she usually wore. For once in her life her temper had been her salvation. If only she could stay angry, she might survive.

There was a nasty bruise on her wrist where Jacob had grabbed her, but she had nothing that would cover it. She shrugged uncaringly and slipped into a bright yellow tank top and blue jeans. She had just started to comb out her hair when she slammed the comb on her dresser. *To hell with him.* She had never cut her hair because Jacob had liked it long, but that was finished now. She was going downstairs to the beauty salon; they could crop it all off, for all she cared.

She was nearly at the salon entrance when she was grabbed from behind. A knot of fear twisted in her stomach as she turned, half expecting to find the man from the previous night. Her jaw dropped in amazement when she found Jacob sitting there, his face set.

''If you want a scene, I will certainly oblige.'' His

voice was low, but Jillian knew by its tone that he meant every word he said. "I warned you last night about cutting your hair, and I'm warning you again. Do I make myself perfectly clear?"

She stared at him for a long moment, then snapped, "Perfectly!" Snatching her arm away and swinging her hair over her shoulder with an arrogant toss of her head, she marched off to the coffee shop.

Only Norm, Elaine and Kathy were there. She joined them, ignoring their speculative glances. By unleashing the raging anger she felt for Jacob, Jillian was experiencing a relief from the anguish she'd been suffering. She felt like throwing a glass of ice water at him when he joined them, but she suppressed the urge with great difficulty and instead ignored him completely.

They were nearly finished breakfast when she felt his eyes on her. She raised her head to give him a frigid stare, but her fury abated when she saw the look on his face. His eyes were fixed on the purple bruise, his face pale as a fleeting expression of revulsion swept across his features. With a slam he set his coffee mug on the table and mumbling his excuses he wheeled around and left the shop. Jillian's anger drained away, leaving her empty and numb.

THAT EVENING she had just finished dressing for the first show when there was a light knock on her door. She adjusted the long full sleeves of her white satin suit as she went to answer it.

A uniformed bellboy was standing there, a small gift-wrapped box in his hand. "Miss Lambert?"

Jillian nodded, a puzzled look on her face as he handed her the package. She absently closed the door and walked over to the desk, completely baffled by the gift. Slowly she unwrapped the mysterious package, a long slim box. Then she gasped. Inside was a wide silver-filigree bracelet set with tiny sapphires. It was exquisitely crafted and obviously very expensive. A card fluttered to the floor as she lifted the bracelet out of the box. Her heart plummeted when she turned the card over and recognized the handwriting. It said simply, "I'm sorry."

Jillian stared at it blankly as she wrestled with the conflicting emotions that stormed within her. Anger, love, compassion, resentment: they were all there. What was she going to do? She tried the beautiful piece of jewelry on her bruised wrist as her eyes smarted with unshed tears. Should she keep it or should she send it back?

Swearing violently under her breath she sent the overnight case that had been sitting on the desk crashing against the opposite wall. *Damn, damn, damn!* Why did he have to add to her bewilderment and confusion with this unexpected acknowledgment? His reaction at the breakfast table had told her more clearly than a spoken apology how disquieted he was by the mark he had left on her wrist. He sincerely regretted hurting her physically, that she knew, but didn't he realize that his unyielding cold attitude hurt her far worse?

She braided her hair and wrapped it into a sedate coil at the back of her head. Then she unclasped the bracelet and held it in her hand. Smiling wryly she turned and left her room.

She felt Jacob's eyes on her later as she walked into the spotlight onstage, but she didn't have the courage to meet his gaze. As she reached for the mike her sleeve pulled up, revealing the sparkling bracelet on her wrist. He took a deep breath and she was aware of the look of relief that flashed across his face before his expression became fixed and unreadable again.

Jillian sighed as she walked to center stage. Obviously the bracelet was not intended as an olive branch.

JILLIAN AWOKE WITH A START the next morning to find herself in unfamiliar surroundings. She gave herself a mental shake when she finally realized where she was, her smile softening when she looked at the beautiful bouquet of long-stemmed white roses on her dresser. Norm had presented them to her the previous night at the close of the last set. The thoughtful gesture had bolstered her sagging spirits, and she had thanked him warmly.

Jacob had been totally aloof and cool, but even his attitude hadn't spoiled the pleasure she had felt.

She rolled over on her stomach and rested her head on her hands. The shows had been fairly successful, considering that they had had such a short time to work together. The next two days would add polish and give them a more professional sound.

Jillian was feeling rather concerned about David, though, for he had developed a sore throat midway through the evening. By the time they had concluded their last set, his voice had sounded harsh and grating.

Jillian continued to lie there for a while, contemplating the situation, then she rolled over and got out of bed. She felt slightly at loose ends in her new environment. At home there would have been a number of things she could do, but here she felt completely lost. She started toward the shower, then changed her mind, opened a dresser drawer and found her swimsuit. She would go for a swim before she went down for breakfast.

She was interrupted just then by the harsh ringing of the telephone. Sweeping her hair behind her shoulders she sat on the bed and reached for the receiver. "Hello."

"Hi. How's it going?" It was John.

"Just fine." She wished it really was fine and that she wasn't beginning to feel like an overextended rubber band inside. She had already realized that Norm's suggestion of a one-month trial period before she signed a contract was just as much for her benefit as for his.

"Jill?"

"Sorry, John." She had been so deep in her own thoughts that she hadn't heard what John was saying.

"I said, I'm going to the horse races at Northlands this afternoon. How about coming along?"

Jillian considered his invitation only for a moment. Why not? There wasn't going to be a rehearsal because Norm didn't want to push David, and besides, she and John always had such fun together.

"That sounds like a terrific idea. Do you want me to meet you there?"

"No, we'll pick you up about eleven-thirty so we can have lunch before the races start. Brian is coming with us."

Jillian couldn't help laughing. Brian had been with John the night before at the lounge; they had sat at a stage-side table. The two of them had made rather a production out of ogling her, much to her amusement and Jacob's disgust. Brian and John had been good friends for the past couple of years, and Jillian had become well acquainted with the antics of the zany New Zealander. He was tall, dark and handsome, his mustache giving him a dashing, slightly piratical look. She knew that John was obviously planning something and that Brian, being Brian, would be the first one to fall in line with any of John's devious schemes.

"It won't work, John, but I appreciate your interest."

John laughed. "Oh, what the hell. It might set Jacob back a step or two, and besides, we'll have a blast."

Jillian fell back on the bed laughing. "You are completely incorrigible!"

John lapsed into a heavy Polish accent. "See you at ewewen-tirty, my darlink."

"At eleven-thirty." Jillian hung up the phone, then lay with her hands behind her head, chuckling over John's absurd antics. Suddenly she froze, her insides quaking with apprehension as she heard Jacob's voice outside her door. She didn't relax until she heard it slowly fade away down the corridor. Then she pressed her fingers to her temples as she closed her eyes and tried to still the upheaval within her. She would have to get a grip on herself or she would never stand the strain that Jacob's hostilities imposed upon her. Damn, why did everything have to be so difficult? She got up and headed for the shower.

She had decided to wear a light yellow dress that was particularly becoming on her. It made her eyes

greener than usual and accentuated the bronze highlights in her hair. She pinned her hair into a coil at
the back of her head, then slipped on her white sandals and picked up her handbag, glancing at herself
in the mirror before she turned and left the room.

It was exactly eleven-thirty when she stepped off
the elevator and started to walk across the lobby.
Brian, who was already leaning casually against the
front desk, straightened up when he saw her approaching. He came toward her eagerly, his hands
outstretched in a touching, expressive gesture that
was pure melodrama. Brian, above all else, was a
brilliant actor.

Jillian smiled at him, her eyes dancing with humor
as she took his hands. "You really don't have to go
that far, Brian. No one is watching, you know; you
could have just said, 'Hello.'"

"Oh, but you're wrong there." He caught her face
with one hand to prevent her from turning around.
"John's brother has been sitting over by the fountain
staring at me ever since I came in, and I have a rather
strong impression he's taken a hearty dislike to me."
He grinned at her wickedly. "I think he recognized
me from last night."

Jillian couldn't really see the sense in explaining
that it was she whom Jacob disliked. She could feel
her face grow pale and it was all she could do to keep
from turning around as she left the lobby, unaware
that Brian's hand appeared to be resting possessively
on her back.

SHE RETURNED TO THE HOTEL half an hour before
show time. The relaxing, carefree afternoon had dispelled much of her tension, but her high spirits were

soon deflated when she noticed Jacob sitting in the corridor off the dressing room. He had on his bright blue vest and pants, with a white satin shirt. Her chest contracted painfully, partly out of apprehension, partly because he looked so damned handsome.

His face was set and he was obviously angry. "Your sense of timing is remarkable, Jillian. You have a little over fifteen minutes before show time."

She was about to make a sharp retort but stopped herself. "I'll be ready," she replied calmly.

He caught her by the wrist as she started to move past him. "And I wonder what exactly you'll be ready for?" His voice was like ice, but Jillian couldn't read his face in the dim light. He continued to hold her arm in a viselike grip, then with a snort he released her and wheeled rapidly toward the stage.

With a sinking feeling Jillian watched him go. She had only to appear and his malice toward her flared.

"Jill?"

She turned around to find Norm watching her. She sighed and gave him a weak apologetic grin. "I know, I had better get ready."

"You still have plenty of time." He took a cigarette from the pack he was holding in his hand. "Jill, I think you had better know what's happened." He paused and lit the cigarette, the flame of the lighter throwing his face in dancing shadows. "We've had some bad news. We called the doctor in for David; his throat is badly infected, so he won't be able to sing for at least a week." Norm hesitated, then took a deep breath. "I'm sorry, Jill, but Jacob is going to have to do the lead vocals with you."

Jillian felt as though a giant hand had squeezed all the breath out of her. Singing with Jacob was more than she had bargained for! But she knew that Norm had no other choice. She certainly wasn't familiar enough with the routine or the material to carry it alone.

"Jill?"

"That's fine. I'll manage." She hoped that she could.

"Keith will take over the emcee duties and David insists that he's well enough to play, so we'll fly with a full flock." Norm started to say something about Jacob, then changed his mind. He squeezed her shoulder reassuringly and grinned down at her. "You know, Jill, you're a damned sight tougher than you look."

Jillian wasn't too certain what he meant, for she could never recall being referred to as frail. She could see the humor twinkling in his eyes, so she grinned up at him and patted him smartly on the cheek. As she turned to go she realized that Jacob had been sitting on the runway watching the exchange between her and Norm with a grim look on his face. It had probably appeared to be an intimate interlude between them, but Jill was feeling so dubious about the performance that she dismissed it completely from her mind.

Actually, the performances that night went far better than Jill had expected. There were a few rough spots, but the customers were both enthusiastic and responsive. Jillian found herself withholding much of the emotion and energy she usually radiated when she sang, but that was a barrier she had to erect. Twice she felt as though her defenses were threatened, but somehow she managed to keep control. As always, she and Jacob were in perfect, beautiful harmony, their voices blending into a oneness that was so very special. It had been an unnerving experience.

Norm joined the group after the last performance, a keen speculative look on his face. Jillian could tell by his brief comments that he was pleased with the way she and Jacob sounded together. He fell into step with her as they returned to their rooms. Draping one arm casually across her shoulders he gently held her back, allowing the rest of the group to walk ahead.

"Jillian, I've made a couple of observations tonight that I would like you to be aware of."

"And they are?"

"One is that you've been holding back, especially tonight, and you don't have to when you're singing with Jake. You aren't doing yourself justice and you aren't really being fair to the boys."

"Norm, I—"

"I know why, Jillian. But I also know that there's a rapport between you and Jake that creates a sound that's unique. I could hear the beginning of it tonight, but it's going to be up to you. Jake won't push you, you know that."

Jillian looked up at Norm, her face drawn and pale. "Norm, do you understand what music can do to people like Jacob and myself? It's such an extension of our emotions that it can become something almost physical."

"I understand that, but I also know it's a problem the two of you are going to have to solve. You walk around looking miserable, and Jake sits in his room and broods. You both have developed plastic exteriors, and that's not like either one of you. When you're together, neither one of you is recognizable as you really are. But that's something only the pair of you can deal with. My professional concern, at this point, is for the band.''

They waited for the elevator in silence. Jillian knew that the group shouldn't have to be affected in any way by the personal problems of its members. In all honesty, she knew she had not given her best tonight. As they entered the elevator Jillian turned to face Norm, her face reflecting her own inner turmoil.

"You're right, Norm, about my performance. I guess I'll just have to try harder.''

He hugged her against him and smiled down at her. "That's all I ask, kid." The door was sliding open as he put both arms around her and dropped a friendly kiss on her forehead. As they turned to step off the elevator they found Jacob silently observing them, his face set, his eyes narrowed. Jillian tensed; she knew that look. Without saying a word she stepped off the elevator and walked past him, her eyes glued straight ahead.

"Very touching!" His voice was hard and cold, full of insinuations.

Jillian whirled around and stared at him in disbelief. He had made it plain that they were finished, that he could barely stand the sight of her. He didn't want her, that was obvious, but he didn't want anyone else to have her, either.

Her temper blazed as she noticed Norm grinning broadly behind Jacob. She realized then that Norm either had anticipated Jacob would be there or had glimpsed his wheelchair through the opening door. That kiss had been deliberately and cunningly staged.

Their behavior was deplorable and her anger soared. "As far as I'm concerned, you can both go straight to hell!'' Turning around, she stomped down the hallway and through the open sitting-room door. The other band members looked at her in amazement as she marched through the room, her jaw set and her eyes flashing green fire. Throwing open her bedroom door she slammed it violently behind her. Then she yanked off her clothes, tossing them angrily in the general direction of the closet. She had just thrust her arms into the sleeves of her pale blue dressing gown when her door burst open and Jacob rolled into the room, his eyes flashing.

She tied the belt with shaking hands, then whirled to face him. ''Get out!''

''The hell I will until I find out what's going on.'' He wheeled his chair over until he was directly in front of her.

''Nothing is going on, except in your obviously suspicious mind!'' Her voice was trembling. She tried to back away from him but found she was trapped against the bed. Suddenly his hand shot out, and with one powerful twist he threw her onto it. Before she could scramble out of his reach, he dived after her and grasped her roughly by the hair. She winced as he yanked her head back and glared at her. The muscle at the side of his jaw was jumping as he spoke through clenched teeth.

''Don't play games with me, Jillian. You and Norm looked damned cozy when the elevator door opened. He's had enough problems in his life without you toying with him. He's been a good friend and I'll be damned if I'll stand by and see him hurt by you!''

The injustice of the accusation inflamed Jillian. ''I have never in my life toyed with anyone, nor am I about to now,'' she hissed. ''Furthermore, what goes on between Norm and myself is strictly our own business and absolutely none of yours! What difference does it make to you, anyway? You've made it very plain that you loathe the ground I walk on!'' Her voice was still low and tight but her flaring anger was giving way to hurt. God, how he could hurt her.

He tightened his grip on the coil of her hair and wrenched her head around to face him. Jillian grimaced and her eyes filled with tears of pain as the pins tore loose and her hair came spilling down. She brought her hand up to untangle his clenched fist but Jacob seized her wrist and held it in a painful grip above her head. She shut her eyes and tried to stop the tears but their source was a new pain—a pain of absolute wretchedness and futility. She really didn't think she could bear it. Jacob felt nothing but anger and resentment toward her, and that cold reality stabbed through her. It was over; everything was gone.

The guilt that she had endured for so long engulfed her and suffocated any anger that remained. It was little wonder that he felt the way he did about her. If she had responded faster at the time of the accident, she could have saved him from injury. But she hadn't. Remorse washed through her like acid, cutting away all restraints.

Her voice was ragged. ''I can understand why you loathe the sight of me, Jacob, and I don't blame you.'' She swallowed with difficulty, ''I know I could have prevented it from happening—'' Her voice broke under a new wave of desolation.

Jacob's savage grip slackened as he stared down at her, but his face was as hard as granite. ''What in hell are you talking about? What could you have prevented from happening?'' He gave her a sharp rough shake. ''What are you talking about?''

Her voice was barely audible. ''The accident.... If I had caught Rogue before....'' She closed her eyes, her face a tortured grimace as the terrifying picture of Jacob's body being trampled beneath Rogue's pounding hooves rose in her mind. Why hadn't she reacted faster? Why hadn't she realized?

Suddenly she had to escape. She fought to free herself from his restraining grip, but his arms easily imprisoned her. He stared down at her in horror and disbelief as her guilt-ridden words penetrated his anger.

''Oh, God—no, Jillian!'' His voice was hoarse and tormented, his body heavy upon hers as he buried his face in her tangled hair, his arms like steel bands around her.

Something burst within Jillian with a rending force and she clung to him, inundated by an overriding relief. To be locked in his powerful embrace once again was the most shattering, yet poignant feeling she had ever hoped to experience. Something that had almost withered and died within her surged to life. She hung onto him and wept until she felt enervated and helpless. She loved him so much. And she needed him as she never had before. His arms were a safe and secure harbor in a tumultuous frightening sea.

The loneliness, the awful hurt, the doubts were washed away as she clung to him and sobbed, purging herself of the hollow ache that had been a part of her for so long. He held her immobile beneath him, somehow sensing her absolute need for the comfort of physical contact. For long beautiful moments he held her, his heart pounding against hers, his breathing ragged, until finally her tears were exhausted. Time passed and she became subdued and quiet; an ethereal serenity drifted around her.

Gently he caressed her tearstained face with his fingertips. She closed her eyes as she relaxed against him, his presence healing the old wounds like a balm. There was such a profound need for this physical closeness that it blotted out all other conscious thought. It was strange, almost out of context, for there was no hot driving passion or erupting volcanic emotions—just this powerful need to hold.

The city grew quiet as they lay wrapped in each other's arms, their bodies molded together in an embrace that soothed their torment and provided comfort from the loneliness that had haunted them both.

He stroked her hair, then let his hand rest on her cheek, his voice a gentle reprimand. "Jillian, you must never again blame yourself for what happened. It was a freak accident and *no one* was to blame."

She stirred against him. "But if I had acted immediately instead of—"

Jacob pressed his fingers against her lips. "It may have seemed to you that you reacted in slow motion, Jill, but you didn't. Something like that happens so fast and is so unexpected...." He sighed against her temple. "I had no idea that you held yourself responsible for the accident, and I feel rotten to think that you've carried that unnecessary guilt around for so long. I just couldn't talk about it when I was in the hospital, and I didn't want anyone else to discuss it, either. I'm sorry, Jillian. So very sorry."

She tightened her arms around him protectively as she heard the pain in his voice. "Don't, Jacob." She lifted her head to look at him, and an ache of compassion twisted her heart when she saw the misery in those dark eyes. "There have been too many painful barriers—"

Once again he covered her lips with his hand as he shook his head. "Not now, Jill. I know we need to talk, but I can't handle it right now." She felt him take a deep shaky breath. Then he relaxed his viselike hold and eased her away from him.

She caught his face in her hands, her eyes imploring. "Don't go! Please, Jacob, don't go." He ran his fingers absently through her hair, his eyes clouded as she whispered, "It's been such a long time." Her voice broke, treacherously revealing the quintessence of her feelings.

He watched her for a moment with solemn unfathomable eyes. Then with a soft reluctant sigh he relented to her entreaty and gathered her against him, cradling her head on his chest. He continued to comb his fingers slowly through her hair until it fanned out over them in a thick auburn cascade.

She longed to talk to him, to ask him about his new life and his exciting career. She wanted so desperately to fill all the empty chapters of time that had separated their lives. But he was still reserved and withdrawn, and she didn't want to risk shattering this new tenuous link. So she said nothing.

The eerie morbid sound of a siren sent an icy chill through Jillian and she shivered. Jacob's arms tightened around her, and her eyes misted when she felt the whisper of a kiss against her hair.

CHAPTER EIGHT

"JILLIAN."

Her mind swam through a mist as she drifted into semiconsciousness. She didn't want to wake up and dispel the illusion of being enveloped in a warm and secure embrace.

"Jillian." Reluctantly she stirred, and for a brief unpleasant moment she thought it had all been an elusive dream. But the arms that were holding her were miraculously real. She opened her eyes to the bright sunshine of early morning. Sleepily she smiled up at Jacob, who was watching her with a soft contemplative expression.

He smiled at her, his eyes unexpectedly warm and untroubled. "It's morning, Jillian. If we don't want to contend with knowing looks and cute remarks, we had better get up."

She stretched with catlike grace, then smiled up at him, her eyes shining with a glow of happiness that she hadn't felt for a long, long time. Jacob watched her for a moment, then flicked the end of her nose in a gesture that was carried over from their childhood. He eased his arm out from under her and swung his legs over the edge of the bed. With reluctance Jillian watched him leave; she wished that he would stay and talk, but that was hoping for too much.

After he hoisted himself into the wheelchair, she

reached out and touched his hand but felt him stiffen. He was wary and guarded, and she knew she must keep the moment light and unthreatening or he would withdraw from her totally.

She grinned at him, her eyes dancing. "If anyone asks where you've been, you can tell them that you were hiding from that big blonde who was drooling over you last night." The spark of mischief in her eyes became a wicked gleam when she realized there was a sudden flush rising beneath his dark tan. "You know the one I mean, Jacob—she sat at the table closest to the piano and kept sending you drinks all night."

Jacob was actually blushing. His eyes narrowed threateningly as he made a menacing gesture at Jillian. "Damn you, Jillian Lambert!"

Jillian couldn't suppress her laughter any longer. "Why, Jacob, I do believe you're blushing!" She raised her eyebrows innocuously, her eyes sparkling. "I wasn't sure if you had noticed her or not."

Jacob tipped his head back and laughed, then grimaced with wry embarrassment. "Notice her! Everybody in the damned lounge noticed her. For one awful moment I thought she was going to come up onstage. God!"

Tears of laughter were brimming in Jillian's eyes and she wiped them away with the back of her hand.

Jacob gave her a pointed look, his eyes glimmering with dry amusement. "It wasn't that funny, Jillian."

Jillian struggled into a sitting position. "But it was...when she stood up and...and gave her hips that little wiggle—" She couldn't continue as she was overcome with laughter.

"There's no way you could describe that as a 'little' wiggle—she must have weighed three hundred pounds. The way she threw those hips of hers around I thought she was going to demolish that whole section of booths." Jacob grinned at her, his eyes flashing. "If you don't stop laughing, Jillian, so help me, I'll strangle you!"

Jillian shrugged her shaking shoulders as she mopped her eyes again. "I can't help it! If you...could have seen the...the look on your face—"

"The look on my face was one of pure terror. If she had come up on that stage I would have been absolutely trapped. And you—*you* have the nerve to sit there and laugh about it!"

Jillian was finally able to compose herself enough to speak. "When we started the last verse to that song, I couldn't figure out why it sounded so strange I glanced over—" she took a deep breath in an effort to quell another burst of laughter "—and you were hanging onto the edge of the piano as though your life depended on it."

Jacob grinned. "It did. That's when her escort, or whoever, was trying to wrestle her out of the lounge. I was afraid she was going to get away from him and come thundering back to attack me."

"Poor Jacob." There wasn't an ounce of sympathy in her voice as she laughed at him.

He shook his head slowly and grinned. "That's show biz!" There was warmth and laughter in his eyes, and Jillian's stomach felt as though the elevator had just stopped too quickly as she met that mesmerizing gaze. She managed to smile at him, but her world began to roller coaster wildly as he reached out and softly caressed her lips with his fingertips, his touch lingering and very gentle. She stared at him, her breathing arrested.

Without another word he turned and propelled himself toward the door. He opened it, then turned and flashed a smile that stopped her heart. "See you later." It was more than a casual empty phrase; it was a promise.

She hadn't meant to fall asleep again after Jacob left. She had buried her face in his pillow, relishing the lingering traces of his presence, and had drifted off into a relaxed slumber. It was nearly eleven o'clock when she awoke. She had a quick shower and dressed, then slipped quietly out of her room.

"Running away, or are you just going out for breakfast?" Jillian jumped at the unexpected voice. She whirled around to find Jacob sitting behind her, a teasing grin on his face. Her breath caught when she saw him. He had on beige slacks and a navy-and-beige-figured shirt that accentuated his fair hair and his California tan. She had to resist a powerful urge to reach out and touch him.

"Scare me like that again and I'll give you a very realistic portrayal of a hysterical woman. It's a wonder I didn't scream and wake everyone up."

"You aren't a screamer, Jill."

"Well, I'm an eater. Coming for breakfast?"

Jacob closed his door and turned to follow her down the corridor that led to the sitting room. "Why don't we go for a drive first? I want to see if I can still find my way around."

Jillian laughed, her voice disbelieving. "I hope you can manage better in a car than you did on the buses. I remember getting lost more than a few times with you, Jacob Holinski."

He made a wry face. "Ah, yes—the Edmonton transit system. We always did need extra transfers, didn't we?"

"Well, we were on a first-name basis with more bus drivers than students," Jill laughed.

Jacob rolled out through the sitting-room door as she held it open for him. "Let's take a chance and strike out on our own scenic tour, okay?"

"All right. But you have to feed me sometime."

"I promise." He continued to wheel himself down the hallway, then he paused and looked up at her. "Jill?"

"Hmm?"

"It's good to be back." His voice was quiet.

Jillian swallowed hard as she reached out and touched him lightly on the shoulder, smiling down at him.

"It's good to have you back, Jacob." She was relieved that her voice did not betray the flurry of hope she experienced. Nothing more was said, but her heart was pounding wildly as she followed him into the elevator.

In the lobby Jacob spoke to the desk clerk, then returned to where Jill stood waiting. "Come on. They're going to bring my car around to the front door." She walked beside him through the lobby, aware that several pairs of eyes were upon them. They had to wait only a short time until a sleek powerful-looking Porsche pulled onto the ramp. Jacob opened the passenger door for Jillian and waited while she slipped in. Then he closed the door and wheeled around to the driver's side. She watched with guarded interest as he hoisted himself in, collapsing his chair and sliding it into the specially designed space beside his seat. He made it all look so easy.

After shutting the door he turned to Jillian. "Miss Lambert, do you want to be hot and windblown or cool and collected?"

Jillian laughed. "Hot and windblown, I think, Mr. Holinski." She certainly was not feeling cool and collected. With a touch of the controls, the sunroof glided back and the windows opened. The engine responded with a muted snarl as they moved out into the traffic.

LATE IN THE AFTERNOON they ended up in one of Edmonton's many picturesque parks that nestled in the beautiful river valley that wound its way through the heart of the city. Stretched out on the grass in the shade of some stately old elms, they shared a lazy companionable time filled with laughter. Both of them deliberately avoided any topics that might disturb the smooth but tenuous surface of their newfound harmony. With the ease of old friends they talked idly about family and acquaintances.

Finally there was a lull in the conversation. Jacob lay stretched out on the grass, his hands laced behind his head as he watched two gulls soar overhead. Jillian sat with her long slim legs outstretched, her back propped against a tree. She watched the gulls briefly, then let her gaze fall on the man beside her.

He glanced up at her, his voice very quiet. "You haven't changed, Jillian."

His comment took Jillian by surprise. She could tell by the tightness around his mouth that he had been reluctant to say it aloud. It was almost as though some invisible force had dragged it from him.

She sensed that he was cautiously and hesitantly reaching out to her as a friend, and with a surge of compassion that made her ache inside, she acknowledged the overture.

She laughed softly, a hint of derisiveness in her voice. "Now, that's not true, Jacob. I've changed a great deal. I've learned patience; I've learned not to be impulsive; I've learned to control my temper; I've—"

"Learned to lie a little, as well, I think." There was humor flashing in his eyes as he rolled over on his side and propped his head on his hand. He tried to suppress a grin as he looked up at her.

She smiled at him sheepishly, then made a face. "Well, maybe... just a little. You made me sound like such a monstrous bore when you said in that very solemn voice of yours that I hadn't changed!"

He tipped his head back and laughed, tossing a handful of grass at her. Jillian could almost see him shedding his reserve and caution like a discarded shell.

"All right, Miss Lambert, I take it back. You have changed!"

She gave him a satisfied smug look, her eyes dancing. "So have you." She drew her knees up and clasped her arms around them so that she wouldn't reach out and touch him as she wanted so much to do. "You really have, Jacob. Your style of music has a whole new dimension that's very exciting. There's a zing to it that was never there before." She laughed down at him as she narrowed her eyes. "I really could punch you for your damned bullheadedness, though."

The last vestige of aloofness fell away as Jacob

visibly relaxed. He stared up at her, his face creased with a frown. "What in hell are you talking about? You've lost me somewhere."

"You were always so certain that it would be impossible for you to make a living with your music, that you wouldn't even consider it. Now Norm tells me you're making quite a name for yourself in the States. How did he ever manage to get you moving in that direction—did he put a gun to your head?"

Jacob shook his head. He gave her a dry pointed look but his eyes crinkled disarmingly with amusement. "Very nearly. I went under stiff protest, but Norm ignored my lengthy objections. Once I was involved, everything just seemed to fall into place. It's been really frustrating at times, and I've been known to tear up a score or two—"

"I'll just bet you have," snorted Jillian, stretching out on her stomach in the cool lush grass. "I think it's really terrific, Jacob, and I'm so proud of you."

Deep in thought, he unconsciously reached out and began to play absently with a thick lock of Jillian's hair, which tumbled across her shoulders and spilled onto the grass beside him. She had to steel herself against the arousing warmth that spread within her.

He glanced at her, his eyes thoughtful. "It drives me crazy sometimes. You know how you get a fleeting sensation about how the harmonies for a phrase of music should sound but it's so elusive? I've spent hours and hours agonizing over six or seven bars of a song—"

"And then at three o'clock in the morning it's there, as clear as crystal."

He smiled at her, his eyes reflecting the old familiar rapport, which caught them up in a gentle intimacy. They exchanged a look of complete understanding, which filled Jillian with a warm glow. Jacob finally broke the spell as he sighed and dropped his eyes. They were on dangerous ground and Jillian knew it. With an ease that hid her sudden nervousness, she shifted the conversation into a safer vein.

"Do you live right in Los Angeles, Jacob?"

"Not anymore. I tried it for a while when I first started doing a lot of arranging, but I found I needed peace and solitude to do my best work. Two years ago I bought a house that overlooks the ocean. It's in a beautiful secluded spot, Jillian, and I've come to love the sea. It suits me."

The ocean would suit him and his moods: deep, intense, ever changing. A comfortable silence descended upon them as they both became immersed in their own thoughts. The sounds of children playing drifted across the park, punctuated by shrill screams of excitement and the barking of a dog.

"What have you been doing, Jill?"

Jillian plucked at a clump of grass. "Teaching, studying—I have my master's now—but I haven't been moving any mountains."

He grinned. "I read your résumé, Jillian Lambert. It didn't sound as though your life has been exactly sedentary."

She laughed. "Between my impulsiveness and your damned brother's machinations, there have been one or two moments that were slightly jarring."

"I saw you on TV."

Jillian felt as if she had been hit by a locomotive. After the shock had eased a little, she sat up and stared at him, her eyes wide with stunned amazement. "When?"

Jacob smiled wryly at the dumbfounded look on her face. "Twice, actually. I saw a commercial promoting Edmonton's Klondike Days when I was in Toronto, and there you were." He hesitated, pressing his lips together in a hard line, and Jillian suddenly realized he had never intended to tell her this.

"And the second time?"

Jacob wouldn't meet her eyes, and there was definite reluctance in his voice. "I was in New York doing the musical arrangements for a TV special. It was last winter during the National Hockey League playoffs. I had followed the Oilers fairly closely—I guess it was the old home-town pride of watching the local team make good." Jacob finally looked at Jillian, and she could see from the expression in his dark solemn eyes that it had been a bad experience for him.

She managed to smile at him, hoping to dispel some of the tension that was building. "So you turned on the TV to watch the Oilers in Edmonton and you saw me singing the national anthem, right?"

"Right." His response was clipped.

She reached out and patted his shoulder with a casual laugh. "If I had known you were watching, I would have waved."

Jacob twisted his head around to look at her, his eyes hooded. Jillian was feeling very vulnerable and uncertain because of his revelations, but she managed to camouflage her feelings as he studied her face. Finally she tipped her head down, her hair screening her face from his penetrating eyes. If she had switched on the television to find Jacob singing the national anthem at a hockey game, it would have absolutely shattered her, and she had the strangest feeling that it had had the same effect on him.

She snapped back to reality when she felt his hand cover hers, and she lifted her face to look at him, her eyes dark and dilated.

"I meant it when I told you this morning that it was good to be back, Jillian."

Her throat tightened. It had cost him dearly to admit that. She managed to smile a slightly shaky smile. "And I meant it when I said it was good to have you back, Jacob."

Nothing more was said. He released her hand and stretched out on his back, closing his eyes. There was an aura of stress around him and she realized that he was silently withdrawing from the look of raw pain he had seen in her eyes.

She lay down on the grass beside him and rested her head on her arms, absently watching a small black ant struggle with a bread crumb three times its size. What could she possibly say to reinforce the fragile bond between them? She would accept his terms, no matter what they were, as long as he didn't shut her out with the cold hostility he had barricaded himself behind since his return.

With trembling fingers she reached out and touched his rigid jaw. "I've missed you like hell, Jacob." She bit her lip with uncertainty, then impulsively continued. "What I've missed the most is the compatibility we shared. I could talk to you about anything that mattered to me, no matter how personal or how painful it was. I always knew you'd understand."

She took a deep breath to ease the pressure within her. "Whether you realize it or not, you were my mentor—especially when it came to music. But your attitudes and beliefs have always had an impact on me, even as a child."

Jacob turned his head and looked at her, then slowly reached out and laced his fingers through hers, his touch giving her the courage to go on.

"There was always a special kinship between us that I've never experienced with anyone else. You're the best friend I ever had. We could fight like tigers, but there were never any grudges or hurt feelings, never any petty games between us."

Her eyes filled with tears but she made no attempt to hide them from him—she was speaking from her heart and he knew it. "You never sat in judgment; you challenged me to think. You have the qualities I value most in a friend—trust, intelligence, humor, compassion. I could always lean on you for support, and I miss that, Jacob. More than anything else, I miss that." The tears were coursing down her face unchecked.

She saw him swallow with difficulty. His voice was tortured as he whispered hoarsely, "I miss that, too, Jillian, more than I can say." The deep breath he took shuddered through him, almost as though it was painful for him to breathe. "Trust usually grows so slowly, Jill, and it has to put down so many delicate roots before it's really strong. All through our childhood, even though I was so much older than you, I trusted you." A soft smile of reminiscence lighted his eyes. "Remember when I confided in you, as serious as hell, that I was madly in love with Amanda Peters?"

Jillian propped herself up on one elbow, their clasped hands resting on his chest. "Allan and John threatened to pitch me into the dugout if I didn't tell them who your girl friend was."

"And you stuck your chin out—you were always

leading with your chin, Jill—and said they could drown you but you weren't telling.'' His eyes were dancing as he laughed. ''So they chucked you in—''

''And you had to fish me out.'' She shook her head in amusement. ''It's a miracle you didn't maim them for life. As I recall, you pounded the hell out of both of them.''

''I think I would have half killed them if your dad hadn't come along!'' His eyes were warm and alive and open. ''Yes, Jillian Lambert—we've been friends for a long time.''

A large red ball bounced toward them and a small boy came dashing up to retrieve it. He smiled shyly as Jacob tossed it to him. The intrusion prevented the awkwardness that might have followed, and Jillian was grateful for that.

Instead they slipped into an easy comfortable conversation about their two nephews, Jacob grinning with tolerant amusement as he listened to Jillian brag about them.

''You'll love them, Jacob. They are so adorable.''

He turned his head slightly and said nothing. She knew from the frown creasing his forehead that something was troubling him deeply. Tentatively she reached out and laid her hand on his shoulder. ''What is it, Jacob?''

He sighed and rolled over on his side, propping his head on his hand as he chewed idly on a blade of grass. When he looked at her his eyes were perturbed.

''Jill, no one knows I'm here except you and John—and Karin.'' He tossed the grass aside and ran his hand through his sun-streaked hair. ''I extracted a promise from John that he would say absolutely nothing to the rest of the family. I thought I might go home this Sunday, but I know now that I'm not ready for it.'' His face was suddenly disheartened, and he rolled onto his back again and laid one arm across his eyes.

Jillian bit her lip as she blinked rapidly against the now familiar sting of tears. She reached out and took his hand, his fingers curling around hers tightly, telegraphing his distress.

''Jacob, would you like me to phone them and tell them you're in town?'' Her thoughts raced as she sought a solution. ''We could arrange to have a family get-together at my apartment on Sunday.'' She squeezed his hand reassuringly as she went on, her voice soft with understanding. ''It might be easier for everyone if it was off home ground.''

Jacob remained silent for a long time as he considered her suggestion, then he raised his arm and looked at her. ''Would you, Jillian?''

''You know I would.''

As JILLIAN LAY in bed that night, her hands behind her head, her unseeing eyes stared into the blackness and her thoughts wandered unchecked over the events of the past twenty-four hours.

The call she'd made to Sylvia that afternoon had been one of the most painful things she had ever had to do, yet the task that faced Sylvia was even worse. It would be difficult to confront the Holinskis with the news that Jacob was in Edmonton but would not come home—they would be hurt by that. There had been so much unhappiness and pain tangled up in the past six years, and all of it would come pouring back. Mixed in with the good news would be the old painful memories.

A feeling of uncertainty grew heavy within Jillian as she lay there. Jacob had been more than willing to recollect old memories and respond with humor that afternoon, but any reference to their romantic involvement had been deliberately skirted. She was sure that any mention of that part of their life would be met with withdrawal, and she was not prepared to take that chance. It was as though Jacob had erased those memories from his mind, and there was nothing she could do that would make him acknowledge that portion of his past.

There had been that one single crack in his rigid self-control as they had clung together on her bed. That night they had both experienced a strange kind of emotional healing, but Jacob would let it go no further than that.

Jillian heaved a sigh and swung out of bed. She went to the window, drew open the draperies and stood staring down at the eerie vacant streets of the city.

She knew Jacob well enough to comprehend the ordeal he was facing. He had totally severed his family ties, and for a sensitive deep-feeling person like him, that alone would be bad enough. But he was still shackled with the awareness of why he'd left, and until he came to terms with that, he would never know inner peace.

Automatically he was reaching for a source of strength to help him through the emotional reunion that was before him. He badly needed reassurance and support, even though he wouldn't admit it. He was reaching for a hand to hold, and as long as he felt he could do it without any entanglements, he would reach for hers.

Jillian was more than willing to give him that kind of support. But the memory of that one incredible moment when he had crushed her against him left her with a gnawing hunger, one that grew and grew until she could barely stand it. She wanted him; God, how she wanted him. She shut her eyes and clenched her fists against the desire that twisted within her, but there was no release.

THE NEXT MORNING she felt edgy and apprehensive. Her sleepless night certainly hadn't helped the condition of her nerves. The thought of tonight's performances terrified her, and that brand of fear was foreign to Jill. There would be a capacity crowd, which was bad enough, but there would be the added strain of having family there, as well. The entire Holinski tribe would be there, with the exception of Karin. Then Jillian had received word that her own parents were going to arrive sometime during the evening. The gathering might present some very awkward moments for both herself and Jacob, and neither one of them needed that additional pressure now. To make the situation even more difficult, she was experiencing deep misgivings about performing with Jacob. Now that they had reestablished friendly contact, could they continue to perform together without being swept into the passion that music aroused within them, the passion that could easily shatter the crystal-thin veneer overlaying their deeper selves? She felt as though she was facing certain catastrophe.

A knock echoing on the door snapped her back to the present. She took a deep breath and straightened her shoulders resolutely. "Come in."

The door opened and the whisper of a wheelchair pushed everything else from her mind. She was in complete control as she turned around. "Good morning, Jacob."

He grimaced, then grinned up at her lopsidedly. "Who are you trying to kid with that 'good-morning' routine, Jillian Lambert?" The exhausted strained expression in Jacob's eyes filled her heart with compassion. He was feeling the stress, too.

She returned his grimace, then smiled at him wryly. "Myself, mostly. I feel as though I'm teetering on the brink of disaster. I was considering rushing off to nurse my very sick Aunt Nellie."

"You don't have an Aunt Nellie, Jillian."

"I know it and you know it, but Norm doesn't know it."

Jacob grinned broadly, his eyes dancing. "You don't know Norm very well if you think he'd fall for that. No, you'll have to come up with something better, Jillian."

Her brow creased as she considered the possibilities, then a wicked sparkle appeared in her eyes. "Just what is poor Norm going to say when we tell him I've caught Dave's throat infection?" Her voice sounded raspy and weak.

Jacob tipped his head back and laughed, his face relaxing, his eyes challenging her. "That's a little better, but I'll bet you anything he still won't fall for it. He's no amateur when it comes to dealing with duplicity."

Jillian looked at him, her eyes narrowing slightly, her chin thrust out in determination. "I'll bet you anything he will."

Jacob's eyes were speculating as he studied her.

"You're on, Miss Lambert. Now what are the stakes?"

"I said anything—you name it."

He continued to study her with an inscrutable look that made her knees go suddenly weak. "Anything?" The low query was strangely provocative.

She managed to keep her voice steady as the old excitement stirred within her. "Anything. . .except you can't give the game away, Jacob."

"I'll be the original stone face." He grinned at her then, his eyes gleaming. "Come on, let's see you pull it off."

"Just one minute, Jacob Holinski—what's your ante in this bet?"

As he looked up at her he grinned again. "I'll see your 'anything' and raise you an 'anytime.' But then, I've nothing to lose—you'll never do it!"

"I will."

"We'll see."

They found Norm seated with the rest of the group at a corner table of the coffee shop. The manager's welcoming smile faded into a frown of concern.

"What's the matter, Jillian? You don't look very bouncy this morning."

She slumped down in the space beside him as Jacob wheeled himself up to the table.

Jillian avoided looking at either of them as she shrugged wearily and gave a dry hacking cough. "I guess I've caught Dave's infection. My throat was a little scratchy last night but I didn't think too much about it at the time. There was so much smoke in the lounge. But this morning. . . ." Her voice ended on a hoarse croak.

Norm winced and rubbed his forehead in a gesture

of concern. There was a loud groan of dismay from the band members around the table. When Norm looked up, Jacob gazed innocently back at him, his face completely deadpan.

"Can't anything go right for more than two days in a row?" Norm turned to face Jillian and shook his head. "I'm beginning to feel like some sort of juggler!" He reached out and laid his hand on her forehead, then ran his fingers down her neck, checking for swollen glands. He shook his head again. "There's no doubt about it."

When he looked back at Jacob, his face was passive. "It's not as bad as some cases I've seen, but it's bad enough." He sighed. "Now what?"

Jillian looked from one to the other, her expression confused.

Norm patted her hand sympathetically, then shrugged his shoulders. "At least it isn't terminal." He glanced up, and she felt herself blushing when she saw the twinkle of amusement in his eyes. "No one has ever died from an acute case of stage fright, Jillian."

Jacob broke out laughing at the look of wide-eyed amazement on her face as she stammered, "How—how did you know?"

Norm grinned at her, then glanced at Jacob. "What are you two trying to do—add a few more gray hairs to this tired old head?"

Jillian smiled sheepishly, shrugging her shoulders. "Well, not really. Jacob and I had a wager. I said I could pull off this routine and Jacob said I couldn't, so—"

"I hope you didn't bet your life savings. Didn't Jacob warn you that I have second sight where performers are concerned?"

"Well, yes, but. . . ."

Norm looked at her, his eyes dancing as he covered her hand with his. "What did you bet him, Jill? You're blushing like crazy."

Jacob's laugh was low and husky as he looked at Jillian with hypnotic, intimate contemplation. "It's none of your business what she wagered, Norm—but I have every intention of collecting, I can tell you that."

His eyes held hers with a look that suspended time for Jillian, and her world went into a long slow spin. It was there; all the old magic and sexual magnetism was radiating between them like a force field.

Norm looked from one to the other, his face creasing with a broad grin as his eyes glinted speculatively. He tilted his head to one side, his eyes squinting. "I think we're going to have one hell of a show tonight." He nodded his head. "Yep, one hell of a show."

Neither Jacob nor Jillian heard a word he said.

Jillian was strolling beside Jacob as they left the coffee shop, her eyes casually scanning the lobby. Her gaze suddenly locked on two very familiar and dear people entering the lobby through the main doors. She rested her hand on Jacob's shoulder.

"Jacob—you have company."

She felt his muscles bunch as he turned toward the doors. A tremor ran through his body as he recognized his parents, and Jillian knew he was fighting an inward battle for control. She squeezed his shoulder reassuringly and prayed that she herself had the strength to contain the feelings that were threatening to overwhelm her.

Olga Holinski's face was wet with tears as she stretched out her hands toward her eldest son.

"Hello, mom." Jacob's voice was a choked whisper as he hugged her to him. Jillian's eyes blurred with tears as she saw the telltale moistness gather on his lashes, and she battled back a sob as Jacob drew a long convulsive breath.

His mother cradled Jacob's face in her hands, kissing him softly on the forehead. "Welcome home, my son." The gentleness, the tenderness in her voice were very nearly Jillian's undoing. Olga smiled tremulously, then released Jacob as Mike grasped his son in a bear hug, unashamed of his tears of joy. It was that joy, the pure effervescent joy radiating from Mike that shattered the tension that bound them all. The apprehension of this initial meeting was instantly dissolved, and a feeling of jubilation wove a web of happiness and thanksgiving, sealing away all the anguish. It was like magic.

This man and his son had shared a special closeness, and now the son was back and the father was exuberant. Mike always lapsed into his native language when he was excited, and he was undeniably excited now. The rapid-fire Polish poured out, accompanied by his usual expansive gestures.

Jacob listened to his father for a moment, then threw his head back and laughed, his eyes sparkling with affection. "In English, dad! Heaven help me, I haven't heard a word of Polish for five years, and with the speed you're rattling along at—Lord!" His eyes flashed teasingly as he continued, "Besides, everyone will think you're a foreigner!"

Mike Holinski laughed heartily, his eyes twinkling as he patted his son's face firmly. Everyone knew that his one overriding pride was unquestionably his Canadian citizenship. His children would often bait him about his foreign birth just to watch him rise to the occasion and expound volubly on the merits and wonders of his adopted country.

As Jacob sat grinning up at his father, relief swept through Jillian. It was as if the long space of time away had dissolved for him, as well. The tension was gone—at least temporarily.

"Jillian." The voice was soft, gentle, loving. Jillian turned to Jacob's mother and hugged the petite woman to her, her eyes again filling with tears. When Olga clasped her face between her hands, her brown eyes brimming with warmth and affection, Jillian could see a question lurking there and she knew what it was. She shut her eyes briefly, then shook her head. Mrs. Holinski patted her cheek understandingly, but Jillian was aware of the flash of disappointment in the older woman's eyes.

Grasping her hands, she squeezed them reassuringly and whispered, "It's okay. Really. But please, please don't ask any questions about Jacob and myself. He simply wants to forget that that part of his life ever happened."

Olga looked at her for a moment, then sadly, reluctantly nodded her head. "The others will know of your wish from me, Jillian. I had so hoped—"

"Jillian! Ah, Jillian! You are as beautiful as ever!" Jill found herself swept up in Mike's rib-cracking embrace.

She laughed up at him and hugged him fondly. "And you, Mike Holinski, are still the most outrageous flirt I've ever known."

He laughed and kissed her soundly on both cheeks.

"Ah, but one can always appreciate rare beauty, no matter what the age."

"Turn off the charm, Mike. I will not be swayed by it. I know you're buttering me up so I'll come and drive your damned grain truck during harvest again this year."

Mike laughed uproariously as he draped his arm affectionately around his tiny wife's shoulders. "You see, mother, already she sees through me!"

Jillian grinned at the two of them. No wonder the Holinski children possessed such charm and vivaciousness, to say nothing of their spectacular good looks, when they had been parented by two such charismatic, handsome people. Olga was petite, Dresdenlike and so very beautiful, both inwardly and outwardly. Mike—big, rugged, handsome, with an unlimited supply of charm that he dispensed with such flourish. No one could stand a chance against all that.

She turned to find Jacob watching the byplay, his eyes dancing with amusement. *Damn him.* It was almost as though he knew exactly what she was thinking. She felt herself blushing and turned quickly back to the older Holinskis.

"I have room at my place if you would like to stay. I'd love to have you."

"No, no, Jillian. Your mother and father phoned last night to tell us that they are expecting us to share their mini home with them. You know they are arriving today?"

"Yes, I do. They phoned the hotel and left a message for me. I think Sylvia has been doing a lot of sly organizing since I called her about the get-together on Sunday. I've been wondering about her enthusiasm—I'll likely end up with seventy-two people for dinner.''

Everyone laughed, but Jillian was suddenly engulfed in an emotional swell that brought her to the verge of tears. If she didn't get away from everyone she would come apart, she knew. It was all too much, especially with the stress that she had been under for the past several days. She kept smiling, her voice light, but it was all she could do to maintain the facade.

''I have to slip over to the apartment to do a few things, so I had better go,'' she said as soon as she could. Somehow she managed to hang onto herself as both Mike and Olga once again embraced her warmly.

She knew Jacob was watching her, and that alone gave her the fortification she needed to keep control. As she turned to go, he caught her hand in his and held it firmly, compelling her to meet his gaze. Their eyes locked and that old empathy was there, holding them, enclosing them in a world of their own. He knew very well what was happening to her and why she was leaving.

''I'll see you later, Jillian.''

Her smile wobbled as he squeezed her hand. She returned the pressure, pleading with her eyes for him to understand and not be angry. He pulled her down and kissed her softly on the cheek, then released his hold. She could hardly keep from running as she left the lobby.

The snarl of slow-moving traffic and the scorching heat acted as a catalyst, transforming Jillian's weepy mood. By the time she finally reached her apartment, her disposition was one of irritation and frustration.

She smiled wryly to herself as she let herself into the cool dim apartment—what she felt like was a very hot and cranky child.

A long cool shower restored her humor, then she whipped through the chores that confronted her. There was going to be a crowd, so she wanted to have as much as possible ready beforehand.. Arrangements had been made for Ken, Sylvia and the two boys to stay with Mrs. Olsen. Jillian set up roll-away cots in the sun room for Jacob, John and Mark. That left Allan's room free in case the Holinskis should change their minds about spending the night in the mini home with Jillian's parents.

She changed the linen on the beds and was arranging fresh towels in the bathroom when there was a knock on the door. It had to be John. If it was, she was certainly going to put him to work.

When she opened the door, the look on his face was a dead giveaway that he was up to something. "Ho, Jillian, my love!"

She made a face at him. "When you look like that, John, I *know* you're up to no good. What have you done this time?"

He laughed and leaned against the door frame. "Well, I found this poor bedraggled stray wandering the streets and I wondered if you would take it in."

Jillian tipped her head to one side and slanted a doubtful look up at him. He had something brewing, there was no doubt about that. Hearing a muffled noise that sounded suspiciously like smothered laughter, she pushed past him, expectation rising in her.

Jillian was speechless. It really was Karin Holinski standing there with an impish grin on her face. "Karin! Am I glad to see you!"

Karin laughed and embraced her friend warmly. "I thought you might be. After Sylvia phoned and told me you were having everyone over, I decided I just had to come. I knew you could use another pair of hands to help get things ready for that crew." She looked at John and pulled a disparaging face. "And besides, I *know* how useless John is."

Both girls laughed as he squared his shoulders and hooked his thumbs over his belt. "Do I look like the Suzy Homemaker type of guy? Not me!"

Karin rolled her eyes in mock despair and pushed him roughly into the apartment ahead of her. She was nearly as tall as Jillian and carried her stunning beauty with a nonchalance that equaled Jillian's. Her hair was long and thick, the color of ripe wheat, and it framed her heart-shaped face. She had the same flashing brown eyes and long sweeping lashes as the rest of her siblings, but hers were simply more spectacular. Few people could be classed as truly beautiful, but Karin was one of them. There was a pensiveness about her now that added to, rather than detracted from, her classic beauty. Three years previously she had suffered through a brief but disastrous marriage. The experience had left its scars and nearly destroyed the whimsical quality that was once so much a part of her nature.

"Doesn't anyone else know you're here yet?" Jillian asked excitedly.

Karin curled up in one of the large armchairs and sighed with satisfaction. "Just you, Jacob and the half-wit." She gestured toward John and laughed in delight as he twisted his face into a moronic grimace. "After Sylvia phoned, I changed my mind about not coming; I simply couldn't miss out on all the fun of having everyone together. I can't believe everything is working out so well. When Jacob was in Vancouver, he refused even to discuss the possibility of going home.''

Jillian sat down on the sofa beside John as Karin scanned the apartment with an appreciative eye. ''I see wealth and prosperity has arrived in Rejectionville,'' she exclaimed, nodding her approval.

Jillian laughed. In those special carefree days at university, they had coined that name for the apartment because it had been furnished with everyone else's rejects.

''It was either a complete redecoration or a total disintegration—I had to make a choice.''

John threw up his hands in mock disgust. ''If you two start talking about fabrics and paints and other equally boring garbage, I'm going to park myself in front of the TV and watch the ball game.''

Karin stuck out her tongue. ''Well, smarty, why don't Jill and I find out how well you can put your engineering talents to work on the business end of a vacuum? How about it, Jill?''

Jillian laughed and nodded her approval. ''It would serve him right. Besides, that way he won't be able to hear what we're talking about in the kitchen.''

John stood up, his manner disdainful. ''Not *this* knight in shining armor.'' He started for the door. ''I'll pick up some refreshments for the bash instead. Need anything from the supermarket?''

''John, would you? That would be a real help; I wouldn't have to go out later.'' Jillian stood up and headed for the kitchen. ''I'll get the list. Everyone will be here later tonight so you'd better buy some white wine. Oh, and be sure to get a couple of bags of ice cubes, too.''

When she'd left the room, Karin looked up at her brother with a sober, troubled expression. ''Her nerves are stretched to the limit, aren't they?''

John nodded his head, shrugging his shoulders in a gesture of hopelessness. ''I know, but only someone who is really close to her would ever guess it. At times I could slap Jacob silly.''

Karin made a warning motion as Jillian reentered the room.

''Here you go, John, boy.'' She slapped his shoulder playfully as she handed him the list. ''And don't take eight hours getting back with the groceries.''

John gave her a smart salute. ''Yes, ma'am!''

Karin and Jill had always worked well together, so by early afternoon they had everything organized for that evening and the following day. After shopping John had decided to spend some time with his parents and Jacob, so they had the apartment to themselves. They were sitting in the kitchen, their feet up, enjoying a cool drink when there was a familiar rap on the door and a cheery greeting.

''In the kitchen, Mrs. O.''

Jillian's landlady entered the kitchen carrying a large package, which she immediately placed on the counter. Her face registered genuine delight when she saw who was sitting there.

''Well, Karin! Welcome home!''

Karin sprang to her feet and returned the affectionate embrace from her former landlady. ''Hi, Ollie. It's good to be back.''

Mrs. Olsen had never had children of her own, so the Holinski and Lambert offspring had benefited from her warm loving nature. She in turn had represented a much loved surrogate aunt to them all.

"Join us for some iced tea, Ollie?" Jillian waved to a vacant place in the nook as she stood up.

"No, darling, I can't. I would love nothing better, but I have a representative from a large tour group arriving at the office this afternoon, and I must be there when he arrives." Ordinarily Mrs. Olsen was bubbly and enthusiastic about her job as tour coordinator at the worldwide travel agency she worked for, but it was evident by the expression on her face that she would rather have spent the afternoon with the two girls.

Jillian laughed. "Why, Ollie, I do believe that you feel like playing hooky today!"

Her landlady nodded her head emphatically. "That's a fact. Especially now that Karin's here. I didn't know you were coming, dear. It is such a pleasant surprise."

With a smile Karin sat down at the table again and propped her chin on her hand. "If you think *you* were surprised, you should have seen the look on Jillian's face when I showed up at her door."

"I can just imagine! We both miss you here." She looked at her watch and grimaced with annoyance. "Drat! I'm going to have to run or I'll be late. The traffic is bad today and I'll have to allow myself a few extra minutes to get downtown." She picked up the box she had dropped on the counter and handed it to Jillian. "This is for you, dear. I wanted you to have something absolutely stunning to wear tonight...."

Jillian opened the box, folded back the tissue, and let out a low whistle as she lifted out a long gold lamé dress. The cut was simplicity itself, but Jillian had an instant mental picture of how it would look on her. It was sleeveless, with a low-cut neckline that accentuated the soft sweeping folds of the skirt. Under the spotlights it would be absolutely spectacular.

"Wow!"

"There's more, dear."

Jillian removed another layer of tissue paper and shook her head in stunned amazement. A short midriff-length blouse was fastened in the front with a wide tie that came just beneath the bustline. The neckline was again low but in a deep V. The outstanding feature of the garment was the long, very full Spanish-style sleeves that gathered into deep cuffs. But once again it was the material that made the top magnificent. The loosely woven silk-ribbon fabric, a vivid green, had a wide silver thread weaving through it. Slim-legged satin slacks in exactly the same shade of green complemented it. Jillian was speechless; the outfit was breathtaking.

"Now, Jillian, I really must run," Mrs. Olsen was saying.

"Ollie—"

"Never mind. I loved doing it for you." The older woman was out the door, but then her head poked around the corner. "Oh, by the way, I was able to borrow a playpen for Scott, and I've set it up in the small bedroom next to mine. He and Kenny can sleep there, and Sylvia and Ken are to have the guest room."

Jillian nodded in bemused agreement as Mrs. Olsen raised her hand in a farewell gesture and disappeared.

Karin burst out laughing. "She never changes,

does she? Those outfits are absolutely smashing. Good grief, Jill, you'll be a guaranteed success before you sing one single note!''

"But, Karin—" Jillian's eyes filled with tears as she carefully replaced the garments in the box. She looked beseechingly at her friend, then buried her face in her hands.

Karin went over to her immediately and wrapped her arms around her. "Has it been really awful, Jill?" she whispered gently.

When Jillian nodded silently, fighting to stop her tears, Karin brushed her friend's hair back off her face in a maternal gesture, her eyes warm with compassion. "I know. Damn it, but it hurts like hell.''

"It's been awful, Karin. I'm on the verge of tears all the time and I feel as if I'm coming unglued, piece by piece. You know I'm not normally like this, but I can't seem to stop myself."

"Let's go and sit in the living room and talk. I'll mix us another drink.'' She gave Jill a friendly nudge when she hesitated. "Go on. I'll be there in a flash.''

Jillian was sitting on the chesterfield, her hands buried in her hair in a defeated yet desperate gesture when Karin entered with the drinks. She silently accepted the tall frosty glass that was placed in her hand and took a long slow sip. Karin sat down at the opposite end of the sofa and watched her with troubled eyes.

"What's happened so far, Jill?"

Jillian sighed deeply and swept her hair back off her face. "I imagine John told you about my accidental meeting with Jacob?" Karin nodded. "Well, at first his attitude was cold and hostile, but the last two days have been different, thank God. He's been friendly and approachable. Nothing more, but at least that's an improvement over his initial reaction.''

Karin's face was somber as she abstractedly toyed with a lock of her own hair. ''Jill?''

''What?''

''Would you like some advice or do you want me to mind my own business?''

Jill stared at the ceiling for a long time and then turned to look at Karin, her eyes steady. ''I'll listen to the advice.''

''The whole thing is a bad scene—you and Jacob working together—and it won't work. Get out and get out now. If you don't, everything is going to come crashing down and this time it will totally destroy you. You and Jacob can never be just friends. It isn't going to turn out that way, and besides, I don't think either one of you could ever be satisfied with that. It has to be all or nothing, and as much as I wish I could make it otherwise, I have this awful feeling that it's going to be nothing.''

Jillian could hear an ominous ring of truth in Karin's words. *All or nothing. All or nothing. Nothing. . . .* The terror was back—black, ugly and frightening.

CHAPTER NINE

IN THE DRESSING ROOM that night Jillian was feeling unusually apprehensive about the evening performances. As Kathy styled her hair she tried to concentrate on solving mental math problems in an attempt to calm herself. It didn't work. As she fidgeted with the cuffs of the green satin sleeves she smiled wryly to herself. If nothing else, at least the gorgeous outfit Mrs. Olsen had made for her would be a showstopper.

"Well, what do you think, Jill?"

Jillian looked in the mirror and was amazed by what she saw. Kathy had pulled her hair straight back from her face and had fashioned it into a pony tail high at the back of her head. She had then tied a long silver ribbon at the base and crisscrossed it around the thick long fall to the bottom, where she tied it again. The style went with her costume perfectly.

"It's terrific, Kathy!" Jillian complimented her warmly, then stood up and walked toward the door.

"Hey, you aren't going anywhere yet. You're staying here until it's time for your cue." When she turned and looked back questioningly, Kathy laughed. "Come on, Jill, give Elaine and me the fun of watching the guys' faces when you walk out onstage in that outfit."

Jillian laughed weakly. "Then you'd better get out there, or I may lose what little courage I have left."

Elaine came bounding through the door. "Come on. They just went onstage."

Jillian took a deep breath and walked into the corridor that led to the stage runway. The band was singing its theme song as Elaine and Kathy circled through the lounge to the reserved area directly adjacent to the stage.

Keith's voice rang out, "We are Firefly and it gives me great pleasure to introduce our own firefly, Miss Jillian Lambert!" Clenching her shaking hands, Jillian walked onstage into the glare of spotlights, a smile glued on her face. The smile became genuine when she heard several wolf whistles from the audience. She turned to pick up her mike from the piano and her eyes met Jacob's dead on. He closed his eyes and shook his head as if to clear it, then blew on his fingers as though he had just been burned.

Jillian laughed, her eyes dancing, and started into their first duet, an upbeat popularized version of "Baby Face." The song had a dynamic tempo that made it genuinely fun to sing and Jillian grinned at Jacob, openly challenging him to let himself go with the scintillating beat. He hesitated for a second, then flashed a smile, his eyes gleaming as he responded wholeheartedly to the challenge. The music was intoxicating and their performance was dazzling.

They completed the first set, and it was at this point that Keith always introduced the members of the band. "And on keyboards, our arranger and lead male vocalist, Jake Holinski. Last, but definitely not least, our delectable, dynamite lady, Jillian Lambert. And, ladies and gentlemen, don't ever try to tell any of us guys in the band that all good things come in small packages. After all, we have Jill!"

The audience went wild. Jillian made a deep bow, then turned to face the band, her hands raised in a gesture of appreciation. As she did so she found Jacob watching her with a hooded enigmatic look that made her senses swim.

The spell was broken as the curtain closed. Keith gave a whoop of glee, then bowed exaggeratedly at Norm as he walked onto the stage. "Well, Mr. Bossman, we did what you said we would. 'One hell of a show,' and that's what they got!"

Norm laughed and rubbed his hands together. "I don't think the management is too happy right now, though. No one's leaving and they have people lined up all the way down the ramp, waiting for a table. It's breaking their hearts to see all that potential revenue just standing there!"

"Sounds like a perfect time to ask the hotel for a raise, Norm," laughed David as he placed his guitar on its stand.

Norm stroked his chin as he leaned against the piano. "Might be...providing you guys don't bomb during the second set."

Jacob grinned as he settled himself in his wheelchair and turned toward the runway. "It sounds as though Norm expects us to flop. We'd better get our egos inflated by doting relatives now, Jillian. They might be tossing tomatoes at us later."

They wound their way down to the main level of the lounge, passing several tables on their way. Jillian, walking slightly ahead of Jacob, was uncomfortably aware of the curious stares. As they approached one table Jill overheard a girl comment breathlessly, "Good grief, that gorgeous hunk is crippled!"

A slight pimple-faced young man sneered, "Well, he can't be too crippled. That big foxy singer seems to be getting what she wants."

Jillian froze. Drawing herself up to her full height, she gave the young man a look that would strip flesh off bone.

She smiled icily, her voice low and cold. "Some people's disabilities aren't as noticeable as others, darling, even though we all have them." Eyeing his slight frame up and down with disdain she added cuttingly, "But then, yours are quite obvious."

Her eyes were flashing fire as she turned and walked away. As they approached the corner area reserved for the band and its guests, she heard Jacob chuckling behind her. "I wonder if he'll bleed to death before they get out of here."

Jillian's temper was still white-hot as she turned to face Jacob. She opened her mouth to fling a retort at him but instead burst into laughter. The people at that table were indeed leaving.

"Well, at least I've made whoever's first in line for an empty table very happy!" She grinned. She was about to turn around again when a pair of hands covered her eyes.

"Guess who!" The voice was falsetto.

"It's John, the village idiot!" she laughed as she raised her arms to pull the hands away. But when her fingers touched a familiar indentification bracelet on a masculine wrist, she stopped abruptly.

"Allan!" Whirling quickly, she threw her arms around her brother.

Allan hugged her soundly and laughed. "Here I've had this incredible chick for a sister all these years and never really realized it until this gorgeous amazon walked out on the stage tonight. You were fantastic!''

Allan's unexpected appearance was almost too much for Jillian's control and she blinked back the tears that were burning her eyes. Her brother grinned at her, a knowing gleam on his face, then squeezed her shoulder understandingly as he stepped past her.

"Hello, Jacob. Welcome home." His voice was deep with sincerity as he took Jacob's outstretched hand.

Jillian swallowed hard against the aching contraction in her throat when she saw the disquieted look on Jacob's face. He was very deeply touched by Allan's unexpected arrival and he was having a struggle maintaining his control. She moved to his side and rested her hand on his shoulder.

He glanced up at her, then took her hand in his, his grip painfully tight as he turned his gaze to Allan. "It's good to be back, Allan." His voice was husky.

Allan grinned as he motioned to his sister. "Do you really think she has any claim to fame, or did you hire her just to keep her quiet?"

Jacob's face relaxed as he laughed. "No comment!" He grinned up at Jillian, his eyes sparkling with devilment. "She has a wicked backhand and I don't feel like testing my luck again."

Jillian turned scarlet and she tried to free her hand from Jacob's grasp. He laughed softly as he maintained his hold. "No, you don't, Jillian Lambert. I feel much safer when I have some control over you."

Allan looked from one to the other, then grinned broadly as he led the way back to their table.

The intermission turned into a boisterous celebration. At the insistence of Jacob and Jillian, the band members and their wives joined the two families at the large corner table. Jacob later admitted that it had been a mistake—having John and Allan together was bad enough, but adding Keith and his keen wit was too much.

By the time the break ended, Jillian's sides were sore from laughing. Reluctantly she excused herself to go and change for the next performance.

Kathy was still fussing with Jillian's hair when Norm walked into the dressing room. He let out a long low whistle when he saw her second new costume.

"That outfit is something else, kid, especially on you. You'll knock 'em dead."

Jillian pulled a saucy face. "I didn't think that was the intention."

He laughed as he leaned against the door, an appreciative look on his face as he cocked one eyebrow. "We'd better think about hiring a bodyguard for you. Ah, but then I didn't really come in here to leer at you. I wanted to let you know how pleased I am with the performance tonight."

He paused as he lit a cigarette and took a deep drag. "Do you want some personal and professional advice?"

Jillian nodded, secretly amused by the fact that she had been asked so often recently whether she wanted advice. She would get it anyway, even if she said no.

"Push him tonight, Jill. You have the power and range to do it. Make him really open up."

Jillian looked at Norm, knowing exactly what his intentions were. She took a deep shaky breath and nodded. "I'll try, but I honestly don't know if I have the courage."

Just then Kathy patted Jillian's hair. "There, you're all done."

Jill turned to face the mirror. The hair in front of her ears was swept up and fastened high on her head with elaborate topaz-colored brilliants. The rest spilled down her back in a shimmering cascade.

"They're into their lead-in!" Kathy announced excitedly. "Scoot!"

Jillian stood up and walked out to the edge of the runway. Norm squeezed her hand as she went by him.

"Go get 'em, kid."

"Ladies and gentlemen, our very own firefly, Miss Jillian Lambert!"

There were no butterflies in her stomach or fixed smiles this time as she walked out onto the stage. Beneath the chorus of loud whistles and cheers she winked seductively at Jacob as she picked up the mike from the piano.

His eyes seemed to devour her as he throughly appraised her soft curves beneath the gold lamé dress. He raised his eyebrows and spoke in a husky voice that was edged with humor. "This is getting better and better!"

They exchanged a charged look before Jillian moved to the center of the stage. Their first song was one that had been sitting at the top of the charts for weeks. It had a heavy pulsating beat, and Jillian was suddenly caught up in its rhythm, her body moving with the throb of the music. Jacob's eyes never left her.

The whole performance was electrifying. The momentum grew and grew until Jillian felt as though she had attained a new plateau of existence. She knew she had never sung the way she was singing now.

They were into the song they used for an encore when she felt a surge of power within her, which carried her into a dimension of such depth that a new energy was released. She was soaring, and Jacob was with her all the way.

Reach out, reach out and touch me, babe
Touch me in the darkness of the night
Reach out, reach out and touch me, babe
Hold me close in the dawn's velvet light
I need your love to survive
I need your touch to come alive
Reach out, baby. Reach out

Like a dream, it was all there. He had shed his facade; his barriers were down, and he was projecting as he never had before. The song ended, but a charged atmosphere remained, enveloping them in a world of their own. The curtain closed. Jacob was watching her, his eyes smoldering, his breathing rapid, and nothing could break that spell.

"Okay, this is Jacob's and Jill's spot," Keith said hurriedly. The other men moved off the stage as Jillian fought for control. She took a deep breath as the curtains slipped silently open. The applause was deafening, then suddenly the audience was on its feet.

Jillian was only vaguely aware of Jacob's voice. "Thank you. Thank you very much." His words were husky with emotion. "You have been a marvelous audience to perform for." More applause.

"Now, ladies and gentlemen, Jillian and I would like to do a very special dedication tonight for some very special people who are in the audience. We made an impulsive decision at intermission to do this song, which is a particular favorite of theirs. It's an old, very beautiful love ballad with a slightly classical flavor. For those of you who are not classical fans, let me explain that vocalists use a different technique when singing classical music. So please, don't be alarmed at what's happening up here—and take heart, the song isn't very long.'' Jacob paused until the laughter subsided. "For those of you who are classical buffs, we hope we can do the song justice. Ladies and gentlemen, this song is dedicated to our parents.''

The bank of stage lights dimmed and a single spotlight framed them in its muted amber light, cocooning them in a mellow glow. Brilliants of gold sparkled from Jillian's dress as she moved to the piano and paused, her hand resting on its polished surface. Jacob was watching her, his dark flashing eyes communicating a warmth that was as heady as warm brandy, and Jillian's senses reeled with that look.

The surroundings faded away as Jacob began to play, and she closed her eyes as she surrendered her emotions to the poignant mood of the music. She raised her head and looked at Jacob as he began to sing, his deep rich baritone throbbing with a spellbinding potency. When her voice blended with his in harmonious perfection, Jillian felt as though he was physically reaching out to caress her. The melody wove them within a spell of enchantment, carrying them into a sphere of their own. It was their song, and they were reaching out to each other without restraint, without doubts.

Jillian was unaware of the audience or anything else around her. She was singing for Jacob and Jacob alone. Tears glistened in her eyes as she told him, through the poetic beauty of the lyrics, how much she loved him. And Jacob did not deny that love.

The audience was hypnotized into total silence by the performance. There wasn't one person in the lounge who didn't realize he was witnessing something extraordinary, something incredibly beautiful. It was as though the magic between Jillian and Jacob spilled over, drawing them all within its spell. As the curtain swept shut, there wasn't a sound or a movement for several seconds; then the magic was shattered by a thundering ovation.

But behind the shimmering curtain the magic held. Jillian stood transfixed, tears streaming down her cheeks as she looked at Jacob, her eyes pleading. Slowly he raised his arms toward her, his face a study of inner torment. Without being consciously aware that she had moved, she was swept into his arms. Gathering her across his lap he pressed her trembling body against his as he buried his face in the fragrant cascade of her hair.

His voice was a muffled, fragmented whisper as he crushed her against him. "I love you, Jillian. God knows I've tried to put you out of my life, out of my mind, but I can't. I love you and there's no way I can ever stop."

Jillian clung to him, her body shaking with the repressed sobs of her devastating happiness. She moved her head and felt his face wet against hers. As she raised her face to kiss him, he caught her head and pressed it against him.

"Not now, love," he whispered hoarsely against her hair. "God, not now. There's no way I could stop myself, and this isn't the time or place." Jillian tightened her arms around him fiercely. It didn't matter—he was holding her, needing her, and that was what mattered beyond all else.

The rest of the evening passed by in a fog for Jillian. Changing her outfit, meeting her family for a final drink—absolutely nothing was in focus until she and Jacob were finally in his car on their way to her apartment. She felt as if her bones had dissolved. She closed her eyes and rested her head against the back of the seat, unmoving until the car stopped. Then she opened her eyes to find Jacob watching her, his eyes unreadable in the purple twilight of an Alberta summer's night. It was only then that she realized they were parked in a secluded area of the park where they once used to walk.

Jacob pushed his seat back. "Come here, Jillian." His voice was quiet and restrained.

She went willingly. He pulled her into his lap, and her strength drained out of her as he encircled her with his arms and cradled her firmly against him. He shuddered as her own arms tightened around him, and he buried his hand in her hair, pressing her face into the hollow of his neck.

His voice was hoarse and shaking. "God, babe, but I've missed you so.... If you only knew how many times I've dreamed of holding you like this." He took a deep breath, and Jillian felt the rise and fall of his chest as his breathing became more labored. She felt as though she would burst with surging love as desire swept through her like a wild cresting wave. She could feel her tears warm against his skin as she whispered tremulously, "Oh, Jacob! I thought I would never see you again."

With a low groan he lifted her face and covered her

trembling moist mouth with his own, kissing her with an uncontrolled hunger that rocketed them both into a fierce storm of raging ardor. The feel of his hard muscled body against hers was more than Jillian could resist, and she returned his savage kiss with a scorching passion. A wild driving obsession was feeding their inflamed need for each other, and it was pushing them toward reckless abandon.

It wasn't until Jacob tasted blood on her ravaged lips that sanity returned to him, and he forced himself to hold her more tenderly. He held her until her shaking abated, then he turned on the interior light, wincing when he saw her bruised mouth.

"Babe, I'm so sorry. I didn't mean to hurt you—"

Jillian laid her fingers against his lips, her eyes so full of love that it cast her face in a glowing radiance. "You didn't hurt me, Jacob. I felt as if I had died inside after you left. You just revived me."

Jacob's laugh was low and husky as he cuddled her against him. "You've done a little reviving of your own, Jillian."

Switching off the light, he shifted his arm slightly and the electric seat slowly reclined. He continued to hold her as he eased them back, until they were stretched out on the wide comfortable seat. Then he twisted his body slightly until she was lying beside him, his arms holding her so very close. He stroked her back gently, calmly, caressingly, until the tempest in her subsided and she was filled with a warm rich contentment.

There was no need for words. Their bodies transmitted a silent consoling message as they lay wrapped in each other's arms, each of them drawing comfort and pleasure from the presence of the other.

Jillian sighed and stirred against him as she ran her hand beneath his shirt, relishing the feel of his naked skin beneath her touch.

He raised his head and captured her face with his hand as he took possession of her mouth with a tender but stirring kiss. Then he trailed his fingers down her neck and across the swell of her breast to the tie of her green blouse. Raising his head, he undid it slowly, then brushed back the fabric to expose the nakedness beneath.

Jillian's breathing became erratic as a fire of feverish longing ignited within her. Her voice was barely audible. "Jacob—"

He propped himself on one elbow and leaned over her, kissing her trembling mouth with a gentleness born of love. "Easy, babe," he whispered against her mouth. "Any potent wine tastes better when it is sipped slowly." He held her face in his hands and kissed her eyes, tracing the outline with sensual delicate caresses. His kisses moved slowly down to the base of her ear, his tongue moist and probing. He ran his hand up her leg, across her thigh, his fingers brushing across her flat belly in agonizing slowness and up to cup her breast tenderly in his hand. Then gently, so gently, he lowered his head and kissed her where the pendant lay, his mouth searing her flesh with a tormenting sensuousness.

"Let me love you, Jillian."

She raked her fingers through his hair as she pressed her body against his. She was in a swimming haze, aware only of Jacob. He awakened her to a blaze of ecstasy as his touch aroused her to a fever pitch, his mouth warm and tantalizing against her skin. She was trembling and her mind was in a senseless whirl. He drove her passion higher and higher, prolonging the agonizing pleasure that swept through her until she reached a point of near-physical pain.

"Jacob, please."

"No."

"God, Jacob!" She was pleading, her voice an unsteady whisper. His hand slipped beneath the waistband of her slacks, gentle and caressing. She moaned as a hot wave surged through her, then spasm after spasm racked her body. She clung to him, her nails digging into his back. His arms came around her protectively, possessively, as he rolled on top of her, and he murmured softly, his words loving and gentle as she lay shaking in his arms.

Her breath was coming in deep sobs as she hung onto him. He kept talking to her until she finally quieted, then he shifted his weight and lay beside her again. He nestled her head in the hollow of his shoulder, one arm holding her firmly against him, the other hand buried deep in her tousled hair. Silent, peaceful moments passed with only the wind in the trees and the distant hum of far-off traffic disturbing their solitude.

"Jacob, why wouldn't you?"

"You know why, Jillian." His voice was quiet, tender. Jillian felt him kiss the top of her head as he snuggled her closer to him.

"How can you?"

Jacob laughed softly as he continued to stroke her back with long, gentle movements. "I've developed patience over the last few years."

A sudden knifelike suspicion stabbed through her and she struggled to a half-sitting position beside him. "I think you've developed a lot more than pa-

tience. I'd say your...your technique is somewhat
more...sophisticated."

He reached up and caught the back of her head.
"Jillian, don't."

Jealousy ripped through her with a malicious gnawing pain that drove all else from her mind. She twisted
away from him, her voice thick with an awful hurt.
"How can you say, 'Don't'? How would you feel—"

His hand shot out and caught a handful of her hair
as she turned away from him. Gently but firmly he
pulled her back down beside him. His voice was low
and full of regret. "I'm sorry, Jillian. The truth is
sometimes very cruel." She tried to pull away from
him but he held her down. "Will you hear me out?"

Her stomach was a hard cold knot of disillusionment, but she stayed there.

He pulled her hair steadily until she was forced to
look at him. "There were other women, Jillian. I
won't deny it." He held her hard against him, his
voice low with remembered desolation, "But I swear,
they didn't mean a damn. I tried everything to drive
your memory out of my mind—women, booze, isolation." His voice was filled with such wretchedness
that Jillian's anger immediately dissolved. "I was so
sure I'd never see you again." His grip on her shoulder became almost painful as he tightened his hold.
"I know you had to be told. I just wish it hadn't been
tonight of all nights."

Jillian could feel the intensity of the regret within
him. She had enough foresight and maturity to realize that indignation and pride might destroy the
foundation of their fragile relationship. Was it really
so very important? What was vital was that he was
back, that he was with her.

She held him close as a strange compassion filled her; her voice was level and sincere. "It's in the past, Jacob. We'll leave it there."

He gathered her against him once more and they lay quietly wrapped in each other's arms, their legs entwined. Then he raised his head and kissed her with a gentle sweetness.

She encircled his face with her long slender hands as she whispered against his mouth, "Jacob, do you know what you did to me tonight?"

Raising himself on one elbow, he smoothed her cascading hair over his arm. "Yes." He leaned down and nipped her ear, then smiled into her eyes. "But then, it was something I've wanted to do for a long, long time." He caressed the line of her eyebrows, then once again lowered his head, his lips moist and parted as he traced the outline of the locket with his tongue. Jillian felt him tremble as he lay there.

"Jacob, please." Her voice was a bare whisper.

"No." His voice was firm. He lifted her into a sitting position and tidied her hair, then straightened her blouse and slowly retied it. Jillian tried to crawl back to her seat as Jacob adjusted his.

"No, you don't. Come back here." So she lay nestled across him, her head on his shoulder, her arms around his muscular back. Again he held her like that for a long time as he ran his fingers through her hair. "I would have killed you if you had cut it off," he murmured at last.

She chuckled low in her throat as she buried her face against his chest, savoring the masculine smell of him. "I was only doing it to spite you, you know—I was so damned mad."

There was laughter in his voice as he ran his

knuckles along her jaw. "I got the message! You have no idea what a shock you gave me when you slapped me that night."

Softly she caressed the cheek that she had slapped. "That was pure reaction, Jacob; I did it without thinking." She caught his face between her hands and kissed him softly. "Thank you for the bracelet, by the way. It's so beautiful."

His arms tightened around her as he whispered against her mouth. "I felt sick inside when I saw the bruise I'd left on you, Jillian. There's nothing I can say to excuse my behavior, except that having you around was one hell of a predicament for me." He ran his fingers roughly through her hair and caught the back of her head, pressing her face against his neck. "Oh, Jillian, what am I going to do with you?"

She laughed softly. "Well, my love, I made a couple of suggestions and you told me no."

He laughed and shook his head. "Right! Anyway, I told the family that we had things to do—" he grinned wickedly down at her when she laughed "—and that we'd be at your place in a hour or so. We have four minutes to meet the deadline."

"I wonder what they think we've been doing."

"They probably know damned well what we've been doing."

Jill laughed again at his dry tone. As Jacob reached across her and started the car, she made another motion to move.

"Don't go, babe. Stay like that—it makes it handy at red lights." He lowered his head and gave her a long enticing kiss.

"This is the only way to fly," he grinned, switching on the lights and backing expertly out onto the tree-lined gravel road.

A little while later Jacob swung into the driveway behind the looming bulk of the Lambert mini home, then switched off the motor and the lights. He turned to face Jillian, his eyes sending messages that left her breathless.

Her own eyes were wide and solemn as she stared at him, suddenly overcome with a definite unwillingness to leave the seclusion of the car. She didn't want to relinquish the intimacy she and Jacob were enjoying, and she was certainly unenthusiastic about sharing him with everyone else.

Jacob seemed to sense her reluctance, and he reached out and laid his hand tenderly against her face, his fingers tracing the outline of her arching brow. She closed her eyes as she turned her head slightly and kissed the palm of his hand with fervent abandon. She heard him suck his breath in sharply and she felt his body tense.

"Jillian...babe, I don't want to go...." He swore softly as he hauled her roughly into his arms. "Damn it, I don't want to, but we have to go in."

She rested her head on his chest, slipped her arms around his back and sighed heavily. Neither of them moved for the longest time, then she finally lifted her head, looked at him and smiled wryly.

"You know we're in for it from John and Allan, don't you?"

Jacob grinned, his eyes dancing. "Would you like to make another wager about that?"

Jillian laughed and sat up, then made a face at him. "Do you enjoy rubbing salt in wounds, Jacob Holinski?"

"You haven't paid up for the last one, you know."

"That's not my problem."

"It might be your problem when I call you on it." There was a suggestive timbre to his voice that made Jillian's spine tingle with excitement. She kissed the tiny dimple at the corner of his mouth, then twisted around and settled back in her seat, straightening her creased clothes.

As she opened the door of the car she flashed him an impish smile. "I'm not the least bit worried about it, Jacob. After all, you're bound and determined to keep me an innocent."

He laughed as he opened his own door and lifted out his wheelchair. "Don't bet on *that*, my love."

Jillian's knees went suddenly weak and she took a deep breath to steady the tremor that ran through her. As she climbed out of the car, she became aware of voices and bursts of laughter drifting from the back of the house; everyone was obviously out on the patio. She collected Jacob's flight bag from the back of the car, then walked around to the other side of the Porsche. She felt as though she was floating as she waited for Jacob to settle himself in his wheelchair. The sensation was compounded when she realized he was watching her with a provocative, knowing look. Catching her hand, he pulled her down and gave her a sizzling kiss that had her heart doing crazy flip-flops. As he released her he laughed softly. "No, never bet on that, babe."

Letting go of her hand, he started wheeling himself across the grass to the front door. Jillian was certain that her feet never touched the ground as she followed him. She held the door open for him as he spun his chair around and backed it over the threshold. She could have helped him navigate the obstacle but she sensed he would be annoyed if she tried, and she didn't want to do anything that might mar the harmony between them.

Jacob looked up at her questioningly as he turned to go down the hallway; she was deliberately blocking his way. She smiled at him seductively, her eyes gleaming with something more than mischief as she bent down, her lips moist and parted, and covered his mouth with hers. The kiss was anything but innocent and both of them were breathing hard when she finally pulled away.

He stared at her, his eyes hooded and dark as he smiled that slow, irresistible, sensual smile that always created havoc with her senses. All he said was, "Oh, Jillian."

They were greeted with loud whistles and cheers as they joined the group of people scattered around the huge patio.

John walked toward them, making an elaborate show of checking his watch. "How wonderful that you two finally decided to join the rest of us. We were about to send out a search party, not that either of you probably needed rescuing." He grinned wickedly as he relentlessly continued, "You didn't need rescuing, did you, Jillian?"

Jillian could feel a hot flush creeping up her neck as all eyes fastened on Jacob and herself. Jacob's own face was perfectly serious as he looked up at his brother, but she could detect a gleam of pure devilry in his eyes.

"Why should she need rescuing? I just wanted to reacquaint myself with some of my favorite local... attractions."

Jill turned scarlet, yet in spite of her disconcerted fluster she had to bite her lip to keep from laughing. Most of their relatives had gracefully accepted Jacob's explanation for their late arrival at face value, and no one appeared to interpret the subtle innuendo.

Norm, however, gave them a penetrating look as he reflectively swirled the amber liquid in his glass. "Those attractions must have been something else— you're blushing like crazy again, Jillian," he said in a voice loud enough for only the two newcomers to hear.

Jacob laughed as he caught her hand and began tracing erotic patterns in her sensitive palm with his thumb.

Jillian was unwittingly rescued from her dilemma by Allan, who strode over to them and grabbed the handles of Jacob's wheelchair.

"It's about time you got here. We've decided to tune up and we need a baritone and an alto for the performance of the century. John says we couldn't wheeze our way through the scales anymore and I say he's wrong."

John laughed. "I warn you, Allan, the neighbors will think we're a pack of yowling alley cats, and they'll start pitching shoes at us."

"Don't you believe it. Besides, Ollie said they were away on holidays. We can still do it, can't we, gang?"

There was a chorus of affirmatives, and everyone gathered around.

"Don't let Allan organize this, for Pete's sake," warned Ken. "He'll have us singing Christmas carols and World War I songs."

Allan shook his head and grinned. "I wouldn't stoop to that! Why don't we start off with that medley of barbershop songs we used to do at banquets?"

Everyone groaned loudly, and John protested, "Don't even suggest it! I'm still sick to death of—how many times did we sing 'Katie' and 'Down by the Old Mill Stream'? It must have been a thousand."

Allan grinned at John, his eyes sparkling with mischief. "Then that leaves us with the Christmas carols and the World War I songs."

Jacob laughed and motioned to his mother. "Come on, mom—you're going to have to take charge or we'll never get this thing together!"

Olga Holinski smiled and laid down the shawl she was crocheting. "I think perhaps you are correct, Jacob."

Norm had sat down with Bill and Cora Lambert, Mike Holinski and Mrs. Olsen. His face split with a broad grin as he called, "How did you ever keep them under control, Mrs. Holinski? Did you need a whip?"

Olga turned and smiled at him, her eyes sparkling with amusement. "There *were* occasions when I felt more like an animal trainer than a music teacher."

There were hoots of protest from the singers, until their former teacher turned to face them. "Please, children, you must stand together."

Jacob looked at Mark and grinned wickedly. "Go on, Mark—that means you'll have to stand with the girls the way you used to!"

Mark laughed and held up his hands in refusal. "If you think I'm even going to try to sing as a boy soprano, you're out of your mind!"

Olga pursed her lips in an expression that they all knew meant business. "Mark, you will sing baritone with your brother." She motioned to him. "Go." She started maneuvering them into position. "Ken, you will sing bass. Mark and Jacob, you stand here. Allan, you will be second tenor, and John will be first tenor. Karin, you will carry the high soprano."

Sylvia shot a disgruntled look at Karin and Jillian as she maneuvered her short pregnant body in between them. "And here I thought I was forever free of the humiliation of being sandwiched between you two Goliaths."

Karin made a face at her sister. "Serves you right for being a mezzo-soprano, Syl." She moaned. "High soprano! My eyes will pop out of my head when I start reaching for those high notes—my own mother is trying to destroy me!"

Sylvia giggled and jabbed her sister in the ribs with her elbow. "Don't you dare get us laughing, Karin, or mother will turn us to stone with that famous look of hers."

"That would be preferable to sudden death when I pop a blood vessel. I haven't sung high soprano in years."

Jillian couldn't help it; she started to laugh, her shoulders shaking as she tried to suppress her merriment. "If you don't sing it she'll make Mark do it, and I think he'd suffer more than a ruptured blood vessel!"

"Girls, you are not paying attention." All eyes riveted on the petite woman standing before them.

"Are you chewing gum, Allan?" Allan sheepishly took the gum from his mouth and dropped it in a flower pot as they all heckled him.

Olga Holinski's eyes scanned the group, then she motioned to Jacob. "Sit up straight, Jacob." Jacob straightened up, his eyes dancing. She quelled the ripple of laughter with a stern look. "Such postures! How can you sing with fullness when you stand so?"

Everyone of them straightened up, and suddenly it was as though they had been transported back in time and they were once again students under her direction.

"We will do 'Sound of Music' first," Olga said decisively. She gave them their notes and no one doubted her accuracy; she had perfect pitch. As in countless performances, she softly sang the first few bars of music: "The hills are alive with the sound of music. . . ." Then she nodded her head and raised her hands.

In perfect unison they all breathed in, then began to sing in fabulous seven-part harmony. As they did they were no longer doctors, engineers, farmers, no longer teachers, parents—they were once again student performers. With unwavering eyes they watched the woman who had taught them and loved them, who had inspired each one of them with an everlasting love for music. The sound was rich and full as they each gave their personal best for Olga Holinski. And it was beautiful.

They sang several old favorites, then rounded out their impromptu performance with "Ghost Riders in the Sky," a special request from Bill Lambert. They finished to a round of enthusiastic applause from their small audience.

John laughed and staggered across the patio to pour himself a drink. "I think I've ruined myself. That was a dirty trick, mother—pitting your favorite son against a powerhouse like that. Ken's bass was bad enough, but with Jacob and Mark both singing baritone, I had to sing my brains out to hold my own.''

Allan slapped him on the back as he neatly swiped the drink that John had fixed for himself. ''That's assuming that you had brains to begin with, John.''

The laughter was interrupted by a small voice. ''Are you having a party, mommy?'' Kenny was watching from the sun-room door, Scott's chubby hand held firmly in his.

Sylvia started toward the pair, a determined look on her face that clearly said, *back to bed*. But Karin and Jillian sprinted past her, and they each swept a nephew up in their arms.

Jillian gave Kenny a hug, ignoring Sylvia's protest. ''Yes, pet, we're having a party. You're just in time for the cake and ice cream.''

Kenny looked from his aunt to his mother, who was standing with her hands on her hips and a firm look in her eyes. ''Can Scott and me stay up, mommy?'' he asked her beseechingly.

Karin didn't give her sister time to respond. She hitched Scott across her hip and smiled at Kenny. ''Of course you boys can stay up. If mommy says, 'No,' Auntie Jill and I will sit on her.''

Kenny giggled and looked at his mother. ''They wouldn't, would they, mommy?''

Sylvia sighed her capitulation, then smiled dryly at her small son. ''They probably would.''

Kenny wiggled in Jillian's arms and grinned impishly. ''You can put me down, Auntie Jill. She won't put me back in bed now.''

Sylvia rolled her eyes heavenward as Jillian

laughed and set the boy down. Jacob was watching, his face suddenly pale beneath his tan, his expression solemn and tense as Kenny walked over to him and studied his face.

"You're my Uncle Jacob, aren't you?"

Jacob's voice was low and very husky. "Yes, I am, Kenny."

A strained hush smothered the murmur of conversation as Kenny considered his uncle with steady sober eyes. The silence dragged on as the boy stared, then he nodded his head, satisfied with his assessment.

"I'm glad you came, Uncle Jacob. I like your face."

Jacob lifted his nephew onto his lap and swallowed hard. "And I like your face, Kenny."

With the open honesty and complete trust of a child, Kenny threw his arms around his uncle's neck and hugged him. Jacob closed his eyes as he clasped the small boy to him, his face rigid and set with an iron control.

Jillian's eyes filled with tears and her throat ached as she fought to swallow a sob. It was obvious to her that Jacob had been profoundly touched by the ready acceptance of the nephew he had never seen before. She wiped the tears away with the back of her hand and looked away. She couldn't watch the heart-wrenching scene or she would break down completely. She glanced at Karin and that was nearly her undoing, for her friend's face was also wet with tears.

Kenny's eyes were wide and earnest. "I knew you were my uncle because you sit on our piano and my dad says I look just like you. Do I look just like you, Uncle Jacob?"

Jacob managed a shaky smile as he looked down at the small boy on his lap. "Yes, I think you do look just like me." His smile broadened and his eyes became teasing. "But don't I get tired sitting on your piano?"

Karin walked over and sat Scott down on Jacob's lap, too, and ruffled Kenny's hair. "You help Uncle Jacob look after Scott so I can help mommy and Aunt Jillian fix us some food, okay?"

Kenny nodded, then reached over and pulled his brother's thumb out of his mouth. "Don't suck your thumb, Scotty. You'll get bent teeth."

Jillian and Jacob exchanged amused glances over the top of the two boys' heads, and there was a relaxed openness in the look. All the hurdles were behind Jacob now.

CHAPTER TEN

JILLIAN STRETCHED and rolled over on her back, then tucked her hands behind her head as she absently watched the curtains billow and flutter in the early-morning breeze. A smile appeared as her thoughts wandered back over the events of the night before. Having the two families assembled together after so long a time had been fantastic. She was sorry that the other members of Firefly hadn't been able to attend the party, but she'd been pleased that Norm accepted Jacob's invitation. He had provided the link to Jacob's new life with a casual ease, and his easygoing personality and natural wit made him seem like a member of the family.

Norm had been very quiet for a time, and Jillian was certain that the presence of Kenny and Scott reminded him painfully of the terrible loss of his own children. But it hadn't taken him long to be totally won over by the two boys. Scott had taken a particular fancy to him and in fact had fallen asleep in Norm's arms. Jillian's smile softened as she recalled the tender protective look on Norm's face when he finally carried the sleeping toddler into the house and tucked him into bed.

Jillian glanced at the clock. It was only eight o'clock and she hadn't gone to bed until almost five, yet she was wide awake. She might as well get up.

She turned her head and looked across the bed at Karin, who was still sleeping soundly. Jillian smiled with warm affection. There had been a sparkle about Karin that hadn't been there for a long time, and she had a sneaking suspicion it had something to do with the attentiveness of one Norm Kent. If only....

She eased herself out of bed and crept to the window. Her parents had parked their motor home in the driveway beside her bedroom window. Their curtains were still closed, so Jillian guessed that they and the senior Holinskis were still recovering from their unusually late night. Slipping into the dressing gown that lay at the foot of her bed, she tiptoed to the door of her room, opened it quietly and went out into the hallway.

She had her hand on the knob of the bathroom door when she changed her mind and silently opened the door to Allan's room. Mark lay sprawled on his stomach, his face to the wall, his breathing deep and even.

Her face softened as her attention became engrossed by the sleeping figure in the other bed. Jacob lay on his back, one arm on his chest, the other flung across the bed. His hair was disheveled, the sweat-dampened curls clinging to his temples. His face was relaxed and calm, with his long thick lashes and arching brows accentuating the chiseled features and square jaw. He looked like a sleeping Apollo, she decided as she stood there for a long while watching him. Then she moved to the side of the bed and softly, so softly, kissed his slightly parted lips, her mouth lingering on his. When his eyelids fluttered, she raised her head and watched for a moment until his breathing steadied. Then she turned and silently but reluctantly left the room.

In the living room she paused and listened. The house was totally silent. She went to the door, opened it and stepped into the hallway, hesitating by Mrs. Olsen's door. That apartment was also silent, so she slipped into the sun room where she found Allan stretched out on his cot. Arms linked behind his head, he was watching two flies circle the light fixture in the center of the ceiling.

Jillian fought down a surge of laughter, not wanting to wake John, who was snoring slightly on the other cot. "That looks wildly entertaining." She whispered, her voice shaky with repressed laughter.

Allan grinned but continued to watch the flies. "Fascinating."

"Come on, I'll make you a coffee."

"I don't think I can carry my head that far."

Jillian was really struggling to keep from laughing out loud. "Could you carry it that far for a Bloody Mary?"

Allan's eyes lighted up. "For a Bloody Mary, I'd carry it to Calgary."

Jillian returned to the kitchen, and by the time Allan arrived she had his drink mixed and sitting on the table. He was wearing only a pair of denim cut-offs and he definitely looked the worse for wear. She burst out laughing as he collapsed into the chair and took a long swallow of his drink.

"You look awful, Allan. What time did you get to sleep?"

"Who's been to sleep?"

"Not at all?"

"Nope. John and I became involved in one of our pointless philosophical discussions. He finally called it quits about half an hour ago."

"And you became enthralled with flies."

"Love flies." Allan drained his glass and started to laugh with Jillian; then he grabbed his head and winced.

Taking the glass he handed her, she acknowledged his beseeching look with a good-natured nod of her head. She fixed him another drink and a large orange juice for herself, then walked into the living room. "Let's sit in here."

Allan followed her and flopped down on the floor, gratefully accepting the glass she offered him. "The apartment looks terrific, Jill."

Jillian curled up on the chesterfield and took a sip of her juice. "Glad you like it. When are you coming home?"

"I am home."

She shot him a questioning look, then her face broke into a pleased smile as she saw his confirming nod.

"I thought you had another two months!"

"Well, I should have, but I studied like hell and managed to pull off some really good marks. Anyway, I received word a week ago that I had been selected to fill that vacant post in surgery at the hospital here, so I can finish my postgraduate practical in Edmonton. I had three more weeks of classes, but when Sylvia phoned and told me that you and Jacob were together in a band, I went to the chief of surgery and lied through my teeth, saying there was a family crisis. Alas, here I am!"

"Terrific!" Jillian's eyes shone with pleasure.

"Now, can I have my old room back?"

"There's a couple of bodies in there that you'll have to toss out first."

Allan grimaced and laid his hand on his forehead. "I'll do it first thing tomorrow." They laughed, then fell into a companionable silence, both of them enjoying the quiet. Jill shut her eyes and rested her head against the back of the sofa.

"Jill?"

"What?"

"How's things with you and Jacob?"

Jillian sat up and studied her bare feet. "Would you accept 'hopeful'?"

"No."

They fell into a reflective silence again, then she asked, "Allan, do you know anything about this treatment Jacob is considering for his back?"

Allan was suddenly intent on the drink he was swirling around in his glass, his face pensive. He looked at Jill, then stood up, walked over to the fireplace and set his tumbler on the mantel. He rested his elbow there, then turned to face her again.

"Yes, I do."

"Did Jacob mention it to you?"

"He spoke about it briefly last night." Allan pushed himself away from the fireplace and sat down beside Jillian. He hunched over, his arms resting on his knees, his hands clasped in front of him.

Jillian reached over and swept the lock of hair on his forehead to one side. She and Allan were alike in so many ways. They possessed the same coloring, very similar features, the same temperament. She looked at his rugged masculine face and realized what a stabilizing force he had been for her.

"Please, Allan, I need to know."

"Okay, Jillian," he said finally. "There's a clinic in Israel that is doing some very impressive work with the psychological rehabilitation of physically handicapped patients." He looked at her, his eyes clouded with concern. "If Jacob's paralysis *is* psychosomatic, it would probably be the best place to send him—"

"But you never agreed with that diagnosis."

"No, I never have. I'm convinced either that something was missed or that he suffered permanent damage from the spinal hematoma. I would give my eyeteeth to get him into hospital and do a thorough neurological examination of his spine, but I don't know if Jacob would ever consent to it. He's made up his mind that he's going to Israel—and I'm afraid he's in for a big letdown."

Jillian's face was creased with a worried frown. "I still can't understand why Dr. Paulson even considered psychosomatic paralysis. . . ."

Allan shrugged his shoulders as he leaned back against the cushions. "I suppose now that I have some experience behind me, I can see why Paulson arrived at that conclusion. Most of us don't fully understand the magnitude of the psychological trauma that faces someone like Jacob—someone who has to fight his way through a long and very painful convalescence, knowing that he might never completely recover from his injuries."

He reached for a cigarette, lighted one and inhaled deeply. "I think I'm just beginning to understand it myself. It can be very frightening and very discouraging; it's not infrequent that patients consider suicide at some point. But Jacob was so different. He is, without a doubt, the most intelligent, talented, passionate, disciplined person I've ever met. Because of the type of person he is, I think Jacob felt he should have been able to master the resentment and hostility he felt."

Allan hesitated, his face thoughtful as he toyed absently with the ashtray. "It was a superhuman task. Other people in similar circumstances are more likely to indulge in binges of self-pity and fits of hysteria, but Jacob never once allowed the anger to surface. He suppressed it all—the anger, the bitterness, the fear, the discouragement. Paulson probably felt that Jacob's rigid self-control was a negative psychological attitude and that his attitude was seriously affecting his recovery. If I didn't know Jacob the way I do, I probably would have agreed with the diagnosis one hundred percent. As it is, there is that possibility that Paulson was right."

Jillian's eyes were glimmering dangerously with barely controlled anger, and Allan smiled knowingly as he watched her face. "Jillian, if you lose that fiery temper of yours, I won't say another word."

She clamped her teeth together and flashed a look of disgust at her brother. "I'm not defending Paulson, nor am I criticizing Jacob, Jillian. I just want you to look at the situation rationally." He fell silent for a moment, then reached out and took her hand in his. "I told Jacob last night that I thought he should have some tests done before he goes ahead with his plans to go to Israel for treatment."

"What did he say?"

"Not much—he said he'd think about it. Apparently he hasn't gone near a doctor since he left here."

"Allan, if there is a medical reason for Jacob's paralysis, is there any possibility that something might be done to correct it?"

"It would be a very remote chance." He released her hand and stood up, walked to the window and stared out of it. "But I can never stop believing in medical miracles for people like Jacob. There's some very promising research being done in the field of microsurgery now, and I hope and pray that someday there's going to be a major breakthrough that will allow us to repair spinal-cord injuries. Someday we're going to have the technology to do it.''

Jillian's smile was one of warm understanding. ''And Allan Lambert plans to be a part of it.''

He grinned and nodded. ''He sure as hell does.'' His face sobered as he looked at her. ''I'll do everything in my power for him, Jillian. You know that.''

She smiled at him and bobbed her head in acknowledgment. ''Yes, I know that.'' After sitting there deep in thought for a few moments, she bounced off the couch and walked toward the kitchen. ''Are you going to help me cook breakfast for this horde or are you going to have a shower?''

''Do I have a choice?''

''No.''

Allan laughed and tossed a cushion at her retreating back. ''Then I guess I'll help with breakfast.''

IT WAS LATE SUNDAY AFTERNOON when Jillian waved goodbye to Ken and Sylvia. They were the last of the Lloydminster crowd to leave; all the others had left earlier in the day. Mark had taken off shortly after breakfast, as he was the pitcher for a district fastball team that was playing in a tournament that day. The senior Lamberts and Holinskis had left together, taking their two small grandsons with them. The boys had been promised a picnic and a swim at Elk Island Park, and Kenny had been wildly exuberant about seeing the buffalo herds that roamed within the park boundaries.

Jillian smiled to herself as she walked down the driveway toward the backyard. She had been so pleased when Ken and Sylvia, despite her sister-in-law's condition, had extended an invitation to the entire Firefly troupe to spend whatever time they had between engagements at the farm. Their invitation had been enthusiastically accepted, for none of the others had ever had an opportunity to spend time on a farm. She was beginning to realize how much she took Ken's and Sylvia's warm hospitality for granted.

The scene in the backyard was a homey, comfortable one. Dan, David, Keith and John were playing a game of lawn darts while Elaine and Kathy relaxed in the shade of a huge old Mayday tree, finishing a macrame plant hanger Jillian had never completed. Allan was sound asleep in the hammock, and Norm and Karin were stretched out on the grass, deeply engrossed in a backgammon game. Jillian grinned—a perfect way to spend a Sunday afternoon. She frowned slightly when she realized Jacob wasn't on the patio. He must have gone inside.

Entering the apartment, she found him sitting in the living room, his head tilted back, his eyes closed. She could feel the exhaustion and tension radiating from him, and could see from the tightness around his mouth and eyes that he was also experiencing a great deal of pain. She went over to him and laid her hand gently on his shoulder, aware of the dampness of his body through his light shirt.

"Jacob." He raised his head slowly and opened his eyes, and she bent down and brushed his lips with hers as he gave her a halfhearted smile. "Why don't you go and have a bath and lie down for a while? The bedroom will be cool and it's so hot in here." She deliberately kept her voice easy, casual, devoid of the compassion she felt for him.

"Maybe I will."

"I'm going to make a lime punch." She smiled at him mischievously. "If you trust me, I'll bring one in to you after I satisfy that howling mob outside."

He looked at her speculatively, his eyes warm. "*Can* I trust you?"

"Yes—" she winked at him provocatively, her eyes dancing "—but just this once, mind you."

His eyes narrowed but she could see the glint of amusement in them.

She carried a large tray filled with two big pitchers of the frosty drink and a platter of cold watermelon slices out to the shady patio. There were lazy murmurs of approval at the sight of the refreshments.

Norm vaulted onto the cedar deck and came toward her. "Here, let me take that."

"Thanks."

"Where's Jake?"

"He won't be out. Norm, do you know if he still carries medication for the spasms in his back with him?"

"No, he doesn't. Is it bad?"

"With Jacob, you never know. I'll mix him a good stiff drink, then do some therapy on him."

Jillian couldn't help smiling wryly at the dubious look that flashed across Norm's face. "Don't look so worried. I learned how to do it when he was still in the hospital. In fact, I used to be rather good at it."

Jillian returned to the house and fixed Jacob a tall ice-filled drink that contained a hefty shot of vodka. She paused at the door to the bathroom and tapped lightly.

"Come in," he called.

Jillian entered, then laughed delightedly at the sight before her. Jacob sat chest deep in bubbles in the big old tub.

"Bubble bath?"

He nodded his head, a droll look on his face. "It's...strategic."

"Oh, very! Cute, too." She handed him the drink and watched the expression on his face as he took a sip.

"Is this the standard lime punch or is it fortified?"

"It's fortified."

His eyes were provocative and appraising as he let his gaze sweep slowly over her, making her very aware of the brief white shorts and halter top she was wearing. "Fortification is definitely what I need around you, Jillian." Her pulse was racing as she turned around and left the room.

Jillian was relieved to find that Allan's room was indeed very cool and shaded. She had drawn the draperies and was folding back the covers when Jacob entered the room. He had on only a pair of white tennis shorts. He had obviously shampooed his hair, which lay in damp tight curls around his face. It made him look extremely boyish, and she ached to run her fingers through it.

"Get into bed, Jacob. I'll be right back."

She returned to find him lying in bed flat on his back, his knees flexed, his eyes tightly closed. She could tell by the drawn expression on his face that he was feeling very uncomfortable. Uncapping the bottle she was holding, she spread some of the lotion on her hands. Without saying a word she bent over him and began to rub his legs with strong slow strokes.

Jacob lifted his head. "You don't have to do that."

"I know I don't have to. I want to." She continued massaging his legs for some time. "Roll over, Jacob."

He hesitated, then rolled over, resting his head on his folded arms. "You sound as though you're talking to a dog." She laughed as she applied the lotion directly to his back, then knelt on the bed, straddling his body. She started working low on his back, using the technique she had been taught.

Jacob groaned with gratification. "Jillian, you have no idea how good that feels."

She worked slowly and thoroughly, struggling against the overwhelming urge to let her hands become caressing. She worked up his back, across his shoulders and down his arms, well aware of the strength and power there. She paused at the base of his neck, then with firm circular motions of her long fingers began to massage the back of his neck and his scalp. He sighed and rolled over, and she could feel the remainder of the tension ease out of him.

Her own emotions were beginning to run rampant. She bent down and kissed his temple lightly, then moved from the bed. She could tell by the look on his face that he was much more comfortable. He brought one knee up, then reached out an arm, catching her hand in his. Gently he kissed her fingertips.

Suddenly his eyes flew open. "Cucumber?"

Jillian laughed as she sat down on the floor beside the bed. "Well, it was either Cucumber Body Lotion or Chanel. I thought I would rather have you smelling like a salad."

He grinned at her lazily. Jillian leaned her back against the bed, her arms around her knees. She simply didn't dare touch him now.

She felt his hand at the knot of hair at the back of

her head. The heavy braid uncoiled, the plaiting loosening. Jillian shut her eyes as Jacob began to comb his fingers through her hair until it was completely loose and cascading down around her in a wild tumble. She grasped her hands together tightly as he continued to fondle it, glad he couldn't see her face. His gentleness was stirring up a wild clamor inside her.

"It smells marvelous." His voice was quiet, appreciative.

"So do you."

He chuckled lightly as he continued to play with her hair. "Were you in my room this morning?"

"Yes."

"Did you kiss me?"

"Yes."

"I *thought* my dreams were more realistic than usual." He was running his hand up the back of her head, then letting the full length of her hair slip through his fingers with absorbed fascination. Her desire was mounting, but she would not break this special spell.

His movements became slower and slower until they stopped completely. Jillian knew by his breathing that he had fallen asleep. She turned and gently removed a handful of her hair from his hand. She sat watching him for a long time, her eyes brimming with tears. God, how she loved him.

A few hours later Jillian was alone in the kitchen finishing the last of the dishes that had accumulated through the day. Allan had taken Karin, Norm and John with him to the airport to collect the rest of his baggage, and the others had returned to the hotel to take advantage of their one free evening a week.

Putting the last plate away, Jillian closed the cupboard doors. She was singing softly to herself as she walked into the living room. Selecting a favorite tape, she inserted it into the deck and adjusted the volume on the stereo, then stretched her hands over her head and arched her back as she moved to the music.

Her stomach felt as though she was on a rollercoaster ride when she realized Jacob was sitting silently in his wheelchair watching her.

"Hi. How long have you been here?" Her voice wobbled treacherously and she could feel herself blushing, although she wasn't certain why.

Jacob grinned, his eyes teasing. "You'd think I had caught you with your hand in the cookie jar, Jillian. Or do you have your hand in the cookie jar?"

She pulled a face at him, then leaned over and gave him a soft kiss. "Now I do."

Jacob's breath caught in his throat as he grasped her by the back of the head, holding her mouth against his. His lips were warm and demanding on hers as his other hand moved slowly up her ribs. His hand rested firmly under her breast and Jillian's knees went weak. Jacob sensed her mounting desire and gently pushed her away.

His eyes were desolate as he looked up at her. "Oh, Jill. I wish—"

Softly she laid her fingers across his mouth. She knew instinctively what he was going to say, and she also knew from deep within her heart that now was the time to reveal all her feelings to him. She knelt in front of him, gently cradling the face that was so dear to her in her trembling hands.

"Jacob, I love you the way I do because of the person you are."

His face was so drawn with the conflict that stormed within him that it stabbed her like a knife. Allan's words echoed through her mind and she knew that Jacob needed, above all else, to be certain of her.

"I love you, Jacob, and I want you and I know that I could never feel about another living soul the way I feel about you. You are my other half. You are my best friend, my companion, my confessor, my conscience, my lover."

She stroked the tension lines around his eyes with a tender caress as she saw the unhappiness there. "I don't give a damn if you are blind, deaf, deformed or crippled; it's the person inside I want. I can never be emotionally independent from you." Her voice was low, intense and weighted with deep sincerity. "I need you, Jacob. You are my soul."

Jacob was completely overcome, his face torn with the multitude of feelings she had stirred within him. He put his arms around her, cushioning her against his powerful chest as he sprawled to the floor with her. Then his hand slid up her back and in one deft movement he unfastened her halter top, brushing it away. He took a deep shuddering breath, gripping her to him as his mouth took hers with a hot demanding desire. She could feel his heart thudding against her naked breasts as he pulled her beneath him.

He lifted his head and looked deep into her eyes, desire blazing uncontrolled between them. "Oh, God, Jillian, but I love you, baby. I know this is all wrong but—" He lowered his head, groaning softly as he kissed her with a frantic passion. All his restraint was gone.

The slamming of the front door and a babble of

voices snapped them back to cold reality. Jacob bolted into a sitting position and lifted Jillian against him as he smoothed her thick hair down her back. He leaned back against the hearth of the fireplace, burying her flushed face against his chest as his arms tightened around her.

The door of the apartment swung open and Allan stuck his head in. "Come on out to the patio, you guys. It's cooler out there."

"I'm sure it must be." Jacob's voice was casual and controlled but tinged with dry humor. "We'll be out in a while."

Jillian heard the door close. "Damn him! Damn him! I could strangle him with my bare hands," she seethed through clenched teeth.

"And I'll help you." Jacob's voice was taut with frustration, but there was laughter there, too. "Allan always was notorious for his bad timing."

"Jacob...." She looked up at him imploringly.

He kissed her gently, completely in control once again. "Sit up for a minute, babe. Here, let's get you dressed before some other clod comes bursting through the door."

Jillian sat up reluctantly and reached for her top. Jacob held her by the shoulders as he swept her hair down her back with one hand, letting his eyes roam over her.

"I love you, Jillian." It was a quiet statement that filled Jillian with radiant hope.

"Don't doubt me, Jacob."

Softly he wiped away the trickle of perspiration between her breasts with his knuckles, then cupped her face in his palms. "I don't. Not now." He gave her a fleeting kiss, then let her go. Reaching for one of the big lounging cushions, he tucked it behind his back, obviously enjoying the vision before him.

She could feel a flush rising in her cheeks as she tossed him a saucy look and with shaking hands tried to put on the halter. "You are a devil, Jacob Holinski."

"And you are a very tempting witch, Jillian Lambert."

A moment later she looked at him helplessly and let the halter fall loose. "I can't do it up."

He grinned and cocked one eyebrow. "Turn around then." Hooking the back clasp, he swept her hair over his arm and pulled her back firmly against him. "I need to hold you for a while, babe."

She snuggled closer against him, his arms circling her breasts, her face resting against his cheek.

"Jillian, will you give me a few days to try to come to terms with myself and all that's happened?"

It was beautiful music. "You know I will," she whispered. She would sell her soul for him and he knew it.

MONDAY'S PERFORMANCES were charged with a dynamic current that had left Jillian aroused and edgy. Firefly had never sounded so good. They had been together all the way, right through the entire evening, and they had been sensational. Jillian was slightly annoyed when Norm called Jacob aside at the conclusion of the evening to discuss some business matters. She wanted so much to talk to Jacob, for the entire evening had been so exhilarating.

She stood in the middle of her room and contemplated a hot bath. She'd have to do something or she knew she'd never settle down. The soft light from the lamp by her bed washed the room in a gentle warm glow that was strangely soothing, but Jillian knew she needed to do something to drain off the pent-up energy that had her feeling like a caged cat.

She sighed, undressed and slipped into a brief cotton nightie, then started brushing her hair. All at once she snapped her fingers and tossed the brush on the dresser. She knew what would do the trick.

She went to the closet and lifted out her guitar case and laid it on the bed. Opening the lid, she lifted the instrument out and ran her hands lovingly over the polished finish. She had started taking lessons four years ago and had been amazed how quickly she learned. Granted, her extensive musical training had been a definite asset, but right from the beginning she had felt a tranquil inner empathy for this instrument. It seemed to suit her moods far more than a piano ever could.

Setting the case on the floor, she sat cross-legged in the middle of the bed and cradled the guitar against her, then ran her thumb slowly over the strings, her keen ears attuned to any discordant notes. After making some minor adjustments to the tuning, she bent her head and began softly to play some of the poignant Spanish songs that she loved so much.

Time slipped by as she lost herself in the rich beauty of the music. She was totally unaware that Jacob had silently entered the room and was sitting quietly in the shadows of the entryway. The magnificence of the haunting passionate music surrounded them both as he sat silently watching her, listening to a sound that was full and rich and captivating.

Jillian sighed as she finished the song and made a motion to rise.

"Don't."

Her head jerked up and her startled eyes widened when she realized she had an audience. Her voice was husky and a little breathless. "I didn't know you had come in."

"I know." He wheeled himself over to the bed, reached out and took her hand in his. With a tenderness that made her hurt inside he gently kissed her palm. His voice was thick as he whispered, "That was very beautiful, Jillian."

She shivered as she leaned forward and took his face in her hands, softly kissing him on the mouth. She felt him shudder as his mouth opened beneath hers, and the gentle kiss turned into a deep and passionate assault. Jacob buried his fingers in her hair and she responded to him with a hunger that was propelling them beyond the bounds of control.

He was breathing hard as he slowly, reluctantly set her away from him, then gently caressed her cheek with his fingertips. "Jillian...babe...."

Jillian could sense the terrible battle that was tearing him apart inside. He wanted her, yet he wouldn't take her until he came to terms with all the conflicts that churned within him. He could be driven beyond his will of steel but she didn't want to trap him that way; she loved him far too much to cause him any more pain.

With a massive effort that cost her dearly, she moved away from him slightly and smiled softly, her eyes filled with love. "I'll behave, Jacob."

Jacob looked at her, his brown eyes dark with an inner torment that sent a spasm of pain through her. His jaw was clenched as he took her hand in his. "Jill, I don't know where I am right now. I have so much I have to work through before—"

She laid her finger on his lips, her eyes soft with compassion. "Don't, Jacob. Don't look like that. You said you needed time, and I'll play by your rules. I promise."

Jacob sat hunched in his wheelchair, his face grim, almost angry. But there was such a desperate feeling of loneliness radiating from him that Jillian could barely smother the threatening tears. Once again, as in the past, she sensed he needed some gentle comforting.

"Jacob, come up on the bed."

"No, Jillian."

"I only want to hold you, Jacob; please trust me."

His face was unreadable as he stared at her for what seemed to Jillian like endless minutes. His mouth was set in a taut line when he finally relented, positioned the wheelchair alongside the bed and lifted himself up beside her. Jillian laid the guitar on the floor on the opposite side of the bed, then swept her hair over her shoulder.

He took a deep shaky breath as she slipped her arms around him and stretched out beside him. His arms came around her as he molded her fiercely against him, his despair nearly a tangible thing. Her throat contracted painfully as she held him, his head cradled against her breast. Tears blurred her eyes as he murmured her name. With gentle undemanding hands she stroked his back, massaging away the tension across his shoulders. Just to be able to hold him in her arms filled her with a deep contentment. The smell of him, the weight of his body against hers, the feel of his hands upon her back tranquilized her into a state of euphoria. She held him as the moments of time slipped away into the silence, and little by little she could feel the strain and tension dissolving within him.

"Jillian, when did you start playing the guitar?"

"I started taking lessons about four years ago."

He shifted his position so that he was lying on his side. Propping his head on his hand he smiled down at her, his eyes like rich brown velvet.

"There's a special kind of enchantment in your music when you play the guitar, Jill."

She smiled at him. "You always said I was a witch."

"That you are." He ran his fingers slowly through her hair and let it slip through his hands until it was spread across them in a shimmering mass of burnished copper. "Will you play for me now?" His voice had a husky quality to it that seduced Jillian. She longed to feel his mouth, moist and warm, against hers, tantalizing her senses. Silently she sat up, leaned over him and touched his mouth with a whisper of a kiss, then retrieved the guitar.

Jacob arranged the pillows behind his back so that he was in a comfortable sitting position. Then he reached toward his wheelchair and took out a thick pad of drawing paper and a pencil.

Jillian curled her legs under her as she hugged the guitar to her and began to play. The serene music drifted around them, enfolding them in its beauty and secluding them from a world of uncertainty. As Jillian played, Jacob sketched her, his eyes fired with the intense need to capture the essence of the picture before him.

When she finally laid the instrument aside, Jacob's eyes seemed to devour her with restrained hunger. As though drawn against his will, he leaned forward and untied the thin straps across her shoulders, easing the nightie down until it lay draped around her hips.

Jillian's breath caught in a sob as she felt his hands on her naked skin. She closed her eyes as the shock waves of desire hardened her nipples and twisted in her belly. Jacob raked his fingers through her hair until it was cascading around her like a gleaming cloak, then he gently caught her chin and changed the angle of her head. There was such a heavy throb within her that she could barely move, and her breasts rose and fell with her labored breathing.

"Jillian."

She opened her eyes and gazed at him, her pupils dilated as the ache within her grew. His eyes were searing her as he drank in every detail of her naked torso.

"God, but you are so beautiful." His voice was a ragged whisper. "Babe, I need to paint you like that—with the light casting warm shadows across your skin."

Jillian didn't move as she watched the impassioned desire kindle a blaze in his eyes. He reached out and gently cupped her breast in a trembling hand, then leaned forward and covered the rosy tip with his mouth, his tongue scorching her. She had to clench her hands into tight fists to keep from touching him. He raised his head and his gaze locked onto hers; there was a silent exchange that needed no words. Without speaking he picked up the pad from his lap, flipped the page and began to sketch her.

Jillian felt divorced from reality. There were no impassioned embraces or soul-shattering kisses—in fact, Jacob seldom touched her. Nevertheless she felt as though he physically caressed her with every stroke, every shading he made. Occasionally he would reach out and trace the line of her jaw or the full curves of her breasts, his hands lingering as though he was absorbing the purity of line through his touch. Jillian was mesmerized by the depth and power of the keen sensual awareness that was woven around them. It was a bond that could never be fragmented.

Sweat dampened Jacob's brow and his hand became less and less steady. His voice was gruff as he finally whispered her name and reached out and hauled her down against him. His arms came around her, crushing her against his hard rugged frame. Their bodies were welded together as the heat of their desire became a raging inferno, and they clung together with a primeval need, yet he made no move to take the release she offered. Even so, there was a fusion between them that gave a release of a different type, a release beyond description, and their denial heightened the beauty of it.

THE MAUVE FINGERS of dawn were pushing back the dark curtain of night and weaving the sky with threads of gold and crimson when Jillian awoke. She was still wrapped closely in Jacob's arms, his body warm and hard against hers. She lay quietly, reluctant to disturb him. His breathing was deep and even, his breath warm against her temple. If she had one wish, it would be that this beautiful tranquil moment could go on forever. She had wanted him desperately the previous night, and she knew he'd had little control left when he had gathered her against him. But she had not given way to her inner maelstrom. She had promised him time, and she could, at least, give him that.

She closed her eyes as she savored the contentment, the comfort of waking up in his arms. There was a hint of his after-shave still clinging to him, mixed with the musky smell of his maleness. The feel of the smooth skin at the curve of his neck beneath her cheek, his hard muscled chest pressing against her breasts, his thighs beneath hers were sensations that would be forever engraved on her mind.

The steady rhythm of his breathing altered, and his arms tightened around her as he murmured her name. Slowly he stroked her naked back, then with an abrupt stiffening of his body he came fully awake. She didn't move, and gradually his body relaxed and he once again began to caress her back.

"You're a good man to wake up to, Mr. Muscle."

Jacob laughed at her perfect takeoff of the TV commercial. "You're not so bad yourself."

She tipped her head back and looked up at him, her eyes dancing with amusement. His own eyes were warm and easy as he smiled back at her, and with a slow deliberate movement he slipped his hand up her rib cage until it rested on the fullness of her breast.

"You do test a guy's resolve first thing in the morning." There was a wealth of humor in his voice but a hint of warning in it, as well.

She raised her brows in feigned innocence. "I? Not I, sir!"

"Oh, yes—you!"

"I suppose if I get up to get dressed, you'll charge out of here?"

His eyes crinkled at the corners and a warm gleam came into them, highlighting the flecks of topaz. His tone was dry. "Not very likely." She started to sit up but he pulled her back down, his voice rich with laughter. "I've changed my mind." He wrapped his arms around her and buried one hand in her hair. "Are you cold?"

"If I said yes, what would you propose to do about it?"

"When did you start loading your questions? Now tell me, are you cold?"

"Yes, I am."

He reached over her, caught the opposite edge of the lightly quilted bedspread and pulled it over her.

"That's called cheating, Jacob."

"That's called maintaining the status quo."

She laughed, draping a leg over his and snuggling against him. A thought flashed into her mind and her face grew sober. "Jacob, have you kept up with your painting?"

"Um hmm."

She knew she was treading on uncertain ground but she had to know. Would he tell her? "What have you been painting?"

"You."

She tried to raise her head to look at him, but he held it firmly against her chest. Tears of wonder blurred her vision and she swallowed hard against the lump that was growing in her throat.

"I've done three of you, Jillian, and I know they're the best work I've ever done." His voice was low and quiet but there was a redolence of satisfaction in it.

Jillian was caught strangely off guard. Three? Norm had spoken about two canvases. She frowned as she tried to find suitable words in which to phrase her query. But she didn't need to ask.

"Remember that day you and I went riding? It was during Christmas break and you were riding that big black gelding your dad was training. We were racing across that field behind the barn, remember?''

"I remember." She would never forget it. The race had been an earnest one. She had managed to pull ahead for a short distance, but Rogue had closed the gap. Jacob had reached out and swept her off her mount, but her weight had dragged him off his own horse. They had tumbled unhurt into a drift of snow, Jillian sprawled on top of him. Their laughter had evaporated as he caught her face and pulled her head down, giving her such a blistering kiss it was a wonder it hadn't caused an early thaw.

"One other painting was from the day I gave you your ring." He slipped his fingers down the chain around her neck and touched the ring. "We were on that old wooden bridge and you were leaning against the rail. The sun had set your hair on fire."

Jillian was having a silent battle trying to control her tears. The tremor in his voice made the agony he had suffered very real for her.

"The last one was done of you the day I caught you in the swimming hole."

The mood of fragile poignancy was shattered as Jillian bolted upright, her face scarlet with embarrassment and horror. "Jacob, you didn't! How dare you!"

He tipped his head back and laughed, his eyes dancing with delight. "Jillian Lambert, how can you possibly convince me that your indignation is justified when you sit there in an unconcerned state of... undress."

She shot him a scathing look as he pulled her back into his arms. His laughter was low and provocative as he cuddled her firmly against him.

Jillian couldn't keep the amusement out of her voice. "That was a damned sneaky trick you pulled that day."

"There was nothing sneaky about it and you know it. I dived in as bold as brass."

And he had. It had been a stifling hot July day and she had been on her way home after taking lunch out to the men who were haying. She'd almost passed the narrow winding dirt road that led to the swimming hole when on impulse she decided to go for a swim. She had put the truck in reverse and backed down the road, then swung into the rutted lane.

The swimming hole was really an old gravel pit that had had to be abandoned because of an underground spring. It had provided the Lamberts and Holinskis with hours and hours of boisterous amusement. Ringed with a dense thicket of willows and saskatoon bushes and several huge old spruce and poplars, it was private and secluded, the water cool and crystal clear.

Jillian's mother had wrapped a roaster filled with warm fresh buns in an old discarded beach towel. Jillian had dug the towel out of a box in the back of the truck and had wormed her way through the dim tunnel of the overgrown trail, ducking beneath the tangled branches. On the narrow grassy bank she had shed her boots and jeans, then tugged off her T-shirt. After a moment she had shed her panties and bra, as well. There wasn't the remotest chance anyone else would come and she hadn't been skinny-dipping since she was a child.

She executed a neat clean dive into the pool, the cold water tingling and refreshing against her hot naked skin. As she swam underwater she relished the feel of the water eddying around her and through her heavy hair. On the other side she stood up in water waist deep and wiped the droplets off her face.

"Very nice."

Her head jerked around and her eyes widened with alarm when she realized Jacob was leaning against a big poplar tree, his thumbs hooked in the waistband of his blue-jean cutoffs, his face split with an unholy grin. He was shirtless, and the muscles across his chest rippled beneath his bronzed skin as he straightened up and kicked off his sandals. Jillian abruptly sank down, her hair spreading out like a massive copper fan as she swam to deeper water. She surfaced in water up to her shoulders and glared at Jacob, who stood on the edge, watching her through hooded eyes.

"What are you doing here, Jacob Holinski?"

"I came for a swim."

"You're supposed to be in Lloydminster for parts." She was flustered and sputtering.

"I was on my way home when I saw you pull in here, so I decided to stop for a swim."

"Well, go away."

"Really, Jillian, is that any way to talk to your future husband?"

"Jacob, please—" Her plea was in vain as he dived in, his long body cleaving the water as silently and as smoothly as an arrow. The ripples from his dive sparkled in the sun as Jillian did a deep duck dive and swam underwater. She hadn't gone fifteen feet when Jacob's arms came around her. He twisted her around as he pulled her effortlessly against him and propelled them to the surface. She had time to gasp a lungful of air before he dragged her under again. His arms encircled her and held her against him as he kissed her slowly, sensually, the deep clear water wrapping them in its cool liquid embrace. They drifted to the surface, where, with a quick agile twist of her body, Jillian flung her arms over her head and slipped smoothly out of Jacob's grasp. She struck across the pool with long strong strokes in the direction of her clothes.

Jacob laughed as he easily intercepted her, catching her firmly by the ankle and hauling her under. When they resurfaced it was in shallower water, and he held her firmly as he laughed down at her and swept her streaming hair back off her face.

Then, suddenly, his eyes darkened and his face became deadly serious as he gathered her against him. His voice was very low and uneven as he muttered her name, and all thoughts of escape fled from Jillian's mind as he lowered his head. His mouth slanted across hers with a merciless searching kiss that left her senseless, and she felt as though she was indeed drowning.

She had clung to him as every ounce of strength drained from her. Jacob's hands had roamed her body, his unrestrained caresses driving her deeper and deeper into a whirlpool of desire where only Jacob existed. She had been conscious of nothing but him and the chaos he was creating within her. Finally he had moved away, his breathing rough and harsh, his chest heaving. The water had lapped beneath her breasts and her hair swirled silkily around her in the sun-kissed waters as she looked at him with wide smoldering eyes that had told him wordlessly of her raw naked yearning. He had stared at her like a man gazing at a vision.

She knew now without asking that that was how he had painted her. She wanted to bury her face against his chest and give way to the tears that were choking her, but she lay quietly in his arms, then swallowed hard.

"Jacob?"

He laid his hand along her jaw and lifted her face, his eyes dark and brooding.

"Jacob, do you still swim?"

He continued to watch her as his dark look of regret faded and a slow smile lighted up his eyes. "I've been known to do a lap or two. What exactly do you have in mind?"

"Well, there's a swimming pool here in the hotel and there won't be anyone else there at this hour...."

The smile turned into a wicked grin. "By any chance are you inviting me to go skinny-dipping?"

She grinned back at him and punched his shoulder in rebuke. "No, you foul man! I just thought—"

"That it would be like old times?"

Jillian tensed with alarm at his comment, but she relaxed when she could find no hint of bitterness in his eyes.

Jacob leaned over and kissed her soundly, then rolled away and sat up. "I'll meet you there in fifteen minutes!" He reached over and spanned her chin with his hand, his face grave and deadly earnest. "Thank you, Jillian."

She turned her head and kissed his palm, then smiled softly at him, her voice very low. "Thank you, Jacob."

She didn't move for some time after he wheeled silently out of the room. She was filled with such a turbulent mixture of feelings that she couldn't begin to sort them out. She wanted to sing with elation, yet at the same time weep with sorrow. She wished she could predict what was going to happen. Sighing heavily she swung her feet to the floor, glancing down when she felt something cold and slick beneath her bare feet. The drawing pad.

With a shiver of apprehension she picked it up and flipped the pages until she found Jacob's sketches of her.

A heavy ache filled her chest as she looked at them. The sketch he had done of her while she was playing the guitar had captured the tenderness, the serenity she had felt as she played for him. There was something so pure, so innocent about it that it brought tears to her eyes.

The other sketch she could barely stand to look at. She wanted to destroy it, but she couldn't bring herself to do so. He had drawn her sitting on a pedestal, remote and unreachable, but the essence of her deep yet unsatisfied love for him was captured in every stroke. It created the illusion that the figure in the picture was drifting out of reach and would soon be engulfed in a swirling mist. The stark, haunting, desolate picture filled Jillian with a cold ominous dread. If Jacob ever painted her like that, it would be because he had once again left her.

CHAPTER ELEVEN

JACOB DIDN'T HEAR her enter. He was hanging on the edge of the pool, his elbows hooked over the edge, his chin resting on his hands as he stared out over the city through the floor-to-ceiling windows. He was totally engrossed by the flamboyant splendor of an Alberta sunrise that cast the skyline in a golden halo and painted the sky with vivid slashes of orange, crimson and purple. He was obviously absorbing the bold and magnificent spectacle with the eyes and the soul of an artist.

Jillian experienced a sharp pang of grief for the lost years as she stood silently watching him. His wet hair was a mass of thick boyish curls, his expression one of ageless awe, and there was something subtle in his pose that fleetingly recaptured his youth. Yet there was a vitality that radiated from him that accentuated his masculinity, his virility, his magnetism. It was an enigma. It was also irresistible.

She breathed deeply, then said softly, "Very nice."

He turned in the water to watch her walk across the ceramic-tiled deck and smiled ruefully. "You have a memory like an elephant, do you know that?"

She pulled a face. "Well, I suppose that's better than no memory at all."

His smile faded and there was a twist of bitterness

in his quiet rebuttal. "I'm not so sure I'd agree with that."

Jillian flinched slightly, regretting her flip response. She said nothing, but slipped out of her velour robe and dropped it on the deck. Without looking at him she dived in.

She struck out for the opposite end of the pool with easy strokes, vaguely aware that Jacob had dived, as well. At the deep end she was startled to see his shadowy outline in the water below her. With one powerful stroke he came up beneath her, his arms encircling her waist as he dragged her against him. Like long ago he twisted her around to face him, and his mouth covered hers in a tantalizing fluid kiss that played absolute havoc with her senses. This time Jillian didn't struggle but wrapped her arms around him and returned his kiss with ardor.

They surfaced, both of them gasping for air. There was an old buoyancy in his laughter that had been missing, and his eyes were snapping with a vivacity that left Jillian feeling oddly hollow. It was a look of freedom, a look of exaltation, and his eyes were alive with it. A realization pierced through Jillian: here in the water he was no longer handicapped or trapped; he was released from the prison of his disability. She reacted immediately and executed a deep surface dive so that Jacob would not witness the look of stark comprehension that swept across her face. His frustrations, his anger, his bitterness suddenly became her burden. It was then that the total impact of what he had lost really slammed home for Jillian. For the first time she really understood how he felt and what an impact his disability had on his life. It was a frightening, helpless feeling.

The streets below were coming to life with early-morning traffic when Jillian finally swam to the edge of the pool, her chest heaving as she rested her arms on the edge.

Jacob surfaced beside her and wiped the water from his face. "Had enough?"

She laughed and nodded. "Yes, I've had enough!"

He, too, rested his arms on the edge, his body drifting weightlessly beside hers. He grinned as he reached out and snapped the shoulder strap of her bathing suit. "You didn't need this after all, Jill."

She grinned back at him, her eyes sparkling with a challenge. "When you go without yours, I'll go without mine."

He raised his eyebrows in speculation and a scheming look gleamed in his eyes as he considered her with devastating slowness. "Really? Sound like a very interesting proposition. I'll have to think about it."

Jillian gave him a flirtatious look. "You do that." She patted his cheek smartly, then hoisted herself onto the deck and sat with her legs dangling in the water. "Jacob, I'll have to have a shower and shampoo my hair. Why don't you come down when you're ready and I'll take you out to breakfast?" He would hate it if she remained and watched him struggle into his wheelchair from the edge of the pool.

He reached up, caught her thick braid and pulled her head down to receive his moist lingering kiss. Jillian felt as though her bones were hot wax when he finally released her and smiled that totally disarming half-smile of his.

"You're on, babe. I'll be down in twenty minutes."

She was still in the bathroom dressing when she

heard her door open. Wrapping a towel turban-style around her hair, she wiggled into a pair of white slacks, zipped them up and smoothed the fabric over her hips. Slipping into a long white embroidered peasant blouse, she buttoned it, then buckled a wide green belt around her waist. She picked up a dry towel as she left the room.

Jacob was stretched out on the bed, his hands tucked behind his head. He gave her a thorough appraisal, then grinned. "All you need is a cluster of fruit hanging from that towel and a set of maracas and you could pass for a Cuban dancer."

She stuck out her tongue at him, snatched the wet towel from her head and flung it at him. He caught it neatly and pitched it on the floor. "Come here."

She willingly crawled onto the bed and sat cross-legged beside him. He took the dry towel from her hands as he sat up. Folding the fluffy towel into a thick pad, he wrapped it around the long fall of her hair, then carefully wrung it.

"I wouldn't ever want to let you get your hands on my neck," she teased.

He laughed as he unwrapped the towel and began combing his fingers through her hair, knowing she couldn't comb it wet because it was so thick and heavy. "I'd rather bite your neck than wring it, anyway."

"There have been occasions, Jacob Holinski, when you've threatened to wring it."

"There have been occasions, Jillian Lambert, when you have provoked me into acts of violence."

She laughed joyfully, her eyes closed as she let Jacob's hands work their magic. These quiet times together filled her with warm satisfied pleasure.

"Jill, would you mind if we ordered breakfast from room service?"

Once again they were on the same wavelength. She, too, didn't want to fragment the intimate seclusion they were sharing; she was more than content to have him to herself.

"I'd like that, Jacob."

He stretched across the bed and picked up the phone. As he ordered, she continued to untangle her hair, then turned to face him as he hung up the phone. She shot him a questioning look as he began to unbutton her blouse.

"It's getting wet from your hair," he explained. Unbuckling her belt, he dropped it on the floor, then slipped the blouse from her and draped it over the lamp by the bed. He picked up the damp towel from the bed and tossed it on the floor as well.

Jillian struggled to keep her voice light and not let him see how much he was disconcerting her. "I hate to think what this room is going to look like when we've finished breakfast. You'll chuck a crust of toast here and an old steak bone there.... Do you always toss things around so haphazardly?"

Jacob didn't answer her but instead stared at her with a gleaming determined look that reminded her of an unmanageable child who was testing her authority. He slipped his hand around her back and deftly unsnapped her bra, stripping it off her and flinging it in the general direction of the dresser. Then he gave her a wicked grin, "Always," he replied.

Jillian could feel her face flushing as he folded his arms across his chest and stared at her with a satisfied, smug look. Her voice was slightly breathless when she commented, "I'm sure the bellboy will appreciate your efforts when I go to the door to collect the tray."

His laugh was low and husky as he pulled her back against him, his arms encircling her beneath her breasts. He eased her forward slightly and swept her damp hair over her shoulder. Jill nestled against his chest and sighed as he kissed the hollow behind her ear, his arms a band of warmth around her. The silence was a communication of its own; there was no need to interrupt it with words.

They had both drifted into a light sleep by the time room service arrived. Jillian scrambled off the bed when the soft knock awakened her and she snatched up her blouse.

"Coward," Jacob laughed softly as he watched her fumble with the buttons. She threw him a slicing look as she snatched the folded bills from him.

When she wheeled the trolley into the room, she narrowed her eyes at him. "For two cents, I wouldn't give you one bite of this!"

He narrowed his eyes in return. "Bring it here, woman!"

The meal was a delight. The food was delicious and their mood unhurried, relaxed and happy. They laughed and talked and simply enjoyed each other's company. Jillian smacked Jacob's hand firmly and tried unsuccessfully to suppress a grin when he made a motion to toss a half-eaten piece of toast in one corner. "You must have been one hell of a trial to your poor mother," she groaned.

"My mother thought I was an angel."

"Your mother was blinded by maternal love and didn't see your deviousness."

He grinned at her and stretched out on the bed as she gathered up the clutter and stacked it on the trays. "Speaking of devious natures, I clearly recollect a scrawny little carrot head who would burst into pitiful tears as soon as her big brother Ken came within earshot, wailing that she just couldn't go into that awful hen house to gather the eggs because the chickens would fly at her head and pick out her eyes. And gullible Ken would gather the eggs. Was that not devious, Miss Lambert?"

Jillian had the decency to blush, but her expression was only slightly shamefaced. "Do you know, Ken never did catch on. The only way I could ever get Allan to do anything for me was if I either blackmailed him or bribed him. Ken was always a softy for frail females."

Jacob watched her with amusement. "You were a brat, Jillian Lambert."

She tossed him a disdainful look as she bounced off the bed and stacked the trays on the trolley. "If I was such a brat, how come you associated with me?"

Jacob grinned. "Because I was a brat, too."

Jillian grinned back at him, then wheeled the trolley across the room and parked it outside the door. Checking to make sure that the Do Not Disturb sign was still hanging on the knob, she closed the door and engaged the dead bolt. Then she drew the heavily lined draperies across the window, closing out the bright early-morning sunshine, and crawled back on the bed beside him.

Jacob had kept the bowl of fresh strawberries that had come with their breakfast, and she smiled with satisfaction as he placed one in her mouth. "I could get hooked on this kind of service."

His eyes were dancing as he fed her another lush red berry. "Really?"

"Really." She glanced up at him, then shook her head ruefully as she propped herself up on one elbow. "You're as bad as Kenny, Jacob. You have marmalade on your face."

"Where?"

Jillian leaned over and slowly licked the speck of jelly from the corner of his mouth. She felt Jacob suck in his breath and his eyes grew dark, and she was acutely sensitive to the heavy throb of his heart beneath her hand. The charged tension between them was building; she would have to try to short-circuit it.

Taking the bowl from his hand, she stretched across him and set it on the night table. She retrieved the lone remaining strawberry and stroked his bottom lip with it, her eyes teasing. "This one should actually be mine, I'll have you know, but...." She placed it in his mouth.

Jacob was looking at her, his eyes smoldering with deep potent emotion. Silently he caught the back of her head and pulled her head down. Jillian's lips parted over his and her tight control was shattered like fine crystal as he slowly transferred the strawberry from his mouth to hers with a moist provocative thrust of his tongue. Jillian's eyes fluttered shut as a bolt of hot desire shot through her body, wringing her breath from her. She could barely chew and swallow for the nerve-tingling paralysis that overcame her.

She managed a deep shaky breath, and the ache eased ever so slightly. She couldn't handle the look of naked longing she knew she would see in his eyes. She melted against him, her strength sapped. She could sense him struggling for control, but this time it was beyond him. His arms came around her in a crushing embrace, and with an unleashed savagery he ground his mouth against hers as his need for release, suppressed for so long, burst forth into violent unchecked desire. His strong hands were rough yet oddly tender as he caressed her body with an urgency that could not be curbed.

His scalding kiss was sending a flame of liquid fire coursing through her veins as he trailed his mouth down her neck. She was without a will of her own as she arched against him, knowing only that he needed her, needed her desperately and she could deny him nothing, especially her heated trembling body.

A cold sliver of rationality penetrated her ardor-dulled mind. This once, he needed her to put on the brakes to the seething rampaging passion. This time, it was beyond his control. With a massive, almost desperate effort, she clung to him but somehow forced herself not to respond to his demanding hands.

Her voice was a hoarse ragged whisper, unrecognizable as her own. "I love you, Jacob—and I want you." Her arms tightened around him fiercely. "God, I want you, but you said you needed time and I promised to give you that." His arms tightened convulsively around her, and she caught his face in her unsteady hands. He resisted the pressure for a moment, then he slowly raised his head, his face twisted with an anguish that was appalling to see.

Tenderly she caressed the tight lines around his mouth. "I'm yours whenever you want me, Jacob; you know that, love. I can never commit myself to anyone but you."

He stared at her for a moment, then closed his eyes and whispered hoarsely, "I know that, babe." He rolled her beneath him, his breathing rough and uncontrolled as he held her tightly. "I'd kill any man who laid a hand on you."

His words of violence were somehow very comforting to Jillian. Time tempered their passion, and Jacob's body relaxed on top of hers. He caressed her cheek with his fingers, his voice thick and low. "I need to hold you, Jillian. I need to hold you the way I did last night."

Jillian answered him with her eyes. He kissed her, then eased his body away from hers. Silently she sat up and unabashedly shrugged her blouse from her shoulders. Jacob removed his shirt and dropped it on the floor, then stretched out his arms toward her. He pulled her down beside him and with a muffled curse cradled her firmly against him, her head snuggled against his shoulder. Jillian closed her eyes and tried to push away the feeling of uncertainty that nagged at her.

IT WAS LATE AFTERNOON when they finally awoke.

"Jillian, are you awake?"

"Yes."

"Do you know what time it is?"

Jillian cuddled closer to him, unwilling to move from the intimate circle of his arms. "No, and I don't care."

Jacob laughed as he hooked his knuckles under her chin and raised her face. "Would it mean anything if I said we missed the rehearsal?"

"No."

"Would it mean anything if I said we had less than an hour till show time?"

That provoked a response from Jill, even though it was a disgruntled one. She swore as she reluctantly lifted her head and looked with obvious distaste at the clock on the bedside table. With a groan she lay down and stretched lazily against him.

"Damn it. Do you think they'd miss us if we didn't show?"

Jacob hugged her and chuckled. "Perhaps, perhaps not." He held her for a while longer, then with a sigh of regret shook her gently, his voice firm. "Come on, Jillian Lambert, up and at 'em."

She started to roll away but was stopped short. There was a touch of smugness in her voice as she replied, "I can't. You're lying on my hair."

"Woman!" He raised them both into a sitting position, then swept her hair into a reasonably tidy fall down her back. As he kissed the curve of her shoulder Jillian couldn't suppress a little shiver of pleasure. Jacob caressed her naked back, then leaned against the headboard, his hands laced behind his head. His eyes narrowed as he grinned. "Now, my lovely, get dressed."

Jillian threw him an impudent look in an attempt to disguise her fluster. "And what are you going to do while I'm dressing?"

Jacob smiled a slow suggestive smile that did nothing to calm Jillian's rioting senses. "I'm going to watch."

That night, Firefly put on performances that were so charged, so electrifying that they literally stunned the audience. The sexual voltage that crackled between Jacob and Jillian was so intense that every single person in the audience was aware of it. Their harmonies were so pure and their timing was so exact it was almost uncanny. Jillian was singing for Jacob, and everyone from the bartender to Norm knew it.

But later that night, Jillian found the drawing pad on the floor beside her bed. Two sheets were missing, their removal leaving jagged raw edges that stirred a feeling of dread within her.

JILLIAN FLOATED THROUGH the following days in a haze of happiness. She was breathtakingly radiant, and Jacob seemed mesmerized by her. He was relaxed and easy, openly possessive of her in a protective, demonstrative manner that exhilarated her. There was a new vitality between them, and neither one of them gave a damn who knew it.

The momentum of Firefly never slackened, and their performances were receiving fantastic reviews. Consequently their reputation as top-flight performers was spreading like wildfire, and they were playing to packed houses every night of the week.

This night was no exception. The customers nearly brought the house down with a thundering ovation after the last set. Jillian and Jacob were so engrossed in each other as the curtain swept shut that they were completely unaware of the audience's response to their final encore.

Jillian had been leaning against the piano at the conclusion of a particularly provocative love song. Jacob reached out and caught one of her hands, and without taking his eyes off her he slowly, sensuously kissed the palm of her hand. She laid her hand on his jaw, then gently traced its outline with the tips of her fingers. The gesture spoke volumes. Neither one of them was remotely aware of the impact it had had on the audience until they walked into the lounge, where they were greeted by noisy, enthusiastic applause and loud cheers of approval. Jillian blushed as Jacob repeated the gesture, only this time his eyes were dancing with devilment. The audience loved it; but then, so did she.

They joined the others at the crowded, noisy Firefly table. Jillian waited for Jacob to position his wheelchair at the end of the table, then slipped into the low comfortable chair beside him. Allan and John were among the others, as was Karin, who had stayed on for a while after the family reunion. Jillian smiled softly as she glanced across the table at her friend. Norm and Karin were crowded together in the corner of the booth, apparently unaware of the crush or the commotion of voices around them. God, but she hoped that there was untainted happiness ahead for them both.

Right from the beginning it had been obvious that there was a powerful attraction between Karin and Norm, but both of them had been very cautious about any involvement. They had each suffered so much that they were wary about exposing themselves to further disillusionment and pain, but a profound trust was obviously developing, eradicating the doubts and uncertainties. They had been together constantly the past few days, and Jillian couldn't believe the change in each of them. Norm had shed years, had lost the lonely tortured look that had etched his face with such grim lines. And Karin— there were no words that could adequately describe the glow of happiness that enveloped her.

"Do you want a drink, babe?"

She rested her hand on the padded armrest of his wheelchair as she looked at him and shook her head, "No, thanks, Jacob."

He slipped his hand under her hair, and she shivered as he leisurely began to massage the nape of her neck. He grinned at her lazily, his fingers caressing as he ran his hand down her spine with tormenting slowness. She sighed and closed her eyes as his touch worked its special brand of magic.

Jillian felt herself blush when she opened her eyes and found Norm watching them, a knowing, amused look on his face. She quickly averted her eyes and unconsciously fingered the pendant. Her breath caught when she realized that Jacob was watching her with absorbed interest. Deliberately she let the pendant slip through her fingers. Jacob watched with intense fascination as the locket crept slowly down her bare skin to the soft swell of her breasts until it was hidden from view by the neckline of her dress.

The others were deep in conversation, so only Norm was aware of the current that flowed between them, and he was watching with obvious appreciation and delight. His grin broadened as he draped his arm around Karin's shoulder.

"Knowing soul that I am, I predict that we are going to have A-1 performances from now on." All eyes focused on him. His eyes danced sagaciously as he raised his drink in a mock salute to Jacob and Jillian.

Jacob grinned and tipped his head in acknowledgment, then he turned and rested his arms on the table, his fingers trailing across the wildly beating pulse in Jillian's wrist. "Go and change, babe," he said. "We're going for a drive." He caught her hand as she stood up. "Would you please bring me another shirt?" She started to walk away but he held onto her hand, his eyes flashing. "And, Jillian, you will get completely dressed, won't you?"

The night before, she had changed into a deep blue wraparound dress before they left the hotel to go over to her apartment. As she walked back through the lounge, Jacob had had a strange feeling she had very little on underneath. He had found out later that he had been right, and she knew intuitively that it had nearly driven him crazy.

She winked at him, then walked away, her hips gently swaying.

His car had been waiting for them when they arrived at the front of the hotel. Jacob stripped off his tan vest and orange satin shirt and tossed them in the back seat as soon as he got in. He slipped into the shirt she'd brought, opened the sunroof and the windows, then reached for her. "Come here."

She curled across him, her head on his shoulder, her breasts pressed intimately against his bare chest. As she did so he looked down into her sparkling green eyes, his voice softly threatening. "Damn you."

She looked up at him, her expression innocent. "Why?"

"Jillian, you are not completely dressed!"

"I didn't think you'd notice."

He flashed her a wicked smile as he ran his hand under her top and caressed her naked breasts. "Like hell!" He put the car in gear and pulled onto the nearly deserted street.

Her laugh was husky. "One of these nights you're

going to get stopped for having me draped all over you.''

He pulled up at a red light and bent his head to give her a long thirsty kiss. She was breathless and trembling by the time the light turned green.

''Let's go to the apartment, Jacob.''

''Jillian, I want to talk to you tonight, and you know damned well we do very little talking at the apartment.''

''We talk, love. It's called body language.''

He laughed and very deliberately put both hands on the steering wheel. ''Yes, and what conversations!''

They drove on, wrapped in a warm silence, the night air cool and refreshing. They had a satisfying number of red lights before Jacob pulled the car off the road onto a viewpoint that overlooked the city. He switched off the engine and the lights, then slid his seat back. His arms came around her, holding her fast against him as his mouth moved over hers with a tantalizing softness.

He eased his grip on her and unwillingly lifted his head as he felt her warm response to his searching kiss. Sighing heavily, he pressed her face against his chest and began to stroke her hair. There was an air of brooding introspection about him that made Jillian feel slightly uneasy, and she felt suddenly cold as she tentatively touched his lips with her fingers.

''What's wrong, Jacob?''

He didn't answer but his arms tightened around her, his embrace communicating an inner turmoil.

She caught his face in her hands, her eyes perplexed. ''Jacob?''

He sighed, his voice clipped and unsteady. ''Jillian, do you know all the reasons why I left five years ago?"

Jillian tensed as a heavy knot of uncertainty and dread settled in her belly. So...the time had come to face the cold and unpleasant past.

She took a shaky breath, her voice very low. "You left because you thought I would come to resent your disability and you didn't want me to be tied to a man in a wheelchair." She pressed her face against his chest and closed her eyes tightly against the feeling of catastrophe that was growing within her.

Jacob rested his face on top of her head, his voice ragged with anguish. "That was part of it, Jillian. But there was something else...."

Suddenly she was unable to tolerate the despair she recognized in his voice. She knew what he was about to tell her, and she realized the confession would be hell for him. "Jacob, I know that Dr. Paulson told you that your paralysis might be psychosomatic."

She felt him stiffen and raised her head to look at him, but his face was unreadable in the dusk. His hand closed on her shoulder, his grip painfully rough. "How did you know that?"

There was such a band of fear in her chest that she could barely whisper. "When you left, Allan was certain you had been told something that influenced your decision." She swallowed nervously, then continued. "He thought perhaps you had developed a tumor and didn't want anyone to know. He managed to see your medical records—"

"And he told you." The chilling ring of anger in Jacob's voice frightened Jillian. She moved back onto the passenger seat and leaned against the dashboard of the car, her hands clasped together. The glow from the distant streetlight slanted through the windshield and cast her pale face in its muted light.

"Yes, he told me."

The silence was grinding, oppressive, and it raked along Jillian's taut nerves.

When Jacob finally spoke, his voice was heavy with bitterness. "Well, Jillian, what was your reaction when you found out—didn't you feel repulsed?"

There was something about his cutting brittleness that fired Jillian's temper and she flared at him, her voice seething. "Did you think I was so shallow that I would find that repulsive, Jacob? Did you honestly think that I would view psychosomatic paralysis as a weakness, a flaw in your masculinity?"

She saw him wince as his hands tightened on the steering wheel. "I was so hurt, so bewildered after you left that nothing mattered—nothing. I didn't give a damn whether I lived or died. It seemed as if my life had become an awful, torturous, never ending nightmare. It was bad enough when I realized you believed I would resent your being crippled, but when you actually left, when you disappeared out of my life because you doubted me, it damned near killed me, Jacob!"

The old pain and agony came boiling back with such a power that she felt as though she was being ripped apart. She couldn't stand it; she had to escape. She fumbled blindly for the door handle, unable to see for the torrent of tears that was streaming down her face.

Jacob's arm shot out and caught her around the waist. Roughly he dragged her onto his lap, his arms crushing her against him in a brutal embrace. She tried to struggle free but his hold was unrelenting.

"Don't, Jillian. Don't cry," he whispered hoarse-ly. His fingers were trembling as he tenderly wiped away her tears with the palm of his hand. "God, I'm sorry, babe. I didn't mean to lash out at you."

His words were fused with such regret and such heartfelt misery that Jillian's anger gave way to shame for her angry outburst. She raised her head and with infinite tenderness kissed him softly on the mouth. He shuddered, his arms tightening around her as his mouth moved hungrily against hers. Then he caught her face with his hand and pressed her head against his shoulder as he took a deep shaky breath.

"Ah, Jillian, I lose my senses when you kiss me like that. . . I can't think straight. And I have to talk to you tonight, babe. I have some explaining to do."

She turned her head slightly and kissed the strong curve of his jaw. "About what?"

He sighed as he ran his fingers through her hair, his hand cradling the back of her head. "I've been living in a kind of hell these last few days; I just didn't know how to tell you about Paulson's diag-nosis. I've been dreading telling you—and I never once considered the possibility that you might already know. It never entered my head." He kissed her gently on the forehead, then sighed again. "When Paulson told me that he wanted me to see a psychiatrist, it was the last straw. I simply couldn't face that—it seemed like a kick in the gut when I was already down. I couldn't accept it, Jillian, nor could I face the ordeal of having to tell you and my family, so I bolted."

"Jacob—"

"Shh, babe," he whispered softly. "I need you to listen." He stroked her temple with his thumb as he continued, "I read about a clinic in Israel that's developed quite a reputation for its psychological treatment of disabled veterans."

Jillian lay quietly in his arms as he told her about the clinic and why he felt the treatment was optimistic. "I'm making arrangements to go, Jillian. It's my only hope."

He didn't speak for a moment, and Jillian experienced a nagging feeling of trepidation. She stirred uneasily in his arms, but he didn't seem to notice. "I talked to Allan about it yesterday and he said he'd give me all the assistance he could. But he felt it would be wise if I had a thorough neurological examination done on my spine first." He lifted her face and looked down at her with solemn eyes. "I'm being admitted this morning for the tests, Jillian."

The feeling of trepidation gave way to cold hard fear as Jillian stared up at him, her face drawn. "Jacob, what if...?"

Jacob kissed her parted lips and forced a fleeting smile that didn't quite reach his eyes. "I'm not going to do any second-guessing, Jillian." His face grew sober as he traced his finger across her lips. "Allan said I would be in the hospital two or three days...."
He hesitated for a brief moment, then went on, his voice firm. "Jillian, I want you to do me a favor."

"Anything, love."

"I want you to promise me that you won't come to the hospital while I'm there."

"But, Jacob—"

"It's going to be a bad time for me, babe, and God knows, I've hurt you enough already."

She caught his face in her hands, her eyes imploring. "I know it's going to be difficult—that's precisely why I should be there...."

Jacob looked at her, his eyes filled with warm tenderness. "No, Jillian—please, babe, I have to do this on my own."

She closed her eyes and rested her forehead against his jaw as she fought down the urge to reason with him, knowing full well that if she pressed the issue he would only withdraw from her.

He hooked his thumb under her chin and forced her head up. He didn't say anything, but his eyes were asking her to yield to his request. She looked at him for a long time, then reluctantly nodded her head.

He smiled at her softly as he slowly brushed a wisp of hair from her face. "Thank you, Jillian."

Her eyes were glistening with unshed tears as she begged, "Don't doubt me, Jacob."

He bracketed her face with his hands, his eyes steady and unwavering as he met her gaze. "I don't, Jillian. You are the one certainty in my life." He stroked her damp cheeks with his thumbs, then closed his eyes, his face twisted with a grimace of anguish as he embraced her fiercely. "God, you're more than that—you're my weakness, my addiction, and I need you, Jillian. God, how I need you." He buried his face in her hair and Jillian hung onto him as her tears coursed down her face.

They remained wrapped in each other's arms, each of them drawing strength from the other, until the sky turned pink with the false dawn.

The skyline of Edmonton lay before them as the rising sun caressed the clouds with tinges of pink and mauve that soon blazed into a passion of flaming orange and red. Far below them, the river caught fire with the reflected light and a flock of pigeons rose up, their glistening wings touched with amber as they swooped toward the sun. The fiery sphere crept above the horizon, washing the silver gray cubes of the towering office buildings with a blaze of glory as they burst into reflected flame.

Jillian turned her head to look at Jacob, her breath catching in her throat. In the glow of dawn he looked like a pagan god cast in bronze. "God, you're magnificent," she breathed.

Words were beyond Jacob as he looked down at her, at her shadowed face framed in the molten gold of her hair. He groaned as he clasped her in an embrace that bordered on desperation. It would be a picture that he would carry in his mind until the end of time.

EVEN THOUGH it was mid-afternoon, Jillian was in the coffee shop finishing her lunch when Norm entered. He raised his hand in a friendly salute when he spotted her, then weaved his way through the scattered tables.

He grinned at her as he slid into the chair opposite her. "Where have you been? I've been looking all over for you."

She blushed slightly and laughed. "I just staggered out of bed a little while ago."

"What happened to Jillian, the early bird?"

"The early bird died young," she responded dryly.

Norm stripped the cellophane wrapping off a new package of cigarettes and wadded it up. "I wondered how long you'd last." He opened the cigarettes and offered Jillian one. She shook her head. After lighting one for himself he leaned back in his chair and exhaled slowly. "Jillian, are you worried about these tests of Jacob's?"

She laid her napkin on her plate and pushed it away, then rested her arms on the table. Her face was very solemn as she looked at him. "I am feeling apprehensive about it; he's avoided this for five years, Norm. I'm afraid it's going to be difficult for Jacob to accept the results, no matter what they are."

Norm sighed as he leaned forward and hunched over the table, his face perplexed. "He told me the whole story yesterday when he explained why he was going into the hospital." He twirled the butt of his cigarette against the rim of the ashtray. "This waiting must be hell for you."

"It is."

"Are you going up to see him today?"

"No, he asked me not to."

Norm reached across the table and covered her hand with his, his touch reassuring. "Hang in there, Jill."

She smiled at him ruefully. "I will." There was a brief silence, then she questioned softly, "Can I do a little prying, Mr. Kent?"

He turned his head to face her and cocked one eyebrow. "About what?"

"About Karin."

He smiled at Jillian, his eyes dancing. "Are you afraid I might corrupt her?"

Jillian laughed and shook her head. "I don't care if you corrupt her or not—you're making her happy, and that's what matters."

Norm's face sobered abruptly and he butted his

cigarette, his expression contemplative. "Do you think that I can really make her happy?"

There was no doubt about the depth of concern in that question. Jillian's smile was one of genuine sincerity. "Yes, I do."

"There's a seventeen-year age difference, you know."

"Does that worry you?"

"A little."

"Has Karin told you that there's a fifteen-year age difference between her mother and father?"

Norm nodded, his brow creased with a troubled frown. Jillian's eyes were glimmering with suppressed amusement as she added softly, "I don't think that concern is going to carry much weight with Karin, Norm."

"Maybe not, but if we were to have kids, I'd be sixty years old when they're in their teens."

Jillian propped her chin on her hands and considered Norm's reasoning, then shrugged slightly. "Mike Holinski managed beautifully. The question is, are you planning on being an old sixty or a young sixty?"

Norm's taut face relaxed into a lopsided grin. "You don't argue rationally, you know."

She smiled at him. "That's your fault. Your concerns weren't rational ones to begin with." Her face grew serious. "There's one very important question that I don't think you've asked yourself, Norm. Could you really let her go—could you bring yourself to hurt her by walking away from her now?"

Norm stared at Jillian, then slowly shook his head. "No," he said, toying with the ashtray on the table for a moment. Then he lifted his head, his eyes dark and intense. "What was her husband like?"

Jillian sighed as she stretched out in her chair. "He was handsome, charming, clever, witty. An only child, and his parents were extremely wealthy. He always got everything he wanted—and he definitely wanted Karin." She smiled crookedly when she saw the grim, set look on Norm's face. "But he was also irresponsible, self-centered, extremely jealous of her and, toward the end, unbelievably cruel. He nearly destroyed her before she left him, and she's disillusioned and very, very wary because of it."

"Do you think she'll ever get over it?"

Jillian smiled warmly and touched his hand. "She's already over it, thanks to you, Norm Kent."

"You know she's flying back to Vancouver today?" Norm's face was unreadable.

"Yes, I know. But I also have a very strong hunch that she's going to be coming back."

Norm didn't say anything for a moment, but when he spoke, his voice was husky. "Yes, she's coming back."

Jillian felt slightly comforted. At least there was happiness on the horizon for Norm and Karin.

FOR JILLIAN THE WAITING was very nearly unbearable. Each hour seemed longer than the last, and with each passing moment the feeling of apprehension and isolation grew within her, gnawing at her calm facade. The time inched by and she felt more and more lost and alone. The nights were the worst, for her nightmare reoccurred with ominous predictability, impaling her synthetic confidence with its hellish reality.

By the third day of Jacob's hospitalization she was edgy from tension and exhaustion and very much dreading the thought of another performance without him. She had spent most of the day wandering restlessly around the hotel, unable to convince herself that she was overreacting.

Finally she sought the sanctuary of the sitting room and made a concentrated effort to pull herself together before the show. For a while she stared out the window at the dark heavy clouds that were rolling in from the west with menacing swiftness. The weather certainly didn't do much for her present mood.

"Jillian?"

She turned around to find Norm standing in the doorway, and she experienced a twist of uneasiness when she realized his expression was one of anxiety.

"Is there something wrong, Norm?"

"Have you heard from Jacob today?" His voice was strained and uncommonly brusque.

Suddenly she felt as though she was suffocating. "No. Why?"

Norm swore as he came toward her. "I just phoned the hospital, Jillian—I wanted to check on Jacob. They told me he had discharged himself early this morning."

Jillian could feel the blood drain from her face as her stomach contracted into a hard knot of dread. She sank down on the sofa, her legs weak beneath her.

Norm sat down beside her, his arms resting across his knees. "I tried to contact Allan but I was told he's in surgery all day." His eyes were full of concern as he looked at her ashen face. "I left a message for him to call."

Jillian closed her eyes and shivered with a sudden piercing cold. Norm took her hand in his. She opened her eyes and gave him a twisted smile. "Then I guess we'll just have to wait, won't we, Norm?"

She never knew how she managed to make it through the performances that evening. The curtain had barely closed on the last song before she was off the stage. She took several deep breaths and forced herself to walk calmly through the lounge, but as soon as she was down the ramp she flew to the elevators. Her heart pounded crazily as she dashed into one as the door was sliding shut. The elevator moved with agonizing slowness up to her floor. She squeezed through the elevator door before it was fully open, grabbed up the skirt of her dress and ran down the corridor, bursting into the sitting room. She reached Jacob's door and swung it open.

The room was empty. Where was he? She went to the phone and with fingers stiff with fear dialed the number to her apartment. It was late but she simply had to talk to Allan.

She let it ring several times; there was no answer. With a feeling of rising panic she replaced the receiver in the cradle and left Jacob's room, her mind swimming in a fog. She opened the door to her own room, her motions trancelike, her mind not registering.

"Hello, Jillian." Allan was standing by her bed, his hands rammed into the pockets of his jeans, his face drawn and worried.

"Where is he?" Her voice was tight and scared.

Allan hesitated. When he finally spoke, his voice was strangely passive. "I don't know."

"Don't lie to me, Allan. Don't, for the love of God." She was shaking so much she could barely whisper.

"I'm not lying."

She sat down weakly on the edge of the bed and stared up at her brother. "What happened?"

Allan sighed heavily, then slumped into the chair by the desk. "It was a bad scene, Jillian."

"Tell me." It was a quiet yet desperate command.

Allan sighed again, then looked at her. "We did a myelogram and x-rayed his spine, using all the current techniques." His face was an expressionless mask, and Jillian's carefully nurtured optimism withered. That look meant bad news.

"We found a minute bone fragment sequestered in the spinal cord. It had migrated through the sheath and abscessed, leaving a thin wall of scar tissue around it."

"Then Paulson did miss something." Jillian's thoughts were confused and disjointed. "But I don't understand, Allan—you expected to find something like that."

Allan went to the window and stared out. "That's the problem, Jillian—it wasn't there before."

Jillian looked up at him sharply, her forehead creased with a bewildered frown. "What are you saying?"

"We went back over every single X ray that had been taken of Jacob's back—and then we went over them again, and again. There wasn't one single indication of a bone chip in any one of them." He rubbed his eyes with his hand, his shoulders slumping with exhaustion. "My theory is that the fragment was lodged against the vertebra. The reason it didn't show up when Jacob was injured was because the radiologist neglected to do an oblique-angle X ray— it wasn't standard procedure then. When we did one of Jacob this time, we could see where the fragment had splintered off the vertebra.''

"Allan, I don't understand. . . .''

He turned to face her, his eyes full of misery. "The chip was caught in the space between the vertebrae and the actual spinal cord. It was harmless, Jillian, or it would have been if it had been detected immediately. When extensive therapy was begun on Jacob, the only damage to his spinal cord was the hematoma. That's all—nothing else. The records prove that. The therapy shifted the fragment and it slowly penetrated the outer sheath of the nerves—that probably accounted for the extreme pain Jacob experienced during therapy. This type of migration doesn't happen overnight; it would take several months.''

The grim facts finally began to register and Jillian's eyes widened with horror. An ugly sickness swelled within her as the ghastly reality of what had happened finally penetrated her numb mind.

She stared at Allan as she groped for clarification. "Are you telling me that up until therapy was started on Jacob, his paralysis was caused by the bruising—and that that healed without any permanent damage?''

"Yes.''

"And during the therapy, the fragment was slowly injected into the spinal cord, causing permanent paralysis?''

"That's exactly what I'm saying.''

Jillian felt as though she was going to be ill. This couldn't be happening. It couldn't be happening! Her lips were stiff, her body frozen by shock. "Would the doctors have been able to remove the fragment if they had detected it six years ago?''

Allan stared at her for a long time, then he slowly exhaled, his voice clipped with suppressed anger. "It was so small that it could easily have been fished out between the vertebrae."

"Oh, God!" she groaned as she buried her face in her hands. It was such a cruel, sadistic twist of fate. Silence hung in the room, suspended by the unyielding and tragic facts.

Jillian dropped her hands, looked at Allan and whispered raggedly, "Jacob...how did he...?"

"It was pretty bad for him." Allan began pacing back and forth, his face set. "When I told him that we'd discovered a small bone splinter embedded in his spinal cord, he seemed almost relieved. I was going to leave it at that—I couldn't see any reason to dump the whole story on him now. One of the doctors from occupational medicine did a thorough evaluation of his condition, and he felt that Jacob had enough strength in his hips and upper thighs to be successfully fitted with braces. Jacob responded very positively to that idea—it would give him considerably more mobility."

"What happened? Who told him...?"

"I don't know what made him suspicious—whether an intern inadvertently said something or if he just started to piece together several unanswered questions. Anyway, he went down to see the radiologist who had done his spinal workup and questioned him about the old X rays. Dr. Mah tried to sidestep his queries, but Jacob became very persistent. Mah called me down when Jacob finally demanded to see his old X rays, and we had to level with him then."

"What did he say?"

"He just stared at me with the coldest look I've

ever seen and said, 'I see.' I tried to talk to him but he asked me to leave.'' Allan sat down in the chair and folded his arms across his chest. ''I stopped in to see him this morning before I started surgery, but he was sleeping. He'd had a rough night after the myelogram—he developed a pressure headache from it, and they can be damned near unbearable—and I don't imagine he slept much last night. Anyway, I didn't want to wake him. I thought I would have a chance to talk to him when I came out of surgery.''

Jillian was beginning to feel very frightened, and she twisted her hands tightly together in an odd defensive way. ''Where can he be?''

''I don't have a clue, Jillian—he's not at John's and I've checked all the hotels.''

Her throat was so constricted that she could barely speak. ''Do you think he's disappeared again?''

Allan crouched down in front of her, pried her hands apart and held them in his. ''I don't think so. Norm checked his room—all his stuff is still there—and then he drove out to the airport tonight to see if he could spot Jacob's car. It wasn't there.'' He squeezed Jillian's hands reassuringly. ''We're almost certain that he hasn't left the city.''

Jillian wished she shared their confidence, but a foreboding sense of uncertainty was twisted around her heart.

SHE DIDN'T LEAVE the suite the following day, hoping against hope that he would come back. Norm came into the sitting room about an hour before show time and sat down in the chair beside her. He winced when he saw the white mask of her face, a face that had been so vibrant such a short time before.

"Jill?"

"Yes." Her voice was brittle, controlled.

"You're going to have to work solo tonight, kid. David's voice is in bad shape again. Okay?"

"Yes."

He reached out to take her hand, then changed his mind and clasped his hands together. "Jillian—" his voice was edged with uncertainty, but he heaved a deep sigh and continued "—I think tomorrow we're going to have to start revamping the program. We'll have to start working on some new material."

She looked at him pointedly. "New songs for a female soloist." It wasn't a question but a flat toneless statement.

"Yes."

"May I have a cigarette, please?" Norm lighted one and handed it to her. Jillian took a deep drag and lay back as the dizzying light-headedness swirled through her. "You've heard from him, haven't you? He won't be back, will he, Norm?"

"I don't know. When he phoned he said not to expect him." She looked at him with expressionless eyes, and he swore violently under his breath. He knew that all Jillian's emotions were suppressed behind an icy wall. He hoped for her sake that the wall didn't crumble.

"Come on, kid. It's nearly show time."

Jillian's professionalism carried her through the evening. They were halfway through the last program when her senses started to tingle. She scanned the darkness, and her breath caught as she saw shards of light reflected from stainless steel. She knew that it was Jacob's wheelchair.

He was gone when they finished the act. Jillian

flew upstairs, her blood pounding through her veins in a mixture of dread and anticipation. She paused briefly in front of Jacob's door, then tried the knob. It was locked.

She rested her head against the door frame, her body trembling with relief. He was back. Now what?

She managed to get back into her room and into bed before her strength deserted her. She spent another sleepless night listening for sounds from the next room.

It was midmorning before she gathered together enough courage to approach his room. Her face ashen, she knocked on the door, her eyes hollow with fear.

"Come in."

Jillian's heart stopped its wild racing at the sound of his voice and began to beat with certain, slow dread. She felt as though she was wading through deep water, for she knew with cold certainty that it would not be a warm and loving Jacob that she faced.

Nor was it.

He was sitting in his wheelchair at the far end of the room, his face gray and unyielding. "Sit down, Jillian." It was a command. She sank into the chair by the desk, her eyes never leaving his face.

"Jacob...." Her voice was strained and quiet. He stared at her and she shrank inwardly at what she saw there.

"I've a few things to say, Jillian, and it isn't going to be pleasant. But I want you to listen, anyway, and I don't want you to interrupt. Do you understand?" His voice was so cold.

She nodded mutely.

"I had a very illuminating consultation with the doctors, Jillian." The sarcasm was thick, brutal and ugly. "But I imagine Allan told you all about the chain of events." He paused and stared at the floor for a long time, then continued, his voice a snarl of anger. "It was not quite what I had expected to hear—to find out that the permanent damage was incurred *after* the accident." He looked at her, his eyes flashing with barely controlled rage. "It wasn't exactly comforting to find out that it wasn't an accident that crippled me but monumental irresponsibility."

He gave Jillian an icy stare as she opened her mouth to speak. "Don't try to patronize me, Jillian. This isn't a bag of garbage that you can neatly dispose of. If I resented being crippled before, I sure in hell am going to resent it far more now."

The anger and pain in his voice knifed through Jillian, and he twisted that knife viciously when he sneered, "Can't you understand, Jillian? Can't you grasp it? If I had had a proper medical examination I wouldn't be sitting in this damned wheelchair now!" In a burst of hatred and violence he slammed his fist into the frame of the wheelchair. This display shook Jillian to the core, for she had never in her entire life witnessed that kind of reaction from him.

"Jacob, please listen—"

"You listen, Jillian—for God's sake, listen to what I'm saying!" He clenched his hands into white-knuckled fists. "I could have been standing here on my own two feet, and my life wouldn't seem like a never ending desert of emptiness and futility."

He looked at her, his eyes burning and intense. "I'm a physical person. I need to hold, to touch, to feel. Do you have any idea what I would give to be able to hold you in my arms and dance with you just once more in my life? I can never, never again have you walk into my arms. I miss all that. I miss it like hell, and when I'm around you it's damned near unbearable. If I didn't want you the way I do, it wouldn't mean so damned much to me.'' His face was twisted with contempt as, at long last, the bitterness, the frustration, the resentment came boiling out.

"Oh, yes—I love you, Jillian, and God knows I want you, but I can't have you the way I want you, when I want you. Every physical contact has to be neatly calculated and arranged. Seldom can it be spontaneous. It's driving me crazy. I feel like some kind of trapped animal that's being tormented with a glimpse of freedom. I hate having restrictions and limitations imposed on me.

"I found I could cope with my disability, accept it to a degree, when I left you. I was living in a hell of loneliness—you were on my mind constantly. It was a torture of the most excruciating kind, but, by God, it's worse when I'm around you.'' He stared at her, his gaze fixed.

Jillian moved to go to him, but he stopped her cold. "No!'' He took a deep breath. "You come any closer and I'll leave.'' But his voice had lost some of the intensity.

"In time I would crush you, destroy you, break you. I hate what I'm doing to you now, but I know what I'm capable of. I can't change the way I am, the way I feel. I've tried. God, how I've tried.'' His face was twisted into a grimace forged by agony. His voice was desperate. "I can't justify what I'm doing to you, Jillian. I just know I have to.'' Then he stopped.

His eyes were like knives, his voice suddenly deadly. "It's finished, Jillian. I'm going back to California just as soon as Norm can get a replacement for me, and under no circumstances will I ever see you again."

Jillian sat in paralyzed silence.

"It isn't going to be easy. It's going to be the same agony all over again, but I can't go on this way. Can't you see, Jillian? It isn't you I doubt. It's myself. I resent what's happened to me—and I think there are times when I could come to hate you as passionately as I love you."

He saw the unbearable pain in her face but went on relentlessly. "I'm positive of that." His voice was a tense whisper. "It's either destroy you later or leave you now."

With that, he rolled out of the room and closed the door firmly behind him.

CHAPTER TWELVE

THE TENSION SPREAD like a cancer.

Moment by moment, hour by hour, Jillian drove herself through the following nightmarish days with a will born of desperation. She pushed herself to the extreme edge of her physical limits and was balanced tenuously on the brink of her personal breaking point. She seldom slept and rarely ate. Her acute wretchedness gave her an air of fragility that was alarming to everyone close to her. Her face was etched with a tortured look; her singing projected her despair with a throbbing haunting quality. Jillian was on the verge of shattering and everyone knew it.

Jacob alienated himself from everyone with a cold impenetrable determination, his face rigid with bitterness, his eyes steeled with hostility. He attended rehearsals and performances but sealed himself off from any other association. He wanted contact with no one and erected a barrier that was unbridgeable.

Jacob's and Jillian's personal ordeal created an immense strain for everyone associated with Firefly, but they handled it with a professional detachment that was admirable. They were turning out performances of the highest caliber and were building a spectacular reputation. They were on their way, but their success was based on Jacob's musical genius and Jillian's ability to deliver. It was an uncertain foundation, to say the least, and they knew that, too.

Allan was obviously worried about Jillian. It didn't take a physician's eye to see that she was functioning on sheer willpower alone. She absolutely refused to talk about what had happened or what Jacob had said to her in their final encounter, but it was apparent she had been decimated by it. She had moved back to the apartment and she spent as little time as possible at the hotel, but even that disassociation didn't relax her stiff reclusion.

Allan was finally able to arrange his schedule at the hospital so he had the weekend free. It took considerable coaxing to persuade Jillian to go to the farm with him. They would be able to spend only Sunday and part of Monday there, but he was certain she desperately needed the break. Allan could understand her reluctance, but he knew he had to get her away before she collapsed under the strain.

When he phoned home to tell his parents that they were coming, his mother had told him that Sylvia, Ken and the boys had gone to Regina for a few days. He was relieved about that, even though he felt slightly guilty about it—Jillian didn't need a crowd of people around her now.

He had assured Jillian that he wouldn't tell their parents what had happened, but he'd said that only to keep her from worrying about it. He had every intention of confiding in his father, who had a special talent for being able to put any situation into a commonsense perspective. His mother, on the other hand, would be terribly upset if she found out what had happened. Jacob's tragic accident and his disappearance had hit her very hard; she loved him like a son.

Jillian was packing with little enthusiasm and a certain amount of dread. She had refused to go home with Allan until he promised that nothing would be said about the break in her relationship with Jacob. Her acquiescence had been practically wrung out of her—the thought of trying to erect a facade of normality left her feeling spent and lethargic. She simply had no desire to try to appear bright and relaxed. She didn't want to see anyone, didn't want to talk to anyone; she simply wanted to hide from the world.

Closing her small suitcase, she carried it into the living room and silently handed it to Allan. He took it, then opened the door, his face set with concern as she walked ahead of him, her bearing one of a lifeless mannequin. The effort, he knew, was costing her a terrible price. It was obvious she was nearly exhausted.

By the time they hit Highway 16, Jillian had fallen into a deep untroubled slumber. She slept until they swung into the Lambert drive three hours later, and Allan shook her gently. Then she adjusted the reclining seat into an upright position and brushed a few wisps of hair from her face. Shivering slightly, she shook her head.

"You really crashed, Jillian. Feeling better?"

"I feel as if someone slipped me a Mickey Finn! You didn't doctor my coffee this morning, did you?"

"Nope—not that it didn't cross my mind."

She smiled ruefully and pulled her heavy sweater around herself as she shivered again. It was such a gloomy overcast day, the sky a dense washed-out gray.

Allan followed a gravel road that curved around the "big house" and wound through a thick stand of willows, birch and spruce. When Ken and Sylvia married, the senior Lamberts had built a neat attractive bungalow in a picturesque secluded corner of the yard. The arrangement had worked very well for everyone, for Cora and Bill Lambert made a point of never interfering in the lives of their children.

Jillian stumbled slightly as she climbed out of the car. She still felt half-asleep—listless and drained, as if her body weighed a ton. She was so damned tired.

As they entered the house Allan called out, "Your darlings have arrived!"

"I'm here, kids." Bill Lambert was in the kitchen hunched over his untidy desk, his pipe clenched in his teeth, a pile of horse magazines spread out before him. He rocked back in his chair, balancing his weight on the two back legs as he grinned up at them. "Wasn't expecting you for another hour or so. Mother's just gone into town to church."

Allan pushed some of the magazines aside and sat down on the corner of the desk. "We got away earlier than we expected, and there was hardly any traffic. We wanted to catch you loafing."

Bill Lambert snorted. "Cheeky brat." He grinned at his son with open affection, then caught Jillian's hand, pulled her down and kissed her soundly on the cheek. "You're looking kind of pale, honey. Aren't you feeling well?"

Allan shot Jillian a quick glance as he intercepted his father's query. "I think she's been fighting the flu all week." He glanced up at his sister, his expression one of masked concern. "Why don't you go to bed, Jill? You look as though you could do with some more sleep."

Jillian looked down at her father and smiled weakly. "Would you mind if I crawled off in a corner, dad? I am feeling rather dopey and I know I'll have to have my wits about me if we play cards tonight."

Her father patted her hand. "Off you go. Can't have you falling asleep at the card table."

Jillian kissed his weathered cheek and hugged him. "Okay. I'll see you two later."

Allan watched her leave the kitchen, his face set in a worried frown. His father struck a wooden match on the heel of his boot and, holding the flame over the bowl of his pipe, slowly drew in on it. Then he rocked back in his chair again and looked at his son through a haze of blue swirling smoke.

"You never could lie worth a damn, Allan."

Allan shook his head and smiled ruefully. His face sobered as he looked at his father with serious eyes. "Dad, could we take a stroll down to the barn?"

Bill Lambert nodded his head and stood up. He scooped his battered Stetson off the lamp on his desk and stuffed his tobacco pouch in his back pocket as he turned toward the door. "Come on, son—I have some new horses I want to show off, anyhow."

They walked in silence along the winding path that snaked through the trees.

Bill Lambert puffed on his pipe, then spoke softly. "It's Jacob again, isn't it, Allan?"

"Yeah, dad. Damn it—"

The younger man's voice was husky, and his father, sensing his disquietude, draped a comforting arm around his shoulder. His voice was steady, reassuring. "Maybe you had better tell me all about it."

Allan coughed in an attempt to ease the tightness in his throat, then unburdened the whole miserable unhappy story, from Jacob's unexpected return to

Edmonton to his final cold and brutal withdrawal. By the time he'd finished they had reached the stable and were sitting in the tack room. Allan sat straddling an old wooden chair, his arms draped across the back. His father was sitting in a battered old rocker, his feet propped on an old crate, the smoke from his pipe encircling his head. The aroma of the burning tobacco subtly blended with the smell of oiled tack, saddle soap and the sweet dusty scent of dried hay and clover. Only the neighing of a horse and the sound of shod hooves prancing on a planked floor broke the silence.

Bill Lambert took the pipe from his mouth and studied his son. "How's Jacob?"

"Bitter, withdrawn, angry. He looks awful. Damn it, dad, I was caught in such a hell of a trap. Professionally I knew that Jacob had every right to know the truth, but privately I wish I had lied to him."

"You did the right thing, son. Maybe not the easiest but it was still right." Bill Lambert cradled his pipe in his hand, his arms folded across his chest. "And I think you're right about encouraging Jillian to move on with the band. New places, new people— I think it will be best for her."

"I hate to see her so badly hurt all over again. I wish to hell Jacob had never come back."

"Now, son, that's a pretty hard thing to say. It's his home, too, and from what you've told me, I have a feeling that Jacob would never have looked her up. He may have intended to, but I think when it came to the final crunch, he would have stayed away from her. It hasn't been easy for him, either. He's a gentle, caring person by nature, Allan, and I'll bet my bottom dollar he's going through his own private hell right now."

Allan sighed and stood up, then swung the chair away. "He is, dad. It's such a hell of a mess. I wish it could have worked out differently for both of them."

"It might yet; Jacob hasn't left. If he had really made up his mind, you know damned well he would have packed his bags and gone, band or no band."

Allan walked to the dust-covered window and stared out, his hands stuck in the hip pockets of his jeans. "I guess you're right. I just wish Jillian wasn't in such a state."

"She'll come through it, son. She's made of tough stuff. Her big problem now is that she's obviously exhausted—and she needs to dump a load of tension. But she will. She'll have a right old beauty of a temper tantrum or something, and that will clear the air." Bill Lambert tipped his hat back on his head and nursed his pipe as he contemplated the toes of his boots. "She's a lot like your mother, Jillian is. She loves hard and deep. There's nothing shallow or transparent about her. Her strength will get her through." He grinned at his son, his eyes twinkling. "One hell of a woman, your mother."

Allan turned and gave his father a straightforward look, his voice filled with respect. "And she married one hell of a man."

Bill's voice was gruff with emotion, but he grinned. "Nice to know you approve of the old man. Makes all those snotty noses seem worthwhile."

Allan laughed and slapped his father on the shoulder. "Come on, 'old man'—let's go look at those new horses that you probably spent my inheritance on."

Bill Lambert stood up, chuckling to himself as he

followed his son into the barn. "Brat," he said affectionately.

JILLIAN DIDN'T WAKE UP until late afternoon. Then she rolled over on her back, her hands tucked beneath her head as she stared unseeingly at the petit-point pictures of *Pinky* and *Blue Boy* that hung on the wall opposite the bed. She was feeling more relaxed than she had for some time, she realized, and she no longer felt as though she was coming unglued.

"Hello, pet. Awake at last."

Jillian smiled. "Hi, mom. Great company, aren't I?"

Her mother sat down on the edge of the bed and patted her daughter's hand in an age-old maternal gesture. "Just knowing you're in the house is nice."

Jillian regarded her mother with deep affection. The children had all inherited their mother's flamboyant coloring and her temper, but she had also endowed them with their natural musical ability.

"What time is it, mom?"

"Going on five. Allan and your father rode over to the west pasture to check the cattle, so they probably won't be back for supper until six." Cora Lambert studied her daughter. "You don't look well, dear, and you've certainly lost weight."

Jillian's voice was level as she looked directly at her mother and lied. "It's the hours. I've always been an early riser and it's an old habit that's hard to break."

"I suppose it would be difficult. How's Jacob?"

"He's fine."

Her mother gave her a quick look, then began to pleat the hem of her apron. "Jillian—"

Jillian squeezed her mother's hand, deliberately interrupting the intended question. "Mom, we're friends. That's all. You always told us kids that we could never go back in time—and we can't."

Cora sighed and patted her daughter's hand. "I know. I had so hoped. . . ." She leaned over, picked a thread off the carpet and rolled it into a ball between her fingers. She sighed again, then changed the topic. "Your father has been complaining that he never gets baking-powder biscuits anymore. Do you feel like whipping up a batch for supper?"

Surprisingly, she did.

The evening was like a reprieve from hell for Jillian. After supper they played a cutthroat version of canasta that left Allan and his father howling with pain and licking their considerable wounds. Jillian and her mother were a murderous team. After that, Jillian worked for a while on a rug her mother was hooking, then went to bed and slept again, undisturbed by the terrifying nightmare.

MORNING CAME like a ghost out of the darkness. It slunk across the land in a mist of fog as the night sky faded into an ominous gray. The weather filled Jillian with an anguish that made her feel panicky; she felt a desperate need to escape.

She dressed quickly, slipped silently out of the house and walked through the mist-dampened trees toward the barns. Her panic abated to the dull ache that had become her silent shadow.

An odd suspended sensation of foreboding crawled along her spine as she entered the gloomy barn. For a moment she hesitated, then a cold shiver shot through her as a stallion's scream echoed with terrifying

shrillness, slicing through the eerie shadows. Her skin
shrank with a chilling apprehension as she was drawn
down the dim alley toward the solid reinforced box
stall at the end of the stable. The stallion screamed
again and hooves lashed out against the thick planks
of the enclosure. Her nightmare became a living
reality as the animal reared, violently slashing out
with his forelegs, his nostrils flaring, his eyes wild as
he tossed his head.

Rogue. The black devil.

As Jillian looked at him, the unknown fear fell
away and she stared at him with a frigid dispassion.
She had been vaguely aware that her father was using
him as a stud—no one could deny his magnificence.
She watched his restless caged prancing, and she felt
no terror, no fear. Just hate, a fierce black hatred inside of her. She turned and walked back to the tack
room, her face set with ruthless loathing.

Snatching a bridle off a wooden peg, she lifted her
unused saddle and blanket off the saddle rack, carrying them back down to the alley to the box stall,
where she set them on the floor. She gathered up two
long thick ropes from a hook by the stall and checked
the heavy metal clasps on the end of each rope. Then
she went to the heavy solid gate and waited.

The stallion slashed at the gate with a foreleg, his
finely molded head tossing, and with an expert twist of
her wrist Jillian snapped the two lines onto the heavy
lead ring on his halter. She secured one line to a huge
ring on the wall outside the stall. The other rope she
threaded through an identical ring on the opposite
side of the alley. Holding the end of that line in her
hand, she pulled back the heavy wooden bar slotted
across the gate and slid back the heavy metal bolt.

Then she swung the gate open. As the powerful high-strung stallion bolted from the stall, she yanked the rope and pulled it tight. Rogue was hauled up short. He was cross tied, unable to move forward or back.

With deadly calmness, Jillian approached him. He stood quivering, his eyes rolling as a nervous lather appeared on his withers. Carefully double-checking everything she did, she slipped the bridle straps underneath the halter, then saddled him. Finally she forced the bit of the bridle into the trembling horse's mouth. She secured all the buckles, then rechecked everything. Moving to the animal's side, she swung fluidly into the saddle.

The stallion tensed his muscles and tried to throw his head as she tested the rigging. Jill was impervious. She gathered up the braided-leather reins, then stretched out and unbuckled the clasp of the halter with a smooth practiced twist. The restricting tether fell away.

The split second the halter and rope dropped, she hauled the stallion's head around and rammed her heels into his flanks. Rogue bolted down the alley and out into the heavy fog.

The reins cut into Jillian's uncalloused hands as she fought to control the plunging horse. She would break this bloodied bastard who had robbed her of any chance of happiness. She would ride him until he dropped. She would break him as he had broken Jacob.

Fiercely he fought her, fought the restraining bit in his tender mouth. But Jillian's will was law. She brought the wild lunging animal around with a rough and heavy grip, then brought his head under control. With a vicious kick she drove him forward into the bit and he leaped ahead. In two powerful strides he was in a full gallop. Jillian let him go, her face set and unrelenting.

IT WAS NEARLY an hour later when Bill Lambert strode into his son's bedroom. "Allan, get up!"

Allan rolled over and looked blankly at his father, his mind fuzzy from sleep.

"Get dressed, son. Jillian's gone and she's taken Rogue!"

"My God!" Allan sprang out of bed, his mind suddenly alert with urgency.

"Be quiet, boy. Your mother's still sleeping and I don't want her to know. I've got the horses saddled and waiting outside. Jillian's gone through the pasture so we can't take the truck." With that, he turned on his heel and left the room.

Allan tucked in his shirt without buttoning it, rammed his bare feet into his boots and followed his father. It would be a hell-bent-for-leather ride.

JILLIAN WAS SOAKED with sweat, and every muscle in her body ached as she turned Rogue homeward. She hadn't been able to do it after all, but somehow it wasn't important anymore. She had ridden him torturous miles before sanity returned and rationality won out. She couldn't bring herself to break the spirit of such a magnificent animal—and Jacob wouldn't want her to. Besides, nothing would change if she had; it wouldn't erase the agonizing emptiness.

Her arms felt dislocated from her shoulders and her hands were raw and bleeding. The rough braided reins had been yanked repeatedly through her sweating palms as she fought to control the wild fury of the stallion. The blisters that had formed were broken and the flesh was rubbed raw. She wrapped the bloody, sweat-soaked reins around her hands, unable to hold them any longer without having them slip through her numb fingers.

She held her hands low on either side of the lathered black neck, her arms extended slightly so that the stallion was forced to tuck his head in. Jillian had him totally in control, but she wasn't sure who was more exhausted, she or the horse. She could feel him trembling beneath her, but still he danced along, thick spumes of foam flipping from his bridle as he tried to toss his head. She spoke softly to him as she tried to ease him down into an easy walk, but Rogue continued to fight the restraint. She kept talking to him in a soothing low voice, and his ears twitched alertly.

She was unaware of the rapidly approaching riders until they were almost upon her. Then she heard her father whistle in amazement and admiration. "Damn it, will you look at that! She's got that black devil prancing along like a high-stepping park horse. Nobody could ever handle him but Jacob—hell, we haven't even been able to get a bridle on him since the accident."

It wasn't until they rode alongside that either Allan or Bill Lambert fully realized the condition of both rider and horse. Allan sized up the sweating lathered animal, then looked at his perspiring exhausted sister. It was obvious that she had ridden him miles. Then he noticed the state of her lacerated hands. *Bloody miles,* he mused silently.

JILLIAN WAS HALF AN HOUR LATE for Monday's rehearsal. She and Allan left the farm later than they should have, and they encountered heavy traffic once they hit the city. Allan tried to argue her out of going, but she ignored him.

The group was working on an instrumental arrangement when she walked into the banquet hall. Norm was sprawled on a chair by the stage, his long legs stretched out in front of him.

"Hi! We wondered if you were coming."

"Allan and I went home for the weekend and we were late getting away," she explained.

Norm motioned toward the stage. "There's some new music for you on the piano."

She nodded and walked over to the piano, somehow managing to keep herself from glancing at Jacob as she reached for the music. Her heart raced with alarm, however, when his hand shot out and caught her wrist, twisting it to expose her palm and the ugly raw abrasion across it. He didn't look at her face but grabbed her other hand, swearing when he saw an identical wound. He knew.

His grip tightened as he looked up at her, his face suddenly gray. "You rode him." It was a ragged tense statement.

"I rode him." She eased her hands out of his, picked up the music and walked away, her eyes burning with unshed tears.

BY THE TIME Jillian returned to the apartment late that night, she had developed a pounding violent headache that left her eyes glazed with pain. Allan was still up, watching a late-night movie on TV, and he gave her a tablet that was a powerful painkiller. Very reluctantly she took it. He didn't realize that her adamant stance in refusing any sedatives during the past sleepless nights was based on fear. She knew the medication would trigger an apathetic drifting state of mind that would dull her rigid control and weaken her determination to shut out everything completely.

The medication, however, sedated her so completely that she didn't move for hours. When she did awake, she had to fight her way through the heavy lethargic fog of drug-induced sleep. She stared hard at the clock on her bedside table, willing her eyes to focus on it. Four o'clock. Another hour before she had to get up. She let the heaviness engulf her as she closed her eyes once again. . . .

A face was beginning to take shape in the gray semiconsciousness—a face that she dared not allow to become a distinct image. She bolted upright in bed, fighting the dizziness and nausea that swept over her. She pushed back the damp tendrils of hair with hands that trembled, then buried her face against her upraised knees, willing herself into a state of numbness as she disciplined herself by taking long deep breaths. She must not lose control, not for a second, for she knew if she ever allowed one small crack in her veneer, her entire world would crumble like a bursting dam. For that reason she had not given in, had not once wept, had refused to discuss the situation with anyone since Jacob had told her of his decision on that fateful morning. She had erected all her defenses; it was the only way she could survive.

And Jillian was a survivor. Her inborn instinct for self-preservation, for life, was strong enough to overcome her desire simply to stop struggling.

She lay back down and stared vacantly at the ceiling. Her days seemed strangely nonending now, one drifting into another with a relentless emptiness that was punctuated only with evening performances and an occasional afternoon rehearsal. Nothing mattered anymore.

She had never realized how much she'd subconsciously built the past five years on the vague hope that Jacob would somehow, somewhere, sometime once again become a part of her life. Never realized it until she was faced with this complete definite rejection.

It was over; she knew that without a doubt. An inner pain that was never ending, never changing, held her, but she was powerless against it. It numbed her senses and paralyzed her mind. The only relief was when she was performing, but even then that awful loneliness was there.

She sighed heavily and crawled out of bed. She could still feel the unpleasant side effects of the medication. At the window she experienced a peculiar sense of relief as she swept back the curtains. It was raining. The drizzle was beating a gentle hollow tattoo on the pane, and there was solace in it that she found soothing, comforting. She stood for a long time in the silence of the dusky room, then turned away from the window reluctantly. She had better start getting dressed or she would be late for the first show.

She had just stepped out of the shower and was toweling herself dry when she heard the front door close. Slipping into her caftan, she walked out into the living room.

Allan was standing just inside the door sorting through the mail he had brought in with him. His hair was beaded with moisture, his squall jacket damp and clinging.

He gave Jillian a hard look as she entered the room. "Hi. Have a good sleep?"

She gave him a halfhearted smile and arched her eyebrows ruefully. "I'm not some aged geriatric patient with a pacemaker, Allan."

He grinned back at her and tapped her under the chin as he walked by her on his way to the kitchen. "But you, Jill, make me feel like some aged geriatric doctor with a pacemaker—you worry the hell out of me when you hardly ever sleep."

There was a tiny spark of humor in Jill's eyes as she followed him. "If you were worth your salt as a surgeon, Dr. Lambert, you should be able to install an on-off switch in my back. Turn me off when you want me to sleep—that would handle your concern very nicely!" To be permanently "off"...she pushed the grim thought from her mind. "Would you like a coffee?"

"That would really hit the spot." Allan seated himself at the kitchen nook and started scanning one of the magazines he had carried in with the mail. The solitude was shattered by the jangle of the phone. "I'll get that, Jill. It's probably the hospital," he said.

When he returned to the kitchen a few moments later he found Jillian staring out the window, her face a mask. She turned to face him, knowing immediately by the look on his face something was wrong. "What's the matter?"

He hesitated, then took a deep breath. "That was Dr. Blackwell. He's just received some bad news."

Jillian was filled with a feeling of uneasiness as she recognized the grim set of Allan's face. "What is it?" Her voice was quiet, controlled.

Her brother hesitated for a moment before speaking. "He just received word that his son was seriously injured in a car accident in Vancouver."

"Oh, no!" Jillian's voice was filled with compassion as she touched his shoulder in a gesture of concern.

Allan grasped her hand in his. He paused, hating himself for what he had to tell her. "Jill, remember I was telling you about the surgeon from the States who is going to be performing that specialized surgery in Toronto next week?"

Jillian nodded.

"Well, Blackwell had been asked to assist. He was to leave tonight."

Without Allan saying another word, Jillian knew what he was going to tell her.

"Blackwell wants me to go in his place. I told him I would. I have to be on the eight-o'clock plane for Toronto tonight." He hesitated briefly, then continued reluctantly. "I'll be gone about ten days... maybe longer."

By sheer willpower Jillian stifled the panic she was experiencing and somehow managed to keep her voice level. "Allan, don't worry about me, please. I'll be fine." She patted his cheek reassuringly and even managed a smile. Under the pretense of pouring the coffee she turned away from him, but it was so he couldn't see the uncertainty in her eyes. "I'm not helpless."

But she was. She was helpless against the unbearable emptiness that kept dragging at her like a menacing undercurrent, threatening to pull her under.

CHAPTER THIRTEEN

THE GRAY OVERCAST SKY continued to hang over the city all that week, the drizzle dreary and persistent. But when Jillian left the hotel after the last set Thursday night, the sky had finally cleared.

When she arrived home she made herself a cup of instant coffee and took it outside to the patio to drink it. She loved the smell after a summer rain—everything was so fresh and clean. The perfume from the flowers was more intense, more beautiful in the dampness, and the soft whispering breeze gathered up the scent of each flower and carried the fragrances in a delightful mixed bouquet.

The quiet enchantment was shattered by the distant discordant jangle of the telephone, and she hurried inside. Who on earth would be calling her at this time of night? She swept her hair over her shoulder as she picked up the receiver.

"Hello."

"Jillian, it's Ken. Is Allan there?"

Suddenly she was very cold; intuitively, she knew that something was desperately wrong. "He isn't here—he left for Toronto on Tuesday. What's wrong, Ken?"

"God, I hoped Allan would be there. It's Sylvia."

His voice broke and a sickening fear washed through Jillian. "What's the matter with Sylvia?"

He sounded frantic. "We had to rush her up by ambulance—we just got in." His voice broke again. "Jillian—"

"Where are you, Ken?"

"In emergency at the University Hospital."

"I'll be there in ten minutes."

"Jillian—" his voice was hoarse and shaky, and she heard him take a deep breath before he continued "—could you phone Jacob and John? She's going to need a transfusion—she has that AB blood type, and the blood bank here is low. They're trying to locate other donors now."

Jillian closed her eyes as she rubbed her hand across her forehead, her own voice tremulous. "John's not here, he's in Fort McMurray this week." She heard Ken groan in despair. "I'll get in touch with Jacob and we'll be there as soon as we can."

"Tell him to hurry, Jillian."

"I will."

She pressed down the button on the phone, then listened for the dial tone. A silent heartfelt prayer pounded through her brain as she dialed the hotel's number. "Please, God, not Sylvia. Please, not Sylvia."

She felt immobilized with a terrifying dread as she waited for Jacob to answer the phone. What if he wasn't there? What if...?

"Yes?"

"Jacob!" Her voice caught on a sob and she swallowed against the painful tightness in her throat. "Jacob, Sylvia had to be rushed to the University Hospital tonight. Ken just phoned and she needs you—she needs a transfusion and the blood bank is low on type AB." She was shaking so badly she could barely stand. She rested her forehead weakly against the cabinet door of the wall unit and stiffened her muscles against the trembling. "Oh, Jacob, Ken sounded so frightened, so worried—"

"I'll be there in fifteen minutes to pick you up."

"You go ahead... I can get there on my own—"

"Wait for me, Jillian." The phone clicked in her ear.

Jillian stood staring at the receiver in her hand for a split second, then she sprang into action. She grabbed a small suitcase from the hall closet and hurried into Allan's room. Ken wouldn't have bothered to change; he had probably come straight in from the field. She went through Allan's clothes and packed some socks, clean underwear, a shirt and a pair of slacks. Rushing into the bathroom she gathered up a new toothbrush, toothpaste and a disposable razor.

What else might Ken need? Shoes. Would Allan's shoes fit him? She dug through the closet, found a pair of loafers and tossed them in the suitcase. Then she grabbed a sweater off the shelf—she remembered how cold hospital waiting rooms could be at night.

Was there anything else? She shut the lid, then opened it again and packed a sweater for Jacob. She closed the lid and snapped the locks shut.

Setting the suitcase in the hallway, she went into her bedroom and pulled a sweater out of a drawer. She threw it over her arm, picked up the suitcase and her shoulder bag and headed for the door.

Jacob's car was just pulling up in front of the house when she closed the front door behind her. She ran down the walk as Jacob leaned over and pushed open the passenger door for her. She swore when she cracked her shin with the suitcase as she swung it into the car. She slammed the door, and the powerful car leaped into motion on the deserted street.

"What did Ken tell you when he phoned?"

"Just what I told you—not very much. He was trying to locate Allan, who had to fly to Toronto to assist in some specialized surgery."

Jacob checked an intersection, then ran the red light. "How long have they been here?"

"They just arrived."

"Did she have any trouble with her other pregnancies?"

"No, she was fine."

Nothing more was said until Jacob wheeled into the emergency entrance.

"Use the ramp, Jacob," she told him.

He threw her a quick glance. "I can't park there."

"Don't worry about it."

Jacob shrugged and parked the car in front of the entrance doors. The uniformed guard walked over to the car as Jacob swung his wheelchair out and snapped it open. Jillian was out of the car like a flash and was standing by his chair when the guard reached them.

"Hey, bud, you can't park that car here."

Jillian retrieved the car keys from Jacob's shirt pocket and rammed them into the guard's hand. "You'll have to park it."

"Hey, lady, I ain't no car jockey!"

She was several inches taller than the guard and she used every inch of that advantage as she leaned over him, speaking in a voice that was low and slicing. "This man has been called in as a blood donor for an emergency. If you haven't the decency to park it, then you'd better find someone who will." She picked up the suitcase and started to walk away. "Leave the keys at the desk for Holinski."

"Yes, ma'am."

She looked at Jacob, her voice no longer edged with authority. "Come on, Jacob."

"Yes, ma'am," he replied. If the situation hadn't been so serious, she would have sworn that he was teasing.

Jillian wasn't surprised to see the crowded waiting room, even at two o'clock in the morning. When Allan was interning he had often cursed the heavy load on emergency at night.

She turned to Jacob. "I'll check at the desk and find out where Sylvia is."

He nodded, taking the suitcase and sweater from her and laying them on his lap.

Jillian approached the desk and spoke to a harried-looking nurse. "Excuse me, please."

"Yes, can I help you?"

"Mrs. Sylvia Lambert was rushed in from Lloyd-minster tonight. Her brother was called to give blood—she has AB positive."

"Oh, yes, I remember. We called in other donors, as well. If you'll wait here for a moment, I'll find out where you're to go."

"Thank you."

The nurse disappeared down a corridor, and Jillian leaned against the wall and studied the people in the waiting room. They seemed to be so isolated from one another, each individual carefully erecting invisible barriers to protect himself. They seemed so depersonalized and flat, so single dimensioned—

A voice interrupted her thoughts. "Miss, this is Dr. Carter. He admitted Mrs. Lambert."

Jillian glanced up, and her body stiffened involuntarily as she experienced a frightening flashback. Dr. Carter had been the intern on duty when Jacob's already critical condition had worsened drastically. The memory of Jacob, unconscious and deathlike, being rushed to surgery returned sharply to Jillian's mind.

Dr. Carter gave Jillian an odd look as she pressed her hands hard against her thighs and took a deep shaky breath. His brow creased with concentration as he peered at her through his thick glasses. "I know you from somewhere, don't I?"

She nodded and had started to reply when he snapped his fingers, a look of satisfaction on his round face. "I remember now. It was a few years ago—your fiancé was admitted after being badly trampled by a horse. That's it, isn't it?"

"That's right, doctor."

"Well, I'll be darned. As I remember, he gave us some very bad moments."

"Yes, he did." Jillian tried to smile as she shifted the conversation away from a time she'd rather not recall. "How's Sylvia Lambert, Dr. Carter?"

"She was taken directly up to surgery. Is she a relative?"

"She's my sister-in-law. We were notified that she would need a transfusion. Jacob's here now; where do we go?"

"Right! Mr. Lambert said her brother was coming. We'll look after that right away." He turned to the desk and said something to the nurse, then took Jillian by the elbow. "Come on, I'll show you where to go." He looked at Jillian and smiled apologetically. "I'm afraid I've forgotten your name."

"Jillian—"

"Jillian, of course. I always thought your name suited you so well."

They approached Jacob, and Dr. Carter smiled broadly at him as Jillian said, "Jacob, you remember Dr. Carter."

Jacob's smile was slightly forced as he stretched out his hand. "I most certainly do. I thought you would have abandoned this place by now."

The doctor shook Jacob's hand and shrugged. "No, I've become a permanent fixture here. Mrs. Lambert is your sister?"

"Yes. How is she?"

"To be quite frank, I don't know. They took her straight up to surgery. I do know she can use some of your good red blood, so we'll take care of that first." Dr. Carter clasped the handles of Jacob's wheelchair.

There was something just a little too practiced, too casual about the tone of his voice, and Jillian felt her insides shrink with alarm. She had become expert at interpreting doctors' comments when Jacob was fighting for his life, and she knew by the tone of this one's voice that Sylvia's condition was critical.

Her voice was calm, but the look on her face was one of fearful comprehension. "It's very serious, isn't it, doctor?"

The man sighed and looked at Jillian, his expression one of solemn resignation. "Her uterus ruptured. She's lost considerable blood." He stopped in front of the elevator and pushed the button, then stuck his fist in the pocket of his lab coat. "She's in the best possible hands. The human body has tremendous recuperative abilities—but then, you both know that." He wheeled Jacob into the elevator and selected a floor, then looked at Jillian with owlish eyes. "This must bring back some very unpleasant memories for you—"

"It does." Jillian cut him off abruptly before he could say anything more. She would never forget those long terrifying hours when Jacob's life was suspended by a thread. Never. The memories of them came hurtling back as they left the elevator and began walking down familiar corridors, through familiar swinging doors, by familiar nursing stations. She bit her bottom lip in an attempt to smother the helpless, frightened feeling that was growing within her. It didn't help when she realized Jacob was watching her stricken face with a peculiar stare.

She was relieved when Dr. Carter directed her to a small waiting room, then rolled Jacob through another set of doors.

By the time they returned, she had managed to collect herself somewhat. Dr. Carter escorted them to another floor of the hospital, through a set of fire doors and past another nursing station to a dimly lit waiting room. There Jillian set the suitcase on the floor by the well-worn sofa and laid her bag and sweater on top of it.

"You two wait here and I'll see if I can locate Mr. Lambert," the doctor said. As he started to walk toward the door Jillian turned to face him. "Dr. Carter, do you have a cigarette, by any chance?"

He dug a pack out of the pocket of his white lab coat and tossed it to her. "There's matches inside. I'll check back with you if I find out anything."

Jillian lit a cigarette with stiff fingers and walked to the window, where she looked out on the vacant parking lot. The puddles of rainwater were shining in the yellow gleam from the streetlights.

Why did one waiting room have to be a carbon copy of all the others? She was almost certain that if she looked in the corner behind the door she would find the same soiled orange chair in which she had spent so many fearful hours. The lounge even smelled the same: floor wax, stale cigarette smoke and fear.

She looked blindly out the window as she experienced the same cold stab she had felt when the doctors told them it was doubtful that Jacob would live through the night. She thought of Sylvia and Ken, their two small boys and the unborn child. Clenching her teeth together, she blinked back the tears that were threatening. She must *not* come apart. No one must know what an ordeal this was for her, and no one must know how frightened she was. The thought of something happening to Sylvia was simply too grim to consider.

"Was it so bad, Jillian—after the accident?"

She didn't dare look at Jacob. "Yes, it was bad."

She heard the whisper of the wheelchair behind her but she didn't turn around until he touched her arm. "Put on your sweater. You look nearly frozen."

She avoided his eyes as she took it from him and draped it around her shoulders. "I brought one for you—it's in the suitcase. These damned waiting rooms are either too cold or too hot."

She didn't move from the window as she heard the suitcase being opened. With the force of habit she reached for the chain around her neck and fingered it with gentle caressing strokes. She wished Allan was here. She would call him in Toronto just as soon as she found out what Sylvia's condition was.

"When did Allan leave?"

"Tuesday night. He was asked to fill in for another doctor in some very specialized surgery." Her fingers worried with the pendant, her face pale and drawn. "He won't be back for two weeks." She turned to face Jacob. "Would you like a cup of coffee?"

He nodded, his own face grimly set. Compassion filled Jillian when she saw the tiny pulse pumping in his temple. He was suffering with muscle spasms again.

She returned shortly with two plastic-capped Styrofoam cups of hot black coffee. Removing the lid from one, she took a sip and raised her eyebrows in surprise. It was really good. From past experience, she had found that it usually tasted like a strong mixture of cough medicine and burnt cabbage.

Jacob was stretched out on one of the settees, his arm draped across his eyes, his lips compressed into a hard line. She set the coffee down on one of the end tables and strode out of the room. She couldn't just stand there and do nothing when she knew he was so uncomfortable. She came back with an armload of pillows, and without saying a word she folded two of them together and arranged them under his knees.

For a moment she thought he was going to tell her to go to hell. "It's going to be a long night, Jacob," she warned him softly.

He sighed with restrained impatience, then nodded his head.

When she finished arranging the pillows, she had constructed a solid comfortable support that had his knees flexed and most of his weight distributed on his buttocks. There was a soft sheen of perspiration on his skin and a tautness around his full sensual mouth that made her want to cry. She tucked the remaining two pillows under his head and shoulders, then removed the cap from his coffee and broke away a U in the brittle plastic lid, firmly replacing it on the cup. He would be able to drink it without spilling it and without moving from his semireclining position.

She took a deep sharp breath as his hand brushed against hers and lingered briefly before he took the cup from her. He was watching her face with unfathomable eyes. "Thank you, Jillian."

"You're welcome." She retrieved the pack of cigarettes from the window ledge, then sat down in the chair beside him. She swore silently at her fumbling fingers, then swore aloud when she burned her fingers on the match. "Damn!"

"Serves you right." There was no slicing sarcasm in the mild rebuke, but instead a hint of humor. Jillian inhaled deeply, then coughed as the smoke burned her lungs.

Jacob reached out, took the cigarette from her and butted it in the battered tin ashtray on the coffee table. "If you must do something to pass the time, bite your fingernails."

She experienced a flutter of amusement at the dryness in his voice, and a tiny smile played with the corners of her mouth. The bubble of humor was abruptly burst when she saw the telltale smudges of paint on his fingers. So he had been painting. . . .

The picture he had sketched of her sitting on a pedestal flashed into her mind like a blinding neon light, piercing through her insulating numbness. In only a few short days the band would be leaving Edmonton, and she would never see Jacob again. She forced her mind shut; she couldn't stand the thought of his leaving.

"Jacob. Jillian." Ken was walking across the room, his face haggard and gray. Jillian sprang to her feet and went to her brother. He hugged her hard, almost desperately, and she could feel the anxiety in him.

"How is she, Ken?"

He took a deep shaky breath and surreptitiously wiped his eyes as he released her. "She's in surgery now—no, don't get up, Jacob." Ken released Jillian's hand with a painfully firm squeeze, then collapsed in the chair near Jacob. Jillian sat on the wide arm of the chair and put her hand on her brother's shoulders. He rubbed his forehead, his eyes dull with exhaustion and despair.

Jacob's voice was quiet. "Tell us whenever you're ready, Ken."

Ken rested his head against the back of the chair and closed his eyes. "She hadn't been feeling well all day. She was getting ready for bed—it was about ten o'clock—and she fainted. Sylvia had never fainted in her whole life! I rushed her into the Lloyd hospital, and her doctor was really concerned. The baby was in a breech position, which was bad enough, but then her blood pressure began to drop. The anesthetist was out of town and there was no one else to administer the anesthetic for surgery. Anyway, he didn't want to waste any time so he put her in an ambulance and sent her here. I guess surgery would be risky in Lloyd, anyway, because of her blood type. Before we left he gave her an injection to stop the contractions—he was certain she couldn't deliver naturally with the baby in that position."

Ken raised his head and stared at his clenched fists, his voice ragged. "We were just on the outskirts of Edmonton when she went into heavy labor and began to hemorrhage. She lost so much blood by the time we reached the hospital that she went into shock—apparently the uterus ruptured. It seemed as though everything that could go wrong did."

Jacob and Jillian exchanged concerned, alarmed glances as Ken dragged his hand across his face.

Jillian was afraid to ask, but she had to know. "The baby?"

A flash of paternal pride lighted up his eyes. "We have a beautiful healthy daughter."

Jillian reached out and caught her brother's hand, her eyes brimming with tears of relief. "Oh, Ken, Sylvia will be so thrilled."

He smiled softly. "She's a little doll. She has a headful of flaming-red hair and a temper just like her aunt's."

Jillian smiled at him, then sobered suddenly as Ken covered his face with his hands, his voice breaking. "Sylvia...she looked so...so frail, so still when they wheeled her into surgery."

Jillian squeezed his hand. "Don't let yourself think about that, Ken. She's going to be okay. The waiting is awful, but you simply must believe she's going to be fine."

Ken looked at his sister, his eyes dark with worry. "It's this damned waiting...not knowing."

"I know. Just believe—really believe—that in a week or ten days she's going to be at home with that precious baby in her arms, giving you hell because you forgot to gather the eggs."

There was a glimmer of a smile in Ken's eyes. "You and your power of positive thinking."

"Jillian's right, Ken. Sylvia has always had amazing recuperative ability. She's in good condition—and she's a fighter."

Ken looked at his brother-in-law. "I know. I'm so damned glad you two are here—" He grasped Jacob's shoulder, his voice low with genuine relief. "Besides bringing your much needed blood, I just feel better having you around." He glanced at his sister, then ran his hands through his hair. "I feel so chewed up inside—but I guess you know how I feel, Jillian."

Jillian was aware that Jacob was watching her with eyes that were narrowed by some inner thought, his jaw set like unyielding granite.

Ken tipped his head back and stared at the ceiling, "I would feel one hell of a lot better if Allan was in that operating room."

Jacob's eyes were solemn and thoughtful as he contemplated what his brother-in-law had said. He tucked his hands beneath his head as he shifted his gaze and stared across the room with brooding introspection. "Perhaps it's a good thing he's out of town. It would be a rough situation for him—trying to separate his personal involvement from his professional role, knowing that we were depending on him to work a miracle."

Jillian stood up and walked to the window, staring out at the predawn sky. Love and compassion swelled within her with an aching tenderness. There was so much self-reproach in Jacob's words, such a burden of regret for putting Allan in that position himself.

"Mr. Lambert."

As Dr. Carter came toward him, Ken rose abruptly, his white-knuckled fists clenched at his sides. "My wife...?"

Dr. Carter shook his head as he sat down on the coffee table. "No word yet. It will be a while before we hear anything, I'm afraid. I just wanted to let you know we've had five more blood donors come in. The Red Cross keeps a file of donors who have uncommon blood types; we've had to call in this bunch before."

Ken's shoulders sagged wearily as he sat back down. "Could I get their names and addresses from you? I'd like to thank them for doing what they did."

"Sure. No problem." Dr. Carter took a cigarette from the package lying on the table and lighted it. "I was just over to the nursery to see that daughter of yours. She's doing just fine—in fact, she's kicking up quite a storm."

Ken's face softened into a tender smile. "I was there when they delivered her...." He swallowed hard, his voice suddenly very husky. "It was just before they took Sylvia—" He clamped his mouth shut, and Jillian could see the muscles tense in his jaw.

Dr. Carter laid his hand on Ken's shoulder. "Try not to worry, Mr. Lambert. The surgeon who's operating is one of the best. Your doctor in Lloydminster is to be commended for sending your wife here straightaway. It's the wisest thing he could have done." The doctor absently brushed some cigarette ashes from his pants. "By any chance are you related to Allan Lambert?"

Ken nodded. "Yes, he's my brother."

"He's one hell of a doctor and a brilliant sur-geon—but don't tell him I said so!" Carter glanced at Jillian, then back at Ken, his eyebrows raised ques-tioningly.

Ken interpreted the look and grinned ruefully. "I guess I have to claim her, too—Jillian's my sister."

The man laughed. "Thank heavens! I was begin-ning to think we had an epidemic of red hair." He stood up and stifled a yawn. "Speaking of redheads, would you like to take a peek at the young lady?"

Jillian's face lit up. "Oh, could we?"

"Sure." The doctor grinned, his expression one of a mischievous adolescent. "I haven't broken any rules for—let's see—at least three days."

Jacob laughed and sat up, then looked at Ken. "Are you coming, Ken?"

"No, I'll stay here, Jacob—in case there's word about Syl." He stood up and combed his fingers through his hair. "I'd give my eyeteeth for a quick shower right now."

"There's one just a couple of doors down you could use," offered Dr. Carter. "Just ask the nurse at the desk for some towels."

"I raided Allan's closet and brought you a change of clothes, Ken—they're in the suitcase."

Ken shot Jillian a look of gratitude. "Thanks, Jill."

Dr. Carter motioned to the others. "Come on, let's see how the terror of the nursery is doing."

Jillian's expression was one of enraptured awe as she stood looking through the nursery window at the tiny sleeping baby in the nurse's arms. She was beau-tiful.

Dr. Carter beamed proudly, then glanced down at Jacob. Realizing that he was unable to see the baby's face from his low vantage point, he strode into the nursery and gently removed the bundle from the arms of the startled nurse, then carried the baby into the hall.

He frowned sternly at the two of them, his voice falsely severe. "Are either of you contagious?" They both shook their heads.

"The nurse will probably have a stroke over me 'flouting regulations,'" he confessed.

Placing the baby in Jillian's arms he grinned with immense satisfaction as her eyes shone with delight. His grin softened into an understanding smile as he saw the tears glistening on her long lashes.

Her face was a picture of tenderness and wonder as she took a tiny fist in her hand and softly caressed the back of it with her thumb. The baby was absolutely perfect, even if she did have red hair.

After she'd held her new niece for a moment, she bent over and placed the baby carefully in Jacob's arms, her hair falling around them like a gleaming curtain.

He looked up at her and their gaze locked and held, the old magic casting its spell as his eyes softened and he smiled. The baby frowned, then started to make sucking sounds with her rosebud mouth. Jacob laughed softly as he folded back the flannelette receiving blanket and gently touched the riot of red curls.

Dr. Carter watched the entire byplay, his hands clasped behind his back, a smile of smug pleasure on his face. "Don't you two have one of those yet?"

Jillian sucked in her breath in a painful gasp as

Jacob stiffened, his eyes instantly shuttered. His voice was clipped. "No."

"No? You'd better get her one, man!"

Jillian deliberately let her hair screen her face as she straightened and stepped back. She felt as though Jacob had slapped her. The temporary respite from her unhappiness was swept away as reality came pounding over her like a mighty wave.

Somehow she managed to retain a mask of composure. Returning to the waiting room, she was relieved to find Ken asleep in a chair. She stood at the window, her arms clasped around her as she stared fixedly out, her determination wrapped around her like a mantle of armor. She marshaled every bit of self-discipline she possessed to keep her mind blank and unregistering. Such was her power of concentration that she was unaware when Jacob returned and sat with his dark eyes riveted on her.

Jillian allowed nothing to penetrate her shield until the surgeon came to tell them that Sylvia was out of surgery, her condition stable. The relief that she experienced then was so overwhelming that it left her weak and shaking, but she hung onto her control with resolute tenacity. She didn't dare give way to the tears of profound thankfulness that were choking her.

The sun was above the horizon when a nurse came for Ken. Sylvia was awake and asking for him.

Jillian felt naked and exposed after he left; she didn't want to be left alone with Jacob. She tensed nervously when he spoke. "Come on, Jillian, I'll drive you home. Ken will likely stay with Sylvia."

Her first impulse was to refuse, but then she remembered about Jacob's car. It was anybody's guess where it was parked, and there was a definite possibility that it would be inaccessible to him. And he looked so exhausted.

With strong misgivings she nodded her head. "I suppose we may as well go. Ken won't need us now."

It was a good thing she had remained with Jacob. She had difficulty locating the Porsche, and when she finally spotted it she found that the cars parked on either side were so close that Jacob would never have been able to get his wheelchair in between them. She was only beginning to realize the countless frustrations that someone confined to a wheelchair faced.

She faced a few more herself when she tried to figure out the hand controls on the car, but eventually she managed to ease it out of the tight parking spot and maneuver it around to the main door, where Jacob was waiting for her. She couldn't help smiling at the dry and slightly cynical expression on his face as the car rocked to a halt beside him.

She slipped out of the car and walked around the front of it toward him.

"I presume you don't want to drive?" he asked.

The look she gave him was one that questioned his sanity. "You'd have to be out of your mind to trust me with that machine."

He didn't respond but wheeled around the car and hauled himself in, stowing the chair in its space and closing the door. Then he looked at her with an intensity that left her unprotected against the censure in his voice. "I trust you, Jillian. It's myself I don't trust."

Her eyes fell away from his. The bitterness was there, burning with its destructive flame.

Jillian was so numbed with exhaustion by the time she reached the sanctuary of her silent and empty apartment that she didn't even have the energy to undress. She sprawled on her bed fully clothed and was almost instantly asleep.

SHE DIDN'T AWAKEN until Ken roused her late in the afternoon. He reassured her that her sister-in-law was feeling well enough to have company and, in fact, had specifically asked for Jillian and Jacob, so she decided to stop by to see Sylvia on her way to work.

Jillian prepared something for Ken to eat, then showered and dressed. She raided Mrs. Olsen's garden and picked a huge bouquet of mixed flowers for Sylvia, recklessly adding a number of roses.

Sylvia, although very pale and obviously weak, was in radiant spirits. She was delighted with the flowers. "They're beautiful, Jillian. Thank you!"

"Your gratitude will be conveyed to Ollie—I snitched them from her garden."

Sylvia smiled impishly. "You're apt to come to an unpleasant end, Jill, when she finds out you've pinched her roses."

Jillian grinned. "For you, sweet sister, anything is worthwhile."

Sylvia buried her face in the fragrant bouquet, then handed them to Jillian, who began arranging them in a vase on the bedside table.

"Oh, Jillian, have you seen her yet?"

Jillian kept her face deadpan as she fussed with the flowers. "Who?"

Sylvia reached out and slapped Jillian's hand and grinned. "Who, indeed! Your brand-new niece, that's who!"

Jillian tucked a few clusters of baby's breath into the arrangement, then sat down in the chair by the bed. "I certainly have. I've even had her in my hot little clutches."

"Did you? When?"

"When you were in the O.R., giving us all nervous breakdowns."

Sylvia's sparkling eyes became serious as she grasped Jillian's hand. "I felt so rotten for Ken. He was frantic with worry and he simply wouldn't believe me when I said I'd be all right."

Jillian couldn't help smiling at the note of exasperation she detected in Sylvia's voice. "These damned men never listen."

Sylvia made an impudent face, then smiled happily. "Isn't she just perfect? I'm so glad she has red hair—I've always thought yours was so beautiful."

Jillian's expression was one of wry skepticism. "She's going to hate you for it, especially when she starts developing those horrible big freckles every time she *thinks* sunshine."

Sylvia giggled, then grasped her stomach as her eyes widened with pain. "Ooh, that hurts." She took a deep breath, then continued. "But your freckles aren't like that—"

"Sylvia Lambert, how quickly you forget! Remember how whenever Allan was put off with me he would sit on me and draw dot-to-dot with a ballpoint pen? Don't tell me you've forgotten that!"

Sylvia laughed, then held her stomach as she tried to stifle her mirth. "Jillian, you have to stop making me laugh...really. It's killing me...ooh."

Jillian smiled fondly at Sylvia, then squeezed her hand sympathetically. "Do you feel awful?"

"No, not really. The incision is really tender and my abdominal muscles are sore, but it's not so bad. I had a shot for the pain just before you came and that helped." She smiled at Jillian, her eyes suddenly brimming with tears. "I can stand anything knowing that the baby is fine. I was so scared she'd.... Well, that's all behind us now. We're just so happy we have a daughter, especially since I can't have any more children."

"What are you going to call her?"

"Lisa Marie. Do you like it?"

"Very much. Lisa Marie Lambert—it sounds perfect."

"Did Jacob say if he's coming?"

Somehow Jillian was able to control her voice. "I don't know if he'll come today, Sylvia. I haven't talked to him since this morning. I went home and crashed, and I imagine he did, too." She was so relieved that she'd sounded perfectly casual. She certainly didn't want Sylvia to suspect anything was wrong; the last thing the woman needed was more worrying.

Jillian deftly changed the topic. "Ken said he would be here about seven. He was going to sleep for a couple of hours."

"He's insisting on staying until I'm released. He shouldn't, Jill. He'll be so far behind."

"Dad can manage for a few days, Sylvia. It's not as if it's the middle of harvest—besides, he'd worry like crazy if he left you here."

"I suppose. Did he phone home?"

"He said he phoned from the hospital this morning."

Sylvia nodded her head in approval, then looked at

Jillian, her eyes assessing. "You've lost weight, Jillian, and you look so tired—"

"Mrs. Lambert, do I have something for you!" A ward aide approached the bed carrying the biggest bouquet of flowers Jillian had ever seen. The woman set them on the wide window ledge beside Sylvia's bed and carefully removed the clear plastic wrap.

Jillian knew immediately whom they were from. Sylvia read the card, then silently handed it to Jillian, her eyes brimming with tears. Jillian had difficulty holding it still enough to read the bold handwriting: "Syl, to you and the most beautiful baby I have ever seen. Promise me you won't ever cut her hair! All my love, Jacob."

The poignant recollection of Jacob holding tiny Lisa Marie in his arms with such tenderness touched an inner chord that would haunt Jillian for a lifetime. Her nails cut into the palms of her hands as she clenched them against the pain of desolation. The future seemed so bleak, so meaningless, so frightening.

Somehow she managed to carry out the charade of nonchalance for the remainder of her visit with Sylvia, never allowing a trace of her inner turmoil to surface. How long, she wondered, could she continue to impersonate the Jillian of long ago?

CHAPTER FOURTEEN

It was another ugly morning—no beauty, no warmth, just cold wet gloom.

Jillian let the curtain fall across the window, then turned and walked out of her bedroom. She didn't think she could scrape up enough energy to push herself through another day. She was weary beyond description, and her head throbbed with a relentless ache.

She found Ken in the kitchen making coffee, his hair still damp from his shower. He frowned slightly when he saw her but didn't comment on her appearance. "Good morning, Jillian."

"Good morning."

He studied her fixed pale face, then turned toward the cupboard and switched on the electric coffee maker, his lips pursed together. He sighed and slowly shook his head before he spoke, his voice deliberately casual. "Are you going to the hospital this morning, Jill?"

"I thought I'd go up about eleven. Is it certain that Sylvia and the baby are going to be released today?"

"It's pretty positive. The surgeon will see her this morning, and if he's satisfied with her recovery they'll release her."

Jillian brushed by Ken and went to the fridge, where she took out a large pitcher. She poured two glasses of orange juice, handing one to Ken as she sat down at the table. "I can't believe how fast they discharge patients after surgery now. It's only been six days! A few years ago they would have kept her in for at least two weeks."

"I don't think the doctor would have discharged her this early if she didn't have mom at home to help her. Besides, I told Sylvia that if she started misbehaving I would chain her to the piano."

Jillian smiled and pointed her finger at him. "Do you know you have a tendency to be a bit of a bully, Ken Lambert?"

He drained his glass and chuckled. "That's exactly what Sylvia said. Ready for a coffee?"

Jillian looked at the glass carafe, her face dubious. "Are you sure it's drinkable? It looks as though it has the consistency of mud."

Ken poured two mugs and slid one across the table to her, then sat down. "Don't get cute."

Jillian warily sipped the strong black brew, then grimaced. "Guaranteed to keep you awake for at least a week and certain to eat a hole in your stomach immediately."

Ken smiled absently as he clasped his hands around the mug. His face became solemn as he contemplated the coffee in his cup, then he lifted his head and looked at Jillian, his eyes unwavering. "I'm not going to pry, Jillian, and I'm not going to start giving you any advice. I just want you to know that if you ever need a place to hang your hat for a while, you can always come home."

Jillian's eyes filled with tears and she covered her mouth with her fingers. She could only nod her head in acknowledgment. If she spoke she would be betrayed by her raw, barely controlled emotions, and her despair would come pouring out.

He looked away, his eyes dark with understanding and compassion. Neither of them spoke for a moment, then Ken took a sip of his coffee and grinned ruefully. "It isn't exactly ambrosia, is it?"

A spark of humor flashed in Jillian's eyes as she shook her head, her voice a shaky whisper. "More like hemlock."

"Brat." He stood up and dumped the contents of his cup down the sink with a look of distaste. "It'll probably do wonders for sluggish plumbing." He rinsed out the cup and set it on the counter. "I want to go downtown this morning. The old Johnson place is up for sale and a real-estate company here in Edmonton has the listing. I'd like to put in an offer on that quarter-section of pasture land. Tell Sylvia that I should get to the hospital about noon, okay?"

"Sure. I have to go down to the hotel for a rehearsal, so I guess I won't see you before you leave for home."

"Probably not. Why don't you come home this weekend, Jill? The boys would love to have you, and Sylvia would be delighted."

Jillian closed her eyes, her shoulders drooping. She sighed, then looked at her brother. "Maybe I will. The lounge is going to be closed on Monday for renovations, so I'll have an extra day."

"You need a break, Jill."

She sighed again. "I know. I'll phone you if I decide to come."

"Good enough." He removed his jacket from the back of the chair and slipped it on. "When will Allan be back?"

"He was supposed to be home this weekend but he's going to stay an extra few days in Toronto. This surgeon from the States is giving some lectures on a new technique he's developed and Allan wants to sit in on them."

"I see. He'll likely give us a call when he gets back. Well, I guess I'd better be off—Sylvia will be anxious to head for home once she's released."

With an unexpected display of affection, he bent over and kissed Jillian on the forehead. She had a nearly uncontrollable urge to throw her arms around his neck and weep on his shoulder.

JACOB WAS SEATED at the piano in the empty banquet hall, working on some new arrangements for the band. Nothing was going right, and in a burst of angry frustration he slammed his hands down on the keys.

"Mother Holinski would have your hide if she heard you do that."

He swiveled around to find Ken leaning against the door, a broad grin on his face. Jacob snorted, then grinned ruefully. "Sometimes I think I should have been a butcher."

Ken laughed as he caught a chair and swung it up on the stage beside the piano, then straddled it, his arms draped across the back. "Somehow I can't quite picture you making a living hacking the heads off chickens."

Jacob grimaced. "When you put it like that...."
He played several complicated chords with casual ease, his head tilted to one side as he listened with absorbed concentration. Then he sighed and shook his head with disgust. "Everything sounds the same to-

day." He looked at Ken as he rested his arm across the top of the baby grand. "How come you're downtown—isn't Sylvia going to be discharged today?"

"Most likely. One reason I came down was to see a real-estate agent. The old Johnson place is on the market and I'd like to buy the quarter-section that borders on the farm."

Jacob's eyes narrowed as he stared at Ken, his expression set and unfathomable, his voice stiff. "That's one reason—what's the other?"

Ken's own face suddenly became serious. "Not to lecture you, Jacob—I think you've probably had a gutful of that already."

Jacob said nothing, but continued to watch him with a wooden expression. Ken continued, "The reason I came was—well, it's hard to explain." He rested his chin on his hands, his eyes squinting. "My life has been pretty content for the last few years. No major crises, no big problems. I never realized how much I took everything for granted. Never really thought about it, in fact, until this episode with Sylvia."

He looked at Jacob, his eyes deadly serious as he recalled the indefinable shock and fear he had experienced. "I did one hell of a lot of thinking when she was so close to death for those few hours. I'd never really sat back and thought about what my life, or the boys', would be like if something ever happened to her. It scared the hell out of me, Jacob. I had never been forced to really assess how important her existence is to me, what it would be like without her. It was pretty damned sobering, I can tell you."

"Just why are you telling me this?" There was a cold vibrating edge to Jacob's voice.

Ken looked at him, his jaw set with unflinching determination. "Because, Jacob, I don't think anyone honestly puts a value on life until someone they care deeply about is seriously threatened."

"Meaning Jillian."

"Jillian, yes—but you, too, Jacob. She's been through that hell and she understood better than anyone how I felt that night." Ken hesitated briefly before he went on. "Jacob, have you ever put yourself in her place? In all honesty, man, what would you feel if I came in here and told you she was dead?"

Jacob's head shot up and he stared at Ken, an appalled, stunned look on his face. "That's a sick thing to say—"

"Is it, Jacob? Is it really? I probably would have had the same reaction if someone had said the same thing to me a month ago. If Sylvia hadn't had such expert medical care she would have died—that's no supposition, but hard cold fact. Think about it." Ken stood up and laid his hand on Jacob's shoulder, his face lined with compassion. "I don't know what's happened, and it's none of my business, but it's pretty obvious that both you and Jill are going through one hell of an ordeal." Ken stuck his hands in his pockets as he stared across the dimly lighted room. "You're family, both of you. And damn it, you matter to me—I want to see you happy." He turned to leave, then paused. "Think, Jacob, before you do something you'll regret for the rest of your life."

Jacob didn't show up for the rehearsal that afternoon, and he didn't arrive at the lounge that night until just a few minutes before show time. He ignored Jillian completely as he wheeled himself toward the stage, his face frozen with a rigid grimness.

Jillian didn't even notice his rebuff. She was deathly pale and her eyes were dark and hollow. There was an aura of brittle tension about her that made her appear fragile and helpless as she leaned against the wall outside the dressing room door, trying desperately to psych herself up for the evening performances.

On top of everything else, she was suffering from an acute case of stage fright. She didn't know how she could possibly force herself out onto the stage and into the glare of the spotlight. She felt as though the brilliant power of the light would strip her of her protective shield, leaving her vulnerable to the probing hostile eyes of the audience. She clenched her shaking hands together and shut her eyes tightly in an effort to gain control. She could feel beads of perspiration forming on her forehead as a consuming tension swept over her.

"Ladies and gentlemen, it is my pleasure to introduce Miss Jillian Lambert."

Jillian pushed herself weakly away from the wall and turned toward the runway, her entire body trembling. The light from the spot encased her in its harsh brilliance as she stepped onto the stage. She kept telling herself that she would calm down once she was past the piano, but it was becoming more and more difficult to breathe. As she reached out for the mike she felt a weird floating detachment and she stared mutely at her shaking hands. Then she was aware that Jacob was watching. His eyes were dark and unreadable, but something in that look fortified her and she somehow forced herself to turn and face the audience.

The night seemed never ending, but Jillian managed somehow to continue until the second-last number of the last set. That song was her undoing: it was the one Jacob had written and it nearly killed her every time she had to sing it.

> Reach out, reach out and touch me, babe
> Touch me in the darkness of the night
> Reach out, reach out and touch me, babe
> Hold me close in the dawn's velvet light
> I need your love to survive
> I need your love to come alive
> Reach out, baby. Reach out.

Her voice faltered as the hopelessness engulfed her, and she felt as though she was being sucked into a gray whirlpool that would never release her. But rescue came from an unexpected source. From behind her came Jacob's subdued harmony, forcing her on. As his voice strengthened, it carried her; it was almost as though he had picked her up and physically held her.

As soon as the curtain swept shut, Jillian laid the mike on the piano, her only conscious thought that of escape. She walked rapidly out of the lounge and nearly ran down the ramp that led to the lobby. She had to get out of the hotel; she felt as though she was suffocating.

Her flight was arrested when she realized a violent thunderstorm was raging outside. Like a woman in a trance, she was drawn to the lobby window by the magnificence of the tempest. The rain was beating down with such fury that she could barely see across the street. There was a blinding flash of lightning, then an immediate clap of thunder that shook the building. The wind lashed with such power that the window trembled against its force.

Jillian felt no fear. Instead, a wild exhilaration claimed her, stripping away her veneer of control. She was welded there, her feelings exposed before the wrath of nature, her blood racing with the power of the rampaging savage elements. Another flash of lightning illuminated her, the high priestess of the storm—the gold lamé gown molded against her like gold leaf, her head crowned with the fiery coronet of her hair. Her face was bathed in sensual awe as raw passion surged through her.

The passion, the tension that surrounded her like a force field was broken by a sound, a movement behind her. She turned slowly to find Jacob watching her, his face set, his eyes flashing with dark emotion.

Their eyes locked and held for an eternity, then something snapped within Jillian as the hopelessness, the utter futility jolted her like a physical blow. She moaned softly and shut her eyes, her face registering the inner agony. It was beyond her endurance, this awful pain that was growing within her. There were no tears to shed, no anger to vent, nothing—just pain. Without saying a word she turned and walked through the lobby doors into the cold lashing rain, into the frenzy of the gale, through the blur of slicing biting gray.

She felt vaguely alarmed when she parked her car in the driveway beside the house; she had absolutely no recollection of driving home.

She dragged herself out of the car, and a blast of driving rain lashed against her as she closed the door. The long skirt of her dress clung wetly to her legs as

she walked slowly down the driveway to the backyard. She stood there for a long, long time surrounded by darkness, her head bowed in wretched
surrender. Then slowly she lifted her face to the black
sky, and the cold slicing rain mingled with her
scalding tears. She was beaten, defenseless—and all
the anguish came boiling out.

She stood there until the storm abated to a steady
chilling drizzle that penetrated through her physical
numbness with a piercing cold. She was cold, so cold.

She climbed the few stairs that led to the patio and
fumbled with the keys she had clasped in her hand,
unlocking the back door and entering the dim hallway. Then reaction to the stress and exposure hit her,
and she clenched her teeth together in a weak attempt
to control the violent shivering that overcame her.
She closed her eyes and slumped against the wall as
exhaustion claimed her.

"Jillian—my God!" She struggled within the
swirling fog that threatened to engulf her and slowly
opened her eyes.

Jacob was wheeling himself down the hallway toward her, his face ashen and tense. He reached out
and caught her arms, pulling her toward him as she
swayed slightly.

"Come on, Jill. Please, for God's sake!"

She was shaking so badly that she could barely
walk, but somehow she managed to stumble down
the hallway and into her apartment, responding to
the sound of Jacob's voice as he continued to urge
her on, his words distant and indistinct. She followed
him into the bathroom and leaned weakly against the
vanity as he turned on the taps in the big old tub.

With gentle hands he quickly stripped off her sodden garments and laid them in the sink. He watched her, his face grimly set, as she got into the water, slumped against the curved back of the tub and closed her eyes.

He sat staring at her for a moment, then tipped his head back and closed his eyes as he slowly massaged the back of his neck. Finally he sighed heavily and wheeled himself toward the door, pausing by the tub when Jillian's eyes fluttered open. He laid his hand along her jaw, his thumb softly brushing her cheek.

"I'll be right back, Jill."

She closed her eyes. As the heat penetrated the terrible coldness, she felt what little strength she had ooze out of her. Little by little the comforting warmth soothed her tense muscles and her shivering abated, leaving her feeling like a limp, lifeless rag doll.

She heard Jacob enter and forced her eyes open when he put his arm around her shoulders and eased her into a sitting position. He cradled her head against his shoulder as he raised a mug to her lips. She tasted it, then shook her head weakly. It was strong sweet tea.

"Come on, Jill, you have to drink it."

She looked at him, her eyes dull with exhaustion. "It's so sweet, Jacob."

Jacob's hold on her tightened. "Please, Jill."

She lowered her eyes and forced herself to take another sip, and another, until the mug was empty. She shuddered at the offensive sweetness, but it wasn't long until the hot drink radiated a warmth within her.

Jacob eased her back into the tub and ran more hot water. His face was taut with concern as he asked, "Is Allan back from Toronto yet?"

She started to tremble again as she shook her head. "No."

Jacob stared at her, his eyes unreadable. "So you're here alone?"

She nodded and closed her eyes, unwilling to witness the troubled expression that settled around his mouth.

Finally she stirred and opened her eyes. "I think I can get out now."

He reached for a terry-cloth bath sheet that was hanging on the towel rack and handed it to her. "Get into bed, Jillian. I'm going to fix you another drink." His voice was low and gruff but not unkind.

She looked at him, her eyes pleading. "I'll be sick if I have to drink another."

He smiled grimly as he turned his chair to leave. "This one will be what the good doctor would have ordered—for both of us."

Jillian somehow managed to creep into bed before Jacob returned. She started shivering again, however, and simply could not will herself to stop.

Jacob wheeled himself into the room and switched on the bedside lamp, then set the tray he had carried across his knees on the table. He hoisted himself onto the bed beside her and piled the pillows against the headboard. Slipping his arm under her trembling shoulders, he lifted her against him, then swore softly.

"Damn. You can't keep that damp towel around you. Lift up for a minute so I can unwrap it." He tossed the towel to the foot of the bed, then carefully tucked the blankets around her shaking body. Picking up the glass he held it against her lips, swearing again as her teeth rattled against the rim.

She swallowed the warm brandy, ignoring the tears that sprang into her eyes as the liquor burned her throat. After a few more swallows she shook her head.

"All of it." His voice was firm.

Like an obedient child she finished it, suppressing a shiver of distaste. He set the empty glass on the table, then reached for his own. She shut her eyes and tried to fend off the dizziness that was threatening to overcome her. She heard his glass clink against hers, then his arm came around her as he eased them both down in the bed. As she lay in the secure warmth of his arms a strange floating lassitude settled upon her, carrying her into an exhausted slumber.

AGAIN THE AWFUL DREAM. Jacob. . . the vicious black horse. . . swirling mist. She struggled but was unable to move. She called out, trying to warn him of the danger, but she couldn't move to help him. Then someone was calling her name and the mist began to clear.

Jacob was holding her firmly against his warm body, rocking her as one would comfort a frightened child. She buried her face against his chest, her face damp with perspiration and tears as the terror of the dream finally faded.

"It's okay, Jillian. Everything will be okay—hush now." Her frightened sobs quieted as he wiped her face gently with his hand. "It's over, babe. There's nothing to be afraid of." He reached out and switched on the lamp, then lifted her face and studied her with sober eyes. "Tell me what happened. What frightened you so?"

She looked at him, then shut her eyes and shook

her head. The grip on her chin tightened and he forced her face up. "Jill—tell me." Once again his voice was firm, determined.

She took a shuddering breath and whispered, "It's a dream I have. You're walking toward me—oh, Jacob, I can't!"

"Tell me." He gave her a gentle shake. "Now, Jillian."

She shivered again, her voice a tremulous whisper. "You are walking toward me, laughing. Just before...just before you reach me—" she took a shaky breath, then forced herself to go on "—a black shadow looms up behind you and it's Rogue. Only... only his eyes are red and his hooves are spurting blood—Jacob, I can't!" She cried out and tried to push herself into a sitting position. Jacob held her against him, his face solemn and concerned as he gently stroked her back.

She jumped when he said sharply, "Your hair is still wet. Sit up."

Jillian struggled into a sitting position, clutching the blankets around her as she suddenly became aware of her nakedness. Jacob unpinned her braid and began to unplait it. When it was completely loose he began running his fingers through it, spreading it out in a riot of color around her shoulders.

She caught his hand and held it tightly as she turned to face him. "Don't do that, Jacob!" Her pale face mirrored her tormented longing, and her voice was soft and husky as she whispered her plea.

Jacob jerked his hand away, suddenly aware of their intimacy. She started to shiver again, but not from cold—the thread of will had finally snapped, leaving her totally vulnerable.

The muscles in Jacob's jaw tensed as he studied her with a dark look that left her feeling faint. He reached out and slowly slipped his hand along her neck until his fingers were buried deep in her hair, his thumb gently caressing her ear.

She closed her eyes in an attempt to dam the tears that sprang into her eyes. His cold brutal withdrawal had hurt her, but this unexpected tenderness was tearing her apart.

She heard him draw in his breath sharply, then he spoke, his voice low and strained. "Is Reverend Williams still the minister of the little church on the corner?"

Her eyelids flew open and she looked at him, her mind confused and bewildered by his unexpected question. She stared at him for a moment, then slowly nodded her head.

Jacob gently wiped away the tears that glistened on her thick lashes, then brushed back a wisp of hair that was clinging to her tear-dampened face. "I'm going to see him today and make arrangements for us to be married Sunday morning."

A stunned heavy silence fell around them as Jillian stared at him in disbelief, her body braced against the sudden overwhelming feeling of uncertainty. She felt as though she was suspended by strings, that she had no control.

"Jacob...."

His face was unreadable behind its fixed unyielding mask. His voice was like a shaft of steel when he spoke. "I want you to think about it, Jillian—think about what you'd be letting youself in for. I want you to make damned certain it's what you want."

He pivoted away from her, then dragged his legs

off the bed. With one powerful fluid movement he swung himself into his wheelchair and rolled toward the door. He paused, then turned to face her.

She was watching him, her face ashen, her eyes wide and dark, her body immobilized by numbness.

There was no gentleness or warmth, but instead a chilling undercurrent of self-directed contempt in his words. "If you decide that life with me would be unbearable, I understand." With that, he turned and left the room.

JILLIAN STOOD STARING out her window at the soft clouds that drifted across the glorious morning sky. Her wedding day....

She closed her eyes and rested her forehead against the cool windowpane, trying to calm the nervous churning in her stomach. For the past three days she had been caught on an emotional roller coaster that rose and fell to harrowing extremes.

She loved Jacob and she needed him; there was no doubt in her mind about that. But could they ever piece together a foundation solid enough on which to build a stable marriage? Could Jacob ever put the past behind him and learn to cope with the bitterness he felt? Could he ever allow her to penetrate the defensive emotional wall he had erected, trust her enough to share with her his innermost thoughts and feelings?

Could she bring some happiness into his life, or would resentment and anger destroy the delicate bond that drew them together? The tormenting questions raced around and around in her mind in a muddle of apprehension and doubt, but there were never any certain answers.

There were moments when she was filled with hope and believed that she and Jacob had a secure bright future stretching before them. Then there were times when devastating doubts would loom up, blanketing her hope in a cloud of despair that left her feeling scared and very much alone.

She had lain awake all night, trying to fight her way through the maze, but she had resolved nothing—except that she was definitely going to be at the church at seven o'clock that morning. That was the only certainty in the whole uncertain ordeal.

What Jacob would do was another matter altogether. During the cold gray hours of very early morning a new ominous thought had overpowered the turmoil in her mind and filled her with a feeling of dull panic. What if Jacob changed his mind and left her waiting at the church? What if he disappeared once again? She tried to push the thought away but it kept nagging at her with an ugly persistence that curdled her blood. What would she do then?

She shivered violently and glanced at the clock by her bed. There was little more than an hour until they were to meet at the church—and Jillian knew it would be the longest, most agonizing hour of her life.

Her back stiff with repressed anxiety, she went into the bathroom and turned on the water in the tub, then twisted her hair up and pinned it securely on top of her head. She poured some bath oil into the churning water under the tap, then climbed in and leaned back, her eyes closed as the warm fragrant water lapped around her in a soothing caress. She was so tired, but the clamor in her mind would not let her sleep and the tension that crackled within her would not let her relax. She was an arrow poised in a drawn bow. Her flight was preordained, her destiny out of her control.

She sighed heavily and slowly began to soap herself with a sponge as she pondered Jacob's attitude toward her since his unexpected announcement about their marriage. He was still unapproachable and very withdrawn, but the cold hostility was no longer there. He had attended the rehearsals and had even spoken to Jillian on several occasions about the music they were working on. But his cool remoteness remained. The day they went for their blood tests and marriage license his manner had been that of a polite aloof stranger. There had been no warmth or gentleness in him, and it had frightened Jillian.

She was still frightened. Somehow, though, she managed to quell the uneasiness that was growing within her and forced herself to concentrate on the routine task of bathing.

She rinsed herself off, then climbed out of the tub and wrapped a big bath towel around her. Automatically she tidied the bathroom, then unpinned her hair and brushed it until it gleamed. She carefully began braiding it, weaving in a dainty edging of old lace as she went. When she was finished, her hair lay across her breast in one thick heavy plait, the ivory of the lace adding a pristine purity to the brazen auburn of her hair. She applied a hint of makeup, then returned to her bedroom. The doubts and uncertainties shrank her stomach into a cold hard knot as she began to dress.

The morning was hushed, sweet with the perfume of flowers that drifted on the gentle breeze. The leaves of the sprawling old elm trees rustled above her head as she walked toward the church, and she smiled softly when she heard the song of a robin. The tall stalks of hollyhock that clustered around the slightly dilapidated chapel swayed gently, their pink and red flowers brilliant against the faded whiteness of the building.

The fresh sparkle of the morning faded abruptly for Jillian when she realized that Jacob's car wasn't there. She felt strangely reassured, however, when she turned up the broken, grass-encroached sidewalk to the church and saw that an improvised ramp had been placed on the low wide steps that led to the vestibule. The weatherbeaten doors stood open, so Jillian entered the dim hushed interior and walked slowly down the center aisle.

Sunlight slanted through the beautiful stained-glass windows, illuminating the old oaken altar with a golden radiance that was almost mystical. Even the drops of dew on the huge bouquet of freshly cut gladioli glimmered like chips of topaz in the softly diffused light. Jillian breathed deeply as a strange peace settled over her. She reached out and with infinite gentleness caressed the vibrant blossoms of the flowers, unaware of the breathtaking picture she made. She was dressed in a long cream-colored silk caftan, her face framed by a softly draped cowl hood, her hair lying across her breast in one magnificent braid. She looked like a Titian Madonna.

There was a murmur of a sound behind her and she turned slowly to find Jacob sitting at the back of the church watching her, his face tensed with some emotion that made his eyes opaque.

Her heart raced wildly when she saw him. She hadn't seen him in a suit since he'd returned, and his appearance was so overpowering that it left her breathless. He looked more rugged, more virile, more powerful, and his blondness and his dark tan were accentuated by the dark brown suit and the crisp white shirt. They stared at each other, neither of them moving for the longest time. Then he moved toward her, his wheelchair whispering across the threadbare carpet.

He was nearly at her side when he paused. Jillian saw him swallow hard, then he silently stretched out his hand toward her. She remained motionless for a moment, then moved toward him and placed her trembling hand in his. Time seemed suspended as a strange, exquisite serenity fell around them.

The entire ceremony had an ethereal, dreamlike quality that consisted of time frames of impressions: kneeling beside Jacob at the altar as they exchanged their vows; the sun warm on their hands as he slipped the wide gold band on her finger; Jacob whispering her name as he took her face in his hands and brushed her lips with a gentle lingering kiss; the soft touch of his fingers as he wiped away the tears that dampened her face.

Jillian was only vaguely aware of Reverend Williams's blessing or of the good wishes of Mrs. Williams and her brother, who had served as witnesses. In fact, reality never penetrated her drifting, unfocused state until they were back at Jillian's apartment. Then the cold undeniable facts hit home with a chilling clarity: she was married to this very remote, withdrawn man.

She felt the warmth drain out of her as Jacob rolled himself into the apartment, his face unreadable and stiff. She shut the door quietly behind him, then set his suitcase on the floor by the chesterfield. She clasped her cold hands together, taking a deep breath before she asked, "Would you like a drink?"

He didn't look at her as he shook his head. "No."

The silence between them was almost tangible by the time Jillian gathered together enough confidence to speak again. She reached out and touched his shoulder with a hesitant gesture. "You look exhausted, Jacob. Would you like to lie down?"

He caught her hand in his and held it tightly as he studied her face. "Will you come in, Jillian?"

She nodded, afraid she would be unable to speak.

He watched her silently for a moment, then he released her hand and rolled past her toward the bedroom. She stood staring after him for a long time, her muscles frozen by a treacherous uncertainty, then she hesitantly touched the wedding band on her finger.

Walking down the hallway she paused by the closet and removed a small dress box and a padded hanger. She entered the bathroom, closed the door softly behind her and stared into the mirror. Her eyes were wide and green, shadowed with dark circles; her face ashen and drawn. She looked terrified—and she was.

With shaking hands she slipped out of her dress, carefully turned it inside out and slipped it onto the hanger, then hung the garment on the hook on the back of the door. She unbraided her hair and brushed it out, then finished undressing. Biting her lip, she opened the box and removed a soft green negligee, and with fixed, manufactured resolve she slipped it on.

It took every ounce of courage she had to walk through the bedroom door and face the alien isolated man who was her husband. She paused in the doorway, the delicate clinging fabric whispering around her like sea foam, her hair rioting around her like a flame.

A drifting detached feeling enfolded her, and the surroundings faded into an unfocused blur. There was no reality except the blond man in the bed who was watching her with dark mesmerizing eyes that drugged her senses. A warm aching tightness twisted in her belly as his deep penetrating stare sent a charge of electricity crackling between them.

The powerful muscles across his chest and shoulders rippled beneath his bronzed skin as he levered himself into a sitting position and stretched out one hand toward her. She began to tremble as she moved across the room, for there was no cold remoteness or soul-destroying bitterness in his eyes now. Instead they were smoldering with a fierce naked passion that was barely controlled. He wanted her and he was going to have her, and that knowledge was Jillian's only conscious thought.

Her blood was coursing through her veins, her breathing erratic as she paused by the bed. The blazing intensity of his gaze deepened, and Jillian was seized by a raw empty hunger as he reached up and untied the satin ribbon that was fastened over one shoulder.

As the silky garment slithered down her heated body she closed her eyes, her hair cascading around her like a fiery mantle, her lips parted. She moaned softly as he placed his hands on her naked thighs and with intoxicating slowness slipped his fingers up the curve of her hips and across her flat midriff. She had no will of her own but was lost to his touch as he gently cupped her breasts in his hands and stroked the hard nipples with his thumbs. A bolt of hot molten desire slammed through Jillian, and she swayed as a sweet, hot, heady weakness surged in her body with the force of an incoming tide.

"Look at me, babe." His voice was thick and husky.

Her eyes fluttered open and she felt consumed by the desperate tormented hunger and the fevered need that kindled his eyes. She was locked into that gaze as he moved his hands over her skin, arousing her to a fever pitch, torturing her with his intimate caresses. She buried her hands in his hair and swayed toward him, pressing his head against her abdomen.

She felt him shudder violently, then his arms tightened around her convulsively as a storm broke within him and all of the unsatisfied desires and the haunting loneliness he had denied for so long demanded release. He pulled her roughly down on the bed beside him, and as naked body molded against naked body, there was an explosion of passion that shattered the last fragment of his restraint.

The blaze was raging out of control. Their bodies were welded together with a fire so ravenous it was almost agony. This was no gentle tender passion, but one that clawed and tore at them, screaming for fulfillment. His desire, his hunger, his desperate need carried her like a chip on a stormy, wild and raging sea, and she was powerless against it. She responded with a passion that was scalding; he was carrying her to the limits of the universe with a white-hot frenzy that seared through her.

His strong masculine body imprisoned her beneath him as he finally claimed her mouth in a hot savage kiss, his hands beneath her hips holding her hard against him in a ruthless urgency. It carried them on and on through a blazing spiraling eternity.

She arched against him as he took her, and she held onto him with all the strength she possessed as at long last the hot rush of release came—pulse after pulse of hot golden release. A hoarse groan was wrung from Jacob as he shuddered violently, his embrace like a band of steel as he held her—held her as if he could never let her go.

JILLIAN AWOKE much, much later, immediately aware of the warmth and security in the strong arms that held her. She was nestled firmly against him, her head on his shoulder, her body relaxed and satiated, still drugged by a serene drifting contentment.

She felt his hand on her chin and opened her eyes as he tipped her head back so that he could study her face. The warm lassitude shriveled within her when she saw the expression in his dark troubled eyes— there was regret etched deeply into his solemn drawn face. He held her face in a firm grip as he closed his eyes, his jaw clenched against some inner tormenting thought.

Jillian felt suddenly cold and very frightened. What was he thinking? What was wrong? Her breath caught on a smothered sob as a knot of panic twisted within her.

He opened his eyes, his brow creased with a frown as he gently caressed her cheek with his fingers. His voice was hoarse and unsteady when he finally spoke. "Jillian—babe—I'm so sorry."

There was a painful ache in her throat when she whispered, "Why, Jacob?"

He ran his fingers through her hair as he cradled her head in his hands. "Because I was out of control—I took you like a savage. I was brutal, Jillian, and I'm so sorry—I didn't mean it to be that way."

Her eyes filled with tears, changing them from hazel to sparkling glimmering emerald as the awful dread was swept away and her face softened with immeasurable tenderness. She laid her hand on his cheek as she gently caressed the tension lines around the corners of his eyes.

"Oh, Jacob, don't regret what happened. Please don't! It was so wild and so beautiful—it had to be like that for us." She kissed him softly, then smiled at him, her eyes shining. "I wouldn't have wanted it any other way."

He studied her face as though he was trying to penetrate some barrier, some facade, but her gaze was unwavering. He turned his head and ardently kissed the palm of her hand, then he took a deep unsteady breath as he caught her against him in a powerful enveloping embrace.

She could feel him tense against her, his voice low and tormented. "Oh, God...when I think of what I've done to you...how I've hurt you...."

She stroked his head as her heart filled with an overwhelming compassion for this deep sensitive man who had suffered so much. "Don't, Jacob. Don't even think about it. If I had to go through that hell again, I would—a thousand times—if I knew this was how it would end. I love you, Jacob."

He raised his head, his face taut with an inner pain as he gently traced the fullness of her bottom lip. "All the doubts and resentments were of my own making, babe. I could never let you go—God, but I need you. I need you to give some purpose to my life, to make me whole again." As he smoothed the hair back from her cheek, his face softened into an ir- resistible smile that seduced her and his eyes kin- dled with a warm light that made her ache inside. "You've filled that awful, empty, aching void that has tormented me for years, Jillian. The song I wrote for you says it all—'I need your love to survive, I need your touch to come alive.'" He lowered his head and covered her lips with his, his kiss warm and vital.

She responded to him, her body soft and surren- dering beneath his. As he trailed his kisses down her throat, then buried his face in the soft curve of her neck, Jillian closed her eyes. A happiness so perfect, so sublime that no words could ever describe it soared within her.

He held her for long beautiful moments, then he eased himself on his back and pulled her on top of him, slipping his hands up her back until he reached the base of her neck. There he unclasped the gold chain, which snaked into a gleaming coil in his hand as he slipped the ring off. Holding her left hand, he placed the jade ring on her finger above her gold wedding band and with touching sincere reverence he sanctified the gesture with a lingering kiss. With shaking hands he replaced the locket around her neck and slowly smoothed the chain between her naked breasts.

She caught his face between her hands, her eyes glistening with unshed tears, and whispered, her voice low, pleading, urgent, "Love me, Jacob. Please love me."

Her tears were warm against his face as he caught

her to him and kissed her, his pliant mouth provoking her, arousing her, tormenting her.

And he was gentle—so very gentle.

JILLIAN GLANCED at the clock and grinned ruefully when she saw the time. Eight o'clock—they had been in bed for twelve hours straight. She sighed contentedly and gently stroked the blond head that rested on her breast. Jacob sighed in his sleep, and a tender reflective smile illuminated her eyes as he stirred against her. It seemed as though the consummation of their love had washed away the residue of the past tragedy, had left them cleansed and free from the miserable loneliness that had been a dark shadow in their lives for so long. It was all behind them now, and with an unwavering certainty she knew that Jacob would be a part of her life forever.

She slipped her hand up his back and idly ran her fingers through his tousled hair, delighting in the silky way it curled around them.

His arms tightened around her as he murmured, "My wife." There was a wealth of satisfaction in those two words.

She cuddled him closer and smiled softly. "I love you, Jacob Holinski—I can't express with words how much."

"I'll settle for actions," he answered promptly.

Jillian laughed a rich throaty laugh as his hands moved possessively along her body. He raised his head, his mouth gentle as he gave her a long searching kiss. Then he pulled away and grinned at her, his dark eyes warm and inviting. "Oh, Jillian! You really are heady stuff."

"Well, you aren't exactly low voltage yourself."

She softly caressed his sensuous mouth, her touch deliberately light and teasing. "Do you have any idea what you do to me?"

There was a roguish gleam in his eyes when he answered. "Oh, I think I have some idea." His eyes darkened and she saw the muscles in his jaw tense as an expression of anguish contorted his face. "How did I ever manage to exist for so long without you, Jillian?"

There was a painful contraction in her chest, but she was determined that the past would no longer haunt them. She laughed at him, her eyes teasing as she caught his head and shook it with mild reprimand. "Through sheer bullheaded orneriness, Jacob Holinski! That stubborn streak is going to be a trial, I just know it!"

He threw back his head and laughed, his eyes flashing. "Are you insinuating that there might be a clash or two?"

"One or two," she understated dryly.

He kissed her, then raised himself up and leaned back against the pile of pillows. His expression softened as he looked down at Jillian, at her dreamy eyes and the soft satisfied smile on her face. Idly he traced her arched eyebrows with his finger, then let it slide down her cheek and across her lips. Her smile deepened as she caught his hand and kissed his palm.

"Come here, babe. I need to hold you." He drew her up against him, and she lay with her head on his chest, her hair falling in a disheveled mass around them.

"This is really happening, isn't it, Jacob? It isn't just another dream?"

Jacob laughed as he smoothed the hair back from

her face. "If it is, I'll kill the bastard who wakes us up."

She laughed softly and tucked her arm around him. A comfortable silence enfolded them and she closed her eyes as he began to comb his fingers through her tangled hair.

It was sometime later when Jacob wrapped his arms around her and held her tightly against him. "Jillian, did Allan tell you that they think that I have enough strength left in my hips and upper thighs to be able to manage with canes and braces?"

Jillian frowned slightly; his voice was too controlled. There was something that was obviously troubling him. She eased out of his embrace and sat up, her eyes solemn as she took his hands in hers and turned to face him. "Yes, he told me."

There was an agitated reluctance about him as his eyes fell away from hers and he began to toy abstractedly with the rings on her finger. "It scares me a little, Jill. When Allan told me that, it was as though I had been set free from a cage...."

"Why the uncertainty, Jacob?" she questioned softly. "Why are you so worried by it?"

His hands gripped hers painfully as he lifted his head and looked at her, his eyes distressed, his face drawn. "If I can't manage—if it doesn't work out, I'm afraid—"

Jillian leaned over and brushed her lips against his, her eyes warm with understanding. "You're afraid that if you discover you can't manage with canes and braces after all, you may react with anger and bitterness and take out your frustration on me. That's what you're thinking, isn't it?"

"Yes."

"My love, don't let that stop you from trying." She caressed his face with her hands, her eyes earnest as she spoke with heartfelt sincerity. "We'll meet those kinds of difficulties together, Jacob. When disappointments and problems are shared with love and understanding, the weight is never unbearable. You may lash out at me, but you won't ever shut me out again. I *know* that...."

Jacob closed his eyes and crushed her against him in a hold that spoke of overwhelming relief and gratitude. He pressed her face against his chest as his arms tightened around her. "Jill—oh, Jillian—you make everything seem so uncomplicated. You bring such strength and reassurance with you, babe."

She lifted her head and looked at him. "I don't think you realize how very much I need you, Jacob. I can tolerate anything as long as I have you there to give me that strength. Without you, there isn't anything that's really worthwhile."

"Jill—"

She covered his mouth with her fingers, her eyes beseeching. "You will try the braces, won't you, Jacob?"

He studied her for a moment, his face serious, then he slowly nodded his head. "Yes, I'll try." For a moment he continued to watch her, then his face relaxed into an amused captivating smile that lighted up his eyes with a touch of mischief. "If you really think it's worth the risk—an all-out clash between my stubbornness and your temper."

She laughed and made a face at him. "I'll risk it."

His hands were working their seductive tantalizing magic on her body, and for a brief moment Jillian was very tempted to submit to the sexual excitement he aroused in her. But she resisted, pushing herself away from him and sitting up.

She leaned over and kissed him, her voice low and husky. "Jacob—don't, love." His eyebrows shot up and she had to laugh at the look of bemusement on his face. "Jacob, there's something I want to ask you, and...well...."

"And you think this might be the best time to ask it, right?" She grinned at him a little sheepishly and Jacob laughed as he swept her hair down her back. "Okay, Jillian, let's have it—and I promise I won't explode. That's what's bothering you, isn't it?"

Her face sobered and she nodded her head, so he hooked his knuckles under her chin. "Tell me, Jillian."

She took a shaky breath, then looked at him squarely. "Jacob, would you like to ride again?"

His face stiffened and his eyes narrowed. She looked down, fervently wishing she hadn't said anything—at least not yet. He caught her again under the chin and lifted her face, disregarding her resistance to the pressure.

"Why do you ask that, Jillian?"

She swallowed against the lump of nervousness before she answered, "They have saddles now that are specially equipped for handicapped people...."

She still couldn't look at him, and she fixed her eyes on the pulse that was beating at the base of his throat. "I read about a riding club in St. Albert that was organized for kids and adults who—"

He jerked her head up roughly, his eyes blazing with...with what? It wasn't anger. "Jillian, are you certain about this?" His voice was charged with a tension that was completely unnerving.

Jillian nodded her head, silently thinking, *don't be angry with me, Jacob, please don't be angry with me.* Aloud she said, "Dad has a horse quarterly at home that has an excellent write-up about them...."

Jacob closed his eyes and hugged her against him, so hard that it drove the breath out of her. "Oh, Jillian! God, do you know what this means to me?"

"Jacob, I can't breathe—"

He loosened his grip and looked down at her, his eyes fired with the same expression that she had seen on the morning they had gone swimming. It was the look of freedom.

Relief flooded through her and she smiled up at him. "Do you want to give it a try?"

"Yes! Certainly, emphatically, yes!"

She grinned at him, her eyes shining. "Good, because I've ordered one for you for a wedding present...."

Jacob hugged her fiercely and kissed her with such thoroughness that she felt dizzy and off balance. She caught her breath, then looked up at him with an impudent grin. "Since you didn't bite my head off, I think I'll be generous and fix you something to eat. You must be starved."

He laughed, his face alive with a lighthearted elation. "My God, Jillian, how can you talk about anything as mundane as food right now?"

She hugged him, then whispered suggestively, "Well, then, I think I'll have a bath. Would you care to join me?"

"With an invitation like that, how can I refuse?" He kissed her, then laughed again. "I think you're going to make my life very interesting, Mrs. Holinski!"

She grinned at him impishly. "I'm going to do my damnedest, Mr. Holinski!"

They sat relaxing in the deep tub, the warm water eddying around them. Jillian lay with her back against Jacob's chest, her head resting on his shoulder. His arms were around her, his hands lying on her breasts. They had been there for some time without speaking, and a drowsy languor had settled upon them.

"Who was he, Jillian?" Jacob's voice was quiet but there was a determined quality to it that meant business.

"Who was who?"

"Don't be cute, Jill—you know the guy I'm talking about."

Jillian laughed as she caught one of his hands and held it to her lips. "Would you believe me if I told you that your brother engineered that whole scene at the hotel?"

"John?"

"Who else?" She twisted around, the water lapping into waves. "He thought you needed to be set back a space or two." She laughed again and pressed her face against his shoulder. "Brian is a member of the theatrical group I belong to. He's a *very* talented actor, and when he saw you watching him he couldn't resist the temptation to prove it."

"I could have wrung his neck."

Jillian glanced up at him, her eyes sparkling with suppressed amusement. "Who—John or Brian?"

He chuckled and stroked her cheek. "Both of them."

"Whatever for?"

"You know damned well why." He held her close,

his voice soft and possessive. "You're mine, Jillian."

Her eyes softened as she brushed back his damp curls. "That's all I ever wanted to be." She relaxed against him, then her eyes suddenly became very serious. "Jacob, when you came to the hospital when Sylvia was rushed in, you had paint on your fingers." She turned her head up to look at him. "What were you painting?"

"You."

She closed her eyes as a familiar tight pain encased her. Jacob saw the fleeting agony on her face and his arms tightened around her reassuringly. "You looked at the sketches, didn't you, Jill?"

She nodded her head.

"I started the one of you on the pedestal—" he pressed her face against his chest protectively when he felt her shudder "—but I couldn't finish it. It was too final." He felt her tears slip down his naked chest and he tipped her face up and softly kissed her trembling mouth.

"I was so afraid you were painting that one. I knew that if you ever painted it, it would be because you were leaving me."

"I can't leave you, Jillian—ever."

She laced her fingers through his. "Then you did the other one."

"No. I'll do that one eventually, but I started something else."

She looked up at him quizzically. "What?"

"The night at the hospital when you were holding tiny Lisa Marie in your arms. Your face was absolutely radiant and you were so beautiful.... That's how I'm painting you."

She sighed contentedly and buried her face against

his neck, loving the feel of his hands stroking her damp breasts. Then she laughed softly. "Now you can follow the doctor's orders."

He frowned. "What do you mean?"

"Dr. Carter told you to get me one of those." Her eyes were soft and lambent, her voice husky. "You are going to get me one, aren't you, Jacob?"

He groaned as he dragged her up against him, his mouth liquid and demanding with a ruthless unleashed passion.

"Let's get out, Jacob."

He brought her chin up and kissed her in a way that destroyed all rational thought. He cupped her breast in his hand, his voice low and throaty, his breath hot against her ear.

"Let's not."

JACOB WAS SITTING by the kitchen window watching Jillian clear away the clutter from their late supper. He shook his head, his dancing eyes belying the woeful look on his face. "If I had known it would take you this long, I would have brought something to read."

She blushed as he gave her a long, slow and very thorough perusal. She had on his shirt and it barely covered her, leaving her long shapely legs to his disconcerting gaze. She made a face at him, then smiled impishly and left the room. When she reentered the kitchen she had the Chinese chest in her hands and she gave him a smug look as she set it on his lap. "If you want something to read, you might start with this."

He looked up at her, a puzzled smile on his face.

"Open it, Jacob."

He opened the lid, clenching his jaw when he realized what was inside. He looked up at her, his eyes dark and smoldering, then he wheeled around and headed for the door.

"Jacob?"

He reached back and caught her hand, yanking her after him. "As I recall, some of these letters were more than a little torrid. We, my love, are going back to bed. You are going to read every damned one you wrote, and I am going to have the pleasure of getting even with you for all the agony you put me through."

She laughed as she followed him into the bedroom. Crawling up on the bed she watched him as he swung himself up beside her and tossed off his robe. "As I recall, Jacob Holinski, none of yours were exactly meant to be read to the family."

He looked at her, his brown flashing eyes holding her spellbound as he reached out and flipped the collar of his shirt. "Take it off, Jillian."

Her cheeks were flaming as she stuck her chin out with determination. "No."

He gave her a narrow threatening look, then opened the box and lifted out the plastic bag. Sorting through the letters he selected one especially dog-eared envelope. He removed the letter, opened it and scanned it briefly. There was a dangerous gleam in his eyes as he smiled wickedly and handed it to her. "Read it, Jillian—out loud."

She shook her head, her face flushed. "No."

He reached out and started undoing the buttons on the shirt. "You owe me, you know. You lost that bet about pulling one over on Norm—you said, 'Anything,' and I countered with 'Anytime,' remember? Well, I'm calling you on that right now." He stripped the shirt from her, stuffed two pillows behind him, then leaned back and leisurely crossed his arms on his chest.

"Read, Jillian."

She gave him a provocative look, then began to read the letter silently. As she read, her eyes widened and she began to blush furiously. "Jacob, I—did I . . . ?"

He was watching her through hooded eyes, a villainous grin on his face. "Read it—now!"

She read. By the time she was finished, her breathing was ragged and she felt as though she was drowning. He leaned forward and plucked the letter from her nerveless fingers, and with a low growl he rolled her beneath him. "Now you are going to pay for that sensuous and very specific piece of literature. . . ."

It was early morning when they finally awoke. The bed and the floor around it were littered with countless letters and envelopes.

Jacob tucked his hands beneath his head and watched with frank unabashed interest as Jillian sat up and began brushing her tangled hair.

He grinned, his eyes dancing. "It's a wonder this place never burned down; these letters are definitely flammable. You're a dangerous woman, Jillian Holinski."

She laughed as she picked up his shirt from beneath the clutter and slipped it on. "You aren't exactly a blameless innocent yourself. You realize, of course—" she made a sweeping gesture at the letters "—that these are censored reading. We'll have to keep them under lock and key—"

Jacob grinned as he interrupted her. "And every year on our anniversary we'll lock the bedroom door and read them."

She threw a pillow at him as she swung her legs off the bed. "I don't think our blood pressure will be able to handle them in our senior years."

Jacob laughed, then reached out and caught her hand, his face becoming suddenly serious. "Jill, time will mellow the passion. It won't always be like this."

She sat down on the bed beside him and gently touched his forehead with caressing fingers. Her expression was solemn, but there was an open honesty shining from her eyes. "I know that, love. I know we'll have our share of fights and disagreements— and there will be disappointments and heartaches. There will be times when we hurt each other and take each other for granted. But, Jacob, I know we can survive all that. Being together is going to mean so much more to us now because of the hell we went through during the last five years." She bent over and kissed him softly, then grinned at him. "Besides, I like you better than anyone I know."

He smiled back at her as he slipped his hand under her hair and caressed the sensitive hollow at the back of her neck. "If you like me so much, how come you haven't made me a coffee?"

She tossed her head and laughed, her eyes sending him a very bold seductive message. "I thought I was supposed to be fighting fires."

He caught her face and pulled her down, his mouth moving across hers with tormenting softness. "And you do that exceedingly well!"

IT WAS AMAZING what the three days together did for both Jillian and Jacob. He looked like a completely different person. All the rigid control and tension that had set his face muscles in an unreadable mask disappeared, leaving him relaxed and open. And Jillian was ecstatic, her happiness radiating from her like sunshine. They were completely refreshed and revitalized as they prepared to return to the hotel for Tuesday's performances.

Jacob appeared from the bedroom looking particularly handsome in a wine-colored shirt with white slacks. He laughed with amusement and a certain amount of pleasure at Jillian's lusty approving look and he pulled her down for a long thirsty kiss.

He ran his hand slowly up her leg and hip, then across her back. "I don't think I like you as much with clothes on, babe. After three days of wearing nothing but skin, I find clothing...restricting."

She gave him an adoring look and kissed him again, then slipped her hand slowly down his chest, unbuttoning his shirt as she went.

He caught her hand and held it against his pounding heart. "Jillian, love, if we keep this up we'll miss the first show." His voice was husky, his words warm against her lips as he raked her hair back from her face. "And since we've already been sidetracked once, we'll have to drive like crazy as it is."

There was laughter in her eyes as she sighed and stood up. She knew very well that it would take very little encouragement for him to say to hell with the drive *and* the show.

They made it to the lounge with eighteen minutes to spare and found Norm pacing back and forth in the corridor backstage, a worried set to his jaw. The other members of Firefly were already dressed in their white slacks and bright green shirts. Concern and apprehension were evident on all their faces.

Norm let out a long sigh of relief when he saw

them, but it was obvious that he was somewhat taken aback at seeing the two of them together. "Where have you been, Jake? We didn't know where in hell you were."

Jacob schooled his face into a blank expression while Jillian deliberately let her hair obscure her own so that he couldn't see the sparkle in her eyes.

Norm rammed his hands into his pockets and stared at them, his eyes narrowed speculatively. "Do you think you could give me some kind of explanation?" There was a touch of exasperation in his voice, and Jillian had to bite her lip to keep from laughing.

Jacob looked up casually, his voice calm. "We went to a wedding."

There was a look of suspicion on Norm's face. "A wedding? A wedding?"

Jacob took Jillian's hand and began to trace idle patterns on the back of it with one finger, seemingly engrossed in what he was doing. He paused, then looked up again, his eyes dancing. "Actually, it was our own wedding." Dumbfounded silence fell upon the group as he continued, his voice casual. "Norm, I'd like you to meet my wife."

A look of absolute amazement swept across their faces, then pandemonium broke loose.

Minutes later Jillian stood in the wings, still slightly dazed by the whirlwind of confusion that had occurred after Jacob's announcement. She laughed to herself at the cunning way he had told everyone. Her train of thought was interrupted by Keith's introduction, and she ran her hands nervously down the front of her green satin slacks as she started to walk toward the stage.

"Ladies and gentlemen, it gives me a great deal of pleasure to introduce our very own Firefly and our brand new blushing bride, Mrs. Jacob Holinski!"

When Jillian walked onto the stage into the glare of the spotlight, she was blushing furiously. *Damn Keith.*

The audience applauded wildly as the spotlight followed her across the stage. Jacob was watching her, his eyes dancing with delight as she came toward him, and he burst out laughing when he saw the pink flush that colored her face. He reached out and with one slow movement carried her hand to his lips and kissed her wrist.

Jillian's knees went weak and her flush deepened, then her face broke into a mischievous grin. She bent down and pressed her warm mouth against Jacob's in a deep searching kiss that left them both a little breathless. The commotion from the audience and the boys in the band finally brought them back to reality.

Jacob's eyes were flashing as she reluctantly lifted her head. "That, Jillian, calls for an encore," he whispered as he slowly stroked her bottom lip. "But we'll get to that later."

She winked at him and squeezed his hand, her eyes glowing. She picked up the mike and sang.

She sang for Jacob.

FREE!
THIS GREAT
SUPERROMANCE

Begin a long love affair with

SUPERROMANCE.

Accept LOVE BEYOND DESIRE, **FREE.**

Complete and mail the coupon below, today!

- -